...cious, Alice H...
atavistic supernatural thri...., a ..., ..., ...
fying dark fantasy. It's breathtaking and merciless, and I can't wait to see what she does for an encore."

—Christopher Golden,
Bram Stoker Award–winning author

"Heralds the arrival of a major new talent in the dark fiction field. Henderson brings tremendous tension, suspense, and atmosphere with this modern twist on the shape-shifter tale. This is one cool book." —J. A. Konrath, author of the Jacqueline "Jack" Daniels mystery series

"A terrific debut. Alice Henderson has the talent to evoke nature as an extraordinarily potent force that is nothing short of breathtaking. [Her] vivid evocation of wilderness places is superb in this page-turning story. A writer to watch."

— Simon Clark,
British Fantasy Award–winning author

"A polished and well-focused novel of raw animal terror. It pits a gutsy, outdoors-loving protagonist against an alluring, shape-shifting demon out of time who lusts not only for her flesh, but also for her extraordinary talent. Alice Henderson deftly crafts her own convincing mythology while telling a compelling, page-turning adventure that makes Glacier National Park itself into a character. Offering crisp action and tingly eroticism, *Voracious* also boasts an environmental subtext blended with astute philosophical explorations of the predator-prey symbiosis. Henderson's first novel is both accomplished and a shining promise of more to come. A winner!" —William D. Gagliani, author of *Wolf's Trap* and *Shadowplays*

"You will tear through this book the way Alice Henderson's monstrous creature tears through its prey. A combination of awe-inspiring setting and deeply personal terror, *Voracious* is irresistible." —Richard Dansky, author of *Firefly Rain*

VORACIOUS

ALICE HENDERSON

JOVE BOOKS, NEW YORK

THE BERKLEY PUBLISHING GROUP
Published by the Penguin Group
Penguin Group (USA) Inc.
375 Hudson Street, New York, New York 10014, USA
Penguin Group (Canada), 90 Eglinton Avenue East, Suite 700, Toronto, Ontario M4P 2Y3, Canada
(a division of Pearson Penguin Canada Inc.)
Penguin Books Ltd., 80 Strand, London WC2R 0RL, England
Penguin Group Ireland, 25 St. Stephen's Green, Dublin 2, Ireland (a division of Penguin Books Ltd.)
Penguin Group (Australia), 250 Camberwell Road, Camberwell, Victoria 3124, Australia
(a division of Pearson Australia Group Pty. Ltd.)
Penguin Books India Pvt. Ltd., 11 Community Centre, Panchsheel Park, New Delhi—110 017, India
Penguin Group (NZ), 67 Apollo Drive, Rosedale, North Shore 0632, New Zealand
(a division of Pearson New Zealand Ltd.)
Penguin Books (South Africa) (Pty.) Ltd., 24 Sturdee Avenue, Rosebank, Johannesburg 2196,
South Africa

Penguin Books Ltd., Registered Offices: 80 Strand, London WC2R 0RL, England

This is a work of fiction. Names, characters, places, and incidents either are the product of the author's imagination or are used fictitiously, and any resemblance to actual persons, living or dead, business establishments, events, or locales is entirely coincidental. The publisher does not have any control over and does not assume any responsibility for author or third-party websites or their content.

VORACIOUS

A Jove Book / published by arrangement with the author

PRINTING HISTORY
Jove mass-market edition / March 2009

Copyright © 2009 by Alice Henderson.
Cover art by S. Miroque.
Cover design by Rita Frangie.
Text design by Kristin del Rosario.

ISBN: 978-0-515-14602-8

JOVE®
Jove Books are published by The Berkley Publishing Group,
a division of Penguin Group (USA) Inc.,
375 Hudson Street, New York, New York 10014.
JOVE® is a registered trademark of Penguin Group (USA) Inc.
The "J" design is a trademark belonging to Penguin Group (USA) Inc.

PRINTED IN THE UNITED STATES OF AMERICA

10 9 8 7 6 5 4 3 2 1

For Norma, who always supported;
Gordon, who ever encouraged;
Becky, who tirelessly read;
and Jason, who always believed

ACKNOWLEDGMENTS

I'd like to thank my agent, Howard Morhaim, for all his work. At Berkley I'd like to thank my editor, Ginjer Buchanan, for being such a pleasure to work with. Thanks to my phenomenal copyeditor, Sandy Su, who did a fantastic and thorough job. I owe much of my inspiration to Glacier National Park, with its jagged, snowy peaks, high alpine trails, and phenomenal wildlife. I hope fellow lovers of this area can forgive the few small liberties I took in my descriptions of the park and its surrounding areas. My deepest gratitude to Jason, for believing in me and being so supportive. And finally, I'd like to thank Norma, my traveling companion, friend, and mother. It was during one of our stays in Glacier National Park that the seeds of this novel were sown. I will always treasure the memories of us hiking along the steep Highline Trail and climbing to Grinnell Glacier.

1

MADELINE was sure she was being watched. She squatted at the edge of the icy river, pausing a moment to dip her hand into the cold water and glance around behind her. For the past half hour, she'd had the most peculiar feeling that someone was following her, keeping just out of her sight. But she was in the wilderness, the far backcountry, and hadn't seen another hiker in two days.

She paused at the bottom of a cliff, a waterfall streaming from the top and plunging a hundred feet to form the river at her feet. Mist plumed around her, beading in her eyelashes. The icy bite of the glacial meltwater stung her hand, but it felt good. The air was so *hot*. She'd never known it to be so hot in the mountains. For the past five days it had been well into the upper nineties. A strenuous four-hour hike had brought her up high into this mountain pass, where waterfalls cascaded over brilliantly green mossy slopes, and marmots scurried through wildflower-strewn meadows before darting back into their safe homes inside rocky slopes.

The feeling of being watched faded. Madeline glanced around her. No one was in sight, just the cloudless blue sky above her and the mountains, immense and snow-covered. It wasn't like her to get jittery in the backcountry.

She let the water cascade over her hand. It made her feel more than cool; she felt free. She was in the mountains, away from her problems and the pressure of decisions. The wind was stronger by the current, sweeping along the water and bringing with it the cold from the glaciers above.

As she sat at the edge of the water, watching the sun bathe the brilliant yellows and reds of the wildflowers, a tremendous rumble thundered against the mountain. She peered upward toward the sound, where the waterfall disappeared above the cliff face. A resonant crack shook the mountain again, making her jump. She went off balance and crashed onto her knees. Icy water swallowed her hands. Quickly she scrambled away from the river's edge and got to her feet. Another deep boom cracked against the mountain, sending a shower of pebbles and sand down on her from the cliff above. Madeline readjusted her backpack and looked up nervously to the top of the waterfall. It was definitely coming from up there. But what could it be? She wasn't close enough to the snowpack for an avalanche.

Boom!

The earth quaked beneath her.

A sudden shrill symphony of whistles echoed up from the marmots. She glanced over to the nearby rockslide remains, and to her surprise saw marmots fleeing down the side of the mountain, at least twenty of them, skittering and leaping and running.

She suddenly knew that she didn't have time. She should have run when she first heard it.

Madeline turned and leapt away from the river, the weight of her backpack slamming against her back as she ran, *thump, thump, thump.*

And then the rumble became a roar, the roar a deafening cacophony of thunder, and in her peripheral vision Madeline saw a wall of water rising up at the top the waterfall, a tremendous wave of white turbulence. And she saw trees in the whiteness, their skeletal roots writhing in the tumult, like gigantic, fleshless hands, flexing and grabbing the air.

Madeline ran, muscles burning with the effort.

She tore across the mountainside, not going down, but going up and across, thinking the water would be less likely to reach her there. If one of those trees hit her in the head, she'd never survive. The air was burning in her lungs now, veins standing out on her neck as she struggled against the weight of her pack that wanted to pull her back.

She thought of dumping it, but there wasn't time. Madeline raced on, trying not to think about the weight or the crashing water, trying just to flee.

And then the water hit her.

With tremendous force she smashed face-first toward the ground, but before the rocks there could cut her, she was swept off her feet in a torrent of water, tumbling and twisting and going under. Her nose filled with water, and she gasped for breath as her head went down into the frigid torrent. The fierce current whipped her around mercilessly, as if she weighed no more than a leaf.

As Madeline struggled to right herself beneath the water, her feet tangled in something hard and unyielding with a million fingers that snaked out to grab her. Rough wood and branches cut into her legs and arms, and she realized it was a tree, rolling in the current beneath her.

The air burned in her lungs. She had to get a breath. Twisting and contorting, she couldn't even flip herself over. It was as if something was holding her down, *trying* to drown her. She struggled more, pushing against the rough bark of the tree while struggling to hold her breath. But she couldn't wriggle free. Her backpack caught in the branches, holding her fast.

Forcing herself to calm down, she unbuckled the straps around her hips and chest, then slipped her arms out. Kicking out vigorously, she broke branches and got free. She desperately swam toward what she thought was the surface. But her grappling hands found only branches and the rough rocks. She bounced against them painfully, cracking her knee and bashing her elbow.

Over and over she somersaulted in the freezing water,

until she was so disoriented she had no idea which way was toward air. Tumbling, crashing, pounding over rock after rock, plunging ever downward, down the mountain.

She grasped desperately at branches and rocks as they passed by over and under and next to her. And then she was careening head over foot, arms flailing in the frigid water, legs scraping painfully against passing granite beneath her, bones connecting painfully with solid rock, jutting edges and boulders and slabs of scraping roughness.

She coughed involuntarily, her lungs out of air.

She tried to swim in the other direction, kicking out frantically. For a second she was fighting through a maze of branches, and then a hard slap of water hit her in the face. Her head reached air. She gasped deeply, saw a moment of blue sky just before the tremendous trunk of a tree spun into her line of sight and connected violently with her head.

A blinding light erupted behind her eyes, and her muscles refused to work as she sank down into the frigid darkness.

2

Several weeks before

WHEN the knock sounded on Madeline's door, she started so badly that tea sloshed out of her cup and onto her book. She looked up from the couch, seeing the outline of someone behind the door curtain. She glanced down at her watch. It couldn't be George. He wasn't due back in town until later that day.

Her stomach went sour as she rose, trying to make out the shape behind the curtain: a woman.

The knock came again, but Madeline stood frozen in the middle of the tiny apartment. After a moment's hesitation she sat back down, opening her book once more. Then the knocking started again. Incessant knocking.

"Madeline?" came a woman's voice from the other side of the door. "Are you in there?"

Who the hell?

"Please, Madeline. It's a matter of life and death. We need you."

Need her? No one had ever needed her before. Avoided her at all costs, but not *needed* her.

"It's my daughter. She's missing."

The book fell out of Madeline's loose fingers. Slowly she rose to her feet, then walked numbly to the door. Pulling aside the little curtain, she saw Natalie Stevenson, a young mother who had often whispered about Madeline at the grocery store or in the line at the post office.

"Your mom told me where I could find you," Natalie said through the glass.

"My mom?" A daze filled Madeline's head. She didn't realize her parents knew anything but her PO address.

"Please." Natalie's tearstained face was pitifully red and swollen.

Then Madeline felt herself opening the door though everything inside her screamed to just lower the curtain and walk away.

Ten minutes later, Madeline raced across a field behind the Stevensons' house, clutching the last thing little Kate Stevenson had been known to touch; a small robot action figure. She tried not to stumble, speeding faster and faster as she leapt through the tall grass. Clearing her mind, she let the images come to her freely.

The little girl in a white dress, playing and laughing behind the Stevensons' house with a stuffed dinosaur and the robot toy.

Two older boys approaching. Teasing the little girl about her dad. "He's a drunk."

The girl, defiant at first. "No, he's not."

The boys continue taunting, malice in their eyes. "Saw him. Wrecked the company car. He's a useless drunk."

The girl, sobbing. "No, he's not!"

"Didn't you hear? Old Man Taggert fired him. You're going to starve. He won't work in this town again."

"No!" The little girl dropping the robot, running out of the yard, clutching her dinosaur. Entering the field at the edge of the property.

The boys laughing, staying behind.

Madeline ran on. The blond grass whipped and stung her bare legs below her shorts.

In a place where the grass was smashed flat, she spotted something brown. She raced to the spot and looked down. The brown, furry face of a brontosaurus smiled up at her. Bending over, she picked up the toy. Emotions swept over her. Images.

The little girl in the white dress sobbing uncontrollably in the grass, chest heaving, thinking about her dad, of the stink of alcohol on his breath.

Memories of a time the girl had spied on him from the stairs as he pulled a bottle of vodka out from behind the worn couch cushions and took a long, deep drink.

The girl kneeling in the grass for a long time, sobbing until her chest shuddered when she inhaled.

Then dropping the dinosaur and running on, toward her secret place, a lightning-scarred hollow tree beyond the old dam.

The girl had left for it just a few moments before.

Clutching the brontosaurus tight under her arm, Madeline raced forward. Ahead lay the edge of the woods. Beyond that burbled the rushing white water of the North Cascade River and the old cement dam, abandoned in the 1940s. She raced to the edge of the woods and entered the forest, the rich scent of sun-warmed pine greeting her. Following the worn path that dam workers had used decades before, she strained her ears for any sound of the girl, but the gentle whisper of wind in the pine needles muffled the sounds around her. A pounding cacophony erupted, slowing her pace, but she realized instantly it was a woodpecker, high in the trees, thrumming away on a decaying tree. She ran on.

Soon the roar of white water replaced the whisper of wind. The air temperature dropped noticeably as the cool air blew off the river. The old dam came into view, a narrow expanse of concrete built over the tumbling teal water. The large turbines had been removed in the '40s, leaving large holes through which the water now filtered.

On one side of the dam the glacier-fed river ran wide and deep. In the beginning of the century, when the dam was still relatively new, a lake had formed on that side of the barrier. But over the years it slowly drained away as more and more cracks opened in the old cement. On the other side of the dam, water gushed from the turbine holes with explosive force, returning to its native river form, free from its man-made confines.

Madeline stopped, staring at that white churning water, a vivid memory of her friend Ellie floating down those seething depths. She couldn't do this. Not the river.

She stopped short of crossing the dam and looked around for the girl. "Kate!" she yelled. The roar of the water filled her ears. Even if the girl yelled back, Madeline might not be able to hear her.

The hollowed-out tree lay on the other side of the dam. To reach it, Madeline would have to walk out over the top of the dam, a narrow ridge of concrete spanning the rapids below. She hadn't crossed that dam since the day she lost Ellie. She couldn't do it again. "Kate!" she called.

Nothing.

Kneeling down into the soft bed of pine needles, she touched the edge of the dam, hoping to get an image that would tell her if the girl had run this far. Her fingers rested on the rough concrete, and images rushed into her.

Kate, reaching the dam and starting across it, hands thrust out to maintain her balance, eyes blurring with tears, barely able to see the concrete ridge under her feet.

Balance failing, arms windmilling, the girl, terrified, falling over the side.

Freezing water engulfing her, desperate swimming, rough rocks banging her knees and scraping her arms.

Then the black mouth of the turbine hole fast approaching, the water sucking her inside. Crashing into a clump of sharp debris on the opposite side of the hole, held there, stuck there, lungs burning with lack of air as the water flooded past her body, stealing her warmth.

Trying to scramble free, but too weak against the strength of the current, too hung up in long, snaking arms of old, slimy branches.

Madeline gasped and straightened up.

The girl was drowning.

Or dead already. *Ellie.*

Without thinking, she dropped the stuffed dinosaur and robot, tore off her boots, threw them to the side, and ran onto the dam. Leaping off where the girl had fallen, she drew in a breath as she plunged into the icy cold below. Instantly the numbing water knocked the air from her chest. She fought to the surface, gasped in fresh air, and then plunged back in, swimming up next to the dam. The force of water against her was incredible, and for a moment she didn't think she'd be able to move where she wanted. It slammed her against the side of the dam and held her there.

The turbine holes lay on the bottom of the dam, and she managed to creep downward, using the force of water to steady herself against the dam. Her eyes wide in the clear water, she found the edge of an opening and pulled herself downward to peer inside.

White fabric filled the hole, plastered against the tumble of branches and mud beyond, and she realized it was the little girl's dress, tossed in the powerful current. The hole reached back at least three feet, and Madeline could barely make out the girl's hair-plastered face, just a hint of pale in the turbulence among a dozen twigs and sticks and leaves spiraling madly inside. While the openings in the debris were certainly large enough for water to get through, they weren't large enough for a human to escape.

Snaking her arm into the opening, she attempted to grab Kate, Madeline's arm whipping violently in the current. The little girl wasn't moving. Her hair parted in a gust of current, and Madeline saw with horror that her eyes and mouth gaped open.

Pulling herself down farther, she managed to make contact with the girl's arm. She tugged fiercely, but couldn't even budge her. The current was both helpful and harmful; while it kept her plastered against the side of the dam, it was just too powerful to yank Kate out.

But Madeline tried again, this time reaching both arms into the large hole and grasping one of Kate's legs. Suddenly Madeline slid down farther, crying out underwater for fear that she, too, would be sucked into the hole. But then her position stabilized. Pulling with all her strength, Madeline squeezed her eyes shut, no air left in her lungs. Kate's body gave a little, but she realized there was no way she'd be able to pull her free from the hole and then around the lip and up to safety.

She had to think of something else.

Letting go, she crawled up the side of the dam and burst into the air above. Gasping, she didn't stop to recover, instead gripping the edge of the dam and pulling herself up dripping onto the top.

The glacial meltwater had robbed her of every bit of warmth, her cold muscles rebelling with every movement. She peered over the other side of the dam. If she couldn't pull Kate out, maybe she could yank the debris free from the other side.

Knowing she couldn't fight the current if she just leapt in, Madeline dashed back to the bank of the river, ran around the dam, and waded into the frigid water on the other side. Before her the water roared out of the four turbine holes. Kate lay trapped in the second. Pressing against the wall of the dam, Madeline waded out to the first out spout in thigh-high water. It was too high to leap over, and she couldn't crawl under it because it rushed out flush with the riverbed. Her only option was to wade out farther into the torrent where the current would be less powerful and then burst across the outpour. Leaving the safety of the dam wall, she cut out diagonally, reached the rushing column of water, and then made a dash across it. Instantly her feet swept out from under her, and she desperately kicked and swam, angling back toward the dam. Her feet hit large rocks beneath, and she used them to spring-board back into the shallows next to the dam.

Now she was between the first two turbine holes. She ran toward the second one. Roughly four feet across, the dark hole erupted water at a violent rate. She wasn't sure if she could even thrust her hands into the outpour. Approaching the opening from the side, Madeline braced one foot against the dam and forced her arms into the frigid water. Immediately the water spat her hands back out. She tried again, more quickly this time, and her fingers laced around a thick, knotted branch inside the hole. She pulled, straining, to no avail, the algae on the wood making the branch too slippery to hang on to. The angle was too awkward, not giving her enough leverage.

Not letting go of the branch, Madeline moved forward, plunging her entire body into the outflow and bracing her legs on the dam below the opening. Cold water exploded over her body, bursting up under her chin and spraying out behind her. Throwing her back into the effort, Madeline strained against the branch, gritting her teeth, gasping for air when she got the chance.

The thick branch slipped and shifted a little to one side, and she strained harder. It shifted again and came free in a wave of debris, hurtling Madeline backward into the river with explosive force. Twigs and branches lashed at her arms and legs as she gasped for breath and went under, releasing the heavy branch to the depths below.

Turbulent water tossed and somersaulted her, dashing her against slippery rocks. She found her bearings and righted herself in the current, head bobbing above the surface. Desperately she looked around for Kate, for a hint of white fabric among the deep teal and thrashing whitecaps of the river.

Sun-bleached branches floated by her, twigs, leaves, and then she saw the girl, bobbing facedown on the surface a few feet away. *Just like Ellie.* Madeline swam toward her, coughing up icy water and struggling against the current. Her hand closed around gauzy fabric, and she pulled, reeling the girl in against her body. She turned her over quickly, horrified to see the wide-open eyes, the blue lips of the tiny mouth.

Angling an arm beneath the girl's chin, Madeline swam

on her side toward the shore, a tangle of sodden logs, pine needles, and kinnikinnick bushes. She reached the bank, hauled the girl out in front of her, and then crawled onto the soggy earth beside her.

Immediately she felt for a pulse and was relieved to find one, though it was very weak. But the girl was not breathing.

Madeline's father was a wildlands firefighter and emergency medical technician and had taught her CPR when she was just a kid.

Madeline went to work.

She remembered she had to check three things: airway, breathing, and circulation. Rolling the girl onto her side, Madeline reached into her mouth and checked for obstructions. Her index finger hooked around a small twig and a plug of mud, and she fished them out. Squeezing the girl, she forced water from her lungs. A stream of fluid escaped between the blue lips, followed, to Madeline's great relief, by a small gasp. Quickly she worked to stabilize her, administering a ten-count of mouth-to-mouth. Kate coughed and sputtered, drawing in a ragged breath, her eyes fluttering, blinking, and tearing up. Madeline checked her pulse. It was stronger.

The girl coughed again, flecks of water raining from her mouth.

Madeline had to get help. Knowing it was too dangerous to move her, she spoke softly to her. "Can you hear me?" After a moment, Kate's eyes turned and attempted to focus on Madeline. "I have to get help. You have to lie here very still while I'm gone, do you understand? You could have other injuries, and moving around might make them worse." The girl didn't speak, just continued to breathe raggedly, her eyes dazed and wide. "I'll be back as fast as I can." Madeline didn't like how blue the girl's skin was. Hypothermia. She had to move quickly.

Trying to determine how far they'd drifted downstream, she stood, shivering in her own soaked clothing. "I'll be back," she said, looking back down at the girl reassuringly.

The girl's mouth moved, a whisper escaping her lips.

"What?" Madeline bent down to listen.

"Winthrop," the girl whispered.

Madeline raised her eyebrows. "Winthrop?"

"My . . . my dino."

Madeline thought of the smiling brontosaurus she'd found in the field. "He's fine," she told Kate. "I found him myself. He's waiting for you."

The girl shuddered and coughed again.

"Try to stay awake," Madeline told her, and then dashed off along the riverbank in her sock feet. Avoiding sharp rocks and pointed branches, she soon reached the dam and the worn path. Grabbing her shoes, she slid them on, not bothering to lace them. Stooping again, she grabbed Winthrop and the robot and took off for town.

Madeline reached the Stevensons' house in under ten minutes, a painful stitch in her side and her lungs on fire. Kate's parents summoned the paramedics. The minutes stretched endlessly as they waited. Madeline knew her father would likely be one of the respondents, and she dreaded seeing him, not knowing what to say. The ambulance roared up, and he jumped out of the back, saving her the awkwardness of talking to him by completely ignoring her. Even as she led them back to Kate, he didn't so much as meet her eyes. On the riverbank, the EMTs immobilized Kate on a gurney and transported her back to the ambulance. Madeline placed Winthrop next to Kate's thin arm as they loaded her inside.

Her chest expanded with relief as her father drove away. Another moment of uneasiness over, another moment of their inevitable encounters survived. It hit her powerfully then that when she moved, she wouldn't have to see either parent ever again.

Now she sat in a worn-out cushioned chair in the emergency room, having been checked for hypothermia herself. Luckily she was all right and had changed into dry clothes. Her long, wavy brown hair hung in wet tangles around her shoulders. Across from her, Kate's father wept noisily, holding the girl's robot, and her mother looked exhausted, anxiously glancing up every time a doctor entered the room to talk to a nurse or another family.

As Kate's father cried, Madeline couldn't help but notice the stench of alcohol radiating from him. He smelled saturated with it.

It made her profoundly sad. Paul Stevenson was a nice man, a creative genius who had never been able to realize his dream in life: to make a living at painting. He had turned to drinking just last year and lost his job because of it. The whole town knew about it, and small towns could be as cruel as they were kind. The rumors were tearing his family apart, and Paul wept now, openly and grievously, in the face of such a near tragedy.

The double doors of the emergency room slid open, admitting a gush of fresh air. Madeline looked up. George Newcastle stood there, his eyes searching the room. He spotted her and rushed over. A tall man in his early twenties, with long black hair swept back in a ponytail, George usually exuded calm. Right now he looked spooked.

"Madeline," he breathed, kneeling down and wrapping his arms around her. "I just heard. Are you okay?" The sensation of being hugged always thrilled her, and she welcomed the familiar scent of his wool jacket.

He pulled away and studied her with his intense brown eyes.

She'd known George for a little over seven months, and he had quickly become her closest friend. Her only friend. He'd moved to her little town and rented a house there to save money while attending the university in Missoula. Rent prices there were highly inflated, so he had chosen to commute instead.

He hugged her again, and she was grateful for him, for her life. She could be bobbing down the river right then, sightless eyes staring up at the darkening sky.

She pulled away, not wanting to hug him for too long. He was very nice, but he had feelings for her that she didn't return, and she didn't like the thought of leading him on.

"Thanks for coming, George," she told him.

George slid in beside her. Taking her hand companionably, he whispered, "Any word?"

Madeline shook her head. "We're still waiting."

They returned to silence, listening only to the soft gasps and sniffs from Kate's father.

A few minutes later, the door to the examination rooms opened, and a young Chinese-American doctor with short, spiky hair appeared. He approached them confidently, a pleased look on his face. They all stood up tensely.

"She's going to be fine," he told them, holding his hands out in a placating gesture. "She's suffering from hypothermia and has some superficial cuts and bruises, but she's going to be just fine."

"Oh, God," her dad gasped, bursting into tears again. "I couldn't bear to lose her."

"Well, you're not going to," the doctor reassured him, placing a hand on the man's shoulder. "Madeline here saved her life." The doctor smiled at Madeline and gave her a slight nod.

Kate's mother hugged her husband, then shook the doctor's hand and thanked him over and over again.

"You have some paperwork to fill out, though," the doctor told them.

The mother nodded and then turned to Madeline. "Thank you," she said, her face twisting with emotion. "Words just don't seem enough . . ." Then she grabbed Madeline, hugging her so tightly the air fled from her chest. Madeline grunted from the squeeze. Then reluctantly she released Madeline, gazing at her with such gratitude that Madeline grew uncomfortable. "Thank you," she said again. "A thousand times thank you."

"It's okay," Madeline said quickly. "You're welcome."

"No, it's not enough," Kate's dad put in. "If it weren't for your"—he paused, trying to find a word—"*gift*, then we wouldn't have found her. Our little girl would be—" He didn't finish.

"It's okay. Really." Madeline hated being the center of attention. She just wanted to slink out of there and go shut herself up in her apartment. "You'd better go finish that paperwork," she said lamely.

To her relief, Kate's parents nodded and turned away to follow the doctor.

"Get me out of here. Please," she breathed to George.

She hoped word of this wouldn't get out. She could already picture herself on assignment with the police, going over grisly photographs and murder weapons, her mind filling with images of horror and murder. It was exactly what she'd been avoiding since she lost Ellie.

George put one protective arm around her and led her out of the hospital. She laid her head on his chest, allowing herself a moment of feeling comforted.

She was about to transfer away from her hometown to a college in San Francisco. Two years at the local community college had only served to make her stigma grow, as more and more people met her as the "Weird Girl." She needed to clear her mind before she left and started a new life.

As the hospital doors whooshed shut behind them, she thought of Kate and her loving parents and felt a little hurt. Maybe even a little jealous. When was the last time she'd talked to her parents? Or rather, when was the last time they'd talked to her? Six months? A year? And they lived here in Mothershead.

In the parking lot, George tucked her into his car then went around to the driver's side. "I'll get you home. Bet a hot shower would be nice."

"Yes . . ." she answered distantly.

As he drove, she thought of the promise of San Francisco. She'd never lived in a city that big and relished the thought of being completely anonymous. This town was tiny, full of rumors and small minds, and she wanted out. She was tired of everyone knowing about her and her gift.

When they got to her little apartment, George walked her in, fussing over her to make sure she was okay. She appreciated the fussing. No one had cared since Ellie, and it felt

good. At last she convinced him she was fine and that they'd
meet later for dinner.

Madeline squeezed into the corner booth at the diner, glancing around at the other patrons. She heard the whispering.
Eyes averted as she met them. The waitress stood behind the
counter, serving a platter of greasy eggs to Ed Hanson, one of
the local ranchers. She exhaled with distaste when she caught
sight of Madeline. Looking back at Ed, she whispered something, and he turned on his stool, staring at Madeline. Then
he swiveled back, shaking his head. Madeline caught his
murmur: "Don't envy you, Edna."

Madeline felt for her bracelet under her sleeve, almost un-
consciously. She felt the solid silver, the little box that was the
focus of the piece of jewelry. Latched tightly, the decorative
box held precious cargo. Through the fabric, she felt the tiny
catch, ensuring it was closed. This had become her ritual
when she felt sad or isolated. Sometimes, on rare occasions,
she even opened the box.

After more than ten minutes, Edna finally made it over to
the booth. It was always the same. They hoped Madeline
would just leave, or better yet, stop coming altogether.

"Know what you want, honey?" Edna said, not making
eye contact.

As if Madeline could see into her mind by meeting her
gaze, anyway.

She took a deep breath, summoning up the energy to be
polite to people who never gave her that in return. "I'm waiting for someone. Can I just get two cups of coffee with
cream?"

"Sure thing, hon." Edna pivoted and moved away quickly.
She filled up the two cups then frowned. "I just remembered I
have to check on a delivery in the back." She looked at Ed.
"Would you be a dear?"

He glared at her, then looked at Madeline over his shoulder. "I'm a customer, you know."

"Oh, Ed," she said, waving at him dismissively, then

disappeared through the swinging kitchen doors. Slowly, Ed got up from his stool, picking up the tray with the coffee and dish of creamer. He meandered over to her table and held the tray down, but stopped short of placing the cups on the table. Finally, Madeline reached up and took the cups and dish of creamers. Ed was so busy looking away from her that the tray started to tip. As the dish of creamers slid toward the floor, both he and Madeline instinctively tried to grab it. She got there first, and Ed's hand landed right on top of hers. He yanked it away, eyes wide, and backed up into the occupied table behind him.

"Goddammnit, Ed!" a woman snarled at him. "You've gone and made me spill my coffee!"

"S-sorry," he slurred, backing around the table without breaking his gaze on Madeline.

The bell over the door rang, and a gush of fresh air spiraled into the hot diner. Madeline turned in the booth, relieved to see George. His long, dark coat caught in the wind as he pushed the door shut behind him. He turned then, scanning the diner, his long, black hair hanging freely about his shoulders.

Madeline's breath caught in her chest. He looked different. More . . . vibrant. A spark that hadn't been there before ignited in her belly. His dark brown eyes positively glittered as they surveyed the diner and then fell on her. She gave a small wave, and he navigated his way through the tables to where she sat.

"Hello, Madeline," he said, grinning, his teeth brilliant white against the tanned glow of his skin. Something was undeniably different about him, but Madeline couldn't quite place it.

"Hi, George," she said after a moment. "Have a seat."

He slid into the booth opposite her. "You look good tonight. Are you still doing okay . . . you know . . . after?"

She nodded, though inside the events at the dam had left her shaken. Her hand felt for her bracelet.

"You're playing nervously with your bracelet again," George told her.

"Oh, sorry. It's a habit."

"I've noticed. What's in the little box, anyway?"

"A treasure," Madeline said and didn't expand.

He glanced around for the waitress then, and Edna didn't disguise her horror at having to return to the table so soon. She started over empty-handed, and to save her the trip, George called, "Menus?"

Edna froze as if he'd just pulled a gun on her. "Menus?" she said weakly.

"Yeah," George said, his brow furrowing.

"I can tell you our specials," she offered after a pause.

"That's okay," George said back over the din of the other diners. "I want to peruse it."

"Um . . ." Edna glanced over at the menu box next to the counter, which was full to the top. "You can come up and pick one out . . ."

George wrinkled his forehead, obviously confused. "What?"

Madeline knew all too well what was going on. She nudged George's foot under the table. He turned to her, confused. "She doesn't want to bring the menus, George. She'd have to touch them, see, then hand them to us."

His mouth came open. "You're kidding me."

She averted her eyes. "Unfortunately, I'm not."

He'd seen this stuff before with her. But now his eyes flared, and he turned to Edna. "Bring us the menus now!" he said angrily.

Madeline's face flushed. No one had stood up for her since Ellie all those years ago.

Flustered, Edna looked down and twisted her hands, then hurried over to the menus. Wrapping her hand in her apron, she grabbed two menus and carried them over, dropping one on the table and the other clumsily on the floor.

"And how are you going to deliver the food?" George demanded.

Madeline nudged his foot again under the table, her face hot. Others turned in their chairs and booths to stare. "Thanks," she said to Edna, who was already halfway back to the counter.

George picked up the one from the floor and gave Madeline the clean one.

Then, shaking his head in disbelief, he shrugged out of his coat. Beneath it he wore a dark purple shirt and black pants. The shirt sported a Nehru collar, which wasn't buttoned, and as he leaned over to place the coat on the far side of the booth, Madeline caught a glimpse of a shapely collarbone.

Instantly she averted her eyes to her coffee cup. What was she doing? He'd never been attractive to her before. He'd always been somewhat, well . . . stiff. Good company, but not deep company. Nice eyes but not alluring eyes. But somehow, things were different tonight. Had been from the moment he walked in the door.

She wondered if the recent serious event had awakened something within her, some desire to experience things on a deeper level.

His lips were full and inviting. Surely they hadn't been the last time she'd seen him. She remembered him having a gray, pursed, slash of a mouth. His hair cascaded over his shoulders seductively, strands curling before his face. Every other time she'd seen him, he had his hair pulled back in a ponytail. The effect of seeing it down was dramatic. She even noticed how shapely his body was: lithe, athletic. She tried to look away but couldn't. She was mesmerized, fascinated at how different he looked.

And it wasn't just that he *looked* different. He *felt* different. A wave of something utterly alluring wafted off him. Other people noticed it, too. The woman in the booth behind them half turned to look around the room and ended up doing a full double take when she saw him behind her.

Madeline had been rebuffing his advances for months, and to show interest now would be too weird. They were friends. And friends were much harder to come by than dates. There was nothing powerful or magical in a date. But a friend? That was a miracle. And currently, being the "Weird Girl," she didn't have an overwhelming amount of friends.

"What deep thoughts are burning in that head of yours?"

George asked suddenly, startling her. He took a sip of his coffee. "Oooh . . . ouch. Too hot." He brought a hand up to his lips and touched them gently. Madeline found herself staring. Again.

"Okay?" she asked, averting her eyes.

"Yeah. Just hotter than I expected."

Tell me about it, she thought and then smiled in spite of herself.

He leaned across the table, nearer to her. "What's this big news you wanted to tell me?"

Taking a deep breath, she twisted the amethyst ring she wore on her index finger. It had belonged to her beloved grandmother, Grace. She glanced around, feeling the sheer weight of being unwelcome crushing her chest. "I'm going on a backcountry trek to Glacier National Park," she told him. "Alone. To clear my head, get away from people, from my visions, my 'gift.'" She sneered on the last word.

"Alone? Isn't that dangerous?"

"Crossing the street is dangerous. There's more chance I'll get hit by a car than get eaten by a bear or fall to my death."

"What about just plain getting lost?" he asked. "I read a story about a couple who were hopelessly lost in Glacier National Park. They got separated from the trail and couldn't find it again. Helicopters searched for them. When the rescue team finally found them, the couple was nearly dead and only fifty yards away from the trail they'd been trying to find."

She smiled ruefully. That story was in a book she'd lent him herself. "I'm leaving my itinerary with you, so that if I'm not back on the right date, you can come look for me." She gave him a warm smile. "I'm also slipping a route into my dad's mailbox."

"You're not going to talk to him about it?"

"No . . ." She let the word fall silently, not going into detail.

"But he might have some advice . . . I mean, the backcountry is his terrain."

"It's just a bad idea, George."

"And your mom?"

"I'd rather not have the image of her disdain be the last thing I take into the wilds with me."

"So just your dad and I will know where you are?"

"Well, that and the park service. You know hikers have to check in with rangers before they can go anyway, and so they'll have my route, too." She sighed, looking at his worried face. "Thank you for worrying," she said. "But I'll be okay. I've done this lots of times."

"Alone?"

"Being alone is what this trip is all about. I'm about to transfer down to San Francisco and start a new life. That means new people, new environments, new challenges. I can't tell you how sick I am of . . ." She gestured around at the people in the diner, then at Edna. "Of this. You know what it's like for me, George. All my life most people have shunned me. You're the only one who's stuck around. You and Ellie. I don't want to spend the rest of my life turning people off, weirding them out."

"Those people aren't worth being your friends," George said protectively. "I don't even see why you worry about them."

"Yeah, I know." Madeline felt a flush of defensiveness. "That's because you have a normal social life. You have a circle of friends you've had since preschool, and make new ones all the time. Plus you're gorgeous, and people flock to you."

George shook his head. "No, you are gorgeous. And don't let these bastards make you feel unwanted."

They both fell silent, a lump in Madeline's throat growing more painful by the second. The incident at the dam had brought memories of Ellie crashing back on her, a resurgence of grief so powerful it made it hard to breathe. At last George said quietly, "I think it's a good idea."

Madeline smiled, then almost laughed. The thought of the peaceful backcountry, of not seeing another soul for days or weeks, sang to her like a lullaby. She couldn't wait to get out there.

George stood up and slid into the booth next to her. Putting his arms around her, he pulled her close. Several people gasped when they saw him daring to get so close to her. Over his shoulder, Madeline whispered, "This is going be great. Just me, the mountains, wildlife, and plenty of fresh air." Now, more than ever, she craved it. A vision quest. That's what she needed.

He pulled back, his hand still on her arm. "I'll know where you are. If anything happens, I'm coming to find you."

"Deal," she said. "But I'll be fine."

3

On the mountain

DARKNESS. Freezing.

The murmur of cascading water.

Reality bit at her cut and bruised body, enveloped her in ice, washed around her, cold and unrelenting.

Too tired to open her eyes, she couldn't remember where she was. Her face lay against something smooth and cold. Her arms felt wedged. Something held her steady as the frigid water curled around her, robbing her body of its last bit of heat. With that warmth had bled all sensation, and all she could do was bob on the current.

Water. She remembered water.

A great wall of water.

And then . . .

Blackness.

Madeline exhaled deeply. She was so *tired.* At least her head was above water now. She could just breathe and lie there. But she wanted to sleep. Sleep sounded so good. To rest.

Madeline lay still and let the water toss her about as she breathed in the crisp air.

Somewhere, in the back of her mind, some distant voice nagged at her, told her to pull herself out of the glacial meltwater, but she just couldn't muster the energy to move.

Water, spiraling, no air to breathe.

Hands clutching at her, dragging her down.

Darkness.

Blood. A dark-haired woman with sightless, staring eyes, throat gashed open, spilling blood. A man struck down in a street, the blood-soaked back of his long coat shredded violently. A feeble old man cowering in a corner, shrieking in terror—

Darkness.

Hands. Pulling her out of the river.

A room full of spinning dancers in ball gowns. A cobblestone street filled with the sound of clopping horse hooves. A lone candle burning atop a small piano. An opera house filled with the music of Mozart.

Darkness.

Faint sun on her eyelids.

A deep, kind voice: "Hey, you're awake. I was worried. That's quite a nasty cut on your head."

"Cut?" Madeline said groggily. All she could feel was cold. Deep, numbing cold. She brought a tentative, shaky hand to her forehead, but her hand was so numb it felt like it was asleep. She thought she detected water on her head, but it was slick, like blood. And if it was blood, her head was covered in it. *"Nothing bleeds like a head wound,"* came her mother's voice from somewhere inside her, echoing from a time when things were much easier.

"You're drenched through. You need dry clothes and fast. I didn't want to move you—didn't know if you'd broken anything. But you could be hypothermic. Are your thoughts clear?"

Madeline managed to open her eyes. They came open with a wet sucking sound, and cold water leaked into them from the corners of her eyes. As things came into focus, Madeline saw the stranger kneeling beside her. He was slightly older than her, maybe in his mid-twenties; semi-short, wavy blond hair; a slightly scruffy ill-shaven face with angular features; and haunting green, green eyes.

He left her side then. The first thing she checked, body moving stiffly, was that she still wore her bracelet with its precious silver box securely latched. She did, and it was. She also felt the weight of her pocket knife in her pocket. She hadn't lost everything. She lay blinking in the fading sunlight, blissfully warm on her face. He returned a moment later with a first aid kit. Quickly he withdrew a silver emergency blanket and laid it over her, though she couldn't feel the difference.

She tried to move, tried even to shift her weight, but she felt incredibly heavy and suddenly realized what they meant by *waterlogged*. She felt like the two-ton trunk of a tree.

Rummaging through the kit, he produced some bandages and Neosporin. He held them up and said, "Glad I always keep a first aid kit in my backpack."

"Oh, my backpack . . ." she said faintly, full of regret, remembering shrugging it off desperately in the cold water. "My supplies . . ." But she knew wriggling out of it had saved her life.

"Don't worry about that now." He gingerly dabbed the bandage on the cut. "I'm just going to clear some of the blood away so I can have a better look at the wound." After a moment of dabbing he said, "It's stopped bleeding."

"Where am I, exactly?" she asked, wondering how far she'd been swept away.

"You're way backcountry. Don't know how long you were in the drink."

She squinted, swallowed hard. "Think I floated on a limb for a while." She remembered feeling her arms lodged between branches.

"Probably saved your life." He shook his head slightly. "I hiked about six hours to get out this far." He affixed a bandage with tape and smiled amiably. "Luckily, this is the first backcountry camp on this trail. We should be able to make it back within a day." His smile faded as he studied her intently.

"What is it?" she asked, uncomfortable suddenly under his gaze.

"Do you remember anything you said before you woke up?"

"Was I talking in my sleep?"

He nodded. "Were you having a dream?"

Madeline shook her head, which throbbed in protest. "Not exactly, I . . ."

And then, checking the tape on the bandage, the stranger touched his bare hand to the skin of her forehead, and striking visions flickered to life before her.

A masquerade party—costumed people whirling on a dance floor.

Tinkling notes of a harpsichord drifting down a grand hall.

Climbing inside a horse-drawn carriage on a busy cobblestone street.

Racing in a Model T along a dirt road in pursuit of another car.

Rain falling in sheets beyond a French window.

Fighting off the images, Madeline managed to speak. "No, I don't remember any dreams." She wasn't about to go into detail about her wonderful "gift" with this stranger. Her head hurt too much to concentrate on those elusive visions, and they slipped away. "How bad is it?" she asked him tentatively.

"I don't think you'll need stitches. Just rest and someone to watch over you. Your pupils are a little dilated. Can you focus?" He held up a hand. She nodded. "Do you feel sick to your stomach?"

"Hard to tell. I just generally feel terrible." She struggled to sit up then, suddenly aware of how uncomfortable the ground was. Once up, she realized she was lying on a vast stretch of bleached white driftwood, stripped of its bark over time by the river, jumbles upon jumbles of it carried down over the years and distributed along the bank by the same river that had brought her there. A particularly sharp limb had been under her back. The man watched her sit up, readying to grab her if she got dizzy.

"I spotted your green shirt in the white branches. You were in the water, tangled in those logs," he told her. "I was a little afraid to approach you. Thought you might have been . . ."

"What?" she said, unsteadily getting to her feet. "Dead?" Her legs were positively numb, and she wobbled, barely maintaining her balance.

He nodded.

"And you pulled me out of the water?"

"Yes."

Madeline crinkled her brow. She remembered hands grabbing at her in the water, pulling her down. Perhaps she'd dreamed it. Or maybe it had just been the limbs of a tree. She also remembered the dark visions that had accompanied them.

"When I got closer, I heard you gasping."

"And talking."

"Yeah, that, too, after I picked you up." He smiled. It was a lovely smile.

"I said something embarrassing, didn't I?"

"No, no," he assured her. "Nothing like that. Just stuff about picking your nose."

"Oh, no," she mumbled.

"No, seriously."

He touched her then, and a stream of visions came to her.

Weeping before a flower-strewn casket.

A covered wagon on fire.

Sunset over a meadow ablaze with vibrant wildflowers.

He was a source of powerful images, and she did her best to block any more input from him. It was rare for her to even pick up visions from touching people. Usually only objects gave her images.

One of the only other people she could remember picking

up images from was Mrs. Ferrington, her neighbor, whose sister had been hit by a car in 1917. Mrs. Ferrington, all of six at the time, had been standing not more than ten feet away when it happened. Her sister had lived, with no permanent injury, but the incident itself had traumatized Mrs. Ferrington—left powerful pictures Madeline had picked up on suddenly one afternoon while helping the elderly lady in her garden.

But that was the only person. Except . . . that day in the forest when Ellie . . .

"Are you okay?" he asked. "You look a million miles away."

She came back to the present. "Yeah."

"Anyway, you started talking when I pulled you out of the water."

She tried to steady her mind. What if the terrible visions she'd received earlier were from this helpful stranger, as well? But no—those visions came from hands dragging her under, not out of, the water. Maybe she'd just been delirious.

Still, glancing away from him casually, she tried to see how tough the terrain was, if she'd be able to run from him if she had to. There was a lot of jagged-limbed driftwood and big glacial boulders in the way. It'd be a tough run.

But even if she could somehow manage to get away, she didn't have any supplies. She had no way to purify backcountry water and knew she could catch some pretty nasty bugs from drinking it straight. She could survive long enough without food, but she'd be weak. And what if she had a concussion?

No—it would be best for now to stay with the stranger, she decided. Besides, if he did do those terrible things she'd seen, he certainly didn't realize she knew. He had no way to know of her "gift."

"Are you thirsty?" he asked.

Unless that is what she had been talking about while unconscious.

"Hungry at all?"

Unless she'd given a play-by-play account of his past

crimes while lying half-conscious on the riverbank. That would explain why he was so anxious to see if she remembered what her "dreams" had been about.

"Hello?" he said.

"What?" she asked, forcing a smile.

"I asked if you needed something to drink."

"Thanks, no," she said, making herself talk evenly, calmly. She hooked a thumb at the river. "Had enough to drink today."

He laughed at that. It was a good-natured laugh. "I guess so. Anyway, I'm Noah." He held out his hand, and she shook it. "Noah Percival Lanchester."

A ballroom. Dancing. Candles gleaming in the chandeliers. Warm laughter. No danger. No fear.

She pushed the images away. "That's not a name you hear often," she said, pulling her hand back.

"Yeah. Unless you're building arks or something." He smiled, and it was positively infectious. "The middle one's because my parents are English professors. You know, as in King Arthur's knight." He smiled again.

"Right, but you're missing your armor."

He looked down, as if surprised. "So I am."

"I'm Madeline. And thanks for helping me before I became an ice sculpture."

"My pleasure, m'lady." He bowed graciously, and she laughed. "Well," he said, looking around judiciously, "we've got to get you into some warm clothes. It's amazing you don't have hypothermia. You must not have been in the water for very long. But that cut on your head—we need to get that looked at as soon as we get to the ranger's station."

"How far is that?" she asked.

"About ten miles, I think," he responded. "But the good news is that it's all downhill."

Instantly she thought of her cell phone, of getting the ranger to meet them instead. But it had been in her pack. "Do you have a cell?" she asked him.

"No, though now I wish I did." He regarded her, his smile falling away. "We are going to get you safely out of here."

Noah suddenly glanced toward the river's edge, then bent his head down in a furtive movement that was eerily quick, as if she didn't actually see him move—suddenly he was just in a different position.

"What?" she asked, turning to follow his gaze.

Noah continued to stare in that direction. "Nothing. I thought I saw someone."

"Out here?"

"Well," he straightened up and looked back at her. "I'm traveling with someone else. He left camp this morning to go to a site higher up on the mountain. He's a photographer—wanted to go get some sunset pictures. We're supposed to meet back here in two days."

She turned to regard the river, suddenly feeling scared and a long way from home. She thought about the icy water that had brought her there, shuddering at the memory. "I had just gone over Swiftcurrent Pass. The river just flooded so fast!" she said aloud. "I'd never seen anything like that before." She watched it churn past now, overflowing its usual banks with roaring white turbulence.

"I know! I heard the boom and then *bam*! All this water and logs come tumbling down the mountainside. I've never seen anything like it. There's a glacial lake up there," he said, pointing at the snow-laden peak. "I think all this heat must have caused it to melt completely and break through its ice barrier."

Madeline studied the glaciers on the peaks around her, their deep blue ice cracked in some places from the weight of accumulated layers. She loved glaciers, loved to see the deep black crevasses in the ice perched high on a precipice. But now she was afraid. Her brow knitted.

Noah saw it immediately. "Hey, don't worry," he said gently. "I've got plenty of food, plenty of water, and we're going to hike out of here together."

"Thank you for helping me," she said.

His gaze was warm and genuine. "Of course," he said. "I'm a knight, remember?"

"That's right. Thank you."

"Great. And if I'd just let you wander off, I'd never know how everything turned out. It'd be too much of a cliff-hanger."

"Cliff-hanger?"

"Yeah," he went on. "Something really serious happens and then cut! Straight to commercials, and they make you sit through all those cleaning supply ads with talking bathtubs and animated bald men appearing suddenly in your floor. I don't know about you, but if my toilet suddenly grew eyes and started talking, I'd freak out!"

Madeline laughed out loud. "Well, no cliff-hanger here. I'd love your help."

"Terrific," he said. "Hungry?"

"Waterlogged."

"Of course. Well, I'm going to make some pasta. Maybe the smell of it will entice you to eat. Freeze-dried backcountry food certainly does that to me. Yum! C'mon," he added, gesturing over a little hill. "My camp's just on the other side."

At his camp stood a little purple and burgundy tent, a tremendous backpack with a cup and pan hanging off it, and a little Therm-a-Rest chair. Next to it lay a bear-safe food canister.

"Nice tent," she said, though she was looking at the chair.

"Have a seat," he offered, noticing her attention. "You must be beat."

"I am," she responded, went straight for the chair, and sat down. She always thought Therm-a-Rest chairs were the best, lightweight and compact—just two great cushions, really, with straps holding them together. And they were comfortable as anything. Self-inflating, too. She'd had one in her pack, a lovely blue one. The kind that doubled as a sleeping pad.

"I'll probably never see mine again."

He sat down on a boulder near her and began filling his tin cup with filtered water from one of his bottles. She looked at it questioningly, wondering if she could even get it down.

"How about some dry clothes?" he asked.

She looked at him appreciatively. "Can you spare any?"

"Certainly." He went to his backpack and pulled out a bundle of clothes, a small towel, and a pair of Teva sandals. "You can change in the tent," he offered.

She placed her water on the ground and stood up, taking the clothes from him. "This is great," she said.

The tiny tent, a one-person backpacker's tent, was so small she couldn't even kneel but had to lie down to change. She peeled off her soaked clothes, toweled off with the little backpacker's towel, and put on a warm, dry turtleneck. Fleece pants, a polypropylene shirt and jacket followed, along with a woolly pair of socks. She knew the socks would get wet as soon as she put her boots back on, so she put on the sandals he'd offered her instead. They were too big, but the adjustable straps kept them on. When she emerged from the tent, he was still sitting down on the boulder.

She laid her wet clothes next to the tent and then returned to the chair. He looked at her with pensive eyes. The little crinkles around them told her he spent a lot of time out in the sun, probably hiking and enjoying the outdoors.

"You're lucky to be all in one piece."

"Yes." She went silent, eyes huge, as she remembered gasping for breath, the cold, the tree branch slamming into her head.

"Are you okay?" he asked, studying her face.

She looked at him, trying to swallow back the lump of fear that welled up in her at the thought of the freezing water. She felt the bandage gingerly with tentative fingertips. It stung a little. But she was alive. "Yeah," she said finally, meeting his eyes. "I think I am okay."

"I'm glad," was all he said.

He stood up then, rummaged through his pack. He began to set up his camp stove, screwing the fixture into a little tank of butane.

"Thank you," she said, shuddering suddenly at what might have happened to her if he hadn't been there.

"You're welcome." He smiled at her. He really was handsome. She stared a little too long. Then, to cover her staring, she averted her eyes and picked up the cup of water. She wasn't used to people treating her like just another person. Anonymity had its blessings.

He looked satisfied that she was drinking and grabbed the food canister. She watched him move efficiently, rummaging through his pack for plates and cups. The sun dipped below the mountain, and now the blue sky deepened in hue. Before them lay a vast glacial field covered with yellow glacier lilies and vibrant pink and red Indian paintbrush, all wavering in the gentle breeze. A deepening shadow overcame the field as the light faded, taking on the soft shades of twilight.

Dinner was a slightly crunchy, gooey concoction—freeze-dried noodles in Alfredo sauce—and before they were finished, darkness had taken over. A full moon rose in the east, tremendous and yellow, casting light over the field and the forest of pines that lay beyond. Noah whistled, wiping out the dishes, while Madeline continued to sit and rest, finally feeling warm. Her long hair was almost dry, too.

As she watched Noah work, a sudden, furtive movement on her left caught her attention. She jerked her head to follow it and saw a dark shape darting across the white of the drift logs.

She squinted and leaned forward in the chair, trying to make out what it was. The figure was squat, low to the ground, moving too quickly to be a bear, but way too big to be a wolverine. Its wet fur gleamed in the moonlight, but she couldn't even make out the basic shape of the animal. *Wolf?* she wondered.

"Noah," she said quietly, "look over there." She pointed toward the jumble of tree trunks where the dark figure crouched, now immobile. She had the familiar feeling that it was watching them.

Noah stopped cleaning the dishes and turned to face the spot. "What is it?" He sounded alarmed.

"Not sure . . ." She studied the spot but now couldn't make out the animal at all. After years of wildlife watching, she'd trained her eyes to take in the slightest movement. Sometimes that was all that alerted her to a lone pika gathering grasses along an old lichen-covered rockslide, or a herd of goats leaping about on a mountain slope. But now she didn't see any movement.

"What did you see?" Noah asked more nervously now, abandoning his dishes altogether. He squatted down beside her and peered intently at the logs.

She glanced at him, seeing his worried expression. "I'm sorry. I didn't mean to scare you. It wasn't a grizzly. It might have been a wolf, but I'm sure you know it's just a myth that a wolf will attack a human—"

"That's not what I'm worried about." He held up his hand in a gesture of silence and studied the trunks along the riverbank intently. "Was it moving quickly?"

"Yes," she said, bewildered about his worried state. The only animal that could potentially do them harm was a grizzly, and it certainly had been no grizzly.

"Stayed low to the ground?" he asked, peering out into the deepening shadows.

"Yes. Look, what do you think—"

"Shh . . ." Now Noah was listening intently, too, though Madeline didn't know how he could hear anything over the roar of the river.

But she listened, too. Wind in the subalpine firs. The high cry of a night bird. And always the roar of the unrelenting water.

"I think you'd better change into your hiking boots," he said.

"But they're wet and—"

"All the same," he insisted, never taking his eyes off the jumble of logs. "I think you'd better put them on. I think we need to leave."

She studied his face, bewildered. He was alert, nervous.

She looked around. Her boots lay on the other side of the chair. Beyond lay the alpine meadow, the wildflowers now lost in the darkness. "We can't hike down now in the dark."

"We'll have to. There!" he said, so suddenly that Madeline started, causing her heart to pound.

And she saw it.

The dark, hunkering shape crept through there again, darting in and out of the logs, furtive and quick, weaving closer and closer to them. She could see now it didn't have wet fur at all, but oily black skin which glistened in the brightening moonlight. The animal was lithe and muscled, moving efficiently, though she still couldn't see enough of it to tell what it was.

"Quick," Noah urged her, placing an insistent hand on her shoulder.

Madeline shucked off the sandals and pulled on her wet boots, knowing they'd soak through the dry socks in a matter of seconds. Quickly she tightened the laces.

With her boots on, she turned her eyes back to the logs. The creature had stopped, and Madeline felt eyes burning into her. And then she watched as it put a paw on one of the logs. It was dark against the white of the wood, distinct in the gleaming moonlight.

And Madeline saw immediately that it wasn't a paw at all, but a hand. A hand as black as charcoal, with impossibly hooked claws that bit into the wood.

"He's got the advantage," Noah said grimly.

"He?" Madeline asked with bewilderment. *"He?"*

Noah didn't seem to hear her. "I can't fight him like this. I can't endanger you. If I could find someplace for you to hide . . ."

"Fight him— What's going on? What is that thing?"

He turned to her then, his eyes full of fear. "I'll explain on the way down the mountain. But right now, we've got to get you somewhere safe. C'mon!" He stood up and gestured for her to follow. "There's an abandoned skiers' hut just over that rise." He pointed to a cluster of trees on a hill. "It's not the greatest, but we'd be more protected than we are now. Okay?"

Madeline nodded, feeling bewildered.

Moving to his pack quickly, he threw everything inside haphazardly and zipped it up, leaving the tent standing some distance away. He grabbed the chair with one hand as he slung the pack over his shoulder. "Let's go," he said, and she caught a glimpse of his eyes in the moonlight, haunted and terrified.

4

THEY ran down the mountain in near dark, trying to leave the animal behind. Exhaustion seized Madeline, and she knew she couldn't run for very long. Her wet boots felt as heavy as small European countries.

She followed Noah closely, the pack slapping violently against his back as he struggled to strap it down. For a moment she didn't think she could keep up, felt her breath failing her, lungs laboring too fiercely as they tore across the lily-strewn meadow. Behind her the furtive rustle of grass told of the thing's presence close behind.

Then, much to her relief, the old, falling-down ski hut came into view, nestled amid some trees. As they drew closer, Madeline could see that most of the windows were broken, and that one side of the roof had fallen to ruin. The door hung on one rusted hinge. As soon as they reached it, Noah shoved the door open and nodded for her to go inside. She slipped by him, her eyes adjusting to the thicker darkness inside. It was cold and dank, a chill that felt decades old. Instantly a musty smell greeted her, and she wrinkled her nose, holding back a sneeze.

Noah followed her in and, pushing harshly on the handle, convinced the groaning, rusted door to close. Madeline tried to make things out in the gloom. The windows were broken but too small for the creature to fit through. Obviously the place had been built to last under the pressure of many feet of snow, but now it was in ruin, and she wondered how strong and determined the animal was. Madeline thought with those claws it could tear right through the rotten part of the roof.

Beneath her feet lay a soft bed of wet, windblown pine needles and dirt. The chill sank into her bones, and she began to shiver, trying to keep her teeth from chattering.

Noah walked to her and tried to warm her by rubbing her arms. After a moment of looking at her gravely, he said, "I'm going to lead him away from you. You're in no condition for a long jog down the mountain. I'll be back." Quickly, he shrugged off his pack and put it at her feet. "It's only a matter of time before he finds us in here. Maybe I can make him think we went a different direction."

Before she could think of what to say, he wrenched open the rickety door, disappeared through it, and closed it after him.

And then Madeline was alone, standing in the center of the cold building, the wind whistling through the shattered windows. She was freezing. For a long moment she stood stiffly, listening until her head ached with tension, too afraid to move, wondering when Noah would be back, and if he was okay.

An image of the clawed hand on the log flashed in her mind, and Madeline moved toward one wall of the old hut so that her back wasn't exposed. She longed to move around, to get her blood flowing, but she couldn't risk the noise. She stuck her tongue between her chattering teeth to muffle the sound.

She waited silently, hugging herself.

And then she heard tree branches cracking outside. From where she was standing, she couldn't see what might be out there and was afraid to look out anyway. She waited a moment longer.

The rustling drew closer. If it was Noah, he would probably say something to let her know it was him. Now the branches moved just outside the nearest window. Madeline braced herself to fight.

The door moved in the frame, and Noah appeared, replacing the door behind himself. It groaned on its single hinge. Instantly he saw her fighting posture and held his hands up to show her he meant no harm. "Didn't mean to startle you." Then he came toward her. "He's following us, all right. But I think I managed to lead him away. He won't stay confused for long, though. We should move now. My fleece looks good on you. Warm?"

He said the last bit in the same urgent tone of voice, and it took her a second to register the question.

"Yes, thanks," she lied, eager to be on the move. "What are we going to do?"

"I'm not sure. Going to think of something now."

The chill sank into Madeline's brain. She couldn't think of anything, her mind muddled. *Hypothermia.*

"You've get to get down the mountain. There's a backcountry ranger station not far from here." Picking the pack up from the ground he said, "Turn around." She did so. "Just about everything you'll need is in this pack . . . food, water . . . the map." He slid it on her shoulders and turned her back around.

"But—"

"Don't argue with me." Working quickly, he buckled the straps at her hips and chest. "You've got to move fast. Don't stop, no matter what you hear. Just keep moving. Agreed?"

Madeline didn't know what to say. She didn't even have time to think or begin to sort out what was happening.

"Agreed?" he repeated urgently.

Finally, Madeline nodded.

"Good. I'm going out there again. As soon as I'm out of sight, I want you to run as fast as you can. The trail is not far from here. Angle northwest. We're only about a hundred yards—"

The sudden cacophony of splintering wood cut him off. In

an instant the door splintered to nothing, and a dark figure filled the frame, a flash of teeth in utter blackness.

Noah turned and lunged toward the door, impacting violently with the creature, sending them both tumbling out into the forest.

"Run!" he screamed. "Run now!"

For a second Madeline couldn't move, couldn't bring herself to rush toward them. A gleeful howl pierced through her shock, and she came to life, rushing toward the door and out into the woods. The two struggling figures tangled several yards away, and after glancing at the moon's position, she dashed toward the northwest.

Behind her she heard Noah scream, long agonized shrieks, and then he was silent. Panic and terror filled her as she ran, darting into the shadows of trees, praying the thing wasn't loping after her in the dark.

Forty-five minutes later, having located the trail, she made her way through the forest. So far she'd heard no sounds behind her. The chill that had settled in earlier had fled with her panicked run. Though her hair was still damp, the fleece jacket and polypropylene shirt had trapped in the heat. Sweat trickled down her back.

The ground leveled out, sloping only slightly downward.

During the day, she would have passed someone on the trail and asked for help. At this hour, though, backcountry packers would be nestled warmly in their tents. She envied them and pushed on.

Without a flashlight, she continually tripped on large tree roots and rocks in the path, feeling grateful for having her boots instead of the sandals.

The ranger at the backcountry station could help her. In the summer, backcountry rangers usually patrolled the trails and manned the few stations scattered about in the wilderness. Hikers were required to sign up for passes before camping in the backcountry.

She'd signed up for a pass herself, though at a ranger station on the other side of the mountain. She'd written down four days from now as her expected return date. They wouldn't be looking for her for quite a while yet. Madeline pictured dogs and helicopters sweeping the other side of the mountain, friendly light and sound breaking through the impenetrable darkness.

She let herself pretend that a search party really was looking for her, and the thought cheered her a little.

A sudden scuffling made her go still, as if a fatal crack had split open beneath her skating feet on a desolate, frozen pond. Barely daring to pant in the darkness, she listened, straining her ears.

She could hear something breathing to her left, just off the path. Her hair stood up. Quickly she moved to the cover of a nearby pine. Peering intently, she tried to make out shapes in the moonlight.

A dark, sinewy shape slunk from one tree to the next. Madeline wished it were a bear but knew it wasn't. It moved upright, and though bears could walk on their hind legs, the movement was always cumbersome and lumbering. This creature was agile and quick as it moved, slipping from shadow to shadow. It was almost a shadow itself, with no features, just smooth, inky blackness.

As it moved onto the trail, Madeline caught sight of its face and bit back a scream.

The thing had turned to face the moon, and she saw its eyes: two huge, luminous red discs in an inky face, reflecting back the moonlight, flashing eerily. The mouth parted to reveal a row of hideous, sharp teeth, then turned up in an eager smile as the thing scanned the darkness.

It was hunting her, and it loved it.

5

QUICKLY Madeline left the trail, making her way through the underbrush and pines. Several times she glanced back toward the creature, hoping Noah was near it. But she didn't see anyone. Had it *killed* him?

Panic crept into her belly. She struggled to keep it in check, her head whipping from side to side, trying to find a hiding place. For a moment she couldn't catch her breath, felt her lungs constricting in terror.

To her left, a little bit ahead, Madeline saw a small clearing in the center of which stood three huge boulders very close together. Maybe she could hide behind one of those, wait till the thing had passed.

Briefly she wondered if she could outrun it, then quickly brushed away the image of it gaining on her in the darkness: she, slowed down by her wet boots and pack: the thing, preternaturally quick and relentless, tearing into her back and neck, opening ragged wounds—

Madeline steadied her mind. Glancing behind now, she couldn't see the creature, though she dared not look for very long. Wincing as she stepped on three splintering sticks in a row, Madeline pushed for the clearing.

When she got to the edge, she slowed, not wanting to dive out into the open, to be in plain sight in the brilliant moonlight.

But the rocks looked like the best hiding place.

She burst through the trees and into the clearing. Where two of the rocks met was a crevice just wide enough for her to hide in, and the shadows there would completely cover her.

Quickly she ran to where the two rocks met and threw the pack in first. She sat down, stuck her legs through the opening, and then pushed herself farther and farther in with her arms. Soon the rock's shadow overtook her, and with one more push she was deep inside the crevice, pulling cobwebs off her face.

There was little room to move around. She lay down, glancing furtively out of the opening, desperately hoping the thing hadn't seen her crawl in. She could see the silvery blue trees of the forest glowing in the moonlight and suddenly wondered if she should have gone in headfirst, so she could kick the thing if it found her in there. But glancing at the inky blackness at her feet, she realized having her head trapped at that end with limited ability to look out would have been too terrifying.

She waited beneath the rock, not taking her eyes from the treeline, and wondered how smart the thing was.

And then she saw it.

The creature emerged from the treeline into the clearing, long, black, lithe body moving furtively, nose turned to the wind, sniffing eagerly. She looked for any hint of features besides the eyes and mouth—hair, wrinkles—but saw none. Its shape was humanoid yet streamlined, a three-dimensional shadow come to life. Its claws met its fingers seamlessly, one flowing into the other. It had no ears.

As it sniffed, she felt a tiny surge of relief and hope when a breeze greeted her face. The wind was blowing toward her, making it difficult for the creature to catch a scent of her.

Dropping low to the ground, it crept about, just as comfortable on all fours. Smelling the rocks and moss, the flowers and grasses, it snapped its head up and stared directly to where she lay in the shadows, its huge, luminous eyes reflective in the moonlight.

Madeline's heart almost stopped.

The thing crept forward slowly and paused after a few feet, sniffing the air again. It lowered its head and scanned the rocks.

Then, just when Madeline expected it to come leaping out to her hiding place, it turned and retreated into the darkness of the trees, moving along the ground like a sinuous black spider.

Madeline exhaled, realizing she'd been holding her breath while she watched the creature. She stared long at the treeline, waiting for the reappearance of the thing. Nothing stirred there.

Madeline waited. And waited.

She thought of Ellie, felt her mind reaching out to her old friend. In the cramped space her fingers closed over the bracelet and its tiny lockbox.

Ellie? she thought. *Am I going to live through this?*

She tried to breathe in the tight space, her neck cramped as she remained twisted in the crevice. Staring out, she longed to open the little box, to take out its contents. To use her gift for the one thing that brought her peace, feeling closer to her lost friend. The terrible grief over Ellie was so powerful at times her brain staggered over the reality of it, denying it. Now the memory of running for her life all those years ago surged back, her mouth dry and her blood thrumming in her ears. The Sickle Moon Killer. His face of fear and rage, the sound of his pounding steps on the forest floor—

Ellie, she thought, *if you can hear me . . .* She craned her neck farther to see more of the clearing. But she didn't finish the thought. She couldn't ask for protection. Not after what had happened. All she could do was stay awake and hope it didn't find her like the Sickle Moon Killer had.

She lay and watched the trees for so long she lost track of time. The crevice was dark and reassuring, her own safe little

cavern, and after an hour of tense watching, she began to re-
lax and rest a little. The dry fleece and polypropylene under-
shirt felt warm and soft.

Madeline awoke with a start when an owl called out.

A predawn glow filled the crevice, and she realized with
amazement that she'd actually fallen asleep. Light spilled into
her world. Dawn had never looked so good to her before. She
felt overjoyed and relieved that it had finally come.

It was day, and she could find someone to help her.

Carefully she crept out of the crevice, scanning the clearing and trees for any sign of the creature or Noah. She studied
the trees. She felt alone, not like she was being watched . . .

Being watched.

Yesterday, on the mountain, just before the water hit, she'd
had the feeling of being watched . . .

Could it have been the creature, even then, readying to attack her?

Madeline shuddered and pushed off the image. Since acquiring her ability, she'd dealt with the unknown, lived with a
talent no one else possessed in her small town. But this was
something new. In the back of her mind, she'd always known
that her psychic ability could be just another part of the brain
that most did not use. But the creature—she thought of its
round disk eyes, the mouth full of teeth, the shadowlike
skin—was beyond even her expanded scope of what the mun-
dane world held within its ordinary grasp. From here out was
unexplored territory. She'd hoped to come to the backcountry
to clear her mind, decide how to fit her unusual gift into the
usual world. But instead, the world itself had grown unusual,
deeper, revealing more of its supernatural secrets. It was far
stranger, far more frightening and inexplicable than she'd
thought.

She brought a hand to her bandage, not letting the feelings
overwhelm her. She had to concentrate on the present, find
out exactly where she was and how far it was to the ranger
station.

Quickly she unzipped the pack and looked inside. The map lay right on top, and she pulled it out

Noah drinking a morning cup of coffee.

Later, afraid, the thing close behind.

Madeline forced the images away and studied the map. After guessing how long she'd walked the night before, and what kind of time she'd made in the darkness, she figured it was another hour to the ranger station.

Not bad at all.

Stuffing the map back into the pack, she noticed the water bottle. Taking several long pulls on it, she gazed up at the deep blue morning sky, golden clouds set afire in the east. Her head throbbed as she tilted it up, the bandaged gash on her head feeling twice its actual size. She replaced the bottle and stood up. Hoisting the pack onto her back, she buckled it as she began to walk, all the while watching the trees and rocks for any sign of movement. Soon she was back on the trail, rushing toward the backcountry station.

Gratefully Madeline stepped onto the wooden porch of the backcountry ranger station and opened the door. A young ranger sitting behind a beat-up counter looked up as she entered. He was in his early twenties, with straight, dark hair pulled back in a ponytail. She approached the desk, which stood on one side of a small room with a couple of shelves holding books and maps. The ranger stared at her.

"What can I help you with?" he asked. He put down the paper he had been reading. His features were angular and his skin dark, his coloration reminding her of a Romanian friend she'd had in high school. His name tag read Michael Zuwalski.

"Something . . ." She reached the desk, trailed off, trying to catch her breath.

"Yes?" He arched one eyebrow expectantly.

"Something attacked me and my friend in the backcountry."

"A grizzly?" The ranger grew alarmed.

"No, nothing like that," she said quickly, then paused. "Look," she went on firmly, "I don't know what it was."

"It was probably a grizzly. Sometimes people have a hard time identifying wildlife —"

She cut him off. "This was not wildlife. This was a ... thing. It specifically, methodically, went after me and this other guy."

"Who?"

"Noah someone. I don't know his last name. He went after the thing to lead it away."

"You were in the backcountry with someone whose last name you don't even know?"

"No," she shook her head. "I don't know him, he just pulled me out of the river and then the creature showed up and—"

"Wait ... slow down."

"Well, I'd never seen an animal like it before, but it was really smart. It was hunting us. Noah seemed to know what it was," she went on, hoping the story would sound better if she filled it out more. "He went after it. And now I want to send a rescue for him."

The ranger was just silent. He stared at the bandage on her head. "Nasty blow there."

She touched it gingerly and then waved her hand, dismissing it. "It'll heal. But Noah's in real danger."

The ranger remained silent.

"Well? Aren't you going to do anything?" she demanded. "Radio somebody?"

"Are you saying you were caught in the flash flood?"

She nodded.

"Well, look, that thing was bad. It's amazing you even got out. Just about every available person we've got is helping people who were caught in it."

"Well, 'just about every person' must mean you have someone who can help."

"Only for genuine emergencies."

"This is an emergency!" she practically yelled.

The ranger crossed his arms. "Did you see the creature *after* you bumped your head?"

Madeline became flustered. "Well, yes, but I don't see . . ." And then she did. She saw perfectly. He thought she imagined the whole thing.

Exasperated, she said, "It all really happened!" Looking down at herself in Noah's clothes suddenly reaffirmed that.

"Look at these clothes. They're huge on me!"

"So?"

"They're Noah's. He gave them to me before the thing attacked."

"I see," he responded.

But she could tell that he didn't see.

"This guy Noah . . ." the ranger went on, then he trailed off. "Listen," he said finally. "There are a lot of guys out there who'll take advantage of you. Tell you a scary story to make you vulnerable."

"It wasn't like that!" she yelled. "He didn't make this *up,* I *saw* it!"

"Are you sure?" he said, gesturing at her head and leaning over the counter with a condescending look. "That *is* quite a nasty blow."

Madeline grew more and more frustrated. Forced herself to take a deep breath. Normally, rangers were so helpful, but this guy was pure aggravation. "Look. Regardless of whether or not you believe I was attacked by some *thing*, there *is* a guy named Noah out there, and he's in danger." She paused, her eyes falling to the registration book on the desk. "Please," she asked, trying to hold back the anger she felt at that moment. "Could you just look in the book and at least see when Noah's supposed to get back? Maybe he's already overdue."

The ranger remained still for a few moments, then shrugged. "If it'll make you feel better," he said.

"It will."

"Okay." He slid the book over toward himself. Scanned the first page of people who'd signed up for backcountry passes. Flipped backward. Scanned that page. Then the one before, and the one before, and the one before that. Then he went back over them again, and flipped even farther back. "I'm at three weeks ago now. No one named Noah has taken out a pass."

She raised her eyebrows. "You're sure?"

"No one. I can read, you know."

She ignored the rude comment. "Could he have gone without one?"

"Well, that's always possible. It's illegal, you know, but there's not someone standing guard at the trailhead or anything, if that's what you mean."

"I know," she said, sighing. "Then I guess he didn't get one."

"Or he lied about his name." He eyed her intently. "He might have lied to you, you know."

She couldn't believe this guy. "What kind of ranger are you, anyway? Don't you even care?"

"Of course I care!" he responded, his tone softening. "I care that you might have gotten mixed up with the wrong sort of company." He gestured at the book. "There's no Noah in here, so I can only assume he lied about his name to one of us or just didn't get the pass at all. Either way, it's pretty shady."

Madeline fell silent. Was this guy right? Had Noah deceived her? Certainly not about the creature—that had been real enough. But had he really given her a false name? Why would he do that?

Their meeting had been so brief it was hard to be certain. But she did believe that Noah had tried to protect her.

No, she thought. *Why would he lie?* It didn't make sense.

"Look. I don't know what to tell you. I think this guy wasn't on the up-and-up," the ranger went on.

A sudden thump resounded from down a corridor that lay beyond the small bookshelves. They both turned in that direction but saw nothing unusual. Another thump followed shortly afterward. It was dull and heavy, echoing down the corridor. Madeline started violently. She didn't see anything there.

"Huh," said the ranger, wrinkling his brow. "That doesn't

sound good. I better go check it out. Sounds like the generator is acting up again."

Hurriedly he moved around the end of the counter and filed past her, heading in the direction of the noise. Madeline waited for a few moments, then looked down at the backcountry reservation book. Maybe the ranger had overlooked Noah's name.

Glancing over her shoulder, she saw the ranger halfway down the corridor, still headed away from her. Quickly she spun the book around to face her.

The instant she touched it, she saw blood.

Instinctively she pulled her hand away. She had seen nothing else specific. Just a pool of blood on a brown cement floor. Forcing herself to touch the book again, Madeline flipped back and forth until she found the reservations that had been made for the past few days.

And almost immediately she saw Noah's name. It was even at the top of the page. Noah Lanchester.

Madeline furrowed her brow. She didn't see how the ranger could have missed it. It had immediately caught her attention. She looked back down the hallway. He wasn't in sight. Returning her attention to the book, she saw that Noah had taken a three-day backcountry pass and was due back tomorrow. She looked at the initials of the ranger who had checked Noah in. MZ. As in Michael Zuwalski, the same initials of the ranger she had just been talking to. Wouldn't he remember someone he had checked in just the day before? She scanned over the names and dates before and after Noah. Only one other party had gone out besides him that day, a couple who were only going to be gone overnight. Surely the ranger would have remembered him then. And she doubted there was more than one ranger at the station with the initials MZ.

Shuffling in the corridor alerted her to the ranger's return. She rotated the book back around and stood there, trying to look innocent. He emerged from the corridor and walked back behind the counter.

"It was the generator, all right. That thing's always acting up." He gave her a smile, but she couldn't bring herself to smile back. Was he intentionally lying, or was it an honest mistake? She didn't see how he could forget so quickly. And what about the image of blood? It was so vague. The ranger could have just cut himself slicing bread for all she knew. But her gut pulled at her. Something was wrong. She didn't trust this guy. The same sense that told her she'd be safe with Noah was now gnawing at her to get away.

But she had to find help. Perhaps another ranger was nearby.

She waited until he reached the desk again, and then asked, "Is it possible another ranger checked him in?" She hoped he would tell her when the other rangers were on duty, or where she could find them.

But instead he only answered, "No."

Madeline waited a long time, hoping he'd say something further, but he only watched her, tight-lipped, as if waiting for *her* to say something.

"Well," she said at last. "Thanks." *For nothing,* she added mentally and turned from the counter. Shouldn't he at least have offered to assist *her*, if nothing else? She had suffered a "nasty blow," as he had put it.

"Good luck," the ranger told her. "It's wild and woolly out there."

For a second Madeline paused before she went out the door. She almost turned to confront him, to ask him why he was lying about Noah. But then she decided she'd go find another ranger. Something was wrong here, and her instincts told her to get away from him. Somehow she had to find help elsewhere. Noah could be out there, right then, gravely wounded.

Or worse, came a grim voice from within her. With utter clarity, the sounds of his agonized screams returned to her. She ran a nervous hand over her face and left the ranger station, stepping once more into the desolation of the backcountry.

Beyond the building she saw the lone structures of two typical National Park Service vaulted toilets, dry toilets that were a step up from pit toilets. She hadn't stopped for anything but sleep since last night. Her bladder pressing painfully, she headed for the toilets.

The smell of pine was strong in the air as a wind kicked up, blowing down into the valley where the ranger station was settled. Overhead a few clouds had gathered during the night, and Madeline found herself shivering a bit in spite of her warm fleece. *Noah's warm fleece,* she thought.

She approached the dark wooden structures and selected the one marked Ladies, surprised at how little the toilet smelled. The faint scent of citrus from an air freshener wafted in the still air, and a fly buzzed dully at a small, square window. Her boots squeaking on the smooth cement floor, she entered.

Madeline had just locked the door when something wet and warm splashed on her hand. Instinctively she jerked it back, seeing a rivulet of red dribble between her fingers. A few more splatters hit the floor in front of her.

Blood on the brown floor.

Then a thick, warm drool rained down on her head.

Gasping, Madeline reeled back, confused, and looked up. The bathroom had a high ceiling that came to a point, with rafters below it.

And hanging over one of the rafters was a corpse of a man, his face twisted in a hideous scream.

It took Madeline only a second to take in that the corpse was naked save for its underwear and one prominent piece of clothing: a hat.

A ranger's hat.

And then, a second later, her brain registered the cause of the dripping.

The ranger she had spoken to earlier was up there in the shadows with the body, chewing on a tattered leg, digging his nails hungrily and greedily into the raw, bloody flesh.

Then she watched transfixed as the ranger's head suddenly elongated and shifted, becoming more streamlined as the skin grew darker, darker, until it was an inky black. The fingers grew long and wiry, claws springing from the tips. It continued to tear into the body, its brown ranger's clothes stained red, until it looked down at Madeline with the same red disc eyes that had frightened her so the night before.

"Forgive my rudeness. Meat is best when it's still warm," it said in a low voice, a piece of ragged flesh hanging from its mouth.

Madeline's jaw fell open. She had never talked to a ranger at all. This . . . *thing* had killed the ranger and taken its place, shape-shifting from hideous creature to human with so much ease, and now it paused from its meal, looking down on her with hunger, readying to tear into her, just as it had probably torn into Noah up on the mountain.

Wiping its dripping mouth, it leapt down from the rafters, landing solidly in a crouch before her.

Madeline screamed.

6

SHE spun toward the door, the creature leaping up, claws jerking her backpack roughly and raking through the fleece jacket.

Her hiking boots, wet with blood, slid noisily on the smooth floor. In the confines of the vaulted toilet, the thing was close behind her, lunging at her back, trying to drag her down by her pack. She felt claws dig into the jacket again, holding her back momentarily before the material tore free. Quickly she wrenched open the door and ran out into the open, not daring to look back. Her eyes scanned the area for a weapon, but she saw none, just the ground sloping away into the forest. She stopped at the back entrance of the ranger station and ripped the door open. Dashing down a narrow hallway, she burst through to the main room, knocking over a display on wildflowers as she passed it, hoping to impede the thing.

She knew she couldn't outrun it, heard the door slam shut behind her as the thing entered the station.

Then she spied a fire ax propped up by the main door. Lunging at it, she grabbed the handle and whirled around at

full tilt. The creature was too far away, and she spun frantically in almost a complete circle, falling off balance and
stumbling. The ax connected violently with the wooden door
frame and stuck fast.

Panicked, she tried to wrench it free, her hands burning
with friction on the handle. The thing sped forward, a fanged
black figure in a blood-soaked ranger's uniform, now mere
feet away. She gripped the ax tightly, working it quickly back
and forth. Five feet. It began to give way. Four feet. She
wrenched the ax head free. Three feet. Swinging the weapon
with everything in her, she connected with the creature's
chest. Bones snapped audibly. Howling, it spun away, gripping its dark flesh as blood sprayed the room. The handle
wrenched out of her fingers, and she backed away. Screaming,
the creature loped madly away from her, retreating down the
corridor, where it banged against one of the walls. At the end
of the hall, near the generator room it had entered before, it
stumbled, fell, and sprawled across the floor, gasping for
breath.

She could hear the bubbling of blood as the thing attempted to breathe, a direct hit to the lung. It struggled to
prop up on one hand, rose a couple feet, but its clawed, black
hand slipped in blood, slamming its torso back to the floor.

Its body contracted violently, folding in on itself, rolling
into a ball. It twitched, its arms and legs alive with a hundred
spasms. Then it fell still, struggling to breathe in long, ragged
gasps. After several final labored breaths, it stopped breathing and lay immobile.

Madeline turned and tore open the front door, flinging it
back on its hinges and banging it against the wall. Then she
was outside again, scanning the area for a safe place. Only
trails met her sight, snaking off in three directions.

Not wasting another second, she took off toward a kiosk
that housed several maps and trail descriptions, hoping she
could hide behind it for a few minutes in order to catch her
breath and think. Sliding in the dirt near the wooden display,
she flung herself down behind it. She panted, her throat dry.
Peering up, she studied the map. At a glance, she noted that

one trail led straight into Many Glacier, one of the biggest campgrounds in the park. There would be people there. Phones. Rangers who were alive.

Instantly she rose and began running down the path, glancing behind her. She had probably killed the thing, but terror had seized her. Madeline ran until she simply couldn't anymore. The ranger's station was no longer in sight, and she had entered a steep, forested section. Gasping, she slowed to a walk, still looking nervously behind her.

She wondered how far behind her the thing was—if it still lay in a pool of its own blood, dead, or if it was up somehow, resurrected, following her scent. How had it found her? Beaten her to her next stop? Had it anticipated her next move? Loped down the mountain in the silver of moonlight and found the backcountry ranger station, the lone ranger up there—and eaten him?

None of it made sense.

Madeline shuddered. She could feel the terror the ranger must have felt when he saw the thing slink in through the front door of the station. And then when it came at him, claws and fangs tearing him apart . . .

She wondered if the ranger, not quite dead, had heard her come in. If he had been desperately trying to get her attention by banging on the wall of the station. *"The generator's been acting up."* The creature had stridden back there and savagely finished him off while she waited in the other room.

It was incredibly intelligent. It had infiltrated the ranger's station—it *spoke*. The fact that it could anticipate her moves, her thoughts, was terrifying. Even now it might know exactly where she was. If it was somehow still alive.

If only she could somehow touch it, or touch something it had touched, she might know what it was and what it wanted. It hadn't had contact with the backcountry book long enough for her to get any detail other than the blood.

She needed to touch something it had been exposed to for a longer period of time.

Or, she needed to touch the creature directly.

She continued down the trail, pondering, gasping for breath

with her mouth open, a stitch forming in her side. Already the temperature was climbing. She'd never known it to be this hot in the Rockies, and she needed water badly. She had to stop and drink. Up ahead she saw a cluster of rocks. Maybe she could hide in there and drink from Noah's water bottle. She hoped he was still alive, but his screams played intensely and repeatedly in her head, like some gruesome song she couldn't get rid of.

When she reached the huge, granite boulders, she glanced back again. The trail was still empty. Quickly she darted off the path and ran around the side of one of the boulders. There she squatted on a bed of pine needles and flung the pack off her back. Inside she found another change of clothes, including some polypropylene long underwear and a pair of woolen socks. Next to that lay the water bottle. Grateful, she took a long drink, quenching her thirst.

Replacing the bottle, her hands found something smooth and solid. A great sadness suddenly swept over her. Curious, she pulled out the object, a very old hardback book. The spine was well worn and the paper old and spotted with age. She opened it carefully and found graceful handwriting and some field sketches: a flower, a mountain peak. It was someone's old journal, she realized. She read the date on the page she was currently turned to: February 20, 1859. The book had a terribly sad energy to it.

Carefully she closed it, replacing it deep in the bag. Her fingers searched for sun protection, but met something cold and metal instead. Instantly images and emotions leapt into her mind.

Running down an alley in pursuit of a dark figure.

Fear. Desperation.

Throwing open a door to a train compartment and lunging inside, heart hammering.

She withdrew the object, holding it carefully. She knew backpackers carried knives, but those were usually folding blades or pocket knives.

The knife she now held in her hand was a foot-long dagger, encased in a round, ornamentally engraved silver sheath.

The handle was completely metal, and when she drew it out, she saw that the blade was very strange. It had no edges but was round with a pointed end, like a sharpened spike. She touched the point and felt it snag on her flesh. *Very sharp.* She'd never seen a knife like it.

It felt *important*, *vital*.

It looked very old and very well used.

Very old. If Noah collected antiques like this, it would explain the strange images I got from him. An antique dressing table had once given her images of a young girl in a calico sunbonnet, and a cameo brooch had once allowed her a glimpse into the Victorian period, showing her an elegant woman who had strolled with a white umbrella on rainy cobblestone streets.

She put the knife back. After cinching and buckling the pack, she hefted it onto her back again. Fastening the waist and chest buckles, she wondered over the objects she had found inside. Then, screwing up her courage, she prepared herself for the long hike to Many Glacier.

She had just rejoined the trail when she heard shouting. She froze, stepping back away from the trail. She heard it again: a man yelling from the direction of the ranger station. She crouched down, peering out between tree trunks. A figure appeared on the trail, and Madeline desperately hoped that it wasn't the creature. It definitely looked human, though after the ranger's station, that wasn't worth much anymore. No long claws or ink-black sharkskin. She remained where she was, trying to make out if it was a ranger or the creature in another guise.

And then she saw the familiar blond hair and made out the face as he drew nearer.

Noah.

"Madeline!" he shouted, looking around in all directions.

Immediately she entered the path and started running, meeting Noah on the trail. He saw her and ran to her. A large gash ran the length of his cheek, and his face showed purple and blue in more places than not. He'd tucked his tent under his arm, along with her wet clothes.

"Are you okay?" he asked breathlessly when they reached each other.

"Yes" she said, panting herself. "I never thought I'd see you again!" The backpack weighed a ton, and she could feel the veins standing out on her neck. She ached to take it off but was too worried they'd have to start running again.

Noah looked around nervously. "I lost it. Let's go over there, and I'll tell you." Motioning to a large glacial erratic boulder a few feet away, he said, "He won't see us there as easily." They hurried to the boulder and squatted down behind it. "It was quite a struggle up there. It was pretty close for a minute, but I managed to wound him and get away. I found my way here and went inside. No ranger. And the radio's missing."

Madeline gave him a glance over. He didn't have much more than bruises. "You weren't seriously hurt?" She thought of the screams.

He shook his head. "Luckily, no."

"But I heard . . . you screaming."

"Well," he said, looking uncomfortable all of a sudden, "like I said, it was pretty tense for a minute there."

"It's here now," she said. "I know this sounds crazy, but I talked to a ranger, only it wasn't really him . . . it was the creature."

Noah nodded. "It's not crazy."

Madeline glanced toward the ranger station. "I hit it with an ax."

Noah raised his eyebrows. "Really?"

"Yes. But I don't know if I killed it."

"Well, it wasn't in there."

Damn. So it just got up again? "Did you look in the vaulted toilet?"

He raised his eyebrows. "The toilet?"

She cast her eyes down, trying to block out the memory of what she'd seen in the rafters. "It was horrible."

"Another victim?"

"*Another* victim?" She looked at him sternly, wondered

why he knew so much. "I think it's about time you told me what that thing is."

"I can't now. It'll have to wait. We've got to get you to safety."

"But what about the ranger's body in the bathroom?"

"A ranger? Oh, man. That's bad. Did he have a two-way radio on him?"

Madeline stared at him aghast. "Well, I didn't happen to notice." Her voice began to rise, quavering as she grew more upset at the thought of what she'd seen. "I mean, when you see a dead body hanging from the rafters with this . . . *thing* . . . eating it, you don't really think of looking for a god-damn two-way radio." She was shaking. Forced herself to calm down. After a moment, she added, "I'm sorry."

"It's okay. I understand. It *is* terrible." Noah's eyes were wide and sympathetic. "Believe me, I know what it feels like to stumble upon a scene like that. That's why I've got to catch him." After a pause he added, "I'm going to go check the body for a radio."

"Noah, no!" She grabbed his arm as he started to get up.

"We could use it to radio for help, get you off the mountain."

Fear gripped Madeline. "But it could still be in there!"

"He's probably gone by now. I have to take the chance."

"No, you don't! That's ridiculous! Let's just get the hell away."

Noah remained squatting where he was, and Madeline let go of his arm. He glanced around. "Which trail is the one that leads down to Many Glacier Campground?"

"I was already heading that way. Too bad there's not a closer one." She was so tired. She slid the pack off her back.

"Well," he said grimly after a moment, "that is the closest ranger station. "The trail's a little long, but at least it's not steep. There's very little elevation gain. I took this route hiking up here. The way down should be a breeze."

"So it's all downhill from here?"

Noah smiled and looked up at her. "Yep."

She watched Noah as he adjusted the laces on his hiking boots. She wanted to ask him again what was going on, what that thing was, why it seemed to be hunting them. But she was just so tired—her eyes burning from lack of sleep, her back aching, her head pounding—that she didn't think she could thoroughly digest it all, even if he did tell her. She just wanted to lie down in a nice, comfortable bed and sleep for a long time. "Let's go," she said finally.

After repacking the map, tent, and clothes, Noah slung the pack over his shoulders, then buckled it in place.

They stood up, glanced around cautiously, and started down the mountain, the heat of the afternoon still building, humidity closing in around them, stifling and unbearable.

Halfway down the mountain, they stopped in a meadow to rest and eat and found a cluster of boulders to sit on. Catching their breath, they passed the water bottle back and forth.

"Sorry I lost all my stuff," she said, feeling bad for drinking so much of his water.

"Don't be sorry for a second. If you hadn't dumped your pack, you'd probably be dead right now." He took a long drink from the water bottle and surveyed the scene around them. They were hiking down through thick forest, where mosquitoes clustered, buzzing in her ears and biting through her clothes. She'd never experienced a summer so filled with mosquitoes. The muggy heat was perfect bloodsucker weather, and they repeatedly landed in her eyes and even occasionally came close to buzzing up her nose. They filled the hot air with incessant, whiny buzzing. Sweat poured down Madeline's face and back, and occasionally mosquitoes stuck in the droplets of perspiration.

"You doing okay?" Noah asked, studying her face.

Madeline nodded.

"Is your head giving you any trouble?"

In truth the cut stung painfully, especially with the salty sweat seeping into the bandage, but there was nothing that could be done there in the backcountry that wasn't already done. "It's okay," she lied.

"Let me see your eyes." He scooted closer to her on the rock, placing a hand under her chin and lifting her face up so he could get a better look. He leaned in, peering intently into her eyes. "No dilation," he said. "That's a relief."

Suddenly Madeline was aware of how close he was. His eyes were a bright green, and his breath smelled cinnamony and nice, his lips perfectly shaped.

"Everything okay?" he asked, making her realize how much she'd been staring.

"Yes," she said, pulling away. "Glad there's no concussion."

"Any dizziness or blurred vision?"

She shook her head.

"Nausea?"

"No."

"Good. Think you can make it down the rest of the way?"

"Yeah."

He put the water bottle into a net pouch on the backpack and produced two granola bars. He handed one to her and stood up. "We'd better go. We definitely want to get down before it gets dark."

Suddenly Madeline felt exposed, standing up from her cover among the rocks. "Does it get more . . . aggressive at night?" she asked, glancing around nervously.

Noah shook his head, and for a moment Madeline was relieved. Then he said, "It's aggressive all the time."

"Let's go," she said quickly and beat Noah to the trail.

Just before dusk, as they passed their last switchback and looked down a steep hill, Noah and Madeline saw the dusk-to-dawn lights burning at the Swiftcurrent Lodge and camp store. Beyond it lay the paved roads of Many Glacier.

Madeline breathed a sigh of relief. "We made it." She was absolutely exhausted and so thirsty her tongue felt swollen.

"Now we can get that cut looked at," Noah said.

Madeline felt the bandage. It was still affixed securely, and she was impressed by Noah's field dressing ability. She smiled at him as they continued down the trail.

They passed the Swiftcurrent Motor Inn, continuing down the road past the entrance to the campground. Soon they reached the ranger's station, a small log cabin set among the trees. All the lights were off.

Madeline walked up to the door, her head aching. She rapped her knuckles on the wood and waited. No one came to the door.

Noah walked up beside her, and she was aware of his closeness as he knocked even louder on the door. They stood together in expectant silence. "I don't think anyone's here this late," he said finally.

She brought her hand up to her head again. It was really starting to throb. "What should we do?"

Noah glanced around the darkened campground. "My Jeep's parked in a lot here. I say we drive down to Apgar. It's more populated than here, and I'll bet we could find some help there." He looked at her, concerned. "What do you say?"

Madeline was so tired that sitting down in a car sounded like a vacation to the Bahamas. Besides, if the ranger had left this area for the night, even if they called for help from the motor inn, they'd still have to wait for the ranger to drive up to Many Glacier. "Sounds great."

"Okay, then. It's this way."

He left the porch of the ranger station with Madeline following close behind. They walked down the narrow, paved road until they reached another parking lot. A blue Jeep stood among a half dozen other cars, and Noah walked to it.

He unlocked the passenger door and held it open for Madeline, who was touched by the gentlemanly gesture. She climbed in, and he closed the door after her. He entered and started the engine.

Apgar, she knew, lay on the shores of Lake McDonald on the other side of the park, near the west entrance. It would take at least an hour to get there because the road took so many twists. Ranchers owned land bordering on the park, and to get to Apgar, Noah and she had to temporarily exit the park and reenter it farther down the road. She hoped someone was awake on the other end to help.

They drove down Many Glacier Road out of the park, and soon cow eyes gleamed green in their headlights, huge lumbering animals on the side of the road munching grass.

They passed through the small town of Babb at the intersection of Many Glacier Road and the Chief Mountain Highway, which they had to take to get back to the park. The local bar at the intersection was going strong, with beer signs glowing in the windows and live music emanating cheerfully.

He turned right on the Chief Mountain Highway, and they drove through more darkened ranch land. Finally they reached the eastern entrance of the Going-to-the-Sun Road, a precipitous route that climbed up along the peaks through the heart of the park. They reentered Glacier, the entrance kiosk at St. Mary locked up for the night. The visitor center at St. Mary was also dark and empty, so they drove on toward Apgar. Stunning drop-offs emerged on the left as they progressed.

Their progress was slow and winding. At night, Mount Reynolds and the peaks around it stood dark and foreboding, and glaciers clinging to the sides gleamed white in the bright moonlight. At the highest point, they passed the Logan Pass Visitor Center and the trailhead to her favorite trail in the park, the Highline Trail, a narrow path that wound through rock slides, snowfields, and mountain goat–populated forests.

Eventually they began to descend. Aspen forests replaced the stunted silhouettes of kruppelholz, small, twisted pine trees that grew in higher altitudes. Despite the gorgeous scenery, Madeline nodded off repeatedly. She jolted awake just as they passed the Loop, the trailhead where her VW Rabbit was parked. She thought of asking Noah to turn back so she could get her car, but her eyes were so heavy she didn't think it was safe to drive. A few seconds later, she fell asleep entirely.

She awoke when the Jeep came to a stop. Groggily, she opened her eyes, yawned, and peered out. Her head throbbed. Before her lay Lake McDonald, its vast length fading into the distance, its rippling water sparkling in the moonlight.

Noah parked in front of the ranger station, and they got out. Apgar was more active than Many Glacier had been. Lights gleamed from cabin windows at Apgar Village, a collection of cabins for park visitors, and several people milled around by the scenic lake.

They approached the ranger station. Like at Many Glacier, all the lights were off. Just a little way away stood a cabin with its porch light on. Through a window they could see the silhouette of a person sitting at a table and eating. A sign out front read Staff Residence.

"Let's knock," Noah said. "They'll know where to get help for your head." He moved forward, but she stayed where she was. "What is it?" he asked when he realized she wasn't moving.

"We also have to tell them about the backcountry ranger," she said solemnly.

Noah stopped then, walked back toward her slowly, and looked at her intently. "I really wish you wouldn't."

"What? But his body is back there, and—"

"They won't know what they're dealing with," he said, hooking his thumb in the direction of the backcountry ranger's station far away in the mountains.

"We still have to tell them!"

"And how would you explain to them what attacked the ranger?"

"As best I could. I'd tell them what I saw. I'd tell them where they can find the body."

Noah shook his head. "Even if they did track him down, he can't be imprisoned. Believe me, I've seen people try. Place after place. It never works. They'd have to kill him, and they couldn't. Even if they tried. They'd die taking him into custody."

Madeline tried to keep her voice down, though she could

feel it rising as she grew more frustrated, trying to understand Noah's point of view. "If he's aggressive when they try to bring him in, they *may* shoot him."

Noah looked up, exasperated. "It won't kill him. And then he'll escape."

"From a prison cell?"

"From anywhere." Noah's eyes were grim. "Madeline," he took her hand gently, "I've seen this before. I've seen it all. You must believe me."

"Look, Noah," she said, feeling overwhelmed. "I don't even really know you. I appreciate you helping me back there, but I firmly believe a person should report a murder."

"But don't you see they'll just get in the way?" he asked exasperatedly.

"Get in the way of whom?"

Noah looked down and remained silent.

"I can't just ignore what I saw, what I've been through. If these rangers can do anything to stop this thing, then I've got to tell them."

Noah put his face in his hand and sighed. He looked weary. "Okay," he said at last, looking up. "But you'll be endangering their lives. I'm going to leave you here then. It's likely they'll want to ask you a ton of questions, so I'm going to find you somewhere to stay nearby. I'll be back soon."

A ton of questions. Madeline hoped none of them recognized her name. She just wanted to report the murder and be done with it. Montana newspapers had carried a few accounts of her psychic endeavors. If they found out she was "gifted," they might be all over her, asking her to return to the murder scene and see if she could pick up anything—like off the rafters in the outhouse. *I can't go through that. I won't. I'll just report the murder, and if they ask me to use my "ability," I'll just tell them it doesn't work that way.*

She was a bit taken aback and hurt that after all, Noah was just abandoning her on the doorstep of this ranger's house. But he had already done so much for her, she was grateful for that. "Thanks," she said feebly.

"My pleasure," he answered, but she could hear the tension in his voice. He rang the bell on the cabin and then disappeared into the darkness.

She stood there for a few moments before the door opened.

A kind-looking man in his thirties appeared, holding a fork and napkin, looking at her quizzically. He wore a National Park Service uniform. She felt tiny out there on the porch, Noah now gone, and the dark expanse of the park at her back.

"I—I want to report a murder," she heard herself say.

The ranger's mouth opened. "A murder?" he repeated.

"Yes."

He dropped his fork, and it clattered on the wooden floor. "Oh, my. I'd better call a ranger."

Madeline furrowed her brow. "Aren't you a ranger?" She looked at his uniform pointedly. The man was dressed in a khaki pants and khaki shirt, a National Park patch sewn onto his sleeve.

The man looked flustered. "I'm an interpretive ranger. We need a law enforcement ranger."

"Oh," she said and squinted as a flash of pain pulsed in her head. "I didn't know there was a difference."

"Are you hurt badly?" he asked, gesturing at the bandage.

"I should have someone look at it," she replied.

He invited her in, and exhausted, she sank onto his couch and rested her hand on the armrest.

Nights spent reading into the wee hours of the morning.

A kiss with a pretty woman with long brown hair.

He went to the phone and dialed a number.

"Suzanne?" she heard him say from the other room. "I've got a young woman here who wants to report a murder . . . Yes, that's right. Someone's been killed."

7

THE naturalist, Steve Pashalt, she had learned while waiting, opened the door to admit a wide-faced woman with long blonde hair in a tight braid. She, too, was dressed in a park service uniform, only she carried a gun in a holster around her waist.

"Madeline, this is Suzanne Harrett."

Madeline got up and shook the woman's hand, then regretted it almost immediately as the woman all but crushed her fingers. Kind blue eyes twinkled at Madeline, framed by small wrinkles that told Madeline she'd seen a lot of sun in her forty-odd years.

"Just tell her what you saw."

Steve himself hadn't heard the story yet. They'd waited until the law officer arrived. Now she was here, and Madeline found her heart pounding, her hands shaky, and her mouth dry. The request sounded so easy, but to fulfill it, Madeline would have to relive those terrifying moments. She decided to first tell them who had been killed. "It was a backcountry ranger who was murdered," she told them. Immediately, concern creased their faces. It was one of their own.

"Where?" Suzanne asked.

Steve motioned for them to sit down on the couch. He took the hard metal chair next to it.

"In the backcountry," Madeline continued, once seated. "At the Glacier Point backcountry station. Mike Z something."

"Mike Zuwalski," the two rangers chorused.

"Yes, that's it."

The naturalist swallowed. "And you're sure he's dead?"

Madeline pictured the man's body draped over the beam in the vaulted toilet, the blood everywhere, his sightless eyes staring. "Yes."

"At the station itself?"

She nodded.

"I'm going to radio up there," the naturalist said, and left the room, the chair's feet squeaking on the cheap linoleum floor.

For a long tense moment the officer stared at her. "Did you see who killed him?"

She paused, uncomfortable. "Not who . . . *what.*"

"An animal attack? You mean like a bear?"

Madeline shook her head. "No. Nothing like that." Madeline felt herself pulled back to those dreaded hours on the mountain when it had pursued her. "It was almost human. Incredibly smart." She thought of how it cut her off at the ranger station.

The officer looked at her closely. "*Almost* human?"

"Yes. But not quite. It had claws, and these enormous eyes . . ."

Now the officer looked at her, brow creased. "You know," she said again, "sometimes it's hard to identify wildlife correctly."

Madeline sighed. What was this, a practiced ranger speech? But she herself had overheard enough conversations between park visitors to know the officer told the truth. How many times had Madeline heard people call a pronghorn antelope a deer? Or call a hoary marmot a weasel or a groundhog? Sure, you could mix up a black bear with a grizzly bear, or a coyote with a wolf, but this creature had been no wolf or bear.

"Bears can walk upright," Suzanne continued, "and in intense situations, people might confuse them with—"

The naturalist came back into the room, a huge grin on his face. "Just raised Mike on the radio," he said, the look of relief evident on his face. "He says everything's fine up there."

"What?" Madeline cried. Bewilderment swept over her, and she looked at them in astonishment.

"You're sure it was the Glacier Point ranger station," asked the officer, "and not another one?"

"Positive!" Madeline insisted. "I had a map, and—" Madeline stopped short, suddenly realizing what was happening. It wasn't Mike the naturalist had talked to. Just as she had never talked to Mike. "You were talking to the creature!" she blurted. "It was the creature on the radio!" So it truly wasn't dead.

"Creature?" Steve looked at Suzanne in confusion. "It can talk?"

She waved a dismissive hand, as if she would tell him later.

"It was him, don't you see?" Madeline said desperately.

Suzanne patted her on the shoulder. "Now just calm down. We'll work this out."

Steve returned to his seat and said softly and reassuringly, "I've known Mike Zuwalski for four years, and I know his voice. It was definitely him on the radio."

"No! Listen!" Madeline pleaded, shrugging off Suzanne's hand. "The creature, this thing that killed him, it can appear just like him! I thought it was really the ranger, too, but it wasn't. Don't you see?"

Suzanne frowned at Madeline, then stuck her chin out in puzzlement. "What exactly did you see?" She pulled out a notebook and readied to jot down notes.

Madeline took a breath. "I went into the ranger's station. I talked to the ranger there, Mike, or so I thought. He went into a back room to investigate a strange thumping noise. I went to the bathroom, and when I entered, Mike's body was hanging from a rafter, and this thing was eating him."

"Why do you say, 'Or so I thought'?" Suzanne pressed, making a note.

"Because the ranger in the bathroom had been dead for some time. The creature eating him was wearing his uniform. It had changed to look like the ranger."

Suzanne stared at her, then stopped taking notes. "Did you have anyone look at her head wound?" the officer asked Steve, suddenly speaking as if Madeline wasn't in the room at all.

"No, not yet . . ."

"I think we need to call Bill out stat."

"I'll phone him now," the naturalist said, and rose from the chair.

"How did you get hurt?" Suzanne asked.

"I was caught in that flash flood, but look, that's really not the important issue here."

"Looks like she got hit pretty bad," Steve put in.

"No!" Madeline practically yelled. "It's not my head! That thing's still out there!"

"Now, honey," the officer said, her tone gentle. "Why don't you just sit there on the couch and wait for our medical technician? Would you like a cup of tea or a bite to eat?"

Madeline threw up her hands in frustration. "I can't believe this!" But even as she said it, she knew how crazy her story sounded, especially to people who hadn't seen the thing, didn't know what it was capable of.

"We'll get this all straightened out," the naturalist said kindly.

Madeline shook her head in disbelief. "You've got to send someone up there! No—send a bunch of people up there. Armed people. And ask that thing pretending to be your friend Mike a lot of personal questions. I guarantee you it won't be able to answer them."

"We'll do that tomorrow," Suzanne told her. "But first we need to get you better."

"Tomorrow I'll go myself," the naturalist offered.

Madeline couldn't tell if he meant it or not. "Don't go

alone," she told him. She was so exhausted, and it felt like someone had jabbed a shish kebab skewer directly through her temple. She sighed, wanting the pain to ease. Bringing her fingers to her head, she massaged gently. She had done her part. She had reported the murder. Now she had to protect herself. And if the rangers weren't going to help her, if the thing came back, she would just have to face it alone. *Or hopefully with Noah,* she thought, suddenly wondering where he was, if he'd found a place to stay. Preferably a place with five bolts on the door and no rafters.

"I'm going to call Bill now," the naturalist said. Suzanne nodded, and he left the room.

"Do you have a place to stay tonight, honey?" asked the officer.

Madeline nodded. "My friend Noah is finding a place. He should be back any minute." She sighed. "Did anyone else get caught in the flash flood?"

The ranger's mouth fell into a grim, gray line. "Three that we know of, aside from you." She paused. "They, uh . . . they didn't make it."

Madeline's eyes widened as she thought of the freezing water robbing muscles of strength, filling lungs, tossing bodies into jagged rocks and lethal branches.

"But, everything's going to be all right for you," Suzanne added quickly, seeing her response. "You'll see."

But her reassurance felt hollow and empty, and despite the rangers around her, symbols of law and safety, Madeline had never felt so alone and scared in her life.

After the medical technician had come and rebandaged her head, he determined she didn't have a concussion and that she should just get some rest. He gave her some acetaminophen, extra bandages, and first aid tape, and left.

Shortly afterward, as she sat alone with the two rangers again, a rap brought their attention back to the door. In a moment Steve was up and opening it. Noah stood there. She was so glad to see him she almost leapt up and hugged him.

"Noah!" she said, about to launch into the story about how they wouldn't listen to her, how the creature had convinced them it hadn't killed their friend.

"I found us a place to stay," he said before she could get a word out.

She realized he was nervous and didn't want to talk to the rangers.

"Thanks for your help," he told the rangers.

"The ranger in question is fine . . . I radioed him myself," Steve said to Noah.

"Yes," Noah said quietly. "It's just been a long couple of days, and my friend here was really spooked by the flash flood."

Both rangers nodded, and after thanking them again, Noah led her out and shut the door behind them.

"They wouldn't listen to me," Madeline said when they stood alone on the porch.

"It's just as well."

"Just as well?" Madeline said incredulously.

He looked every bit as exhausted as she felt. But his bruises looked a little better. Not so dark.

"They would get killed if they went after him. You must see that by now."

Madeline fell silent. At last she nodded. She looked at him intently. "And you won't?"

Noah sighed and looked out into the night. "Not if I can help it," he said softly, more, Madeline thought, to himself than to her.

The only available accommodation in the entire park had been one cabin at the Lake McDonald Alpine Chalets, just a few hundred yards from the Apgar ranger station.

A small cabin set back away from the lake's edge, next to a burbling creek and surrounded by trees and a few other cabins, it stood right next to Apgar campground. It was a miracle they even got it: someone had canceled a reservation at the last minute. During the summer, accommodation in the park was booked solid. They stood in front of it in the dark, listening to the sounds of night around them: the rush of the creek, a warbling owl in the woods.

"I'm sorry I couldn't get us each a cabin," he told her, "but I'll sleep on the couch."

She nodded. "Thanks. But I already figured you for a gentleman." Secretly she was grateful they only had one cabin available. She hadn't relished the thought of sleeping alone in a strange place tonight.

They went inside. It was a small structure with only a main room and a tiny bedroom. In the center of the living room stood a little wooden lacquered table for eating or playing cards. A couple of folding wooden chairs stood on either side. In one corner of the room sulked an old stuffed chair and couch, upholstered in the ever-popular rough orange brown patterned material that almost came to rule the world in 1972.

They checked the closets and even under the bed at her request. The cabin was small and sparse, built in the '30s, and the bedroom contained only a bed, desk, and a rickety chair. Bathrooms were in separate buildings, shared by all the guests of the cabins. Madeline had seen one of the structures on the way in, a large, lighted building that looked like it had flush toilets and even hot water. The thought of such luxuries after her ordeal almost made her giddy.

After Noah checked the cabin, she collapsed into a chair. In the soft glow of a table lamp, she could clearly see the concern on Noah's face and something else: a profound tiredness. He looked over, caught her staring, and she glanced away toward the windows.

They didn't look very secure. What if the creature came scrambling up the stairs, broke a glass pane in the door, reached in with furtive fingers—

"Will it . . . come? Here?" she asked at last. "Will it find me?"

"No." Noah shook his head. "There's no reason to think that. His attacks are random . . ." His voice trailed off, eyes fixing on the darkness beyond the windows.

Madeline had the distinct feeling he was lying.

8

WHILE Noah unloaded his backpack, Madeline walked the short distance to the bathroom with a toothbrush and toothpaste Noah had bought for her at the campground's general store. She had no money on her whatsoever; no gear to speak of except what she'd been wearing when the water hit. Her clothes lay drying next to the little heater in the cabin. She was still wearing Noah's warm fleece. Luckily she had money nearby, however; she'd stashed her wallet under the seat of her car. Tomorrow she'd get a ride to where her car waited, miles down the Going-to-the-Sun Road at the Loop Trailhead. And then she'd go home.

She had done all she could here. She'd notified the rangers, they hadn't believed her, and Noah was determined to hunt the thing himself. He'd obviously had prior experience with it, and he was still alive, so hopefully he'd be successful. Madeline was lucky she was in one piece, and she felt anxious to go home.

A nagging feeling preyed on her, and she pushed it away. It loomed back up, though, surfacing repeatedly. She could help. She could use her ability.

This was exactly what she wanted to avoid: working on murder cases, sacrificing any chance she had of living a normal life and enjoying her youth, relinquishing whatever innocence and happiness was left to murder and violence.

Loud laughter brought her attention to a cabin a couple doors down from hers. A group of college-age guys sat around a bonfire in front of their cabin, laughing and drinking beer. They looked like they'd come out for a weekend of partying.

She envied their carefree demeanor. They could afford it. Probably their biggest concern was passing calculus or asking someone out for a date.

She walked by them and hesitated before the bathroom door. Closing her eyes, Madeline made a brief wish for a safe bathroom: nothing hiding in the stalls or behind the trash cans, or under the sinks, and especially no bodies in the rafters. Her wish done, she pushed the door open. It creaked on rusty hinges, admitting her to a large, brightly lit bathroom with a white tiled floor and white painted walls. Immediately Madeline looked up. No rafters. The ceiling came to a point above her. Nothing was up there.

Three stalls stood on one side of the room. All three doors were open. Cautiously Madeline crept past them, peering inside each one. The last door was partially closed, and she pushed it open with her foot.

Nothing.

Just a normal bathroom with normal toilets, two normal sinks, and a couple of shower stalls.

Outside she could hear the college guys getting rowdier and rowdier. She heard a beer can being crushed, followed by more laughter and drunken shouting. They turned up their radio so loud it overpowered the droning of a nearby RV generator.

After she'd gone to the bathroom, Madeline took a deep breath and stood before the mirror. Grasping the length of tape, she carefully peeled the bandage aside. Underneath, an inch-long angry-looking gash nestled amid brown and blue bruised flesh. But it wasn't as bad as it felt, and she replaced the bandage. She brushed her teeth and recapped the toothpaste. Taking another long look at the gaunt, exhausted Madeline in the mirror, she sighed, then walked to the door, where she paused. Originally a source of fear, the bathroom, having proved clear, now felt like a safe haven. The creature could be out there, even now, its approach muffled by the radio and the voices of the drunk guys across the way.

Noah said the creature killed at random. If that was true, then it was illogical to think it had followed her here. Except that it had intercepted her at the ranger's station. But now that she was down in civilization, maybe it wouldn't risk being seen.

She wished she'd asked Noah if it hunted in more populated places. She wished she'd asked Noah a lot of questions.

Opening the door, she stepped out into the night. The college guys were now throwing different things into the fire and seeing what effect it had. One of them sprayed something—*Bug spray?* she wondered—into the fire. It spat out flame in a long, flowing arc.

When they started talking rudely about a woman one of them had asked out, she slunk by them quietly, hoping they wouldn't notice her.

"Hey!" one of them called as she began to pass by. "Hey, baby! Come over here!"

She just ignored him and kept walking, as if he wasn't talking to her at all, but to someone else.

"Don't just walk by!" slurred another. "We need some company!"

"Yeah," a third one laughed as if that was the funniest thing he'd ever heard. "We need some company!" The way they said *company* let Madeline know exactly what kind of "company" they had in mind.

Great, she thought, *a perfect end to a perfect day.*

Madeline shot them an unfriendly look, which enabled her to see how many there were, and how far away.

She counted four by the fire. Just as she looked away, she glimpsed one of them get up from his seat and begin walking after her.

Madeline's mouth went dry. At community college last

semester, she'd taken a self-defense class, and she remembered the teacher saying to look around continuously when you were under threat so no one could sneak up on you. She also remembered the instructor saying, "GET him!" which meant strike at the groin, eyes, and throat.

Madeline picked up her pace and glanced behind.

"Shit!" one of the guys said. "Pete's going after her."

"C'mon!" another said. Soon all four guys were up, following her along the road. Her cabin was too far away. She didn't think she could reach it in time. She made a decision and spun around quickly, shouting in a loud, aggressive voice, "What the hell do you want?"

This completely surprised them, and the lead guy stopped. The other three caught up with him.

"Just some company, baby."

"Not a chance in hell."

She waited to see their reaction. They looked unsure. She turned to leave, and then heard one of them start to run after her. She whirled around and came face-to-face with Pete. Hostile brown pig eyes glittered under a crop of blond hair.

She remembered what her instructor said about the "reaction range" and stepped back so she was too far away to be grabbed. At least she could see where all of them were, she thought, looking for an advantage.

"You're a real fucking bitch," Pete said, "you know that?" He stepped forward, and she echoed his move, striking out with her palm and connecting with his throat. He reeled back, grabbing his neck, a hiss of pain escaping from his lips.

One of Pete's cronies lunged out to grab her. She darted to one side, and he missed. They all came closer, and Madeline broke out in a cold sweat. She took an aggressive stance, ready to "GET" as many of them as she had to. Holding her hands up ready to strike, she watched them closely.

The guys advanced, Pete still trying to recover but watching the action. "I'm gonna fucking kill you!" he yelled, frowning mouth raining spittle. As they advanced, Madeline retreated, waiting to kick or hit any of them if they came close enough.

And then she backed into someone.

She hadn't even seen a fifth person—realized he must have flanked her and that she had to whirl around and smash him with every bit of strength she could muster. Madeline spun around, her hand looking to connect with a throat or eyes. But she whirled around in darkness, her hand striking only air, her eyes meeting only the black behind her.

"Someone call for help!" she screamed.

"I can do better than that," said a voice from the darkness. And then she saw a part of the night come alive, straightening up out of the shadows. Two red, luminous disks blinked into view and narrowed in the darkness.

"Holy shit!" one of the drunk guys yelled. She heard someone stumble back and fall on the ground. She had her back to the four guys but didn't care now. The creature filled her vision, and she stood staring at it, frozen.

It placed a clawed hand on her shoulder and pushed by her. Madeline whirled around, not taking her eyes off it for a second.

"You pathetic swine," it growled. "I'm going to slit open your bowels and force you to eat what I find."

The guys stumbled back as the creature approached. One guy in the back broke away and took off down the road. In an instant the creature was down on all fours, loping after him. It met him a few yards away, leaping onto his back and twisting his neck fatally.

Then it spun around, eyes locking on the remaining three. In an instant it was among them, claws slicing open stomachs and throats, slashing at skin, tearing at meat. When it finished, four bodies lay sprawled around its feet. Then one of its hands suddenly elongated, becoming a sharp, gleaming silver spike. The creature reared its arm back and plunged it forward, driving the spike deeply into the closest body. A sizzling sound filled the night, and Madeline watched as the body melted and sputtered, sparked and flamed, then erupted in a cascade of ashes. The creature leapt to the other bodies, thrusting the spike within, filling the night with the sounds of spitting fire. In under half a minute only ashes remained of the bodies, carried away on the wind and soaking into the pools of blood on the asphalt.

And then she was alone on the road with the creature.

The creature stood up before her, the long spike shortening and re-forming into an ink-black hand. She could see the creature bore no mark whatsoever where she'd struck it with the ax. Its black skin was smooth and unscarred. She marveled at its strange, sharklike skin and lack of features. It was shadow come to life. An ebony wraith.

A solid lump formed in her throat. She stood transfixed, watching the eyes in the darkness. They had no pupils, just pools of ruby light.

"Where is Noah?" it asked, its voice low.

She moved backward and opened her mouth, but at first no sound came out. "I—I don't know," she finally managed.

The creature cocked its head and looked closely at her. "He can't be far away. Not with you here." She could hear a hint of a foreign accent but couldn't place it. "After all, he's still trying to make up for it."

"For . . . for what?"

"For letting her die."

It stepped closer, breathed in deeply, then reached one long-clawed hand up to her hair. The claws combed through it gently, and she flinched away. "Does he know about you?" the creature asked.

Madeline frowned, confused by the question.

"Touch me," it said.

Madeline didn't move.

It lowered its hand, reaching to her side and closing around her fingers. Then it raised her hand, placing her fingers on its chest. An overwhelming sensation swept over her—a vast, incomprehensible amount of experiences, thoughts, and emotions—and one extraordinary sensation of age. It was old, older than she could fathom. Heat began to tingle in her fingers, traveling through her hand, up her arm.

And then the visions came, scorching geysers erupting behind her eyes.

A handsome young man, the creature in disguise, she

realized, hopping into a hansom in Victorian London, then laughing, drunk in a tavern, conversing with its next victim, a rosy-cheeked young playwright, a linguistic genius . . .

Stumbling through an alley in Prague, starving, panting, hiding in shadows as a group of Nazi soldiers march by. The last one looks into the alley, sees the creature disguised as a young man in a tattered woolen coat. The soldier, sneering, pulls the gun from his holster and fires into the shadows as a terrible pain erupts in the belly of the beast . . .

In a parlor in Vienna, listening to an amazing pianist, a young woman, so vibrant, aching to tear into her and devour every morsel, to taste that sweet flesh, as tantalizing as the music itself . . .

Coughing, staggering, smelling of goat urine and feces, the creature dragging itself out of a barn in a drunken stupor, not drunk on ale, but drunk on flesh, meat from the body of a traveling bard with the ability to spin tales that spellbound listeners. The creature makes its way toward a castle in the distance. It has a hiding place there, a hidden corner of the catacombs where it can digest undisturbed . . .

Hiding in the shadowed galley of a Viking longboat, waiting for a cartographer to descend into waiting jaws, so eager to devour that knowledge, the thirst for places unseen but for the cartographer's eyes, soon to be the creature's alone . . .

In a grove of trees on the island of Anglesey, stalking a Druidic priest, fires erupting, cries of battle as the Romans invade, all turning to chaos, the Druid lost, wasted, dead before the creature even gets a chance . . .

Stalking the well at Alexandria, chariots rumbling by, the creature memorizing the routine of the Greek geophysicist, imagining the tasty meats of the brain, salivating, adjusting its garb stolen from a fellow scholar and the laurels crowning its head. Soon. So soon . . .

Midnight at an Egyptian festival, the full moon bright on the Nile, the young pyramid architect caught unawares in the grove of palms, the rustling of the trees' fronds muffling the sound of eager feeding . . .

"What do you see?" the creature demanded.

A vague part in the back of her mind, beyond the visions, the anguish, the searing pain, remembered how to speak. But Madeline could see nothing but the visions. Her eyes filled with them, unable to see the creature, the woods. "You . . . were shot," she breathed, "in Prague . . . and before that, you were in London, happy . . ."

She wrenched her hand free and gasped, sights of the real world flooding into her once more. The road. The bathroom. Pine trees.

The creature.

It stared at her, eyes wide, silent.

Neither spoke, Madeline forgetting to breathe. Images still swirled in her head, a cacophony of sounds and smells and images from a dozen other times. She could still smell bread baking in an eighteenth-century Viennese bakery, could taste a bitter root pulled from the earth in ancient Norway.

"Stefan!" Noah's sudden cry cut through the heavy silence between them.

The creature looked past Madeline's shoulder. Then it backed up, retreating completely into the darkness, just melting away. For a second she saw the red eyes moving in black, and then even they were gone.

Madeline heard Noah's boots thumping on the pavement behind her, approaching quickly. She didn't dare turn away, afraid the creature might bound back out of the darkness and take off her head with one powerful swipe.

"Madeline!" He pulled her into his arms, holding her tightly. "Did he hurt you?" Madeline's head pressed against his chest, and he felt warm and reassuring. She shook her head.

"But—I heard screaming."

"It wasn't me," she said and pulled away. Silently she indicated the blood on the asphalt.

"Oh, no," said Noah.

Maybe it was cold, but Madeline just felt relieved. Those guys would never bother her or any other woman again. She felt oddly numb and shaky and just wanted to sit down.

Noah evidently saw this on her face. "What is it? What happened?"

Madeline shook her head. After a long pause, she said, "He . . . he *defended* me."

"What?" Amazement.

"The blood . . . is from these guys who were attacking me. He just came out of nowhere and . . ." Madeline thought of the intensity of the moment, of the creature's claws, fangs, the ferocity of his attack.

Noah looked as surprised as Madeline felt.

"Has this ever happened before?" she asked.

Noah raised his eyebrows in bewilderment. "No. At least, not when I've been around."

"Who—" Madeline swallowed, afraid of the question she wanted to ask. "Who does he usually kill? What sort of person?"

"Two kinds of people," Noah answered. "Carefully chosen victims, and people who get in the way of his pursuit of those victims."

A dark, terrible thought crept into her mind as her savior turned back into her killer. "Do you think he killed those guys so that he could still be the one to murder me?"

"Gods," Noah breathed. "Probably."

"That's terrible!" Madeline almost yelled. "What kind of twisted, demented, screwed-up—" She stopped short when she realized how much her voice had raised. "Why me?"

"In the past, he has always chosen victims of extraordinary talent. Something that sets them apart from the rest."

"You said he killed randomly!"

"I lied. I wasn't sure if he had chosen you as a specific victim, and I didn't want to worry you."

"Well, I'm worried." She swallowed back a painful lump that had suddenly moved into her throat and begun to home decorate. "Exceptional talent?"

Noah nodded. "He's killed writers, inventors, architects, scientists, a classical pianist once . . ." His voice trailed off.

He knows? she thought, unnerved. *This creature knows? "Touch me . . ."*

"Do you know why he'd be after you?"

Madeline quickly shook her head. She just wanted to get

away. Go home. "I guess I'm just one of those people who got in the way."

Noah looked closely at her and then shook his head. "I don't think so; he's *hunting* you. If you were merely in the way, he would have just killed you outright."

Madeline just wanted to slink away somewhere, make herself as tiny as possible. She looked to where it had vanished, though she knew it could probably leap out from anywhere it wanted, tearing them both down to bloody nubs. "Let's go inside somewhere," she said. "Somewhere light."

"Of course!" Noah said quickly.

He took her arm, and they walked back toward their cabin, Madeline glancing behind all the while.

Up ahead, the cabin lay in the shadows of the pines, shielded from the dusk-to-dawn glow of the campground light posts. Madeline was leery to go toward the cabin, nestled in the dark, and she walked slower and slower, until Noah slowed to a stop beside her. "What is it?" he asked.

"It just looks so . . . small, so fragile." She stared at it reluctantly. "Like the creature could tear right through the walls."

He followed her gaze, studying the shadowed building. "I'll be with you. Even if we manage to get some sleep, I'll be right outside the bedroom on the couch."

Madeline screwed up her face in hesitation. "What if he knows which one is our cabin?" She paused. "He could break in while I'm sleeping, slash your throat, then find me in the bedroom."

"Glad to know I'll be so helpful in this dark scenario of yours." The corner of his mouth turned up in a smile.

She shook her head. "Sorry. I'm a little on edge, as you can imagine." Her head pounded. Gently she checked the bandage again.

"I understand. Tell you what, then. We'll go to the cabin. We can lock the doors, latch the windows, drink a cup of tea. I'll stay up and keep guard."

"But you're already exhausted!"

"He needs to sleep, too, you know," Noah said. "Not to

scare you more, but he really likes to draw out the hunt. We probably won't see him again tonight."

"Well, that's reassuring. About as reassuring as if you'd told me, 'Don't worry. We won't get hit with another flash flood until tomorrow.'"

The chittering of a squirrel brought their attention up to a nearby tree. Madeline jumped. "It's just a squirrel," Noah said, putting a reassuring hand on her back.

The woods crept in on her, full of creaking wooden arms and reaching limbs. Then the disturbing hush of night fell over them, all animals save the squirrel quiet in the presence of a waiting, virulent predator. The quiet sigh of wind in the pines was alive with the breathing of the creature, and the chattered words of the squirrel were a terrified warning, uttered sharply and urgently.

"Let's go inside," she said, peering into the darkness beyond the dim yellow glow of the lights. "Now."

Without a word, Noah turned and hurried with her to the cabin. Along the way he fished in his pocket for the keys, producing them as they climbed the two steps to the door. The chilly night air crawled down the collar of her jacket, and Madeline turned to keep watch behind them as he unlocked the door. She sniffed the pine-scented air, in case she could detect some unnatural scent on the wind. Only the familiar river and deep earthen tree smells greeted her. But somewhere out there, somewhere close, she could feel it . . . the heaviness of it staring at her, its red disc eyes narrowed with hunger.

As soon as she heard the lock disengage, she pushed past Noah into the cabin. "After you," he said in a startled voice.

"Sorry, just anxious to get inside. Lock the door! Quick!"

Immediately, Noah entered, slamming the door behind him and reengaging the locks. Madeline sprinted around the cabin, rechecking locks on all the windows. The air inside was damp and chilly, and she shivered in the fleece jacket. After she was satisfied all entrances to the cabin were barred, she returned to the front door to find Noah staring out one of the windows, pushing aside one of the curtains.

She flipped a wall switch, spilling even more light into the cabin, then checked both rooms: the main room and the bedroom.

Noah turned to look at her as she returned to him. The pit of fear had given up its condo in her throat and opted to move into her belly. It spread itself out there, distributing its weight into one uniform mass of dread.

"I want to get out of here. Tomorrow I'm hitching a ride back to my car."

He raised his eyebrows in concern. "Nonsense. My Jeep's here. I'll take you. You don't need to hitch."

"I'd leave now if I thought there'd be anyone on the road at this hour to give me a ride. Can't we leave now?"

Noah shook his head. "He's content to sit tight for now because he knows where you are. Leave, and he'll pursue."

"How reassuring."

"You'd be putting yourself in danger again."

"Maybe," she said. "But I can tell you one thing." She squared her jaw. "I'd feel a hell of a lot safer hitching a ride to my car than sitting here like a waiting duck."

"I think that's a sitting duck," Noah said, looking frustrated with the situation.

"I don't care if the duck is doing a goddamn gold-medal triple lutz. Waiting here is suicide, *precisely* because that thing knows where I am."

Noah walked to her and put his hands on her arms, trying to comfort her. "Stay here with me," he said. "I'm your best chance for survival. I have the only weapon that can kill him. As long as you're here, where I can watch over you, he won't be able to harm you."

She pushed the curtain aside just slightly and peered out. "He's so . . . powerful. How would you fight him?"

"I have a way. I've done it before. I've completely foiled his plans several times."

She looked at him, then, his face determined. Then she looked back through the window. She couldn't see anything beyond the bright glow of the dusk-to-dawn lights. Replacing the curtain, she turned to face him. She felt lost. Muggers could be tackled. Gunmen could be disarmed. But this creature was beyond anything she'd ever dealt with. Her life up to this point, even with its own strangeness, simply had not prepared her to fight a physical, supernatural being. Before last night, she didn't even know such a thing could exist. Now she was expected to fight it. "He's just seems so . . . undefeatable."

Noah stepped closer. "He's not. And I'm going to stop him."

She looked at him doubtfully, but exhaustion crept up on her as she stood there, uncertain.

"C'mon," he said. "You look beat. Why don't you sit down? I've got some clean clothes you can change into."

She looked down at his clothes she already wore, covered in dust from the hike down. "Soon I'll have the whole set."

He laughed. "And you'd be welcome to it. Just to see you warm and happy."

The corner of her mouth turned up in a half smile.

"So how about it? Change into some warm clothes? I'll make us some snacks."

She sighed, giving in. She was still shaking from the encounter with the attackers, and even more so from the visions of the creature. The clean clothes, the food, it all sounded great. Especially the food. "Sounds wonderful. Okay. But . . . what about those guys? Shouldn't we report it?"

"Haven't we been through this already tonight?"

She felt angry and hopeless and shook her head. "I guess we have."

"I'm sorry. I know this is tough." He walked to his backpack and opened the top. Then he stopped and looked at her over his shoulder. "You'll get through this, you know. You really amaze me, the way you've taken all this in stride, your bravery. I really admire you."

She shook her head. "Well, we'll see. Right now I don't feel so admirable. I just feel scared."

While Noah unpacked his backpack, Madeline changed in the small bedroom. She pulled on Noah's clean clothes: a

black and purple Capilene turtleneck that zipped up the front;
black pile pants, the thin, soft material somehow amazingly
warm thanks to the technology of synthetic fabrics; a thick
black fleece jacket with a 200 rating—darn warm. She zipped
up the jacket, pulled on a clean pair of Thorlos socks, and put
on her boots, which were now almost dry. She was glad she'd
kept her underwear on up on the mountain. Wearing Noah's
boxers would have been a little too much. The poor guy had
already given up most of his wardrobe. But by tomorrow, her
jeans and shirt Noah had saved would be completely dry.

As she finished dressing, he knocked on the door.

"Come in," she said.

Noah entered, then leaned against the doorframe. "Looking good. Want me to check that bandage? You've bled through
it."

"Okay." She looked at herself in the wall mirror. Blood
had seeped through the white gauze, and she pulled the bandage aside. The cut on her head looked aggravated and red,
the surrounding tissue a dark blue. An image of the tree trunk
hurtling toward her head flashed through her mind.

Noah picked up the small bundle of bandages and first aid
tape the EMT had given her and joined her by the mirror. He
tore open one of the sterile packages. He removed the gauzy
patch and gently placed it on her forehead. "Can you hold this
in place?"

She reached up and pressed her fingers to the pad.

Quickly he tore off several strips of white first aid tape and
affixed the bandage to her skin.

"It looks a lot better already," he said. "Does it hurt much?"

She gazed at herself in the mirror. "Not really," she lied,
her head still throbbing dully.

"Let's eat. I've got some cheese and crackers . . . not much,
but it's the only food we'll find around here at this hour."

"Sounds delicious." And it did, too. After hiking, even the
simplest food always tasted incomparably good. Cold pro-
cessed lunchmeat on a flabby slice of white bread became a
savory dinner cooked in a French bistro.

He paused at the bedroom door and motioned her through.

As she passed him, she caught an alluring scent, along with something else—some indescribable connection—electricity in her stomach diving down to her toes and back up. She glanced back as he closed the door and caught him staring at her. Quickly, he averted his eyes.

From his backpack he'd pulled a small wheel of smoked gouda and some butter crackers in a plastic bag. Rummaging through the pack again, he pulled out a pocket knife. She wondered about the other knife that lay in the pack, the strange silver spike with the elaborate sheath. The temptation to ask him grew as he unfolded a blade and set the cheese on the small wooden table.

"Sorry," he said with a sheepish grin. "It's the best I can do."

"Looks terrific."

"If I'd known I'd be entertaining a beautiful woman, I'd have brought wine and made my special pasta with mushrooms and cream sauce." He smiled, his eye contact intense.

"Well, if any beautiful women show up, we'll just have to let them down gently."

He laughed, shaking his head.

Instantly she regretted saying it, but having someone call her beautiful was so rare and strange. Usually they desperately tried to avoid her, except George, thankfully. But of course Noah didn't know about her "gift" yet.

She watched as he leaned over the table, muscular arms slicing away at the cheese, strong hand working the knife, cropped blond hair giving way to his lean, tanned neck—

"Thick or thin?"

"Excuse me?"

"Do you like your slices thick or thin?"

"Either way."

"Gosh, you're so picky," he said, grinning at her over his shoulder. "My clothes aren't good enough, my cheese isn't the right thickness. Give a guy a break once in a while."

She laughed and walked over to the table, eager to nibble at the feast. He returned to slicing, and she peered over his shoulder longingly as he placed a slice on a broken cracker.

He turned his head slightly, inhaled. He stopped moving. "You smell good."

She cocked an eyebrow.

"It's the scent of your skin, your breath. You smell—" he leaned forward, breathing her in, "ambrosial."

"Ambrosial?"

"Mmmmm."

"Isn't that what people eat to become Greek gods?"

"Hmm . . ." He looked down at her, his eyes sparkling. "Let's find out." He leaned forward, flexing his teeth, and she grinned and took a step back.

"Noah!" She stopped a few feet away, still facing him.

"How can I find out if you run?" Closing the distance between them again, he said, "Yes, ambrosial . . . as in delectable, savory, delicious." His hand found hers, and a rush of excitement tingled through her at his touch.

"Cheese?" she asked suddenly, her old fear rushing into her. She wanted this part to last—this part where he didn't know she was a freak, where he might just be able to enjoy her company.

His eyes widened, and he leaned back. "Cheese?"

"We were about to eat cheese."

"We were?"

"With crackers."

"I see. Well then." He dropped her hand. "We'll have to do that. I suddenly feel compelled."

He turned back to the table and continued placing the slices on the broken crackers.

"Gouda. My favorite," she said.

He regarded her schemingly out of the corner of his eye. "I'll have to remember that."

They ate in silence, hunger overtaking them. Madeline felt a little strange, too, wanting to stare at Noah but afraid of what might happen if she did. Teetering on the edge of a change, she feared it and wanted to lean back from the brink. Everything that had happened since she'd come to the mountain was so startling and amazing, even considering her already unusual life.

Noah glanced up from his crackers and met her gaze briefly, the green of his eyes eerily the same color as his sweater, almost glowing with intensity. She held his gaze for what felt like a full minute, a vague buzzing inside her creating a pleasant sensation as their eyes met. Then she returned her attention to the crackers.

They finished eating in silence, but the tension between them was so thick, Madeline could feel it hanging over the table like a mounting tropical storm. As she finished, she stood up, brushing crumbs off her shirt. Noah stood up, too, staring at her. He came closer, standing before her less than a foot away. She stood her ground, fighting off her desire to flee. He studied her face, his eyes so intense she couldn't look away.

Then he stepped closer, mere inches away, so close Madeline could feel the heat from his body. Something in his eyes was so powerful she felt her heartbeat pick up, almost as if she anticipated danger.

Noah brought his hand up and touched her shoulder, then ran it along her neck and around the back of her head, curling his fingers gently around the curve of her neck. His touch sent shivers of delight down her back. She felt him move closer, his leg against hers, then his stomach against her own. Every fiber in her being was aware of his closeness, and she relished the sensation.

He leaned down, placing his lips against her cheek, then moved gently along her jawline toward her lips. His breath was sweet and intoxicating, and she drew it in. His mouth drew closer to her lips, the slight roughness of his whiskers brushing along her skin.

He reached the corner of her mouth and kissed her there, sending waves of pleasure through her. And then he kissed her full on the lips, pressing in passionately. At last she moved, bringing her hands to his shoulders and clutching them tightly. He wrapped his arms around her, closing the distance between them, his kisses wild and unrestrained.

They went off balance, knocking a chair over, still kissing. Her hands moved over his back, pulling him closer to her.

His hands moved down, cupping her butt and lifting her up. She wrapped her legs around his waist, and they fell against the wall, her tongue tasting him, kissing along his neck and salty skin. He pulled away from the wall, turned toward the bedroom, knocking a lamp over in the process.

In the ensuing darkness, she felt his fingers on her back grow sharp and wiry, felt claws piercing through her shirt.

Gasping, she pulled her head away and looked at him.

He had changed.

His eyes gleamed red, flashed in the shadows like the eyes of a night creature caught in the light.

She unwrapped her legs and jumped down, but still he held her close to him.

"Don't be afraid," he said, and as he talked she could see all his teeth had gone sharp. "Kiss me." And then he brought his lips to hers again and kissed her still more passionately. Her mind reeled as she tried to take everything in, feeling both afraid and still drawn to him in the same moment.

He must have felt her reluctance, for he pulled back and said, "It's still me. I won't hurt you. It's just that in moments of extreme . . . emotion . . . the change comes over me."

"What change?" she demanded, panicked. His eyes glowed fiercely now, a look of hunger gleaming there. "Noah, I—"

"I'm not like him," Noah said.

"Who, the creature? Your eyes . . . you look ravenous."

He paused, thinking. "I am. But not like you think. It's just that being near you, the way you smell, the way we talk so easily. You've faced this all unflinchingly. I've never met someone so brave. You amaze me." He caressed the side of her face. "I am ravenous, yes, but it's for you. I desire you. I haven't been drawn this way in a very long time."

"But, Noah . . ." Her voice trailed off. She felt a tremble deep within her. What had she gotten herself into?

He pulled away. "Do you feel . . . nothing?"

"Oh, no. I feel something. Believe me, I feel something. But I don't understand." She pushed him away. "You . . . that thing . . . What are you?" she asked finally.

He sighed, dropping his arms. In an instant his green eyes

returned, the red fading. Claws gave way to normal fingers. She couldn't believe it. They just transformed before her eyes, the gleaming sharpness changing to soft flesh and skin. She stared at him, feeling the urge to bolt out of there. Slowly he took her hand, and she cringed at first. But his touch was so gentle, his eyes so pleading, that she let him lead her back into the main room. He slumped down into one of the wooden chairs. Sighing, he put his head in his hands. She pulled up the other chair and waited. "I'm old," he began. "Very old."

He fell silent then, and she wondered if he was going to continue. "What?" she finally said. "You've reached the ancient age of twenty-four?"

"No. Older." He looked intently into her eyes. "I was born in 1739. In London."

Madeline stared. "What?"

"Yes. And when I was twenty-four, something terrible happened."

He went quiet again for a long time, and she realized how hard it was for him to talk about this. His eyes cast downward, and his brow creased. She wondered if he'd ever even spoken these words before.

He swallowed hard. "I encountered *him.*"

"The creature?"

Noah nodded. The rims of his eyes turned red. "But before that, before my life was torn apart, something wonderful happened." He fell silent again.

"What?"

"I fell in love."

She waited.

Noah's eyes grew distant. He looked beyond Madeline, toward the window. "Anna. I first saw her at the opera. She was gazing down at the performers, her eyes bright and excited. I learned later that was her first visit to the opera house. I was immediately enchanted. My family was very wealthy and knew almost every other family of means in Vienna. I begged them to throw a ball so that I could meet her, and they agreed. On the twenty-sixth of May, she walked into my house, that same look of youth and excitement glowing on her

face. I stole her dance card and wrote my name down for most
of the dances, then placed it back by her fan when she wasn't
watching. She laughed when she saw the card." Noah cast his
eyes down. "I still remember her laugh so vividly.

"I courted her for two years, and when I became successful
as an investor, I was ready to propose. But I wasn't the only
one. She had a slew of suitors who regularly called on her. All
this time she'd been learning the pianoforte, and came to play
it amazingly well. She began playing at parties and gatherings,
and many people took note of her exceptional talent. One
such person was a newcomer to Vienna, a wealthy entrepre-
neur with some distant relative who was an acquaintance of
her family.

"He took an intense interest in Anna, often visiting to hear
her play. I thought his interest was purely romantic at first.
But as it turned out, it was far worse than that. He feeds upon
exceptional people, you see. He craves new strengths and abilities and ingests his victims' knowledge, their experiences,
and then uses it to infiltrate yet another group and continue
the cycle." He clasped his hands tightly together, till his knuckles grew white. Madeline resisted the urge to comfort him.
She wanted to hear the story, wanted to understand. Though
at first he'd begun merely to explain to her, now she felt he
was exorcising ghosts of the past.

"One night, Anna's family was away in Salzburg and had
left her behind with her brother, Gregor. He spent most of his
time drinking and carousing and brought all sorts of unsa-
vory types back to the house.

"On this night, he brought home several men to play cards
with. They were all drunk. Anna was playing the piano in the
sitting room. I came by to call on her. She was happily playing; her brother's habits seldom affected her adversely, though
she hated to see him drink so much. A Welshman, Ffyllon,
had passed out on the settee, and Gregor asked me to carry
him to one of the bedrooms. When I got back, *he* was standing over her while she played, and Madeline, you could feel
the lust coming off him. His eyes filled with it, gleaming as

he watched her play. He didn't even see me enter. The other guests had left the room to play cards in the parlor.

"I had been watching for only a second when he began to . . . change. He opened his mouth, revealing a hideous row of sharp teeth, and he lunged down, sinking into her neck.

"I cried out—and that's when he realized I was there. He tore away from her and sprang toward me on all fours, his body becoming more squat and animalistic, his skin darkening till it was completely black. Then he was on top of me, his gray eyes enlarging to red orbs that glowed fiercely. He clawed at me, raked my chest and neck like he was in a frenzy. I fought as best I could, punched and kicked, but it was useless. He had so much *power*! I knew he was going to kill me, and the thought was terrifying. And then above the scuffle, I heard this gut-wrenching sob. He stopped attacking me and turned to the piano. Anna had fallen from the bench and was trying to stand. Blood covered her yellow dress, staining it scarlet down the front.

" 'Get away from him,' she hissed, and I'd never heard her like that before. Her eyes were narrow and threatening, her face contorted in anger and pain.

"He left me there and stalked over to her as I struggled to get to my knees. As he reached her, she lifted her hand high. Something gleamed there, but I couldn't see what. I tried to get to my feet. And then she brought it down on the creature, driving it deeply into his neck. He screamed and bolted away from her, red eyes wide with surprise. He burst from the room and crashed through one of the French doors.

"Anna collapsed. I rushed to her side and cradled her head . . ." Noah's voice cracked painfully. "I could see how bad . . . how bad she was hurt. I took off my cravat and pressed it tightly to the wound. 'The metal,' she started to say, and then she choked. Blood bubbled on her lips." He bit the corner of his mouth. "I remember she said, 'Oh, Noah, I wanted to marry you . . .'

"And then she was gone. Her eyes just went vacant. I clutched her to my chest and kissed her lips and hands, her blood in my mouth. I begged to have her back, begged God, the earth, begged time itself, but still she lay there, lifeless, pale, and limp."

Noah broke into tears, and this time Madeline did get up and put her arms around him. She held him tightly while he cried. He wrapped his arms around her. "It was so long ago, but the pain is still so fresh that the very thought of it breaks me down." He continued to cry, and Madeline brought him closer.

After a while, Noah said from her shoulder, "It was the blood."

Madeline's brow wrinkled. "What?" Gently she pushed him up so she could see his face. His expression was dire, his eyes cheerless and empty.

"The blood," he said again. "When I kissed her hand, I tasted blood. What I didn't realize was that it was *his* blood—the creature's blood. When she stabbed him, it spilled down her hand, and I had ingested it."

"What happened?"

"At first nothing. Full of grief and obsessed with revenge, I wandered the underbelly of Vienna, trying to find someone who knew of the creature. I had one drive: to find the thing and destroy it. Polite society, save one person, ostracized me. That one person was one of Gregor's frequent visitors to the house: Ffyllon. He knew of the creature and its weakness, a certain type of metal. It was this friend who had given Anna the metal, in the shape of a letter opener, and told her of the creature. He wasn't specific, but at the time I got the impression he'd been following the creature for some time. He said Anna had laughed at him when he offered the letter opener for protection, but she had taken it in appreciation of his good story about a roaming, voracious creature.

"A few days later I found Ffyllon's body, murdered by the creature. His journal was on him, and I read it. He had followed the thing to Vienna, worried that it intended to kill a musician named Anna. In his journal, he wonders if the drinks he had the night Anna was murdered were drugged.

With the hunter passed out, the creature had open access to his target."

"Did you still have the letter opener?"

"No. When she stabbed him with it, it must have stayed embedded in him when he ran off that night. Everything happened so fast—" He exhaled shakily.

"Did this friend help you find another weapon?"

Noah shook his head. "No. He disappeared right after that and was killed before he could help me further. I vowed to take up his quest, but spiraled ever downward. Eventually I found a piece of the special metal, though, and had a knife made out of it."

Madeline considered for a minute, then said, "Is it the same knife that's in your pack?"

Noah raised his eyebrows. "Going through my things?"

"I needed to look at the map."

"Ah. Yes, it's the same knife."

Madeline resisted the urge to tell him she'd felt how old and important it was when she'd touched it.

"I thought once I had the knife, I'd just find him and kill him. But it was far more complicated than that. I don't think he has an inherent human form. He can look like anyone he's eaten. Anyone at all. I realized that the hard way when a stranger attacked me in an alley in Cardiff. The creature had taken on another appearance, but I didn't realize it until then. He'd been stalking me not only because I was a witness, but because he had been unable to eat Anna, and he wanted revenge. I slashed him with the knife, but only shallowly. He flew into a rage, twisting and screaming. He tore out of the alley and into the streets.

"For a long time after that I didn't know where he'd gone. He covers his trail well. But little clues, like accounts of people with exceptional talent gone missing or murdered gave me his whereabouts.

"And so I've been hunting him. Across four continents, for over two hundred years, it's all I've done."

He sighed and put his head back in his hands.

Madeline just stared at him, not knowing what to say. Finally she asked, "But how are you still alive?"

Noah stayed silent for several moments, then he looked up at her, his eyes tired and bloodshot.

"The blood," he said. "Over time I noticed . . . changes. I was able to see in the dark. I rarely needed to eat. I was more energetic and started noticing that I was aging quite well. Then I realized it was a little *too* well. Fifty years went by. On those rare occasions when I returned home, I saw that my friends had gotten wrinkles and grown stiff, and I still looked the same. Then they started to die of old age. And I still looked twenty-four. Later, when I was very emotional, when feeling anger or"—he looked at her—"passion, I began to change physically. The more time goes by, the more I change, the more abilities I gain." Noah fell silent.

"What abilities?" The tremble returned within her.

"The power to heal quickly. To see in the dark. To not need much sleep. To change small parts of my appearance, like growing claws. I'm not nearly as powerful as the creature, but I've been learning as I go." He paused. "The usual things won't kill me anymore. I found that out through accidents that have happened over the years. I was hit by a train once. And while it didn't kill me, it took me weeks to heal completely. Still, mere weeks after having my body pulverized isn't bad.

"I began to get completely absorbed with it. I didn't have to fear death anymore and became obsessed with that fact. I even tried to kill myself in a few different ways, just to see if it would work. It never did. But I've longed to die a few times over these last centuries. I just didn't want the responsibility anymore. I just couldn't keep on hunting him fruitlessly, year after year."

They sat together for several long moments.

"What *is* he?" Madeline asked at last.

Noah shook his head. "I don't know. He's either completely nonhuman, a creature all his own, or he's a man like me—a man who was attacked by the same kind of creature, a long, long time ago."

"Why long ago?"

"Because what you've seen me do—the claws, the eyes—has taken me two hundred years to develop. At first I couldn't even do that. I'd try to grow claws, and instead freakish things would happen. Sometimes I wouldn't be able to undo them for a while. Like once I grew fingernails in my leg, and another time a finger sprouted out of my stomach. It was excruciating learning how to control the power, and I still know next to nothing. I think if I'd gotten a larger dose of his blood, I might have more power and be able to control it better, like him. He can shape-shift, adopt the features of other people, change his flesh to metal. If he was ever a man, he was so thousands of years ago." He paused. "But there's something else that makes me think he's nonhuman."

"What's that?"

"He eats people. Has a terrible appetite for them. But I don't feel anything like that. This change that's happening—it isn't bringing with it a desire to eat human flesh. And maybe that's because I was human to begin with but he wasn't."

"Or maybe," Madeline added, "it's because that change hasn't happened to you yet."

"Don't say that!" he snapped. "I'll never be like him."

She was taken aback. "I'm sorry," she said after a pause. "I didn't mean it like that . . . I know you never would have . . ." She thought of Noah cradling his love in his arms as she slipped away, and immediately regretted what she'd said.

"Whatever he was to begin with, creature or human, he was evil. I'm sure of that. And I'm not like that."

"I didn't think you were, Noah. I know you're not. You saved me, remember?"

He closed his eyes. "Sorry. I didn't mean to be so defensive. It's just . . . I've asked myself that same question so many times. 'Am I going to turn out like him?' I have to tell myself no. And I have to keep believing it."

Madeline looked at him intently. She couldn't imagine what it must be like for him . . . to be aging and not know how he'd turn out, if he'd become a beast, to lose someone so special and live hundreds of years without her. "I'm sorry for what you went through," she said, and the words felt inconsequential in the face of such loss. But she could understand what it was like to be different, to be a social freak. And Noah was hiding it from her, just like she had hidden her own ability. But now he'd been honest with her. And maybe she should return the favor. "Noah," she said, after they'd been quiet for a long time. "I lied before when I said I didn't have any exceptional talents."

He looked at her with surprise. "You did?"

She looked down. "Yes. It's just that I came out here to get away from it . . . the negative attention, the imposed segregation. I just wanted to be normal." She sighed, thinking about the traumatic experiences of the last two days. "It hasn't been terribly successful."

Noah arched his eyebrows with curiosity, watching her expectantly.

She was silent for a moment, thinking how best to tell him.

Finally he urged, "What exceptional talents do you have?"

"Well . . . give me your watch."

"What?"

"Don't say anything about it; just hand it to me."

"Okay." He began unbuckling it, and Madeline took in its physical characteristics. It was a digital watch with a green nylon band. He handed it to her, and she opened that door in her mind, letting the images flow. As each one came, she told Noah what she saw.

"You bought this watch in Missoula, Montana," she told him. "It was a hot day, and you'd really wanted a watch with a built-in altimeter, but it was too expensive. After you bought this watch, you drank coffee in a little café called Cool Beans. Once you thought you'd lost the watch, but it turned out that you'd just left it in the net pocket inside your tent. The next time you pitched the tent, there it was." She was quiet for a moment, still holding on to the watch. "Oh, and there's something else . . . your grandfather . . ."

Noah's face went white.

"That's why you were so upset about losing the watch. You thought, 'Can't I have a watch without losing it?' Your grandfather had given you a pocket watch, and you lost it. Just last year. You held on to it for two hundred years, and now it's gone. And you resent yourself for it." She paused. "It's in Scottsbluff, Nebraska. You stopped to drink tea with an older woman, a relative, no, a descendent of your family. You left your pocket watch on her side table. She's still got it. You just have to call her."

Noah just stared at her. She handed the watch back. He didn't put it back on, just held it with wonder as if it contained magic itself. Then he said, "Madeline, that's amazing! How did you know all that?" He sat back and stared at her in astonishment.

"It's a talent I've had for as long as I can remember. I get images, feelings, from anything I touch. I can tell who touched it last, what they were thinking about at the time, where they were, sometimes even where they were planning to go next."

"It's amazing!" Then with a thoughtful look, he added, "Up on the mountain, when I pulled you free of the driftwood, you murmured things about a house in Vienna. I thought it was strange at the time. But now I understand." Then: "So my pocket watch is really in Scottsbluff?"

Madeline nodded, then had to laugh, a tired laugh. "It's nice to have someone react positively to this. I'm not very . . . popular where I come from."

"What do you mean?"

"Well, my parents noticed that I had this 'gift' when I was really little. My dad came home one night with a bottle of wine for my mom, telling her he'd had to work late. I was sitting at the kitchen table, and when he set the bottle down, I touched it. Instantly I got an image of him kissing this other woman. They'd bought the wine together but had a fight, so he came home. I was only six. I described it there on the spot. I didn't know how it would tear my family apart. My mom was so hurt. It's the first time I remember her crying. They got divorced shortly after that and took turns taking care of me. But I could tell both were spooked by me. They didn't want me to touch their personal possessions. Some nights they'd fight about me, how they felt like they had no privacy around me. They hid my ability, told me never to reveal it to anyone. But it was a tough thing to hide. Back then I couldn't control it well, couldn't shut it off. Eventually word got around. I stopped getting invited places. People didn't like the idea of me being in their houses, touching counters, fridge handles, whatever, and getting flashes of things that were personal.

"I had to teach myself to control it, to block out images when I didn't want them. I didn't want everyone's life to be an open book. I didn't want to know their sordid affairs or private longings. I hated it.

"But they never seemed to get that. I hate going into town, like when I need to go the grocery store. My town is so small that everyone knows who I am. They don't want to touch me when they hand me change. Checkers will suddenly close lanes if they see me waiting.

"Only one friend stuck around. Ellie." She looked down at her lap, the pain still unendurable. "But even that changed when I was fourteen." She couldn't bring herself to finish. She'd barely even talked about this with George, the only person she confided in back home. Putting it into words was just too difficult.

"What happened when you were fourteen?" Noah asked at last.

She looked off toward the window, reluctant to answer his question. "A couple years before that, there was a rash of killings in Montana. All the victims were men in their thirties and forties, who were killed while in the outdoors, generally while hunting or fishing. The victims were . . . flayed. Flayed alive, the police realized after autopsies had been performed. And all the murders happened on the night before a new moon."

"Hey . . . I remember this!" Noah said suddenly. "There was a media frenzy! The press dubbed the murderer the Sickle Moon Killer. Didn't he also—"

Madeline nodded; her hands gone clammy. "Yes. He would eat skin from his victims, then regurgitate it. It was a ritual to separate himself from his abusive father. He killed men similar to his father, then ate them, making the men 'blood of his blood,' as he described later in an interview. Then he threw them up to forever divorce himself from those men, in essence rejecting his father on a deeply emotional and biological level.

"The police had no leads. They staked out some likely places, recreation areas, popular fishing sites, things like that, but they never caught anyone. Then suddenly the killings stopped. Police thought something may have happened to the killer, that he himself was killed or put in jail on some other charge. Two years went by.

"But neither was the case. The killer was just reestablishing himself in a new town. A man named Sam MacCready moved in down the street from us, and everyone thought he was pretty nice and quiet, but he gave me the creeps.

"Ellie and I used to go out to this spot near an old dam and hang out and talk. It was one of the few places we could get privacy in that town. We'd go for long hikes and talk about everything under the sun. Our parents. Boys. We both shared a passion for wildlife watching and nature." Madeline paused, the memory of her friend alive. "She never judged me or was reluctant around me. Never treated me like a pariah. She even defended me at times."

She stopped talking, wanting to linger in that warm area of good memories, of her stalwart companion. She didn't want to finish. Finishing meant killing Ellie all over again.

"And what happened?"

Madeline bit her lip. "On one of these hikes, Ellie dropped her bracelet. Her grandmother had left it to her, and Ellie was really attached to it. We backtracked, doing a bit of bushwacking. We'd been eating some huckleberries along the way and had stepped off the trail a number of times. She got ahead of me, went out of sight, hurrying because we didn't have much time before dark." Her voice trailed off.

As Madeline told the story, her mind left the room and the little cabin in Glacier National Park. It moved, tentatively at first, back to that day by the river. Then it rushed, tumbling, crashing back to those memories still so fresh. She felt the weight of the grief, the sheer, shocking power of those images, and soon was no longer in the cabin with Noah at all.

She was back at the North Cascade River, in those last few minutes with Ellie.

Madeline was sure Ellie had lost her bracelet while picking berries. She stopped at a huckleberry bush they'd spent a lot of time at while Ellie moved farther up the trail to look near a thimbleberry bush. As Madeline bent over, searching the ground, a gleam of metal caught her eye. It flashed in the sunlight, some four feet from the path. Madeline walked to it, sure it was the bracelet. But instead she found a knife, recently dropped. The blade was clean, no dirt or sign of lengthy exposure to the elements. She stooped and picked it up, and images rushed into her.

Sam MacCready torturing a man, making slices in his skin and peeling it off like sheets.

The victim screaming as MacCready bent forward for more flesh.

The victim lifeless, cast to one side, wet muscles gleaming in the sunlight, the skin completely gone.

MacCready picking up a handful of skin and pushing it into his mouth, stifling the gag reflex and swallowing, the sweet sensation of the act momentarily overpowering the anguish of his life.

Then vomiting up the skin, MacCready thinking of his father and his cruel eyes, the sting of the old man's hand across his cheek, the pain of his father's fingers digging into his skin as he hurled insults at his little boy.

Euphoria sweeping through him as he looked at the pieces of regurgitated flesh, a ritual to purge himself from his overbearing father and save other sons from their own oppressors.

Madeline threw the knife aside as she fell forward, landing hard on her knees in the dirt. She tried to separate her own mind from MacCready's, but for a long and horrible moment they were one. She forced her eyes to close and tried to dispel the images. But they were too strong, as if she'd been there with him, reveling in his crimes, eating the flesh of his victims.

She stood up, the forest swimming back into view. And before her stood MacCready, his face contorted in fear. He held Ellie in front of him, a knife to her throat. Tears streamed down her face.

MacCready looked down at the knife Madeline had thrown aside, then back up to her face. "You're that girl from town," he said, and Madeline felt the weight of his statement hit her like a punch. "What did you see?"

She shook her head. Ellie started shaking uncontrollably. Madeline noticed then that Ellie had blood on her hands, knees, part of her shirt. MacCready was covered with it.

She tried to formulate a plan, some kind of escape, but her mind was numb. She didn't know how she could wrestle the knife away from him, but there was no way in hell she was going to let him take Ellie. In a rush of anger, she ran straight at him. He jumped back in surprise, and Ellie twisted free.

They ran, crashing through the underbrush with Mac-Cready close behind. In a few moments they hit the river trail, taking off at full speed with Ellie in the lead. Madeline could hear her friend's ragged breath, their footsteps muffled by the blanket of fallen pine needles.

As they rounded a large boulder, a flash of movement streaked down from above. MacCready landed violently on top of Ellie, and she went down hard. Madeline barely stopped short of colliding with them. She darted around MacCready, who struggled to regain his balance. Madeline had almost reached her friend's side when she realized Ellie wasn't moving. She lay on the riverbank, her head against a rock and a stream of blood trickling onto the sand. MacCready leapt toward Madeline, and she dodged out of the way. As he turned, he clumsily bumped Ellie's side, rolling her into the river.

As the current took Ellie's body, Madeline ran downstream and dove in, muscles instantly robbed of warmth. MacCready followed, hitting the water at the same time she did. Coarse hands grabbed her in the icy water and shoved her head under. The roar of the river grew louder as they tumbled through a rapid, Madeline's shoulder hitting a submerged boulder. The jarring bump tore her out of MacCready's grip. She gasped for air and kept swimming, searching for Ellie.

Struggling to keep her head above water, she didn't see Ellie at all. Instead, the cement of the old dam loomed up before her, a barricade across the river. Rocketing fast toward the wall, she put her feet out first and collided with the cement, doubling over and hitting her head on the dam. Gripping the stone with fingers gone numb, she pulled herself out, fighting the rush of the water. Ellie was still nowhere in sight, and Madeline hoped desperately she'd climbed out farther upriver. She stood there for a few tense moments, not sure if she should run back to town for help or keep watching for her in the water.

When MacCready bounced into sight, aiming for the dam, Madeline ran upriver, searching for Ellie. Finally, worried that her friend could die if more people weren't brought into the search, she ran for town.

Madeline went quiet, one hand resting on her silver bracelet. Noah watched her silently, momentarily placing a hand on her shoulder. The forest faded away. The roar of the North Cascade River grew distant, and her heart beat dully, her mind returning to the present, to the little cabin in Glacier, and to Noah. "It's all so vivid still," she said.

"You don't have to finish."

"I know. I want to." She closed her stinging eyes for a moment and then went on. "At the police station, I told them about MacCready and Ellie. They sent out a search party. Searchers found a new Sickle Moon Killer victim in the woods and called in the Feds. But it wasn't until four days later that they found Ellie's body."

"Oh, God," Noah breathed.

"She'd been caught in one of the old turbine holes of the

dam. But she was dead before that, probably on impact with the rock, they think."

"I am so sorry."

"A week later, I went back and found her bracelet." She held up her wrist. "I keep it inside this little silver box. I haven't taken it off since." Madeline felt her throat constrict. "I killed her."

"What?"

"If I hadn't been there, if MacCready hadn't known about my ability, he wouldn't have freaked. She'd still be alive."

"No," Noah said firmly. "You can't think that. You're no more responsible for her death than I am for Anna's." He took her arms and frowned at her. "Do you hear me?"

Madeline didn't respond. It was her fault.

Noah released her. She met his eyes. "The Feds got a search warrant for MacCready's house. In a closet they found skin from all the Sickle Moon killings. They'd got him."

"I remember that . . . his trial . . . the media sensationalized it. He's still in prison, isn't he?"

"No. He was killed in a prison fight last year. I still can't quite believe it. For years I was afraid he'd break out and find me. Now he's gone."

Noah shuddered. "That was a terrible case."

"A lot of people got scared about the whole thing," she said. "Even after he was caught, there was still an air of fear in some campgrounds and fishing spots. They kept me out of the newspapers, but the townspeople knew I'd played a part in his capture. I think a lot of them blamed me for Ellie, too. That experience permanently tainted my gift for me. It cost me my only friend. After that, when I was sixteen, my parents suggested I move out on my own. They still helped me with money, because no one in town would hire me. But they asked me around less and less. I rarely see them now. Until a couple weeks ago, I didn't even think they knew exactly where I lived."

Noah took her hands in his and squeezed. His touch was warm and comforting, full of good energy. She leaned forward and placed her head on his shoulder, and he gently stroked her hair.

"I'm sorry you had to go through all that," he said.

"Thanks," she said softly.

"Your life sounds as lonely as mine."

She pulled away and looked at him. "I'm sorry you experienced such a loss. I can't even imagine . . ." Her voice trailed off.

He closed his eyes and nodded. "We've both been through some pretty terrible stuff."

"Including the last twenty-four hours," she put in.

"Including the last twenty-four hours," he agreed.

A second flesh eater. Madeline closed her eyes in horror. Finally she opened them, regarding Noah closely. "I can't imagine what it's been like for you, hunting him all this time, seeing one person after another killed. How many victims?"

"One hundred and sixty-four that I know of. A hundred and sixty-four whom he targeted and hunted. Maybe more. And then there are people, like that ranger, who just got in his way. It's hard to say how many of those. He covers his tracks well. He can completely destroy a body."

Madeline nodded. She thought of the silver spike plunging deep into the body of the men who had harassed her. Once again she felt conflict. Though he terrified her, she was relieved he had been there. She thought about the hundreds of victims over the years, bodies reduced to ashes.

"This is strange," Noah suddenly said. "He's blown his cover to you. Usually he insinuates himself into a person's life as a friend, then hangs around frequently, learning more about them until he makes his move. Like he did with Anna." Noah looked away painfully. "This whole situation with you is different. Why appear to you as a beast first?"

"Touch me." She'd seen his true self, not a mimic. "How long has he been hunting me?"

Noah furrowed his brow. "For months, I think. At least, that's when he first showed up in this area, though I didn't arrive here until just a few weeks ago when I picked up on his trail."

He grew silent, watching her openly, his secrets laid out.

She stared back. *Months.* And the first indication she'd had of being watched was just before the flash flood hit. They both went quiet, looking at each other, nothing hidden between them now.

At last he stood up, took her hand, and led her to the bedroom. He stretched out on the bed, rolling over on his back, and reached out to take her hand. Gently he pulled her to him, and she laid her head down on his chest. Madeline lost track of time there, feeling his chest rise and fall, hearing the deep thud of his heartbeat. Though they didn't speak, they were united in their thoughts of their pasts, presents, and futures— how all the events leading up until now had brought them to this one moment in time.

Then Noah rolled over on his side, wrapped one arm around her, and pulled her flush with his body. She turned her head to face him. The light from the main room bathed half his face, while the other lay in shadow. Her eyes moved to his lips, and he pulled her closer, mouths inches apart. She could feel his warm breath on her and tilted her head slightly, bringing them closer. Slowly their lips met, and she felt desire bloom within her. She drank in his scent as they kissed still more passionately, their mouths meeting perfectly again and again as if they'd been kissing each other for years.

He rolled on top of her, and her stomach thrilled to the feeling of him. She wrapped one leg around him, and he brought his knee up, half kneeling over her while he kissed her deeply. His lips left her face, tongue darting out over her neck and bringing a moan to her lips. She could feel that his teeth had gone sharp as they grazed against her skin, but she didn't flinch.

He pulled up and looked down on her, eyes gone red and gleaming in the dark. She touched his face, and he stared down at her with passionate hunger. Then his hands traced down her face to her neck, collarbones, then chest. Gently he ran his fingers over her breasts, pausing on each nipple, stroking them, making them erect. She opened her mouth in pleasure, eyes fluttering in her head, and arched her back beneath him.

His hands on her breasts caused the warmth between her legs to erupt into a fire, and he lowered his hips over hers. She could feel the heat of his erection through his jeans, pressing first against her inner thigh, then blissfully between her legs. He moaned, wrapping his arms around her and writhing against her, their lips meeting again. When the kisses grew so intense she felt herself melting away into a fiery abyss, she pulled away.

She needed a moment. Needed to digest everything. Breathlessly she said, "I've got to think about all of this." Just processing that he still wanted to be close to her, even knowing her ability, was a lot.

Noah looked at her with desire, his smoky eyes making it hard for her to turn away. But she had to think, and being this close to him made that hard.

He sighed. "I suppose you're right . . . Despite this strange connection I feel to you, we have only just met." He gave her one more long kiss before meeting her gaze again with resignation. "And we do have a lot of sleeping to catch up on. I didn't get any last night—spent the whole night creeping through the forest looking for you."

Madeline felt a twinge of guilt at that, Noah searching for her while she slept away in the rock crevice. But she hadn't intended to fall asleep in there. "Guess I'll go change into my PJs," he said.

"Okay. In the meantime, I'll check all the locks."

"Again?"

She raised her eyebrows. "Can you blame me?"

He sighed. "No. I can't. In fact, I think I'll check them when you're done checking them."

"And then I can check them again."

Noah smiled, then held her gaze for a moment in silence, his eyes still burning, his lips so kissable—

She turned away, stood up, and left the room. Noah followed her out, got clothes out of his pack, and returned to the bedroom, partially closing the bedroom door behind him.

Madeline couldn't help but glance through the crack in the door. Noah peeled off his long-sleeved cotton shirt in favor of a black T-shirt. As the cotton left his body, her eyes took in the smoothness of his skin, his muscular sides and chest, his flat stomach. His bare arms, working now to pull on the T-shirt, were muscular and toned, his biceps alone as big as a calf muscle. He was perfectly proportioned, inviting collarbones accentuating his already fiendishly attractive chest. And then the T-shirt covered him up.

Madeline swallowed and looked away, feeling oddly embarrassed for gawking. She supposed constantly being on the move, constantly pushing himself kept him in shape. And what a lovely shape. Oh my.

"I think I'll take the couch," she said.

Noah appeared at the crack in the door. "No way! You get the bed."

She shook her head. "You've done so much for me, paid for this place, even, and I would just be too racked with guilt if you slept on the couch." He opened his mouth to protest, but she added quickly, "I insist."

He shook his head hopelessly and gave a little smile. "Okay." Then he turned away to resume getting ready for bed.

Madeline sighed and looked down at the couch, forcing her body to cool down. Parts of her ached for Noah, and she told those parts to cool it. Even though they'd been through a lot together, she barely even knew him.

As she took the cushions off the couch and pulled out the hideaway bed, Noah appeared from the bedroom. "Ready to go brush our teeth?"

Madeline started. "Out there? Again? Where that thing is?"

"I'll go with you."

"I think I'd rather be irresponsible and not brush my teeth tonight. Damn. Why couldn't they make these cabins with bathrooms?"

"Too cheap?"

"Can't I just use a cup and some water from your canteen?"

Noah relented. "Sure," he said. "I'll do the same."

They brushed their teeth in silence, Noah doling out water from his Nalgene bottle, and Madeline just glad to stay indoors, away from the creature.

"Madeline," he said when she was finished brushing, "help me catch the creature."

She looked at him in disbelief. "What?" Her gut sank.

"Help me catch him. With your gift and my knowledge, we could stop him. I can feel it."

She shook her head, her gut wrenching at the thought. "No. I'm just a college student. I'm no vigilante."

"But how can you ignore your gift like that? Especially after you already caught one killer?"

"My *gift*?" she spat. "It's no goddamn gift. It's not some knitted handbag my grandmother gave me. It's made my life hell. You think I wanted to see those terrible things the Sickle Moon Killer did to those men?" She threw her toothbrush and the little tube of toothpaste into Noah's backpack and stalked away. If that thing weren't out there, she would have stormed out of the cabin right then.

Fear. Plain old mind-numbing fear swept over her.

"Madeline," he said. "I know you're hurting. I know it's been hard. I'm just saying that this is your chance to turn that ability around, make it work *for* you."

She exhaled sharply, turning to look at him. "This is exactly what I *don't* want. What I came out here to avoid. Don't ask me to do this. That thing almost killed me! You can't expect me to go up against it!"

He shook his head. "You're right. I'm sorry. I wasn't thinking. I asked too soon."

"Too soon?" she raised her voice again. "No, please don't ask me again. I'm sorry, Noah, but I just can't. I came out here to try to scrape together a semblance of a normal life. Now my life is in danger and frankly . . . I'm terrified."

He stared at her, then his eyes narrowed, and he went into the bedroom, leaving Madeline outside with her ghosts of Ellie and the Sickle Moon Killer. Before he shut the door, he said quietly, "I can see you're terrified. But if you could just think about it—I can take you to his latest hideout, a cabin near here. You could touch his belongings."

Madeline felt so opposed to the idea that she was shaking her head before he even finished.

"Please," he said. "Think about it."

Then he shut the door between them.

With Noah breathing softly in the bedroom, Madeline lay in the main room, unable to sleep. Why had she insisted on taking the foldout bed? Her face still felt flushed in anger at his request. She'd never escape this cursed ability. For a while she'd felt almost like a normal person with Noah. Now her "gift" loomed between them, just like every other relationship she'd tried to have.

Her mind wouldn't rest, kept sweeping over the story he'd told her.

Noah was over two hundred years old.

She thought of the old journal she'd found in his backpack. At the time, she'd never dreamed it was his journal, just some keepsake he'd picked up on his journeys. The temptation to peek inside now was overwhelming. She glanced over at his backpack, which still sat on one of the chairs. But she couldn't invade his privacy like that.

Throwing a worn, yellow blanket aside, a blanket she suspected had been living unwashed on that couch for nigh on thirty years and had probably developed its own rudimentary sense of logic and arithmetic, she crept to Noah's bedroom.

"Noah?" she whispered when she got there.

He stirred.

"Noah?"

"Yes?"

"Sorry to wake you."

"No problem."

"It's just I . . ." She faltered.

From the light filtering in from the main room, she could just make out his shadowed form on the bed. The sheets draped over his body, and he propped himself up on one elbow.

"Your journal . . . is it a record of hunting the creature?"

He nodded. "A spotty record. I'm not very good at journaling. When I first began, I wrote almost every day. Now I write once a decade if I'm lucky. Two hundred years, and I never had to buy a second book." He smiled.

She felt uncomfortable, nosy. "I know this is a terrible thing to ask, but I was curious to look at it. Just to get a better idea of what we're dealing with."

"Hmmm . . . well . . . I guess that would be all right. Just don't pay much attention to the whole 'girl in every city' theme. And that barmaid in France? It was just a fling."

Madeline began to doubt if she wanted to read the thing after all.

"And the herd of goats in Greece was really more of a roll in the hay. Heh."

She rolled her eyes.

"I'm kidding. There was no barmaid. No girl in every city. I may look as dashing as Captain Kirk, but I don't have a gorgeous alien lover on every planet. Not even on this planet." He stared at her from the shadows, a thin slice of light falling across half of his face. "But suddenly I'm not opposed to the thought of being with someone again . . ."

Their eyes locked, and she smiled.

"The journal is in my backpack. Have at it."

She could think of two things at that moment she'd like to have at but opted for the journal. It was a little less daunting and would give a clearer idea of the other thing if she read it.

He winked devilishly at her, and she turned away with difficulty, intent on at least making it to the backpack. When she reached inside and her fingers closed around the diary, though, a great sadness swept over her, the same as on the mountain.

She returned to the sofa, climbed under the nearly sentient yellow blanket, and began to read.

* * *

July 14, 1763
Mountains above Vienna

    I feel that I should keep a record of my tribulations so that, if I am found dead, and someone else takes up the cause, they will at least know something of the creature which I pursue relentlessly, and will be better armed with information in order to stop it.

    I find it too painful to relate the details of how I came to be on this desolate mountain trail, weary from exertion, following a killer. Perhaps later I will be able to write about it. But suffice it to say that Stefan, this thing, this terror, killed my beloved, and I will stop at nothing until he is destroyed.

    For days I have been tracking the vile beast. I spotted the fiend in an alleyway in Vienna and have been following him ever since. Now I trail far behind, however, the high elevation of this mountain pass robbing me of my stamina. My head pounds, chest heaves. I am not used to moving so quickly, carrying so much weight, or steadily climbing upward across slippery, gray talus slopes and melting snowfields.

    The crumbling slope to the right of my path is nearly vertical, leading down to a steep valley far below. On the other side of the narrow, tree-filled ravine lie more peaks, the snowy Alps stretching to the horizon.

    I struggle on, stomach rumbling with hunger. Repeatedly I attempt unsuccessfully to rearrange the uncomfortably heavy assortment of objects on my back: a clunky pot, a heavy bag of rice and coffee beans, an unwieldy canvas tent and its splintery wooden stakes. It is really just a lean-to at this point. I had to abandon the wood for its frame when I lost a handcart wheel over the edge of a precipitous section of trail yesterday. Realizing I would have to leave the handcart behind, I piled what I could into the tent, transforming it into a makeshift pack for my back and continued on, trying to follow the creature's footprints in the mud and melting snow.

    Today as I stumbled across the crumbling stones of a

rock field, the sharp whistles of some nearby rodents caused my head to snap violently in that direction. I know they are just rodents, watching me from their hiding holes in the rocks, but my nerves are frayed. Any sharp noise has me starting anxiously.

I am not used to such hardship. An English aristocrat raised in the heart of London, whose parents moved me to Vienna at the age of 22, the most arduous task I have ever undertaken before this was stumbling home dead drunk from Herr Grusschen's pub, the Heart and Feather, on Bär Strasse. One night two rogues tried to rob me as I tripped and swayed over the cobblestones on a darkened street. I brandished my sword, nicked one of the seedy, bearded perpetrators, though more through drunken clumsiness than skill, and managed to drive them off by spewing a stream of slurred obscenities at them and threatening to call for the authorities.

At the time I bragged about the encounter, embellishing the story without mercy, telling my friends about the murderous fiends I had driven off that foggy night.

That life feels a thousand miles away now. I was so carefree, so naive. What did I know then of "murderous fiends"? Nothing. My entire lesson on murder has been taught by the creature, on that dreaded night two months ago when he tore out my love's throat and nearly ended my own life on the cold, tiled floor of her manor house, as unknowing friends slumbered peacefully a floor above.

The rodents whistle again. I think I am growing accustomed to it. I know nothing of alpine fauna, though it would be nice to catch a juicy, fat rodent and cook it up. I am so tired of rice. My life was once the symphony, the opera, the taverns. I have never hiked this high before. Certainly never carried my own baggage. My feet ache and are covered with blisters, my hands callused and covered with deep, bleeding cracks from the dry air.

July 17, 1763
Mountains above Vienna

Earlier today a rock shifted beneath my feet. Off balance, I leaned forward to compensate, but instead swung forward heavily under the weight of my pack and pitched toward the ground violently. With a painful crunch, I landed face-first in the field of stone, edges of sharp rock cutting gashes in my freezing hands.

I did not rise immediately. I lay there, face pressed against the cold, sharp points, and tried to catch my breath. I am growing so weary, getting clumsy in my fatigue. I have to stop to rest.

It is too dangerous up here to take any chances with exhaustion. I must find a sheltered spot up next to a granite outcrop and set up my pathetic lean-to for the night, even though it is only early afternoon.

I have not been able to sleep. Oh, what I would give for some beefsteak and a stein of ale. Instead I have only salted meats, which I am dreadful sick of, and the never-ending rice.

I must stop now and make a fire, melt some snow, boil the rice . . . My stomach growls now at the thought of it.

July 20, 1763
Mountains above Vienna

Night comes close behind, blanketing the eastern mountains in darkness, while above the clouds burn bright gold, and then intense pink. On the highest peaks, alpenglow shines, painting the mountains an intense shade of magenta and scarlet.

Too exhausted to go on, I have been watching the brilliant play of light. How beautiful it is up here. How I would love to have watched this sunset with Anna.

But I will never have the chance to. That sudden sickening realization presses in on me. My whole life will be filled with moments like this, beautiful moments made hollow by the lack of her presence. There will be a countless stream of things I will never do with her: picnics in the country, carriage rides in the heart of Vienna, making love beneath a canopied wedding bed.

The brilliant red fades to gray on the peaks. A few minutes ago, I clenched my teeth so hard I bit myself severely. Then unable to control myself I screamed, blood spilling from my mouth and flecking the stone beneath me.

I have not seen signs of Stefan in days. I fear I may have lost his tracks for good. How ever will I find him now?

At least I still have plenty of rice, though I am so sick of it I sometimes feel like pitching it over the mountainside and dancing about like a madman.

I have been feeling stranger and stranger as of late. Whereas first I was full of many aches and pains and cuts, I now find I do not have a scratch on me and though tired, I no longer ache. Perhaps I am just growing fitter, or more careful not to cut myself on the sharp rock, but it feels more than that. I feel braver, stronger, more fearless. And ever more mad than the day before. I fear for my sanity.

July 22, 1763
Mountains above Vienna

An amazing thing happened today. I had all but given up hope of catching up to the creature. I was ready to head back to civilization, eat a real meal in a tavern, when I came upon a narrow crevice in the cliff face along which I was traversing.

A putrid smell issued forth from the shadowed recess, and I peered inside. I gasped. Lying there in a stripe of sunlight was Stefan, or what I thought at first was Stefan.

On its back, pure black as it had been the night it attacked Anna and me, sprawled a dead thing with tremendous claws and hideously pointed teeth. The clothes of an aristocrat adorned the body. I bent low, sure it was my quarry.

The killing blow had come from a ten-inch gleaming stake protruding from the creature's belly, pinning it to the ground below.

I touched the weapon, a smooth metal spike that felt cool to the touch.

I shall never forget the visage of that dreadful creature there in the crevice. Its eyes (what were left of them, as one had been partially eaten by some animal) were opened wide as if in terror, and the mouth lay open and twisted as if in a scream.

For a long time I stood in the entrance of the crevice, staring down at what I was sure was the murderer of my Anna, feeling at once relieved he was dead and also intensely curious as to what had killed him.

Was this metal spike made of the very same metal Anna swore was able to injure the creature? If so, who had carried such a weapon?

I leaned in closer for a look and was suddenly seized by curiosity to go through the creature's belongings. I unbuttoned its waistcoat and searched the pockets of its breeches. I came away with several letters and a small pocket-sized journal much like this one.

Retreating from the crevice to read by the bright sunlight, I flipped through the journal.

What I found there left me dumbfounded and amazed.

After reading the entries breathlessly, I learned that this wretched beast in the crevice was not the creature I have been pursuing, but was Ffyllon, the man who had given the letter opener to Anna.

The journal told an impossible story. Ffyllon was impossibly old, and had somehow been alive since the twelve hundreds. One night back then, he and his brother had been working on a written version of the Welsh text, the Mabinogi. As they labored into the wee hours of the night by candlelight, a desperate knock came at the door.

Ffyllon leapt up to admit a bedraggled traveler who complained of starvation. The scribe lived with his brother, Gywnfar, who was a brilliant linguist. The two brothers invited the traveler in and fed him. For three months the traveler stayed with them, talking to both, but mainly to Gywnfar about his work translating ancient texts and his ability to speak over nine languages.

Then one frightful night the scribe came home to find the traveler sitting atop his brother's dead body, tearing flesh off the bones and devouring it. In a fit of rage, Ffyllon fell upon him, pounding the traveler with fists, cups, plates, and anything else he could find. He even bit the traveler, tearing a great hunk from his shoulder.

But the fight was in vain. One strike across the scribe's temple knocked him senseless, and the traveler dragged off the brother's body to eat it elsewhere.

When Ffyllon awoke, only blood remained where his dead brother had once lain. The scribe vowed revenge and left his trade to pursue the mysterious traveler.

Over time, Ffyllon noticed he healed much faster than before. He stopped aging. Years went by, then decades, then centuries as he pursued the creature. He learned important facts about the creature, studied its patterns and habits in order to better destroy it. On several occasions he tried to kill the beast, but nothing worked. Not sword, not musket, not drowning. During one of their confrontations in an alley in London, the creature summoned two gleaming spikes from its forearms, and impaled Ffyllon with one of them. A group of theatergoers passed by, and the creature ran off, withdrawing the spike as it did. It took Ffyllon nearly a year to recover from the wounds, instead of his usual few days. He became convinced that this metal, summoned from the creature itself, was the key to destroying him. If it could wound Ffyllon so, with his special healing abilities, perhaps it could wound the creature, as well.

During Ffyllon's recovery from the grievous wound, he met a group of nomadic storytellers, with whom he stayed while he healed. He told them the story of the creature. In hushed voices they drew away, whispering among themselves. Ffyllon grew full of fear that he had offended and that they would finish him off in his sleep. But instead they produced a gleaming letter opener and gave it to him. The weapon of a hunter, they told him, made from the special metal. He asked where they had obtained it, and they told him many decades ago they had come across the twisted, rotting corpse of a monster, and that knife was sticking out of its belly.

Ffyllon reasoned that, since the blade was left in the body, and the body was indeed dead, in order to kill the creature, the metal had to remain in its body for some unknown extended period of time. Ffyllon himself had only recovered because the creature had run off after wounding him.

Ffyllon's last entry, dated June 20, 1763, stated that he was closer than ever before.

He had trailed the creature to Vienna, where he learned of its next victim, a young pianist named Anna Gordova. Ffyllon had contacted her, posing as a friend of her uncle. He had given her the letter opener made of the special metal so that she could defend herself if he was not there when the creature attacked. To prepare her, he told her the legend of the creature.

I lowered Ffyllon's journal and wondered at the tale told therein. He had not been there when the creature attacked, was instead drugged and incapacitated in the rooms above. And the creature had killed Anna. At least he was not able to eat her body.

I think of this poor man crammed in the crevice of rock. He must have continued his quest, leaving Vienna after Anna's death, and pursued the creature, just as I do. But now he is well and truly dead. His theory must have been correct; the creature stabbed him with one of its gleaming spikes and then left the metal in the wound. The hunter now dead.

My mind cannot grasp the scope of this journal.

Even as I was hunting the creature, so was this poor soul, this man who had turned into a creature after ingesting the beast's blood.

My heart pounds. I myself have noticed my increased healing speed, my energy and power growing daily.

Could it be that I myself somehow ingested the creature's blood? Could the blood that entered my mouth when I kissed Anna's hand actually been that of the beast's from when she stabbed him?

I am terrified.

Will I end up as this poor soul did? Murdered centuries from now in some lonely crevice in the high country, failing in my one mission to bring justice?

Eternal life . . . even just a few months ago, the thought would have enticed me, seduced me. To be young forever, to feel that powerful, that invulnerable . . . would have been a blessing indeed.

But now, like this? To endure this eternity without Anna? To be a monster? The thought revolts and terrifies me.

What am I to do?

July 23, 1763
Mountains above Vienna

After a great deal of consideration, I have decided to persist. I will take the mysterious metal stake and fashion a knife out of it at the next town.

All yesterday I searched in circles for any sign of the direction which the creature has taken, but to no avail. The terrain up here consists exclusively of rocks, with no soil to leave tracks. And I know almost nothing of the art of tracking.

Tomorrow I will head down and find a town where a smith can fashion a sharp weapon for me of this metal.

If still I have found no trace of the creature, I will use the scribe's journal to hunt for other clues. Perhaps the creature has some sort of pattern it follows when choosing victims.

Perhaps I will be able to guess its next move and stop it before it kills again.

July 25, 1763
Mountains above Vienna

*I think I am finished. As I was breaking camp
yesterday, a small rain of pebbles landed on me from
above, where a tremendous granite cliff rose. No sooner
had I rolled up my tent canvas than the rain became a
torrent, pounding me with ever larger boulders. I lost my
footing in the rockslide and careened down the mountain
in the wake of it, landing harshly against a stunted tree,
my legs devastated by the rocks.*

*I have lost the use of them. I fear they are badly
broken, so swollen and black and blue.*

*I have lost all my camping supplies, and have only the
metal spike, this journal, and my pencil left, which
happened to be in the breast pocket of my waistcoat. The
remainder of my food is now lost among the sharp-edged
rocks.*

*At least there is water in the form of snow this high
up, and a few trickling streams. I shall not want for
water. But I cannot drag myself very far. The pain in my
legs is great indeed.*

*Night draws on. I shall have to make myself as
comfortable as possible, perhaps in a large crevice in the
rock to keep the wind off.*

Tomorrow I shall think of some plan of action.

July 26, 1763
Mountains above Vienna

*I am stunned. It is a miracle. My legs, broken just two
days before, have healed. I have only bruises where once
torn flesh and broken bones resided.*

*I can walk, run, even jump on legs that yesterday
were spelling my doom.*

I shall start for town immediately.

August 12, 1763
Vienna

*I returned to Vienna and to my home to regain
strength. I have eaten till I gorged myself, drinking down
ale and beefsteak, savoring the delicious flavor of both.*

I have been reading the journal left by the scribe, and it has put me in a good state of fright, I assure you. This man, Ffyllon, was but a normal, average man before he ingested the creature's blood. Over time, he developed certain abilities, including, as I wrote before, the ability to heal quickly.

This must be why my legs rejuvenated themselves so. I now fear more than ever that I am destined to become a thing like the creature and Ffyllon.

Even now I continue to feel better than ever before, full of energy and vigor. Two nights ago, I cut myself shaving and was completely healed in just an hour. Last night I cut myself purposely, far more deeply, on the arm. Today there is no sign of the gash.

Truly, I have inherited some of this creature's remarkable ability. But its power to change shape? To turn into a shadow? To suddenly grow claws and fangs? I cannot do those things.

Over time, Ffyllon learned to control more and more of his abilities. He writes that the creature can look like anyone it has killed—can change its very countenance to that of another person. Ffyllon could never look like someone else, but he was able to grow claws in emotional moments when he had to defend himself, and over time he could make his skin grow black as shadow, enabling him to move undetected in the darkness.

Can this beast really take on the appearance of other people? The very thought causes hopelessness to bloom inside me. How ever will I kill it if I cannot recognize it?

If I am afflicted with the tainted blood of this creature, then I am more determined than ever to put a stop to its evil. I will use my invulnerability as an advantage and track the beast until my exhausted body breathes its last breath.

August 15, 1763
Vienna

I am not sure where to go next. I have studied and

studied the journal of the scribe and have noticed patterns with the creature. Apparently he assimilates himself into the life of his future victim, always someone of exceptional talent like my beloved Anna. Once he has won their trust, he . . . eats them.

A truly gruesome thing. By digesting the flesh of his victims, he can then possess whatever talent they cherished in life. He also gains certain memories and emotions of the victim.

I will build upon Ffyllon's considerable knowledge and assume that the only thing that can kill the creature may be the special metal which it used to kill Ffyllon. Last week I paid an armorer to fashion a grip on one end of the spike I took from Ffyllon's body. I am ready to resume my hunt.

I have the tool to kill him; now I just need to find him.

August 16, 1763
Vienna
I have made further study of Ffyllon's journal. If only I had access to his earlier writings. I wonder where they could be? If not for the summary in the front of the journal, I would be quite puzzled indeed by the diary's contents.

I have pieced together a few facts: the creature can summon a metal from his very body and use this metal to utterly destroy the victims he does not wish to eat. Ffyllon himself was able to form small bits of this metal. It is gruesome indeed, but he could turn each finger into a metal spike, and then break off that finger if he wanted to fashion a weapon independent of himself. The finger would grow back.

In this way, he could mimic small weapons like the letter opener the nomadic storytellers had given him. The one he gave Anna . . .

Anna . . . if only Ffyllon had been there that night. If only he had stepped in instead of being in a drunken stupor on the upper floor of her house. He wrote after

Anna's death that he had not drunk that much that night and that he suspected the creature had slipped sleeping powder into his ale when he was not looking.

Ffyllon speculates on an interesting idea: he wondered if the reason why he could summon only small amounts of this strange metal was because he had only ingested a small amount of the creature's blood. Had he drunk more, perhaps he would have been able to summon the deadly spikes from his arms as the creature can.

He also recorded this interesting fact: he had managed to wound the creature several times with the small spikes of his fingers, but the creature always recovered, though badly wounded. This further proved his theory that the metal would have to stay in the creature's body for an extended period of time in order to kill it, not allowing it the chance of rejuvenation.

This would also definitely explain why the creature had left its spike in Ffyllon's body on the mountain. Perhaps he planned to return and claim the metal. Perhaps even now he is somehow not whole, as I possess part of his body.

Madeline flipped ahead, skipping several entries. Noah had been getting used to the idea of a creature like this for more than two centuries. It was his life now, hunting Stefan, a daily routine. Madeline's mind still reeled at the thought of other creatures sharing her world. She'd always loved the thought of magic, and as a child had read every book on fairies, dragons, and mythological beings that she could abscond away into her room. But none of that had prepared her for the absolute knowledge that such a thing could exist. And Stefan was no mischievous fairy or griffin with gleaming wings. He was a killer—an intelligent, relentless killer—and a kind of beast too dark for the books that had thrilled her as a child. Stefan was a monster that belonged in forgotten volumes, heavy with age and sealed with a rusting lock. Dark records of hideous creatures described and then hidden away for none to find, as if the sealing of the tome could seal in the beast's power.

She found another entry and resumed.

June 15, 1765
Copenhagen, Denmark
    I can scarcely believe it. I have actually caught up with the brute. I followed a rash of killings leading to Copenhagen over the last two years. Four murders in all, all of people with exceptional talent.
    A poet here is to be honored by King Frederick V of Denmark, and reports have been in the local and larger gazettes. This is just the sort of opportunity to which the creature would be attracted.
    I have started following the poet myself, studying his friends, hoping the creature will reveal himself. I have decided upon a particular friend who watches the poet with a hungry gleam in his eye and who looked quite startled when I strode by him one day.
    I have introduced myself into the poet's circle. Once again my aristocratic status has its advantages. My only doubt is that perhaps I have the wrong fellow. Doubts visit me in the small hours of the night . . . I wonder if the poet is indeed next, and if his friend Jesper is indeed the creature in disguise.
    What if I am planning on killing an innocent man?
    Though I have tracked the killer tirelessly over the last two years and get little sleep, racked with worry, I do not feel the worse for it. In fact, I feel more energized than ever before. I fear I do indeed have the same malady that afflicted Ffyllon, though such a fantastic malady I could never have hoped for. To feel so power-ful, youthful, to be able to heal quickly. It is a miracle, though perhaps a dark one.

June 17, 1765
Copenhagen, Denmark
    A terrible thing has happened! I can scarcely write it

down. Damn my hesitation. Jesper was indeed the villain, posing as the poet's friend. Jesper invited the poet to the opera, where he had purchased a box for the evening.

I followed, repeatedly checking the box nervously during the course of the opera. I saw the creature make its move, dragging the poet down below the lip of the box. I leapt up from my seat and ran to the box, where the creature was already feasting upon the poor man's throat. The unfortunate fellow had not even time to cry out.

I dashed into the box and grabbed Stefan, who had shifted into what I have come to think of as his true form: a shadow of a thing, all black with no features save a pair of red saucer eyes and a mouth full of vile teeth.

As I rushed forth, hand inside my waistcoat to produce the weapon, the creature met my rush, lifted me up effortlessly over the lip of the box, and flung me down.

I crashed painfully into the seats below, injuring several operagoers. A commotion stirred up, the orchestra and singers still attempting to proceed with the performance in spite of it. One woman I had landed on screamed, and I struggled to right myself.

In the end, by the time I had returned to the box, the poet was gone, leaving a bloody trail. I can only assume Stefan dragged off the body to devour in some secret place.

I feel responsible.

How can I take up Ffyllon's sword if I cannot save even one life? And I fear this may be the first in a string of murders I will be unable to prevent.

Spooked, Madeline closed the diary. She didn't want to know this—didn't even want to consider that the one person who knew what was going on had failed in the past.

She flipped through the rest of the journal. The entries grew further and further apart, sometimes only one or two every twenty years.

The last entry, dated February 22, 1922, read, *"Hate my-self. Hate myself. Hate myself. Hate myself."*

Blank pages followed. In the back, a number of pages were filled, listing names she assumed were victims. One column contained the name and the other the fate of the person. "Couldn't save" was written after each name in a scrawling hand. The list went on for pages and pages, almost all with "Couldn't save" written next to them. Only three entries differed. One read, "Died of natural causes before creature could kill." Another read, "Incarcerated in H.M. prison before creature could kill," and the column next to the last name was blank. She froze as she read the name: Madeline Keye.

Horrified, she realized Noah had *never* saved a victim. Not even once. Some had escaped being eaten, but only through coincidence.

Her safe haven suddenly seemed as dangerous as going it alone.

But where else could she go?

At least Noah was knowledgeable, even if he hadn't been successful. She couldn't imagine what it must have been like for him, discovering everything as he went, both the horrible with the good.

She sat for many moments with the book closed on her chest, unsure if she should stay or flee and hope for her chances. She debated for a long time, feeling the terrible sadness of the book sweeping over her.

Madeline checked her wrist, ensuring she still wore the bracelet. She unhooked the latch and lifted the tiny lid. Inside, coiled and gleaming, was Ellie's thin silver bracelet, the one she'd lost that day. She rarely touched it herself, and would never wear it. Locked inside the metal were such powerful images of Ellie that when Madeline touched it, she almost felt her friend was there, like she could talk to her and Ellie would hear her. She touched the bracelet gently, just the tip of one finger resting on its surface.

Images swept over her. Ellie sitting next to her in math class. Ellie and she watching movies on a Friday night, popcorn strewn around them. They'd met when they were five, on the first day of first grade. Huddled outside the gray stone school building that chilly morning, waiting for school to start, they'd begun a conversation with each other, comparing their similar woolly hats. The talk turned toward age and birthdays. Being only five, neither could remember their exact birth date (they left that and the toy-giving to their parents), but they were both sure they'd been born in late October. It was close enough, and they became instant friends.

When the other kids teased Madeline or tried to pick fights because they were scared, Ellie was always ready to jump in and let her fists fly. An intense flash erupted of Ellie standing over one bully on the jungle gym, shaking her five-year-old fist threateningly after shoving him into the monkey bars. Another image sprang up of Ellie thrusting a tree branch into the spokes of a bully's BMX bike as he tried to flee the area after calling Madeline a series of unflattering names. The jerk had flipped up over the front of his handlebars and landed with a terrific smack in the middle of the street. It was a hot July day and the bubbling tar on the street had stuck to the boy's face.

"Ellie." Madeline breathed softly. Her friend shimmered and swam into view, sitting next to her on the foldout couch.

"Hey, Mad," she said softly.

"I don't know what to do."

"I know. And that's okay. You're a good person. You'll figure it out."

"I think you'd want me to help."

"You're probably right," Ellie answered, a wry smile turning the corner of her mouth.

After a stretch of silence, Madeline said, "I think I really like this guy."

"I can see why. He's hot."

"And nice. And he has a noble quality about him, too."

"Your knight in shining armor come to take you away from all this madness?"

"Or maybe to take me into all this madness."

"That's not as good."

"I know," Madeline answered, nodding in the darkness. She watched her glimmering friend, remembering the curve of her brow, the mischievous look she could get in her eye, all the years of happiness they'd had, and all the years that had been taken.

"I miss you."

Ellie met her eyes, sadness glistening there.

They sat in silence then, Madeline not sure of what to say, not needing to say anything. That had been their way in life. They understood without needing to say much.

Finally Madeline closed the latch on the small silver box, Ellie's image shimmering, then vanishing into the darkness. She set the journal aside, her mind drawn back to the Sickle Moon Killer, the story fresh now in her mind. She could distinctly picture his face, that terrible knowledge that he'd been caught, the desperation, needing to get rid of them. She lay awake nights sometimes, terrified he'd escaped from the penitentiary and was on his way to her house. Or worse, already there, breathing laboriously outside her bedroom door, seething with hatred and waiting to crush the life out of her in revenge. The fear hadn't stopped until she learned he'd been killed in that fight.

Her mind traveled over what was to come tomorrow if she agreed to Noah's plea for help. They'd drive out to the cabin where the creature was holed up for its "digestion period." She cringed inwardly. She'd feel any belongings it had there, see if she could get a fix on any future victims. Maybe she would, and then they'd go to the police. They'd contact her hometown police station, or maybe they'd remember reading about her from the Sickle Moon Killer case files. They'd either ridicule her or ask her to participate in the investigation. Maybe they'd even save the next victim's life and catch the killer. What if they wanted more? Piles of dead-end grisly cases, one after the other? This time she couldn't use the excuse of being fourteen years old. Now she was twenty-one and was supposed to be deciding her future. People would expect her to "do the right thing," to give up her innocence and happiness in the service of others, to use her "gift" to identify other killers. They wouldn't consider the horrific images and acts she'd have to relive while acquiring visions.

They wouldn't consider the empty black-hole ache that consumed her after she'd encountered the Sickle Moon Killer. She'd become a hollow, bleak shell.

She alone had to consider herself. And she didn't want that kind of life.

She wanted to transfer to her new college, engage in normal college activities. Go to parties, take fun classes, hell, even write term papers and cram for biology finals on hydrophilic cells and mitochondria. She wanted people to know her for who she was, not her bizarre talent. She wanted people to act normal around her.

She glanced toward the bedroom door. Noah had been hunting this thing for two centuries. He had a weapon but had been unsuccessful thus far. She thought of the endless list of victims he was unable to save. Why would she be any different? She didn't need to hang around him, waiting to be murdered, so much bait waiting in a tackle shop.

Looking out the window at the darkness beyond, she suddenly thought of the goat in *Jurassic Park*, the one tied to the post in wait for the *Tyrannosaurus rex*.

The urge to run suddenly became intolerable. *Listen to your instincts,* she thought. *Know when to get the hell out of here.* Lying still for a moment, she listened for sounds from Noah's room. Silence. Turning her head, she looked at the door. It was still open a crack, and darkness lay beyond. She was almost sure he was asleep. Quietly she peeled the yellow blanket back and swung her feet to the floor. Her own clothes, the pair of jeans and long-sleeved cotton shirt, lay draped and damp over the back of a chair. She dressed quickly in the dark, putting one of Noah's fleece jackets on top. Lacing up her boots, she glanced again at the bedroom. Still silent. Still dark.

Creeping silently across the floor, she reached the front door and pushed aside a curtain. Only trees and a Dumpster met her eyes. No creature in sight. She disengaged the bolt and slipped outside. Turning the lock on the inside knob of the door, she made sure Noah would be locked in safely and then closed the door behind herself with finality.

A chilly breeze blew over her, and she zipped up the fleece jacket as high as it would go, partially covering her face.

She needed to reach her car. She didn't fancy the idea of waiting out on the road at this hour for a car to hitch a ride. Hardly anyone would be driving by, and she'd be out in the open, vulnerable to the creature.

Then she thought of Steve, the naturalist who had helped her earlier. She was in trouble and needed to leave the park. He would understand that. Maybe he'd give her a ride to her car.

Making up her mind, she set off down the paved path, the pines creaking overhead as her boots crunched on loose pebbles. The ranger residences lay only about a quarter mile away, on a parallel road. She'd reach them in no time.

The moon overhead shone bright enough for her to see the path, and she navigated quickly to the main road. She tried not to think about the dense shadows around her or what could be hiding in the black beneath the trees. If the creature *was* there, it was not attacking, which was fine with her. And if it wasn't there, she didn't want to slow herself down by checking every shifting shadow beneath the pine branches. With her ears tuned sharply to the sounds around her, she pushed on quickly, her eyes darting around furtively. If it did jump out and she caught a glimpse or heard a shuffle, she'd be ready. She could dart aside, or maybe even turn and strike out at it. She'd wounded it before. She could do it again.

Up ahead she could make out another road turning off to the left. In front of it stood a small wooden sign that read Private Residence.

She was almost there.

A sharp, snapping twig brought her to a halt. She spun around and heard another snapping branch. Her breath coming fast, fear consumed Madeline. Her feet became lead bricks, her mouth went dry, and though she wanted to run in terror, she couldn't move.

Her eyes wide, she stared into the trees and brush on that side of the road. Another twig snapped. Then the shrubbery began to part, and a dark shape emerged. Madeline ran. Not looking back, feet pounding the pavement, she raced toward the rangers' houses. "Somebody help me!" she yelled, though the plea came out hoarse and not as loud as she'd hoped. Almost at the other road, she dared a look back.

And saw a bear standing in the middle of the road.

She had never been so relieved to see a bear in all her life. She stopped running and turned to face it. Meandering along the pavement, it was a huge, hulking mass of shaggy, powerful limbs and a tremendous head. Its nose sloped distinctly from the forehead, and she took in the dish-shaped face and large shoulder hump. A grizzly. One look at the tremendous white claws scraping on the pavement confirmed it. It looked at her with disinterest and crossed the road to the bushes on the other side. Branches cracking and bending in its wake, the bear pushed into the thick of them and reared up on its hind legs. Placing its mighty paws together, it shucked the berries off a branch and devoured them.

Madeline laughed, breaking the silence, relief bubbling up inside her. Then she stopped short, feeling a little embarrassed, and hoped no one had heard her call for help.

The grizzly moved to the next bush, shucked off some berries. Then it dropped to all fours and pushed farther into the bushes, into the forest beyond and out of sight.

She sighed as she watched it go, but the minute it disappeared she felt the woods press in on her again, every piece of darkness hiding the creature. The presence of that huge ursine predator had comforted her.

But now it was gone, and she turned and hurried toward the ranger's house.

9

MOST of the windows in Steve's cabin were dark. Though she knocked quietly on the door, the sound thundered in the otherwise hushed night. She waited on the doorstep, watching a haze of blue smoke drift through the forest, remnants of the many campfires still smoldering, even at this late hour.

No one came to the door. She peered in a window. A light was on in the back of the cabin. She knocked again. Waited. Knocked harder.

Finally she heard someone stirring on the other side of the door. "Listen, buddy," Steve called through the wood. "There's nothing I can do about your damned beer. You're just going to have to drive to town tomorrow and get more."

She stood silently on the other side, confused.

"Besides," he went on, "if it was that important to you, you should have known they didn't sell it at the camp store and brought more."

Madeline said, "Um . . . Steve? It's me, Madeline, the person who reported the murder tonight?"

"Oh," came the reply. A lock disengaged, and the door swung open. Steve's sleepy face came into view, his eyelids drooping as he focused on her. "Sorry about that. Some drunk guy keeps coming by, asking me if I have beer. He's been driving me crazy all night." He rubbed some sleep out of his eye. "This park's not nearly as bad as the state park I used to work at. But, man, do I get the unpleasant ones." He leaned against the door. "So what's up?"

"Well, actually, I was hoping . . ." Her voice trailed off. It was the middle of the night, and he didn't even know her. But she had to get away. Her life might depend on it. "I was hoping you could drive me to my car."

"What, now?" He squinted at his watch.

"Yes."

He looked back up. "What's the hurry?"

"I'm just . . . freaked out, I guess. I just want to go home."

He scratched his head, his already mussed hair now standing up where he'd ruffled it. "Well, where is it?"

"It's at the Loop trailhead." The Loop was a section of the Going-to-the-Sun Road east of there that made a sharp, hairpin turn. A small parking area lay up there, along with a trailhead that started off some fantastic hikes, including the Granite Park Chalet and Swiftcurrent Pass trails.

He scratched his head again, then ran a hand over his whiskers. "You're freaked?"

She nodded emphatically.

"What, you think the murderer is going to come after you? We did talk to Mike up there, you know. There was no murder."

She looked down, feeling awkward. They already thought she was crazy for what she had seen and didn't believe her at all. "I just feel unsafe," she said finally. "I know you don't think that thing was real." She gently felt the bandage on her head. "But regardless, I just want to go home."

Steve studied her face for a long time. "I don't know if you should drive with that head wound."

Madeline looked at him pleadingly.

His face remained concerned. Finally he exhaled. "What the hell. I'm not getting any sleep here anyway. Besides, I have to see about my winter job in Missoula tomorrow, so I do have to head out of the park. Driving up to the Loop first won't take me too far out of the way."

Madeline felt a little guilty. If she waited until morning, she could get Noah to drive her or take one of the red historic touring cars that had been recommissioned to take tourists from location to location inside the park.

Steve looked at his watch. "I guess if I left now, I would just get there super early. Could even squeeze in a visit with my sister." He dropped his hand to his side, then pushed the door open wider. "Sure. C'mon in. I'll just get changed. Then we can be off."

"Really?"

"Sure." He gestured for her to come inside.

As she entered she said, "Thank you."

"No problem," he said, still groggy. He closed the door behind her and turned on a table lamp next to the door. "Make yourself at home. I'll just be a minute."

Sighing with relief, she watched as he walked off toward the back bedroom. Hope simmered within her at the thought of going home. She felt almost giddy. She was getting out of there!

Turning where she stood, she took in the meager possessions of the ranger: a small wooden table where he ate; two wooden chairs, the finish worn off on the seats and backs; a small bookshelf overcrammed with books. She approached the latter, taking in some of the titles. Many were field guides, the *Golden Guide to Birds*, the *Audubon Society Field Guide to the Night Sky*. But a lot were fiction, mostly mysteries and thrillers. So many books sat on the bookshelf that they were crammed four-deep in some places. On top of the bookshelf, next to a painted, wooden katydid, books teetered and loomed in precarious stacks, readying to topple at the slightest movement of the bookcase.

"You like reading?" she called into the other room, trying to make polite conversation.

"How'd you know? I love it."

She smiled at the teetering books. "Just a guess."

"Just about ready."

"Okay."

A minute later, Steve appeared, threw a backpack down on one of the wooden chairs, and then disappeared into the bathroom.

As she listened to him brushing his teeth, an unsettling feeling crept up on her. She started pacing. Suddenly the windows felt too close, like the creature was out there, peering in through the gauzy curtains, and only had to stretch its hand through the screen—

In the center of the room she stopped, staring at the windows. Part of her wanted to open the curtains and stare out, but she feared that as soon as she pushed one aside, she'd find a hideous dark face with red saucer eyes staring back. But she remained transfixed, as if it were *calling* her to the window, daring her to see if she was right. The room continued to creep in on her, the windows growing closer.

"Well, I'm ready to go," Steve said, appearing from the other room.

"Great." She was already moving toward the door. The wooden floor creaked beneath her feet as she moved. Glancing back, she scanned over Steve's outfit to see if he wore a gun. He didn't.

"Don't you have a gun?" she asked.

Steve shook his head. "I'm not a law enforcement officer. I'm an interpretive ranger. I don't have professional weapons training. But I do have my own shotgun in the car. Why do you ask?"

"Just curious. About different ranger categories," she fumbled, lying. She knew the shotgun wouldn't kill the creature, but if it came down to it, the fiery pellets probably wouldn't feel too good. At the very least it might slow the creature down.

She paused before the door as Steve grabbed up his bag from the chair. Reaching out to turn the knob, she felt reluctance wash over her. And then Steve was opening the door, and they were outside, the cold of night sneaking in through the collar of Noah's fleece jacket. She zipped it all the way up, turning while Steve locked the cabin. She scanned the shadows clustered at the bases of trees.

"My Jeep's in the lot down the drive here," he said.

Together they walked toward the vehicle, Madeline rushing slightly ahead, starting at every night bird rustling in the bushes, and each laugh or shout from loud campers. She wondered if she should tell Steve about the four guys who tried to attack her. There were no bodies, and nothing Steve could do except notify the families. She decided that when she got home, she'd write an anonymous note describing the incident. At least then the families would know. She wondered how many missing people had disappeared without a trace at the hands of the creature.

"You okay?" Steve asked.

Madeline nodded. "Just anxious to get to my car. I really appreciate your taking me."

He smiled, a kind smile. "No problem."

Soon they reached the parking area, and Steve pointed out his vehicle, a green Jeep Cherokee, which waited among five other park service vehicles. He unlocked the door for her and went around the other side. Carefully she opened the door and peered into the cab, then into the back of the vehicle. It was clear. Exhaling sharply, she climbed in, closing and locking the door after herself. Steve got in the other side, fired up the car, and they were off.

"So, the Loop trailhead?" he asked, pulling out of the parking spot.

She nodded.

"Okay." He straightened the car out and exited the parking lot, Madeline still searching the dark outside for any sign of the creature. When he pulled onto the main road, she watched with relief as the speedometer needle climbed, hopefully faster than even the creature could run.

They rode in silence, Madeline letting her head lean back on the headrest, Steve still looking a little sleepy. "I should have made a cup of coffee," he said, rubbing more sleep out of his eye.

"Sorry for the rush. I guess it was just getting to me." She felt safer in the Jeep now, freer. She couldn't wait to be in her own car, speeding toward home. Once in Mothershead, she would talk to the local police. Ever since she'd played a part in catching the Sickle Moon Killer, they'd been kind to her and kept a helpful eye on her, even if as individuals they kept their distance. His capture had meant kudos for the tiny precinct, as they had solved a case that had baffled even the FBI. If the creature came after her, she could rely on them to help her.

They drove on, the headlights playing over the shadowed branches of overhanging pines, the yellow center line glowing reflectively. A pair of headlights appeared over the crest of a hill and another car sped by them, traveling too fast.

"Jerk," Steve said. "So many people speed on these roads. Did you know that vehicle accidents are the number one killer of bears out here?"

Madeline raised her eyebrows. "No, I didn't know that."

"I hate it when people speed here. And I'm just a naturalist ranger. I can't pull them over and give them a ticket, though I'd really like to."

"I don't blame you," she said sincerely.

"Okay. Tirade over."

She laughed.

"Or, wait—here's another. People who don't think park signs apply to them. Like there's always some jerk who thinks the 'Stay off the meadow—it's being restored' sign doesn't apply to him, you know? So he just steps right over the fence and tramples the damaged area some more. Or the jerk who thinks the 'Don't feed the wildlife' sign doesn't apply to him, so he feeds a coyote some lunch meat out of the window of his car. Next thing you know, the coyote is hanging around the road all the time, eating unhealthy human food, and then it gets hit by a car. Even worse than that jerk might be the jerks who see him doing this stuff and figure, 'Hey, if that guy can do it, then I don't see why I can't feed wildlife and trample the meadows.'" He paused to take a breath. "Man, it pisses me off!"

"I can see why."

"I'll say." He paused. "Okay. That tirade's over, too, and I don't think I see any more looming on the horizon anytime soon."

"No problem," she said. "We've all got to vent sometimes, and it sounds like you've got more reasons to complain than the rest of us."

"Except you," he said, glancing over at her. "You've been through a tough time."

She assumed he meant the flash flood and the bump on the head, so she said, "Yeah. My head is still giving me grief."

"Not just that," he said.

"I thought you didn't believe me about the rest of the stuff. That I had hallucinated it."

"I don't know what you really saw up there, but it's easy to tell it terrified you. I don't blame you for wanting to get home. If I'd seen some *thing* up there, I wouldn't be too anxious to stay in the woods."

She turned to face him. "So then you believe that I really saw something?"

He nodded. "Once, when I was eleven, I was out hiking with my dad in Oregon. All of a sudden, I can't explain why, but we both got this really intense feeling we were being watched. A primal fear washed over me, my hair stood up— everything."

Madeline thought of her own feeling of being watched, just before the flash flood hit her.

"And then, all of a sudden, stench. I mean, the most god-awful stench you can imagine—like rotten meat and rancid, chunky milk, putrid, decaying flesh. The smell was so bad and so pervasive that I almost threw up, right there on the trail. I ran ahead, trying to get away from it, while my dad kept plodding along. Finally I turned around to see how far back he was. And something was there, on the trail behind him. I only saw it for a second, following along behind him, and then it darted back into the bushes."

"What was it?"

"Something big. Huge. Way taller than my dad. And covered

with hair. He spun around just as it vanished, and then took off down the trail toward me. He asked me if I'd seen anything. I nodded."

"But what was it?" Madeline asked again.

"I don't know. Bigfoot, maybe? A homeless guy with a lot of hair? I only saw it that one time, and we'd hiked that trail a bunch of times before and since. So all I'm saying is that there's some weird stuff out there. And I don't doubt that you saw something up on the mountain."

And down here, she thought grimly. "Thanks. That makes me feel a little better." But then she thought of Mike, the murdered ranger, and how Steve had no idea that his friend was dead, and how the thing had imitated him, even down to his voice. She shivered, feeling cold even in the fleece.

They traveled on in silence, and after twenty miles they saw the sign for the trailhead on the left. Steve slowed and pulled into the parking area. There, like her own version of the Holy Grail, sat her beloved 1980 VW Rabbit, its red paint gleaming in the headlights, the white and gold racing stripe glowing reflectively.

"Yay!" she said aloud, not able to help herself. "Um, that's my car there, the Rabbit."

It was the only car parked at the trailhead, as if she was the only person to attempt the hike that day, the only one unfortunate enough to get caught in the flash flood.

Before he'd even fully stopped the car, Madeline opened the door, ready to jump out. Then she turned and hugged him. He looked startled, then returned the hug. "Thank you," she told him. "Thank you so much."

"No problem. And now I'll be able to see my sister, too."

She climbed out of the car, and he added, "I'll just wait here till you get the car started."

"Thanks." She closed the door and walked over to her car, resisting the urge to throw her arms around it, too. Instead, she said, "Hello, Rabbit!" Lying down on her stomach, she felt around under the car for the magnetic key holder. Her fingers closed around it almost immediately, and she tugged it off. Inside, safe and sound, rested her spare key. Unlocking

the door, she swung it open, then sank down into the familiar
black bucket seat, breathing in the comfortable smell of her
faithful car.

And realized she hadn't checked the backseat first. Spinning around in her seat, she looked back there. Nothing. Then
she got out, walked to the back and peered in through the
hatchback window. Nothing. Sighing with relief, she climbed
back in the driver's seat and started up the Rabbit. It roared to
life.

She closed the door, locked it, and waved to Steve. He
waved back, watched her for a moment, and then pulled his
Jeep out, swinging onto the road and driving away.

Madeline leaned back momentarily. She longed to return
to her normal life, to the life that made sense. Days ago she'd
wanted nothing more than to escape Mothershead. Now she
just wanted to escape back into its familiarity, put all of this
into perspective. She reached under the passenger seat and
pulled out her wallet, grateful she'd stashed it there. Strapping
on her seat belt, she thought of Noah, asleep back in the
cabin. She hoped he would catch up to the creature soon and
end his long, miserable quest. Maybe then he could have a
chance at a normal life, get back the future that had been
taken from him that night in Vienna.

She backed up and pulled out of the small lot onto the
main road toward home. The moon rose behind her, the road
glowing when she looked back. She wondered about Noah,
and if she was doing the right thing. The sky darkened as a
cloud passed over the moon, and Madeline's lights were the
only ones on the road. Dark shadows of pines rose on both
sides of her, with the looming black mountains beyond. She
felt different, like she never had before: sad and full of a
strange kind of regret. But she couldn't go back. What Noah
asked for was too much. She wouldn't willingly embrace the
very lifestyle she'd been avoiding since the capture of the
Sickle Moon Killer.

Up ahead, lights broke through the darkness, a flashing
sign, she thought at first. But then, as she drew nearer, she
realized it was a Jeep, pulled off on the side of the road. A

police or ranger's vehicle, with flashing lights on the roof, identical to the one Steve drove. She slowed as she drew closer. The Jeep was at a strange angle. Almost upon it, she slowed to a near stop. It was off the road, down in a ditch. The engine was still running; she could see the exhaust pluming in the cold air. She didn't see anyone standing around and wondered if someone was still inside, hurt or unconscious. Cautiously she pulled up on the shoulder behind the car. When she got out, she immediately saw that the driver's side of the Jeep was crumpled in, as if another car had smashed into it and sent the Jeep tumbling into the ditch. But no other cars were in sight.

The smell of gasoline hung heavily in the air, and Madeline could hear the steady trickle of what she presumed was gas leaking out of the damaged tank.

If there was someone in the car, she had to get them out fast. The battery obviously still held a charge, and one little spark could send them up in flames. Quickly she ran to the driver's door and peered in. Her heart sank. Steve sat slumped over the wheel. Grunting, she tried to wrench the door open, but it was too damaged to budge. The passenger door was locked. She took in Steve's condition through the window.

He was unconscious, breathing, bleeding from a head wound. The smell of gasoline reeked strongly, making Madeline feel dizzy and sick to her stomach. She scanned over the car. The radio! Of course. He must have a radio. Maybe help was nearby. She reached in through the shattered window, sliding her hand between Steve and the steering wheel, feeling for the radio. The round shape of a CB handset met her fingers, and she pulled it toward her. Instant dismay filled her when she saw it. It was completely crushed.

"Steve?" she said urgently. "Steve!"

The ranger didn't so much as stir or twitch. He was out cold, and Madeline had to make a decision fast. Already her head was pounding from the noxious fumes. Slowly she reached out to gently touch him. Her fingers brushed his jacket, and suddenly he jerked violently and grabbed her hand. Madeline cried out and reflexively yanked her hand back.

Then he turned slowly to look at her.

And she knew it wasn't Steve in that body at all.

10

MADELINE staggered back, away from the car.

The creature followed, wrenching open the destroyed door with ease and crawling out. Madeline's head spun from the fumes as she watched. He looked exactly like Steve; it was uncanny. The tousled, sandy brown hair, the high cheekbones and narrow chin. But the eyes were all wrong; they had a feverish, haunting quality that the real, gentle Steve didn't have.

"Madeline," he said, straightening up in front of the car. "I had to stop you from leaving." He paused, turning his head and taking her in. "Your gift . . . is amazing." Again she noticed the strange accent she couldn't quite place, just a hint of it in the consonants. "You touched me . . . and you knew. I could feel myself filling you with my memories. That gift is your destiny. You shouldn't run from it. We all have our special . . . talents." Just then the skin on the upper half of his face rippled and turned black, smooth as sharkskin and dark as ink. The pupils widened, engulfing the iris, then the white, until just black remained. The eyes bored into her.

Her mind froze. She couldn't think. She backed away, her eyes filling with the creature and the gas-leaking car. She didn't know which she was more afraid of: getting blown up or torn apart by the creature. If she turned and ran, he would chase her, but at least she'd be away from the car when it went up. If she stayed, she'd get blown to bits *and* torn apart.

Madeline took off. Out of the corner of her eye, she saw him sprint forward in pursuit. Darting away from the ditch, she looked at the meadow ahead and then the road. She knew she couldn't run straight for her car now. If she darted back around, he'd intercept her. The dark meadow was her only option. Maybe she could lose him in the tall grass, get far enough away and then lie flat, out of sight. Or if she gained enough ground, she could double back to her car.

Panting and leaping over tall grasses, she hit the meadow. As her eyes adjusted to the gloom, she could see that tremendous granite outcroppings rose on both sides of her, bordering the meadow. No use darting to the side.

Zigzagging left and right, she leapt over tree stumps and windfalls of old branches. Behind her, the creature threw up branches and pinecones in its wake. Clouds slid away from the moon and made it easy to see anything big sticking out of the ground. She leapt over half-buried logs and large rocks. Chancing a glance behind, she saw a furtive bounding dark shape only twenty or so feet behind. She tripped on a rock, managed to regain her balance, tripped again, stumbled, righted herself.

Behind her the running footsteps thrashed through the tall grass, then took on the eerie quality of loping. It was on all fours. She could hear the rhythmic thump of each foot. In her mind, she could see the creature's black form speeding through the trees, the gleam in its eyes as it hunted her.

A dull *whump* sounded behind her.

She had completely forgotten about the car. Glancing back, she saw bright licks of flame on the road at the edge of the meadow.

Then a tremendous weight crashed into her, sending her sprawling into the grass. The creature landed on her back, his claws curling around her shoulders, his legs straddling her body. With a whoosh, air exploded from her lungs, and she lay stunned, struggling to breathe. Then, slowly, oxygen returned, and she felt the crushing weight of him on top of her. She writhed beneath him, grass sticking in her mouth, pinecones piercing her cheek.

He moved his face down next to hers. Round red eyes filled her view. He had completely reverted to the sleek black creature she'd first seen on the mountain. A shadow with weight. "You give a good chase."

The sound of creaking bones and snapping sinew erupted, and the creature shape-shifted again. She felt him grow very cold and then hot on top of her, the eyes, still near her own, closed as if in ecstasy. A face formed, one she didn't recognize. Chiseled, classically handsome features. Olive skin, shoulder-length black hair falling in front of his face. He snapped open his eyes—deep green. They focused on her.

She jerked to one side, trying to throw him off. "You don't like my real face?" he asked. "But you're the first person I've shown it to in such a long time."

Kicking out at his knees and elbowing him in the gut, she managed to flip herself over and came face-to-face with him. He still sat on top of her. His eyes flashed brightly, hot as embers, momentarily burning her retina. Quickly she punched him in the face, and he grunted but did not move off her. Rearing her hips up, she tried to throw him off, make him lose his balance. But smoothly he matched her moves with his own, never even coming close to falling over.

She struck him in the throat. He coughed but remained stationary. A fury of panic welled up within her, and she grabbed his neck, desperately trying to choke him. But instead, he brought his hands up and closed around hers in an almost tender gesture.

A surging wave of powerful energy hit her. She fell back against the ground, a blinding light enveloping her mind, the creature relentlessly holding on to her hands. Her eyes fluttered in her head; her back arched. A tremor began in her chest and spread throughout her body, her legs and arms shaking violently. Still he held fast. She tried to break the connection, tried to break free.

Too intense. Too intense.

Waltzing, dizzy, at a masquerade ball in eighteenth century France, twirling a blonde-haired woman around the dance floor and laughing giddily . . .

Feasting on corpses on a medieval battlefield, lifting shields and digging into the waiting flesh beneath, licking bones and finding the delectable soft parts . . .

Swimming through frigid waters toward a Viking longboat, the seamen unaware, backs turned, climbing silently over the rail, and then sinking into warm, delicious flesh . . .

Stumbling, drunken, from a pyramid in the Mayan jungle, the hiss of a volcanic vent nearby filling the air with a foul, sulfurous smell . . .

Dragged in a net behind a Roman chariot, a spear painfully jammed between the ribs, gasping for a breath, mouth full of dirt and blood . . .

Standing on the balcony of a sangha in mountainous Tibet, silent snow cascading down, a flurry of flakes dusting stone railings and worn steps, ancient trees . . .

Staggering alone across the vast sands of the Sahara, lips cracked and bleeding, mouth parched, eyes searing . . .

Fighting with a lion over a water hole in the Kalahari, snarling and snapping, the lion lashing out, claws biting deep . . .

Standing outside an ancient Sumerian city, at the edge of a great void, a black opening in the earth, standing transfixed, staring. Then something moving in there, glistening, sinewy, writhing down there in the darkness, then rushing up, up—

Gasping, the creature flung her hands to the side. Madeline lay still, heart pounding, her mind stumbling over the images, her eyes unable to open. "Oh, gods," he croaked. "So far back . . . even I'd forgotten."

Her eyes fluttered and opened. For a minute she couldn't fix on him, her focus swimming. Then the blur dissipated, and she saw him, still straddling her, his head in his hands. He looked completely human now, still in the ranger's clothes, and he appeared—she couldn't believe it—stunned. Upset. Vulnerable, even.

"I don't think I'll kill you after all," he said, taking his hands away from his face.

Heat hit her. The meadow was completely on fire. The reek of gasoline filled the air. The burning car was still intact on the road, but it was utterly consumed in flames and would explode any second.

"The car," she mumbled, spitting out a blade of grass. She could hear the roar of the fire over their labored breathing. Firelight flickered on the granite walls to both sides. She struggled to throw him off. "It's going to go up!"

Coming out of his daze, the creature snapped his head to the road and then turned back to her, his now-human hands gripping her shoulders. She twisted beneath him, trying to get out. A bright flash lit up the sky, followed by a deafening explosion. A concussive blast knocked him off her. She threw her hands up over her head as a rain of debris came down: bits of colored lenses, seat springs, a spark plug. When it stopped, she peered out. The creature lay a few feet away, groaning. Blood dripped from a head wound. Quiet crackling followed the cacophony. She looked back at the car. Flames shot from it, alighting on more of the meadow. The summer had been hot and dry, and the grass went up amazingly fast.

For a second she was five again, watching immobilized as a golden fire roared toward her. She had been on a picnic with her family in the woods, and a hot piece of metal had fallen from the exhaust pipe of their car and set the woods on fire. Her father had jumped up, grabbed a metal rake out of the car, and tried to control the flames by raking leaves and pine needles away, exposing earth. She'd stared on in horror, the flames dancing closer and closer while her father screamed at her to get back. She had, while her mother raced forward to stamp at flames. They'd put it out then. Everything had been okay.

But now flames crawled and spat, drawing ever closer. She got to her feet. The entire expanse of the meadow was ablaze, reaching from one granite cliff clear across to the other.

Blocked from the road, her only choice was to run farther into the meadow. The creature still lay injured, groaning, trying to rise. She ran a little way before stopping in front of a thick branch. If she hit him now, while he was down, maybe she could knock him unconscious. Since she couldn't kill him, it was her best bet. Quickly she ran to the branch and picked it up. It was heavier than she expected, but she carried it to where the creature lay and then hefted it over her head. He rolled over on his back, and his eyes went wide when her saw her standing over him. She brought the branch down hard, aiming for his head. Reflexively he brought his arm up to shield himself, and the branch connected with a sickening smack. The creature howled in pain, and she raised the branch again for a second blow. She struck violently as he tried to roll away. The end of the wood crashed down on the back of his head.

He went limp.

She dropped the branch and ran.

The meadow stretched on a little farther, and she bounded over rocks and logs, her dark, flickering shadow from the firelight making progress difficult.

And then, with a horror, she saw a granite wall loom up before her.

She was trapped. The two cliffs on both sides met here at a tremendous granite outcropping that curled around, meeting the road at both of its ends. She was trapped in a half moon of tall grass and wildfire. Desperately she tried to climb up the wall. It was sheer—no handholds or footholds—and it leaned out toward her, so she couldn't even leap up and cling to the sheer rock itself. She groped along the cold stone wall, smoke reaching her and forcing her to cough. Her eyes teared, blurring her vision. With frantic hands, she felt the rough surface for any nook and cranny, and each time she found purchase she tried to raise herself up, only to fall to the ground again.

It was no use. She couldn't climb it.

Hands bleeding and fingernails torn, she turned to face the fire.

11

BEFORE her, fire raced forward, devouring grass and dead-fall in its wake.

Madeline ran along the granite perimeter, trying to find a break. Acrid smoke filled her lungs. It was no use. The cliff was uncompromising, smooth, tall, and hopeless. Still the fire advanced. She was trapped.

She looked to where she'd clubbed the creature and saw that fire had already consumed that part of the meadow. She only had maybe two minutes before it would sweep over where she stood and then burn itself out against the cliff face.

She leapt at the wall, clawed it, tried to run up it, grab it. Nothing. The angle at which it leaned in toward her made it impossibly steep. She fell flat on her back. It was too late. The fire was coming.

Scorching smoke seared her lungs, and she couldn't get a breath. She spun all the way around, not seeing a single escape route. Panting, she stood there, ready to bolt in any direction, not knowing where to go, her mind reeling and eyes streaming.

And then she heard her father's words, clear and loud, as if he were standing right next to her, just like he was that day when she was five.

"If you're caught in a wildfire, there are three things you can do. Look for a natural firebreak, like a ridge of rocks or water, and get on the other side of it."

She looked at the unforgiving granite cliff and bit her lip.

"If fire is on both sides of you, submerge yourself completely underwater, like in a river or creek, while the fire passes overhead."

No water in sight.

"If there is no water or climbable fire break—"

Madeline gulped for air.

"Bury yourself."

Immediately she stripped off her coat and laid it flat on the ground, then dug into the ground with her bare hands, dumping handfuls of dirt onto the coat. The lack of summer rains made the soil loose and easy to dig into. She dug handful after handful, using her fingers like scoops.

But it wasn't enough. The fire crept closer, and the space she'd dug wasn't nearly big enough to cover her. Nearby lay a large, flat piece of sturdy bark. Grabbing it and using it as a shovel, she piled more and more dirt on the coat. Then it suddenly hit her that the coat was made of synthetic material. If the fire swept over her, the heat would melt the coat right into her flesh. She couldn't use it. She stripped off her long-sleeved cotton shirt, poured the dirt from the jacket onto it, and then flung the jacket away. With the shirt covered, she piled the dirt up next to the hole itself. Desperately she dug faster, sweat dripping off her body and stinging her tearing eyes. Her lungs felt on fire, mucus streaming from her nose.

When the hole was deep enough to partly cover her, she lay down in it and scooped the dirt over her legs. Then as the fire leapt and devoured leaves, closing in on her, she turned on her belly and pulled the dirt-covered shirt up over her torso and head. Quickly she cupped her hand over her mouth. The instant the fire swept over her, she knew. It sucked the oxygen right out of her little hiding hole. Heat swarmed over her body, and the unbreathable air under the shirt grew searingly hot. She cupped her hand tighter around her mouth and squeezed her eyes shut. The heat was so intense that she imagined her shirt had caught on fire and would soon burn into her back, setting her jeans and skin on fire. Desperately she clung to thoughts of her father and his words. *"Cup your hand. Try to keep the air cool in there. Wildfires pass quickly. Just keep calm. Keep calm."* She repeated the mantra in her head over and over as the heat became intolerable. *Keep the air cool?* she wondered. *There* was *no air.* Sweat trickled over her back and dripped from her chest. Had the fire passed over yet? How long had she been lying there? She was dying for a breath. Panic set in as the air became hotter. Involuntarily her lungs gulped for air, but found none. How would she know when the fire had passed? Wait for the heat to dissipate? For the oxygen to return? The air to become cooler? She couldn't remember.

The heat remained intense. But suddenly, a flood of cool air filled her hiding hole. She gulped the air in, her lungs grateful and her head pounding. Did this mean the fire had passed? Why was the heat still so intense? Cool air continued to seep into her. The fire must have passed.

But then the heat turned from intense to painful. Crying out, Madeline involuntarily threw the shirt off herself. Rolling over, she saw that it had caught on fire, igniting the waistband of her jeans, too. Panicking, she rolled in her little hollow, extinguishing the flames. Beyond, the fire had moved on, feasting on the grass at the cliff's edge. Farther out, all the way to the road, the meadow lay blackened and smoldering. Getting to her feet, she checked herself over for flames again, paranoid they were licking up the back of her jeans. Heat burned through her soles, and she realized they were melting quickly. She stamped the flames out on her shirt, which lay a few feet away. Picking it up, she saw that half of it was unsalvageable. One sleeve and part of the front were completely burned, the stench of singed cotton intermingling with the smoke and smell of burnt grass.

The jacket wasn't so lucky. It had completely melted, the sleeves now stuck together. She grabbed it and looked toward the road. To her utter relief, her VW was still there, the road having acted as a firebreak. It hadn't exploded. There it was, covered with twisted metallic debris and charred pieces of plastic from the ranger's car, but it was still intact. Grabbing her shirt by the unburned sleeve, she ran across the blackened meadow. When she reached her car, the melted soles of her shoes slid on the asphalt.

Mucus rattled in her lungs, and then a fit of coughing overtook her. Leaning over, she hacked and hacked, spitting out vile, black strings of phlegm.

Placing her hands on the hood of her car, she burst into a fit of hysterical laughter that ended in another coughing fit. She clutched her car, pressed her face against it, feeling the cold, friendly, familiar metal against her skin.

Ahead on the road, Steve's vehicle sat burning and smoldering, huge plumes of black smoke spiraling into the sky. The stench of charred plastic stung her dripping nose and eyes. The last rollicking flames in the meadow demanded her attention. What of the creature? She scanned the smoking meadow. A few lumps broke its evenness, but they were old tree trunks and stumps. She didn't see the creature's charred remains.

A flash of hopelessness overtook her as she thought of the sheer undefeatable power of an animal that couldn't even be killed by fire. The sense of her own mortality, so recently tested, shook her. And this creature, this *thing*, had no such concerns. It just traveled from country to country, from year to year, feeding on whomever it chose with no consequences.

And what of Steve? She remembered Noah telling her it could look like anyone it had killed. He'd been kind to her, and she had cost him his life. She thought of Steve's sister in Missoula, and how she'd never get a visit from her brother again.

A sudden anger swelled up within as she realized the unfairness, the advantage this creature had over all its victims, past and future. They had no chance. It had been killing for at least two hundred years, and no one had stopped it yet.

Yet.

She had the ability to know where people were going before they were there, to know their motives, their thoughts. So far Noah had only been able to follow along in the aftermath of the creature's killings, racing from country to country but always too late. He needed an advantage if he was going to catch the beast, needed to anticipate the creature's next move.

She could be that advantage . . . touch things the creature had recently touched, know where it was going, whom it had chosen as its next victim. She knew then what she had to do. She had to go back.

She had to help Noah stop it.

12

MADELINE sat in her car, coughing black-lined mucus out of her lungs. She rolled down the window and spat, then leaned her head against the headrest. Its familiarity was comforting, like an old friend cradling her head. For a moment she closed her burning eyes and exhaled deeply.

Immediately an image of the creature, half-burned and desperate, clawing at her window snapped her eyes open. Furtively she glanced out all the windows of the car, the sides, the back. The fire was now smoldering out at the far edges of the meadow, and the air was filled with thick, acrid smoke that drifted lazily with the faint breeze.

Though it was partially burned, she put her shirt back on and shivered in the night air.

The full moon, now risen, set the smoke aglow, giving the eerie impression of a gathering of spirits, floating and ethereal, mingling and drifting by each other, intent on taking over the world of the living.

Beyond the meadow rose the impassive granite cliff, disappearing into the darkness. On the other side of the road lay forest, dense and dark. Madeline reached down and closed her hand around the keys in the ignition. The car sprang to life. She pulled out on the road and did a U-turn. She had only driven a few feet when she saw movement in the back of her car.

Slamming on the brakes, she threw open the car door and leapt out, then ran to the back of the car to peer into the backseat and hatchback. The backseat was empty, but she had a tarp in the hatchback, and beneath it lay a large lump.

She staggered back, not sure what to do, and then remembered. It was an extra spare tire. She'd bought one before she drove up to the mountains. Once she'd been stranded on a remote road with a flat tire and a flat spare, and for this trip she'd brought along an extra.

Even still, for several minutes she started at it intently, waiting for it to twitch or breathe. No movement occurred. Gingerly she approached the car and removed her keys from the ignition. Crept around to the back of the car. Inserted the key in the trunk lock. Pressed the button. Raised the hatchback. Again she stared at it for several minutes. When it still didn't move, she ripped the tarp away. The spare tire lay beneath, along with jumper cables and an oil funnel.

The wind from the open window must have ruffled the tarp. It wouldn't be the first time she'd imagined things in the back of her car. The way the glass of the hatchback slanted, when streetlights played over it, often gave the illusion of something rushing forward from the backseat.

Madeline lowered the tarp over the tire. Mucus rattled in her lungs, and she coughed for several long minutes until her throat was sore. Leaning over, she spat up long strings of black, ropy phlegm. She wiped her mouth on her burned sleeve and looked around.

All of a sudden the road seemed very empty, the shadows deeper, each tiny sound louder. She glanced off the road into the darkened forest, then back to the asphalt itself, scanning up and down the desolate highway. The only sound was the idling engine, huge and cacophonous in the quiet.

Quickly she tucked the rest of the tarp in, slammed the

hatchback, and ran to the driver's door. Wrenching it open quickly, she gave one last look around the car and got in.

Gripping the wheel, she pressed on the accelerator and flew back onto the road, speeding back toward Lake Mc-Donald and the cabin.

"Noah!" Madeline cried, running to the cabin's door. She rummaged around in her jeans pocket and found the key, which she'd forgotten to leave behind. Unlocking the door, she thrust it open. It banged against the wall. "Noah!"

A muffled stir brought her into the bedroom. "Madeline?" Noah said sleepily.

She came into the darkened room and felt her way slowly to the bed. Cool cotton sheets touched her hands, and she sat down on the edge of the bed.

Noah sat up and turned on the light. "What's wrong?" he started. "What in the world happened? Your face!" He brought his hand up, stroked her face and came away with sooty fingers. "And your clothes!"

She looked down. Her clothes were covered in soot and bits of dry grass. Black smudges covered the sheets were she had touched them.

"Did he come back?"

"No, well, yes . . . but listen. I want to help you. I can help you, tell you where he's going to be next. Like you said. Anticipate his next move."

Noah sat up straighter, taking her in, waking up more. "I don't know what to say . . . I thought you didn't want that."

"That was before."

"Before what?"

For a moment she was still. "A brush with death."

"What? Are you all right?"

"I've never felt better," she sighed. "I feel like I finally know what I'm supposed to do, and for once I'm not scared. I see the advantage he has over everyone he's killed and is going to kill. He can be anyone he wants to be, know what they know. The advantages he has are countless: anonymity, the ability to change forms, to dispose of evidence without a trace. He's almost unstoppable. Until now. I can figure out where he's going next, and we can cut him off when he gets there."

Noah stared at her, mouth open. He blinked several times, unable to speak. Finally he worked his mouth, and sound came out. "Yes."

Madeline grinned. "Yes." Her body felt light and filled with energy, exuberant and excited.

"Yes!" he shouted.

"Yes!"

Scrambling to his knees, he grabbed her tightly, wrapping his arms around her and practically crushing the air out of her lungs.

"This is it, Madeline," he said. "I can feel it. We have the advantage. For once, we will be the hunters. We'll close in and destroy him, once and for all."

Noah's Jeep climbed the pitted dirt road in lurches and jostles, and Madeline had to grip the armrest tightly just to stay in her seat. The road climbed steeply through dense pine forest. Through breaks in the trees, she caught views of the mountains beyond.

They'd started out on the smooth, paved North Fork Road, which ran along outside the western boundary of the park. The North Fork eventually turned to gravel, and soon they turned off onto a small, dirt road with only a fire number for a name.

Last night she'd told Noah of the forest fire and Steve's death, hoping Noah would tell her that fire could kill the creature. But he had only shaken his head. She wanted to report Steve's death, but Noah said it would be dangerous to investigating officers while the creature was still in the area, and that she should wait until it moved on. He also suggested she wait to report the four men who had attacked her for the same reason. She guessed he was right but grimly wondered how long this list would get by the time she did indeed return home. If she ever returned home, other than in a closed casket to hide her partially eaten body.

They had phoned in the fire, though, on an anonymous tip, but it had already been spotted, and fire vehicles had been dispatched. The dispatcher told them the fire was under control.

She guessed they'd find Steve was "missing." She felt really sad about him, blaming herself for getting him involved. Maybe Noah was right that night when they got down off the mountain. Maybe she shouldn't have involved anyone else.

The road ahead lay in utter disrepair and looked like it was used only twice a year, if even that much. "How much farther?" she asked as she left her seat and almost hit her head on the ceiling and then on the passenger window frame.

The air was still incredibly hot. Stifling heat filled in the cab of the Jeep as they crawled upward, far too slowly for a breeze to really get going. Madeline could feel that the sky wanted to rain and alleviate the heat, and that when it did, a terrific thunderstorm was likely. But for now there were only a few tiny white clouds in the otherwise bright blue sky.

"Another four miles, I think."

Madeline's mouth fell open. "Four miles!" Four miles on the highway or a paved street was one thing. But four miles on this road could take—

"The rest of our lives."

"What?"

"Estimated driving time."

The truck dived into a pothole again, sending her over Noah's way. The seat belt cinched painfully against her collarbone. "Why," she asked, as her voice reverberated with the rough motion, "do . . . they . . . make . . . Jeep . . . shocks . . . so . . . tight?"

"I . . . don't . . . know," reverberated Noah as they hit a stretch of washboard road that she was convinced had last been traveled by a bulldozer carrying two tons of cement and a brontosaurus with a weight problem. The grooved tracks were so deep that the Jeep seemed ready to bounce them right into an alternate reality.

Madeline looked ahead with fear. Would rifling through the creature's things would be like when she touched the Sickle Moon Killer's knife? Would it haunt her for years to come? The images awaiting her could be worse than those. Suddenly she wanted to turn back more than anything in the world.

It was noon by the time they arrived. The forest was absolutely silent. If she strained her ears, Madeline could hear the muffled fall of pine needles dropping to the soft forest bed beneath. Sunlight streamed through the branches to the forest floor below, illuminating wildflowers and small fairylike rings of mushrooms.

She climbed from the Jeep and took in the cabin. It was tiny, couldn't be more than four rooms. It lay at the end of the long and winding road they'd traveled, and the nearest house they'd passed lay two miles back down the road.

The creature had wanted its privacy.

She hoped Noah was right, that the creature would have no occasion to be here now, no person to devour and digest. No need to build a nest.

"It's isolated here," Noah said after he shut the Jeep door.

"Quiet, too."

Both grew silent as they stood there.

"Too quiet," she added.

Noah smirked. "Yeah. Too quiet. The kind of quiet that makes you think of crimes being committed in the heart of the city. The kind of city that only comes in one size, big, and one flavor, dangerous."

"Thank you!" she interjected, cutting him off. "That's enough Sam Spade for one afternoon."

"My pleasure. Thank you for tuning in to my one-man radio show."

"Don't forget to thank me for tuning in to your planet, too."

"Uh. I'm hurt. Just because I'm a shape-shifter from another time period doesn't mean I'm strange or something."

"Yes, it does. It definitely does."

"Well, I hope that's strange in a good way."

She smiled at him, his handsome face caught in a shaft of soft light. "It is."

He returned the smile and gestured toward the cabin. Her feet had turned to lead. "Are you sure he won't be in there?" she asked, her voice tiny. They crept closer. It was a rental cabin. Dusty curtains hung in the windows, and a sign on the door listed rules for staying there: wash your own dishes, take sheets off the bed when you're done.

Don't eat the help, she thought grimly.

"Ready to do this?" He watched her expectantly. She hated this part of her gift, when people stared at her as if she were about to pull off some kind of miracle. Because it was a rental cabin, this was going to be harder than usual. Objects that had been touched by numerous people offered a hodgepodge of information, oftentimes making it difficult to separate one person's thoughts from another's.

Approaching the door, she once again took in the cabin's small size. "If he does show up, there's not much room to hide."

"I don't think he will."

She studied the cabin reluctantly. "Well, let's do this as quickly as possible."

"Here goes," Noah said, trying the doorknob unsuccessfully.

"Did you really think it would be unlocked?" she started, trailing off as Noah smashed the French door pane closest the knob.

"No," he answered.

Reaching through the hole in the jagged glass, Noah unlocked the door from the inside. Madeline glanced around nervously.

"What is it?" Noah asked.

"I guess I thought the cops could sense a law being broken miles away and would come for us."

He nodded. "I felt that way myself the first few times."

She raised her eyebrows as he opened the front door. "The first few times you broke into houses?"

"The first few times I committed crimes."

She swallowed as he paused in the doorway, waiting for her. "What kinds of crimes have you committed?"

He smiled. "Oh, nothing serious. You know, a little B and E, some minor theft of food and clothes over the years, that kind of thing."

"Oh." She wondered if he was leaving anything out. Centuries of pursuing a killer could warp any person's mind. With an obsession carrying you from year to year, you could very well skew your ideas of where justice ended and madness began.

Noah stepped toward her. "What is it? You look like you're about to run away."

She looked into his concerned eyes and felt foolish. "It's nothing," she said. "Just my overactive imagination." Her gut told her Noah was safe. He was a good person, determined to stop this killer. A lot of people wouldn't be so selfless. It was too easy to roll over and let bad things happen, to not think about others. Most people would have grieved over their lover and then moved on, too scared or too weak to pursue justice when the law failed to deliver. She studied Noah's face, his old, wise eyes, slight growth of whiskers, sandy blond hair curling about his face.

She reached up and touched his cheek, feeling the warmth of his face on her palm. Slowly she stepped forward, closing the distance between them and pressed her lips to his, breathing in the delicious scent of him. He returned the kiss, wrapping a hand around her back, pulling her even closer. Her mouth longed to drink him deeply, and the tip of her tongue came out, lightly brushing his, an electric sensation passing through her. She pulled away, hunger in her eyes, and watched as he slowly opened his eyes, his mouth still parted and wanting.

They watched each other for a few moments, and then she said, "I guess we have work to do."

He nodded.

Madeline touched the doorknob as she entered, expecting to get something. But so many people had touched it over the years, it only gave off static: a wash of feelings and emotions of hundreds of people who had rented the cabin in years gone by.

Beyond the front door lay the kitchen, a modest setup including an ancient propane stove that had probably cooked food when Frankie Valli and the Four Seasons first sang on the radio. Next to it stood a genuine icebox, the kind you actually had to put ice into to cool its contents. In the center of the room stood a Formica-topped table, scarred with decades of use, and two cheap aluminum chairs with plastic cushioned seats, cracked and spilling their polyester stuffing.

Madeline moved about the kitchen, touching the chairs, the table, the stove, the icebox. The last she opened, admitting a terrible reek into the room. Wrinkling her nose, she peered inside. Nothing. But decades of use had taken its toll. Too many people had left food in there to go bad, and the lingering stench was a mixture of rancid milk, overripe cheese, and a sharp garlicky smell that threatened to overtake the kitchen. She slammed the icebox door shut and backed away.

Noah, waiting quietly by the front door, asked, "Anything?"

Madeline shook her head. "Just a lot of white noise."

He raised his eyebrows.

She moved toward him, away from the cloud of stench. "When a lot of people touch something over the years, like these appliances, all I get is white noise: a crazy mixture of the thoughts of everyone who has ever been here. I call it the Bus Seat Effect."

"Bus seat?"

"Yeah. I first noticed it on a bus. My elementary school used these really old buses that had probably driven kids around since the 1950s. Our school district didn't have a whole lot of money. Anyway, I noticed one day, bouncing along on my way to school, that I didn't ever get any specific images when I touched a bus seat. I thought it was weird at the time. I mean, think of all the nervous and terrified kids who had used them for decades. I thought I'd get something— an image of a kid crying over a stolen lunch box, or a vision of a kid getting beaten up during recess by the local bully. But nothing. Eventually I realized that I got no images precisely because there *were* so many kids who had ridden in those seats before me. It was just too much information, a hiss and static of a thousand lives, each with their separate fears and terrors, struggles and triumphs."

"The Bus Seat Effect. Got it. Want to try the other rooms?"

"Sure," she said, feeling mildly sick, and not sure if it was due to nerves or the terrible stench.

Together they made their way through the sitting room, a tiny room sporting an ancient stuffed rocker and a magazine rack complete with wilting copies of *Better Homes and Gardens* dating back at least to the '60s.

Madeline touched all the furniture, the magazines, the lamp. Nothing.

In the small bathroom, she touched the sink, bathtub, shower curtain, toilet. No images.

She moved into the last room, a small bedroom with a bed, dresser, and wooden writing desk with a lamp. Noah lingered in the doorway while she ran her fingers gingerly over the dresser's smooth surface, then the writing desk and lamp. Finally she moved to the bed. It was unmade, recently slept in, the dark green comforter spilling over the bed and onto the floor. The sheets looked new or nearly new; they still had creases in them where they had been folded at the factory. A deep maroon, they weren't the kind of cheap linens that rental places normally stocked. She reached down gently and brushed her hand over the soft cotton of the sheets. Immediately, powerful images swept over her.

The creature, in human form, dark wavy hair spilling about his shoulders, bare olive skin pressed against the sheets, asleep . . .

Still in human form, gasping, nightmare about the black, terrible void, awake, sitting up quickly, glancing about the room . . .

Rising, pacing, staring out the window into the moonlit forest beyond . . .

Falling back on the sheets, sighing, twisting in the covers, moaning, thinking about . . . thinking about . . . Madeline . . .

Quickly she pulled her hand away. Tentatively she reached down and touched the soft sheets again.

The creature in human form, naked and muscular, lounging on the bed, images of Madeline drifting in its thoughts, the scent of her hair, her skin . . . the creature's tongue licking its lips, wanting to taste her . . . then gazing outside at the moon, at the dark silhouettes of the pines against drifting clouds set aglow by the moonlight . . . where was she . . . out there . . . right now . . .

She could feel his thoughts, his need, his desire for her. He wasn't planning on killing her. Not anymore. But he had picked out no future victim because he wasn't finished with her yet.

Madeline wrenched her hand away as if it had been burned.

"What is it?" Noah asked from the doorway, startling her. For a moment, she'd forgotten he was standing there, forgotten where she was, had only felt the creature.

"We have to get out of here now."

"Why? What is it?"

She hurried toward the bedroom door and pushed past him.

"Did you find out who his next victim is?"

She turned, shook her head. "He hasn't chosen one yet. But I can tell you this: it won't be me."

"I know it won't. I won't let him hurt you."

She shook her head. "No, it's not that . . . he doesn't want to kill me anymore."

"What?" Noah's mouth fell open.

"I can't explain it, but he's lost interest in killing me." Madeline couldn't bring herself to say the rest. She felt strange, her mouth heavy and dry, her heart hammering away. What could she say? That the thing lusted for her? That it had some new plan? She just wanted to get away from that remote cabin, return to the civilization of Lake McDonald, and get her car and get out of there. There was nothing she could do right now; until it picked its next victim, she wouldn't be able to get any helpful images. Later, when the creature chose a new victim and she happened to touch something of its then, she could inform the police with the specifics.

But right now, they had the information they'd come there for, and more than anything, she wanted to leave.

"I'll tell you about it on the way," she said. "Let's get back to your Jeep." An image flashed in her mind of the creature entering the cabin, sliding up to her from behind, wrapping its powerful arms around her and crushing her, her ribs snapping and piercing through her skin. She glanced around, saw the empty sitting room and backed up to the front door. "Coming?" she asked, a little too impatiently.

He met her at the front door, and they exited, Noah closing the door after them and locking it.

Once outside, she moved toward the Jeep and noticed something glide fluidly by the back window, then emerge on the side of the car: an inky, nonreflective mass of black among the shiny black paint of the Jeep. The black straightened up, blocking out the grill.

"Madeline," said the shadow, "I hoped you'd come."

13

MADELINE froze in the doorway, Noah behind her, her heart thudding in her chest.

The creature stepped away from the Jeep, the pure inky black of its body suddenly shifting and slipping over its bones in a flurry of movement. Human skin snaked over his body in a matter of seconds; if Madeline had blinked, she would have missed the transformation. Long, wavy black hair cascaded from the head, framing a handsome olive-skinned face, the same face that had stared down at her during the wildfire.

Noah suddenly pushed past her, stepping out into the sunlight before the creature. "Stefan."

"Noah," the creature answered.

Both stood still, glaring, the tension so thick that Madeline found herself staring on morbidly, wondering what would happen. It was the first time she'd really seen them together, steadfast hunter and ancient enemy.

"I see you've found my little hideaway," Stefan said. He turned to Madeline then. "And you've been going through my things . . . seeing what images you can get. My intentions, perhaps? My next victim?" He raised one dark eyebrow, his eyes flashing again, momentarily burning her retina. "Did you learn anything . . . interesting? Have any visions that were particularly stirring?"

He was playing with her. She knew that. Her face wouldn't behave, either; she tried to remain stoic, to not reveal that she'd seen the images of him writhing, thinking of her. But instead her features started to fall apart; her brow crinkled, her mouth turned down at the corners, her eyes blinked rapidly. The creature held her gaze, eyes running through her, into her.

If Noah noticed this nonverbal exchange, he didn't let on. Instead he slung his day pack off his shoulder and unzipped it quickly.

Then one moment Stefan was still by the Jeep, and the next he was latched on to Noah, legs locked around Noah's waist and tremendous, extended claws trying to get at his throat while Noah blocked the blows.

"Noah!" Madeline yelled as he toppled backward, slamming against the side of the cabin. The day pack slumped to the ground, and Madeline ran toward it. She knew what he had been going for: the dagger.

The creature moved swiftly, tearing a bloody gash into Noah's neck. Then it let go and leapt to the ground, its feet no longer human but clawed and elongated. As Madeline grabbed for the day pack, he swiped it up deftly before she could reach it and flung it violently toward the forest beyond. Its arc in the sky was tremendous, so high she lost track of it in the branches. She kept running and slammed into Stefan, who toppled to the ground next to Noah. She scrambled to her feet, dry pine needles jabbing her hands. Stefan leapt up on muscular legs and faced her.

Noah moaned on the ground, grasping his neck as blood trickled through his fingers. The wound wasn't bleeding as much as she had expected. A tense silence followed while she waited for the creature's next move. Maybe if she ran now, she could hunt for the pack, find the dagger, and kill him.

They couldn't fight him without the weapon. Stefan stood between them, his arms slightly outstretched, ready to leap in either direction. Darting to the side, she took off toward the trees, ready to hear the pounding of his footsteps behind her. She ran, kicking up dry soil in her wake, plumes of dust and pine needles. The ground beneath her blurred, dry mountain air stinging her eyes. Not able to hear over her own labored breathing, she chanced a look back.

He wasn't following her. Instead, he had turned back to Noah, standing menacingly over his prone body. She had to find the knife.

Madeline ran toward the shadow of the forest, scanning the ground as she went. She entered the treeline, running and scanning quickly. Every dark lump looked like the day pack but turned out to be a shadowed stump or log. Glancing around at the tree limbs, she made sure the pack wasn't dangling from a branch above her.

She spotted it then, some twenty feet away next to a fallen tree. She snatched it up, then turned back. In the clearing before the cabin, she rummaged through its contents and came up with the knife.

She broke from the treeline, making a straight line for the cabin. But now she didn't see the creature or Noah. She raced to the door, fell panting against the wall, and searched the area for signs of any movement or struggle. She saw none and heard no sound except her own laborious breathing.

She burst through the door, then, knife gripped tightly in her hand. The kitchen was empty. So were the bedroom the bathroom. She left the cabin, running around its perimeter. The back door lay off its hinges, tilted to one side in the doorframe.

They were gone.

On the wind she heard a long, strangled cry, and her gut sank, churning with fear.

14

MADELINE stopped, listening in the ensuing silence for the direction of the cry, hoping for another. Only the sigh of wind in the pines met her ears. The cry of a distant hawk. A creek gurgling nearby. She thought of calling out for Noah but was afraid to give her position away to the creature. Instead, she crept silently around the perimeter of the cabin again, gripping the knife in one hand.

She hoped that Noah had successfully driven the creature away, but her gut knew Noah was no match for the creature. Without the dagger, the most he could hope for would be to knock it unconscious and run away. With a chill she thought of the men who had attacked her, of the gleaming, silver spike that the creature had summoned, driving it deep into their flesh.

She searched the entire area, moving in bigger and bigger circles radiating out from the cabin. She thought the cry had come from the north and searched longer in that direction, but to no avail. An hour passed, then two. She covered every foot of the surrounding area. Sweat clung to her body, stinging her eyes.

If Noah had been successful, even in knocking the creature out, he would have been back by now. She had to get help, get a rescue team going. Right then he could be lying helpless, bleeding to death while she searched fruitlessly.

She returned to the cabin and to Noah's Jeep, flinging the door open. No keys. She was sure he had them in his pockets, but she just wanted to be certain. Quickly she checked the visors, under the seat, the glove compartment, and finally under the Jeep itself to see if he had a spare. No luck.

For a moment she frowned, looking at the steering column of the Jeep. In movies, criminals just touched two wires together and *spark!* They were on their way. She gazed at the tangle of cords hanging from the steering column, a rainbow of twisted cords bound together with small plastic clips. She had no idea which two would start the car if she touched them together. For a second she considered just ripping them all out and touching them all together until she found the right combination, but she thought that might just take the Jeep out of commission completely.

The nearest cabin lay two miles down the road, but when they'd passed it earlier, it showed no signs of occupation. And she knew it wouldn't have a phone. The dirt road meandered for miles through the forest before rejoining North Fork Road on the outskirts of the park. She knew there'd be faster, more direct trails than sticking to the winding road.

At last a terrible wave of déjà vu washed over her as she realized she was going to have to hike down. She couldn't just wait here for Noah and hope he came back. She couldn't be sure that he wasn't lying far away somewhere, wounded, or worse. If she was going to get help, she had to do it now.

Putting the driver's seat forward, she rummaged in the back of the Jeep, pulling out Noah's huge backcountry pack. She could hike out without it, she knew, but there were a few supplies she didn't want to be without. Laying it out on the ground, she unzipped the main compartment. From inside she took the map, a compass, two bottles of water, five mint-chocolate Genisoy protein bars, a purple and black Gore-Tex raincoat, Noah's fleece jacket, and a baseball hat that read

"Banff National Park" above the bill. These she stuffed in the day pack along with a flashlight, and zipped it up. She kept the knife in one hand. Quickly she returned the huge pack to the Jeep and shut the door. Hunkering down beside the car so she'd have at least a little cover, Madeline opened up the backcountry map and studied it.

In a few moments she'd located her position: a graded dirt road that ran from North Fork Road up a ridgeline. She was about thirty miles from the west entrance of Glacier National Park if she took the road. She shook her head. That would take too long. Way too long. She'd have to spend the night out, possibly two. She studied the map closer, and found a nearby trail that cut down into a valley and led to the Polebridge Ranger Station. According to the map, it was a mere 7.5-mile trek to the station, almost all of it downhill. She stood up, slinging the day pack over her shoulders.

According to the map, to the west the trail came within four hundred feet of the graded dirt road. She hiked in that direction, crossing the front yard of the cabin and entering the treeline beyond. Trying to stay in as straight a line as possible, she wove between pines and stepped over logs, avoiding thorny brambles.

The sky rumbled, and a few moments later rain erupted, trickling down through the trees. She paused, pulling out the rain gear and donning the parka.

"Madeline!" A sudden voice crashed in through the quiet pitter-patter of rain on her hood. She turned back around, trying to find the source of the voice. "Madeline!" shouted the voice again. Noah.

"Noah?" she called out, taking the hood down so she could see better.

"It is you!" Peering through the trees, she saw movement back at the Jeep. He ran out from behind it.

When she saw his face as he grew closer, Madeline cringed. One eye was completely swollen shut, the rest of his face bruised and cut. Blood wept freely from the gash in his neck as he hobbled quickly toward her with a painful-looking limp.

"Noah!" she cried, running toward him. Even closer, she saw the full scope of his injuries: a terrible slash in his stomach; blood soaked through the tear in his shirt; ragged, torn skin exposed beneath. A similar gash along one thigh had torn through his jeans. Through it Madeline saw muscle and the white gleaming of bone.

"It's nothing," he breathed, wrapping his arms around her. "I'm just glad you're alive."

"Nothing!" she said in disbelief.

"I'll heal," he said simply. "You should have seen this an hour ago. I could see my own bone marrow."

She winced.

"How are you?"

"I'm fine," she reassured him, feeling the slick of his sweat beneath her fingers as she hugged him back.

"But . . . I don't understand." He pulled away. "Didn't he come after you? Didn't he find you?"

She shook her head. "No."

"But—" Noah shook his head, looked down. Ran a hand over his face, wiping blood out of his eye. "I don't understand. Why wouldn't he come after you?"

Madeline had no idea why. She stood there silently. "What happened?"

After a moment, Noah looked back up at her. "We fought, but I didn't have the knife, so it wasn't much of a struggle."

She cut in. "I found the pack and came back with the knife, but I couldn't find you."

"I'm glad you've still got it. We crashed through the cabin, ended up breaking through the back door. I took off down a path in the back. He came after me . . ." His voice trailed off.

"Go on."

"He gave me one hell of a swipe to the head. I went unconscious. As I faded out, I heard him move off in your direction." He looked down her intently. "I thought he'd get you for sure."

"Well, if he had come after me, I would have been ready." She thought of the knife lying safe in the backpack.

"Damn, you're tough." He held her again, but she didn't feel so tough. She was scared. Damn scared.

"So where do you think he is now?" she asked, hugging him again, placing her head on his shoulder.

They parted. "I don't know. But I think we should get out of here. Fast."

"I'm with you on that." She looked around at the deepening shadows, wondering what they hid. "Let's go."

As they walked to the car, he asked her, "Where were you going?"

She shrugged. "To hike out."

"Just like old times, eh?" he laughed.

"I wasn't looking forward to the seven-mile hike back. As much as I love hiking, fleeing down a mountainside because I'm in mortal peril is getting really old." She paused. Then, looking around she said, "Do you think he'll find us again? I mean, back at the cabin in Apgar?"

Noah gingerly touched the wound on his cheek. "At this point, I don't feel like we're safe anywhere."

She took in his injuries. "I think I should drive. You're in no shape. Do you have a first aid kit?"

He shook his head. "I think it's back at the cabin. But give me another hour. My leg and neck will be just fine."

She gazed at him in amazement. "Not even Neosporin?"

He laughed.

Noah opened the doors to the Jeep, Madeline checking the back end about five times before she was convinced the creature wasn't in there,

"It's not back there," Noah said finally. "Really. I don't think it can change into a box of snow chains. At least, not a very convincing box of snow chains."

She raised her eyebrows. "You're the expert." Hefting herself into the Jeep, she said, "Are you coming or what?"

Noah shook his head, a bemused smile on his lips as he climbed into the passenger seat of the Jeep.

"Should we return to our cabin?" she asked.

"It's too late to go anywhere else tonight." After a long

pause, he added, "Are you going home now? I mean, now that you say you aren't in danger?"

Madeline climbed into the driver's seat quietly, resisting the urge to say yes. She was a changed person when it came to her gift. At least, she was trying to be. Finally she shook her head. "No," she said at last. "I told you I'd help you track him, and that's exactly what I'm going to do."

Suddenly reality dawned upon her. She thought of the centuries Noah had been tirelessly tracking the creature. He still hadn't succeeded in killing him. Classes started in San Francisco in just two months. This was her chance at a normal college life. What was she supposed to do? Postpone classes? She stopped that train of thought. They had two months. Two whole months. And there was a difference now. Until now Noah didn't have her gift aiding him. Now they would know where the creature was. And for now, she knew it would stay close to her, at least until it chose its next victim.

"I'm starving," he said suddenly, cutting into her thoughts. "Are you hungry?"

She nodded.

"There's got to be someplace to eat near the campground."

"No cheese and crackers tonight?"

He shook his head. "There's a diner out on Route 2. Great omelets."

Her stomach grumbled at the thought of it.

"But don't you even want to clean the cuts?"

"That's what restaurant bathrooms are for."

"Of course." She threw the Jeep in gear.

At the diner, a rotund waitress in a burgundy apron and large-collared white dress seated them by a window. The diner was of '50s cinder-block construction, the exterior painted utilitarian gray like an old bomb shelter. Heck, maybe it was one, Madeline thought. But she didn't care. She was starving.

Bright neon signs in the window advertised a Breakfast Special and four kinds of beer.

Inside, attempts at cheery decoration included enough plastic flowers and plants to open their own craft store, and vases at every table held genuine carnations in reds, pinks, and whites.

They sat down in a vinyl-seated booth, the material creaking as they squeezed in.

The waitress, after giving Noah a long, disdainful look, as if he'd been out picking fights in the local bars, gave them each a menu and walked away. Noah excused himself for the men's room and returned ten minutes later, looking infinitely better. He was right; he healed fast. Already the swelling in his eye had receded, and he could now open both eyes. The wounds in his neck and stomach were mere scratches, and the gash in his leg had almost closed completely, just a thin, red line visible through the tear in his jeans.

They made small talk while they glanced at the menu, resuming again after the waitress took their order. Noah looked nervous, glancing out of the large windows now and again at the darkened parking lot. When he wasn't doing that, he studied her intently as she sipped the steaming cup of coffee that tasted like two-day-old peanut shells soaked in hot water. For once he seemed at a loss for words and kept unusually quiet as they munched on their omelets and steaming French toast drenched in maple syrup.

She glanced around at the other customers, most of them middle-aged men and women wearing ranchers' clothes: worn overalls, warm corduroy shirts, and almost all the men in wide-brimmed cowboy hats. She loved that none of them stared at her or whispered surreptitiously. She was a total stranger here.

Country music played softly from a tinny speaker above them. A man sang about his "girl" in a mournful voice, crooning that he would have loved her forever, even if it took all night.

An electronic bell chimed as another customer entered the

diner. Madeline turned to look at him and froze. It was Steve, the naturalist.

Or something pretending to be Steve.

He walked in, giving the waitress an easy smile and removed his ranger's hat. With one hand he fluffed his sandy brown hair to get rid of his hat hair and began following her to a table on the other side of the restaurant. He walked with a bad limp.

Madeline dipped her head low so the creature wouldn't see her and turned to Noah.

"Noah!" she said low, urgently.

He looked up in midsip. "What is it?"

"Stefan!" she whispered.

Noah started, coffee spilling over the table. He winced as it burned his hand, then put the cup down. "Where?"

"Over there." She gestured with her head. "He's being seated, impersonating Steve. Just like he did when he wrecked his car." When Noah remained silent, she went on. "That can't be Steve. You said the creature could only appear as someone it had killed, so what I saw that night in the ditch, the creature imitating Steve, must mean that he had killed him earlier that night."

Noah wrinkled his brow. "Only look like someone he's killed?"

She nodded. "Right?"

Noah swallowed hard. "Right."

"What's wrong?"

"It's just," he cleared his throat, looking over at Steve. "Just so many victims."

"What should we do?" she asked, leaning closer to him across the table. "Confront him? Jump him in the restroom?"

"We shouldn't let him see us. Let's just leave."

Madeline's jaw dropped. "What?"

Noah just stared back at her.

"But you've been waiting for this opportunity. Let's lure him outside and tackle him."

Suddenly, as she watched him from across the table, he ducked his head low and turned it toward the window.

"What is it?" she whispered.

"He's coming over here."

"What?" Fear flopped in her stomach. She turned slowly. "Steve" was walking quickly toward their table.

"Madeline!" he said. "I can't believe it's you. I saw you from across the restaurant. Thought you'd be gone by now!" He continued toward her, limping severely. She sat transfixed, watching him approach. To her amazement, he walked right up to the table. "Can I sit down? My leg's killing me. And I have to talk to you. You won't believe what's happened."

Her mouth went dry. Her limbs felt heavy as sledgehammers, and still she sat, immobile, as she watched him. Here he was, the creature, in the middle of this well-lit diner, talking to her as if nothing was wrong. His gall was unbelievable.

She was blocked into the booth, "Steve" standing in her exit path. Noah just sat there silently, his face unreadable, almost frozen.

And then, to her amazement, Noah scooted over and offered "Steve" a seat.

"Thanks a lot, man," he responded, and plunked down next to him in the booth.

The thing pretending to be a naturalist leaned across the table and whispered to her. "You won't believe what happened. I never should have doubted you!"

She listened, half-dumbfounded by Noah's behavior and half trying to figure out how she could make it out to the Jeep to grab the backpack and the weapon.

"Steve" continued talking. "So last night, after I dropped you off, I kept on toward Missoula. I wasn't two miles away when all of a sudden I see this dark shape standing at the edge of the treeline. At first it's upright, like the shadow of a man just at the edge of the road. Then, as I get a little closer, it drops down on all fours. My headlights lit it up. It charged straight for my car."

He fell silent and glanced around at the other tables to see if anyone was listening. They weren't. Above him the speaker piped out a sad ballad about a dejected man who would do anything to get his lady back. Madeline was beginning to notice a pattern.

"It rammed into my car. Full tilt. Smash. Completely creamed the driver's side. I swerved off the road and into a ditch. The thing came around and opened the passenger door, started climbing in. It was terrifying: absolutely inky black and featureless, more like a shadow than a living thing. But it had eyes—I'll never forget them; huge red saucer eyes—and a mouth full of pointed teeth. It tore a huge gash in my leg.

"I pulled out my shotgun and shot it. Two times at point-blank range. Right in the head and chest. It let out this howl and flew back into the ditch. I reloaded, hit it again. I tried to get out of my side of the car but couldn't. I could already smell gas spilling out, so I quickly climbed out of the passenger side." He looked around again. No one was even glancing over at them. "And can you believe that thing started to get up? I reloaded and fired the rest of my rounds into its chest and ran like hell."

She watched him as he talked. His voice, mannerisms, eyes, all seemed like Steve. She hadn't known the naturalist for very long, but even still, she'd felt a kinship with him. They read the same books. Had similar interests and beliefs. Some people you just liked right away and felt a strong connection to. Steve had been one of those people. Suddenly she was starting to have doubts that this was in fact the creature.

"It's got to be the same thing you saw, right?"

She didn't answer.

He continued. "I hiked for a long time, my leg killing me, and eventually reached this ranger's residence. We radioed for backup. But when we got back there, my car had exploded and burned through a meadow on the side of the road. There was no sign of the creature. No body. No remains. Just the smoldering meadow and strewn car parts."

She looked at Noah, who was listening intently to the ranger. "What happened then?" he asked.

Steve shrugged. "An EMT fixed my leg. I got stitches and some codeine. Went back to my cabin." He regarded Madeline intently. "And regretted not doing more to help you," he added.

"You were plenty of help," she said, leaning even more toward believing him.

"Why didn't you get the hell away from here?" Steve asked.

She stared at Noah. "I thought I could help," she said finally. Reaching across the table, she squeezed Noah's hand. He seemed surprised, but then he squeezed her hand back.

She suddenly thought of a way she could know for sure. She looked uncertainly across the table at the naturalist. "Could I see where it scratched you?" she asked.

Steve raised his eyebrows in shock. "Well, I wouldn't call it 'scratched,' more like 'took a chunk out of my leg.' What, are you into the gory stuff? Shark victims, bear attacks, that kind of thing?"

She shook her head. "It would just put my mind to rest about something." If this was actually Steve, then the wound would still look fresh.

Steve shrugged. "Okay," he said finally. "But you probably want to finish your dinner first."

Just then the waitress approached and set a steaming cup of coffee in front of Steve. "Just want to sit here, hon?"

"Sure," he said, then looked at Noah and Madeline. "If that's okay with you two."

"Oh, perfectly," Noah said, trying to make him feel at ease.

Madeline found she couldn't eat another bite of omelet until she knew for sure if the person at their table was her new friend or her relentless pursuer.

At her insistence, the three of them went out to the parking lot. Steve wore the kind of pants that zipped off into shorts, and he zipped off the bottom half of the left pant leg. Pulling the leg up, he revealed a blood-soaked bandage covering his thigh. Gently he peeled away the white first aid tape on one side and revealed a hideously long gash in his thigh. Brown stitches, over thirty total, ran the course of the wound, which seeped blood at the edges.

Gasping, Madeline took in the severity of the wound, sucking in breath and wincing.

Noah gave a long, low whistle.

"Satisfied?" Steve asked, grimacing as he replaced the bandage.

Noah nodded.

Madeline still wasn't sure. She guessed it could fake a wound, too. She said, "Now give me something personal."

"I beg your pardon?"

"Like your watch or a piece of jewelry."

"What, are you robbing me now, too?"

"Seriously."

After a pause, during which he scrutinized her, he said, "Okay." He reached into his pocket and pulled out a half dollar. "My grandpa gave it to me. Good luck charm."

She grasped the coin tightly and let images come to her.

An older man with a kind face sitting in a blanket-covered chair telling a story . . .

Steve and the woman she'd seen before in the vision from his couch, kissing passionately . . .

Steve hiking along a road in the dark, leg in agony . . .

Steve arriving back at the scene of the fire with backup . . .

This was Steve. She handed the coin back.

"Mind telling me why that was necessary?"

"The creature can—" Madeline began, but was cut off by Noah.

"The creature's scratches can be poisonous. But it doesn't look like he infected you."

Madeline looked at Noah in bewilderment.

Steve sighed. "Well, big thanks for small miracles." Then he looked at Madeline with concern. "But that thing—twelve rounds right into his chest and head. No effect but to stun him. You need to get away from here, Madeline. Get in your car right now and get the hell away."

His words chilled her as the three stood out in the shad-

owed parking lot. Once again she felt vulnerable, uncertain.
Ironically, thinking the creature was right there in the diner
with them had almost been preferable to having no idea where
it actually was. It could be waiting anywhere, hoping to catch
her alone. She shuddered against the chill of the evening.

"Let's get back inside," she said.

The other two nodded, and they turned their backs to the
night, returning to the diner and its cheerful plastic flowers.

Their food had gone cold.

After they ate, and after much debate in the parking lot, Steve
went back to his cabin, and Noah and Madeline returned to
their own. Noah had tried to convince Steve not to get involved, though the ranger was already in it to some extent, as
he had to write up a report about his car. "The other rangers
seemed to think it was a grizzly," he had explained. "They've
been known to take a gunshot and keep moving."

"What do you think?" Noah had asked, keeping mum
about the true nature of the creature.

Steve had shaken his head. "I don't know. But whatever it
is, it's no damn grizzly. It's something otherworldly. And
something lethal."

Noah had nodded, and Madeline and he said no more.
Steve said some armed rangers were doing sweeps of the area
to see what they could turn up.

Back at their cabin in Apgar, Madeline went through the
ritual of checking windows and doors about six times. She
was still hungry, even after their cold, slimy omelets, which
were definitely not "great" as Noah had claimed before. Neither had eaten much of theirs, deciding to pick up something
else on the way home.

Noah had gotten them sandwiches at the little camp store.
Madeline believed hers was tuna salad but wasn't entirely convinced. Noah's, on the other hand, was clearly ham, or possibly
turkey. They munched on the flabby white bread, which was
soaked with a white, tangy, unnamed sandwich dressing, and
chewed at the wilted lettuce bits. It wasn't the best meal she'd

ever had, but it was at least better than the grease-laden omelet.

Already the bruises on Noah's face had faded, and she
could only see them because she knew where to look. The cuts
on his neck and stomach had completely closed, and the gash
on his leg was nothing more than the faintest red line.

"Your healing powers are amazing."

He nodded. "One of the benefits." He grimaced at the
food. "This isn't very satisfying. What a bad night for food.
Nothing seems to taste very good." After a moment, his face
brightened. "Say! What if we rob one of those metal bear
lockers that campers are required to put their food in?"

She stared at him in wonder, sandwich wilting in her hand,
the tuna dripping onto the table, looking for an easy route
back to the sea.

"Hey, it's dark. We could be sneaky! There are probably
hot dogs, Cheetos, you name it!"

She raised an eyebrow. "Do you really want to be awakened by little Billy wailing at six in the morning because
someone with clearly sketchy morality has absconded his
Cheetos?"

Noah frowned, harrumphed, then bit into his soggy sandwich. "I guess not," he mumbled.

She chewed on hers awhile longer, finished it, and licked
her fingers. "Well, I'm ready for those Cheetos now."

Noah stared back at her.

"Well?" She crossed her legs and looked at him impatiently.

"No, no," Noah said, waving a dismissive hand at her. "I'm
a reformed man now. Can't stoop to having 'sketchy morality.'"

"Me and my big mouth." She looked down at her hands.
"And I was already looking forward to Day-Glo orange fingers."

He looked away, chin up, a superior gleam in his eye. "As
attractive as that sounds, you will not be able to corrupt me."

"Shoot."

He looked at her then, closely and intensely, his smile fading completely. "It's amazing you can be high-spirited in such serious danger."

She gave a slight shrug. "Sometimes you have to be or you'd go crazy. At this point, I guess I'm too exhausted to be terrified."

He nodded. "I know what you mean." He smiled again. "Thanks. I haven't laughed in a long time."

She nodded. "Me, neither. What an intense couple of days this has been."

"I'll say."

She regarded him with interest. "This must be normal for you, living your life on the run, always in danger."

He looked away, out of the window. "I suppose I am on the move a lot. But I kind of like the danger."

She laughed. "Are you kidding? I'm so stressed out I keep catching myself clenching my teeth. You actually like this?"

He looked back at her, eyes glittering. "A little bit," he admitted. "Though I don't appreciate being hunted."

She thought of the creature out there, prowling, perhaps even now back on their trail.

"Nor do I," she responded.

"Well, I don't think you have to worry about that anymore."

Her brow crinkled. "You mean you think he's given up now? Before, you wouldn't agree. What changed your mind?"

"I wouldn't say he's given up, but I think if he was dead set on killing you, he'd have tried by now."

"Tried?" she snorted. "I think he already has . . . dragging me down in the freezing water, chasing me down the mountain in the dead of night, almost getting me barbecued in that meadow—"

"Maybe he wasn't trying to drown you in the river. Maybe he was frantic and clutched on to you in panic."

She stared at him in wonder.

"I mean," he added quickly, "his MO is to eat people, not drown them."

"I guess you have a point," she conceded, though she felt

sick at the thought of the river and that thing's claws holding her fast underwater.

"Sorry if I upset you."

"No, no," she said, shaking her head. "I'm just shaken up, I guess."

"Understandably." He leaned over and held her, a comforting hug that made her feel some solace. She was glad he was there. Resting her head on his shoulder, she realized how good he smelled. He noticed her breathing him in and smiled.

"Well, I guess we should clean this stuff up," she said, pulling away.

He still smiled, straightening up. "I'll do it."

She stood up, and he instantly rose to his feet, moving so quickly she didn't see him do it.

His eyes glittered with energy. They stood only a foot apart. The tension hung between them, palpable, lingering. He reached out and touched her arm, caressing down from her shoulder to her wrist, then back up, across her collarbone to her bare neck, his hand warm against her skin there.

His fingers caressed her jawline, and she relished the sensation, closing her eyes momentarily to the arousing caress. He brought his other hand up, stroking her other arm and shoulder, till both hands curled around her neck. He stepped closer. She drank in every sensation.

His thigh moved forward, brushing hers. She shifted her leg so they continued to touch, thigh to thigh. He studied her intently, green eyes roaming over every feature of her face. Then he leaned in, pressing his cheek against hers, the rough of his whiskers gently brushing her skin. He radiated warmth, giving off an enticing scent she couldn't place.

He inhaled deeply, lips tracing over her cheekbone to her jaw, then down to her chin, her neck. She sighed when he reached the sensitive skin there, and she leaned against the table to steady herself.

Still he breathed her in, mouth moving to her neck. His fingers found the collar of her shirt, and he pulled it down slightly, exposing a collarbone. His lips brushed along it, tongue darting out briefly to taste her, her skin humming to his touch.

Reaching out, she grasped his arm, pulled him still closer, stroking down the muscles between his shoulder blades.

And she could smell him deeply now, his skin, his hair. It was different somehow, the oils of his skin more fragrant, alluring. He turned his head to face her, their lips mere inches apart. She could almost feel his spirit tugging at her, an invisible force drawing her closer, irresistible and intoxicating. Her lips felt hot, engorged with desire.

But Noah didn't draw closer. He stayed that inch away, eyes melting into her. She leaned a fraction closer, and he sealed the distance, pressing his lips against hers with such feverish passion that a well of electricity surged through her stomach.

His hand laced through her hair, cradling her head. He kissed her deeply, passionately, his tongue darting out to meet hers. He tasted exquisite, like some rich, tropical fruit. The tip of his tongue carried an electric charge when it entwined with her own.

It hadn't been like this the first time they kissed.

His lips moved from her mouth to her chin, strong kisses then moving along her neck. He tilted her head to the side as his tongue flickered luxuriantly over her skin there. Then his arms wrapped around her tightly, pulling her away from the table as his teeth grazed her skin and then sank in—not painfully, not breaking the skin, but passionately pressing against the muscles there while his tongue caressed her. Involuntarily, her eyes rolled back in her head in ecstasy as he moved to the other side of her neck, sensually biting and kissing her there.

She gripped his arms, his muscles taut from holding her, and gasped with pleasure.

His strong hands caressed down her back, across her stomach, up her arms. His lips returned to hers, and once again she tasted that sweet, delicious taste and breathed in his intoxicating scent.

Swaying, he moved his hips against hers. Their pelvises

pressed together, she could feel him, hot and erect, through his jeans. Turning her hips, she pressed against him, and he sighed with pleasure.

She breathed in deeply, his alluring aroma making her head sing and feel warm with desire. Had he smelled this good before? Something was so different . . . so incredibly alluring. She felt light, swept away, heady and almost swooning. Her body sang at his touch, longing for his hands to roam over her.

"Madeline," he breathed between kisses, sighing her name. "You taste so good. Better than I imagined. Better than anything . . . this way."

His hands ran down her sides to her hips, Madeline thrumming on a wave of desire. Her lips left his, and she kissed along his jawline to his neck, his skin tasting of something exotic she couldn't quite place. Vanilla? He tasted incredible. She wanted to devour him. Gently she licked along his neck, then bit him gently, eliciting a moan from him. She released, then bit him gently again, lower, by his collarbone, and this time he growled, his fingers curling into her.

The growl was deep and throaty, and she wondered if he was changing again. But when she gazed up, he was the same Noah, piercing green eyes meeting her own.

"I'm on fire," he said. "Kiss me."

She did, and he lifted her up, hooking his hands under her thighs while she straddled him. He carried her over into the bedroom and threw her down on the bed, landing on his knees between her thighs. His strong hands stroked the length of her legs, and then he sprang forward, arms supporting him mere inches above her. She longed for their bodies to touch. He lowered his lips, kissing her deeply, and then lowered the rest of his body, pressing down on her, writhing sensually.

"Madeline," she heard him say, though it felt as if he was saying it from some far-off place.

An intense, deep wave crashed over itself inside her belly. Though they were still fully clothed, she felt desire like she had never known, her lips tingling, burning; her stomach rolling in on powerful waves; her chest heaving; her eyes closing with pleasure. She breathed him in, savoring every sensation. Her heart pounded so loudly it felt like it reverberated about the room.

"You feel . . . different . . ." she breathed out.

He stopped kissing her and studied her intently. "Do I?"

She nodded.

He remained staring down at her, his green eyes flashing briefly. Something in those eyes was hauntingly familiar, and yet she couldn't quite place it. He stared at her, intrigued, looking into her. It wasn't the way Noah normally looked at her. His smell, his taste, his kiss, all of it was so different. He *looked* like Noah, but—

Inside, the waves of passion turned to ice. She pushed at him, rolling out from under him while he continued to watch her, transfixed. "It's you," she breathed.

He watched her move away. "I've traveled for so long," he said, reaching his hand out to her. "You can see the journey I've had. You could know me. Without me saying a word."

The pounding continued. She realized now, separated from him, that it wasn't just her heart. It was the door. Someone was there, desperately wanting in.

"Madeline!" Her name. From far off. It hadn't been uttered moments ago by the creature at all but by the real Noah on the other side of the door.

She leapt up, the creature propping himself up to watch her, looking so strikingly like Noah that suddenly she was uncertain again.

Quickly she reached the door, flung it open. Noah stood in the doorframe, chest heaving, face desperate and bruised.

"Thank the gods," he said, drawing her into his arms. "I thought he'd got you!" She clutched him tightly, breathing in his scent. Yes. This was Noah. The hint of sun protection, the wisp of cinnamon.

Then, looking up over her shoulder, he breathed, "What in the hell?"

She spun around. The false Noah stood there, framed in the bedroom doorway.

Behind her, Noah gasped. "But . . . am I dead?"

"No!" she said, not taking her eyes off the creature. "He can become anyone. Noah, you were wrong."

"Back so soon?" asked the false Noah.

Behind her, Noah shook with anger.

"After you tumbled into that ravine, I thought of sticking around to kill you, but," he looked at Madeline, "I had better things to do with my time." He sounded calm, assured, but his eyes held something else in their depths. Maybe sadness, she realized.

Noah was anything but calm. He stepped forward, neck veins bulging, "This is it! You die here!"

He pushed past her and launched into the air, colliding with the creature in the center of the room, a clumsy, rage-driven move that knocked the false Noah sprawling across the floor.

They tangled there violently as Madeline gawked, frozen. It was bizarre to see Noah and his doppelgänger roll across the floor, both wearing jeans and a black T-shirt. She moved in to help and suddenly realized she couldn't tell them apart, had completely lost track of the real Noah. Both even had identical tears in their jeans and T-shirts.

Then one of the Noahs met with a violent kick in the gut and rolled off to the side, momentarily unable to breathe. The other Noah leapt to his feet and ran to Madeline. She steeled herself, ready to punch him in the face if she needed to. "Where's the backpack?" he asked just as the other Noah rose from the floor and struck him in the head with an upraised fist. "Get the backpack!" he shrieked as he fell.

That had to be the real Noah. The creature wouldn't need the weapon to kill, but Noah would. Without taking her eyes off the real Noah, she backed up quickly, groping behind her for the backpack, which she'd tossed down when she entered the cabin.

As Noah struggled and kicked at his doppelgänger, Madeline's hand felt the wood of the chair, then the table, then the canvas of the pack. Desperately she grabbed it, unzipping it and shoving her hand inside. Her fingers closed around the cold metal of the dagger.

Dashing forward, knife in hand, she reached them just as the creature gained the advantage again and flipped Noah over on his back. She raised the knife and thrusting forward, drove it deeply into the creature's kidneys. Howling in agony, he twisted and sprang up, trying to grab at the blade there, wrenching it out of Madeline's grasp as he stood.

But Noah was too fast. In an instant he was on his feet, grabbing the handle of the dagger. With a sharp tug, he slid it out of his twin's back and then brought it forward again as the creature dodged. The blade connected with Stefan's cheekbone. A red gash opened in his face, streaming with blood.

Staggering backward, Stefan brought a hand to his slashed face, eyes bewildered. And there was something else, too: fear, Madeline realized. For the first time, he was afraid.

"So this is what you meant earlier by the 'knife,'" he gasped. "I can see why you were so eager to have it." And then he started changing, Noah's features melting away into the visage of the same olive-skinned man she'd seen him take on before. Long black hair sprouted, taking the place of Noah's blond color, and fiendish claws replaced the fingernails on his hands.

Noah didn't stop, advancing on Stefan with clenched teeth and wild eyes. He struck out once, missed as the creature ducked, and then scored a hit just below Stefan's rib cage, ripping open a hole there as big as a football.

With his right arm, Stefan swung out, connecting with Noah's throat and sending him spiraling back into the wall.

Hacking and gasping, Noah bounced off and surged right back, swinging the knife, darting it in and out like a striking cobra. She'd never seen him move so fast. He must have practiced this scene a thousand times, picturing his moment of triumph.

Noah whipped his foot out suddenly while Stefan's attention was transfixed on the moving blade. With a violent crash Stefan smashed to the floor as Noah's leg swept him off his feet. Losing no time, he closed in, leaping on top of Stefan and stabbing the blade deep into his throat. Then, using both hands, he drew the blade across, ripping open a seven-inch weeping gash in the creature's exposed neck. Blood gurgled and bubbled in the wound as Stefan tried to breathe, his eyes full of terror.

In a frenzy of rage, Noah withdrew the blade and struck over and over again, puncturing Stefan's chest, stomach, neck, and face. Crying in gleeful ululation as each blow landed home, he sent up a spatter of fresh, warm blood with each wound. The creature raised his arms defensively in an attempt to block Noah's blows, blood pooling on the floor, seeping ever closer to where Madeline stood transfixed.

She darted in to help Noah.

And then something terrible happened.

Stefan jolted his hip, hitting Noah and knocking him off balance. The creature turned, twisted, and rose to his knees, grabbing the blade of the knife with both hands. Not as strong as the creature, Noah struggled to maintain a hold on the knife as Stefan whipped it around violently in his grasp.

Then the creature's left hand changed from flesh to metal, the same spike he'd used to destroy her attackers. The flashing metal touched the metal of the blade, melting and seeping over it. Instantly the blade changed form, bursting from Noah's grip. The creature pushed away from Noah, rising to his feet. Where the blade joined the end of the metallic arm, it sprouted a finger, then four more, joining seamlessly with the creature's arm until it was a hand.

Howling in agony, Stefan staggered backward, slamming against the wall. The metal hand grew flesh, fingernails. Chest soaked with blood, throat streaming red to the floor, the creature gasped and sputtered, staring at Noah through tearing eyes. "Thanks," he growled. "I've been missing that part for a long time."

Noah stood up, then froze, staring at the creature running free with blood.

Stefan staggered toward Noah and spat in his face, "I'm coming back for you. And I will kill you."

Then he pivoted, turning toward Madeline. She gasped when she saw him look at her, eyes dark with pain, face smeared in scarlet, deep knife holes in his cheeks, revealing sections of teeth and glistening blood-streaked bone. He stumbled toward her grimly, and she moved out of his way, hearing the sucking and laboring of his breathing. He was hurt badly, close to death.

But now they had no way to finish him.

Sliding in his own blood, he walked right by her to the front door and went through it.

She looked back at Noah. He was still frozen in the same spot but had turned to watch Stefan go. Madeline didn't know what to do. She thought of chasing after the creature, pounding on him until he stopped breathing so he couldn't claim any more victims. But she knew that wouldn't kill him. Noah had said they needed the weapon. And it was gone.

She glanced out the door. The creature was gone now, too.

"Noah," she said, turning back around. He gave no indication of hearing her.

"Noah," she said again softly.

Still he stood there, unblinking, unmoving.

And then he fell to his knees, a great eerie keening escaping his lips. He pressed his blood-soaked hands to his face and sobbed, a terrible long, helpless sound.

15

AFTER kneeling immobile for twenty minutes, deaf to Madeline, Noah staggered into the bedroom and collapsed on the bed. Sobbing, he rolled into a tight ball, his body shaking. Madeline went to him, sat next to him. Stroking his back soothingly, she said softly, "Noah . . . we'll think of something."

But he sobbed even harder at her words and shrugged away from her touch. Still she sat on the edge of the bed, watching his heaving and shaking body.

Mucus streamed from his nose, mingling with tears. Only occasionally he'd suck in a deep breath, shuddering, wheezing, and another great wail would explode from him. It was the kind of crying she hadn't done herself since she lost Ellie, the day she learned for the first time what death was.

She rose and retrieved a big wad of toilet paper from Noah's backpack. Placing it down by his hand, she stood over him, concerned. He pushed it away, mucus already soaking into the bedspread, streaming down his cheek and lips. His crying grew so loud she began to wonder if neighbors would call in complaints.

Then she sat down again, watching him. She sat there for a long time, and his crying only got worse. She didn't think it was possible for someone to cry for that long. She remembered how much her lungs and stomach had ached that day she'd cried for three hours straight.

She tried to talk to him, soothe him, murmur to him, hold him. Nothing helped. He stopped pushing her away and just lay there helplessly, limply, sobs convulsing his body. She lay down beside him. And then, after four hours, he simply stopped. He lay limply, his back to her. Madeline thought he might be asleep, but when she peered over his shoulder she found him staring fixedly at some point in the distance, his mind a million miles away.

"Noah?" she asked softly.

No response. He was far away.

Each breath shook his body, his lungs not yet recovered from the weeping. She continued to lie next to him, her arm cradling him, body spooning him. Soon she drifted off to sleep.

A little later she startled awake, lying next to Noah. He still lay in the same position, still staring at some fixed point in the distance. Her outburst hadn't even made him stir. His eyes, dry and bloodshot, didn't even blink. "Noah?" she asked.

No response.

She looked at his watch. Five hours had passed. Beyond the curtains, light gleamed.

"Noah." This time she shook him gently. His eyes slowly closed, but he said nothing. She decided she should leave him alone for a while, give him some space.

She rose, straightening her rumpled clothes. Quietly she picked through Noah's clothes and grabbed a clean turtleneck and a fresh pair of Noah's jeans. They were big on her, hanging low on her hips, but it was the only pair of clean pants she could find. In the front room, she scrubbed up as much of the creature's dried blood as she could, using a towel and water from Noah's water bottle. She couldn't get it all up, though, especially where it had seeped into the wood, creating a dark stain.

She was careful not to touch any of it.

After a brief, lukewarm shower in the camp bathroom, she stood in front of the steamy mirror brushing her teeth. Her cut looked a lot better, and she didn't think she needed a new bandage. She gently touched the cut and thought about Noah. If he was still lying there motionless when she finished, she'd go out and get them some food. Then she'd have to think of a plan.

They may have lost Noah's weapon, but she still had her ability to sense where the creature might be heading next. Was she no longer in danger? He certainly could have killed her yesterday, but he hadn't. Maybe he was just playing games as Noah said.

She rinsed, gathered up her things, and returned to the cabin. In the bedroom, Noah still lay motionless, his eyes still closed. But the rapid rate of his breathing let her know he wasn't sleeping.

She stared at him worriedly. Was he having a nervous breakdown? Or just a moment of futility? Maybe food would help. She didn't think he'd eaten since breakfast the day before.

She looked at his watch: 1:30 p.m. Grabbing the cabin key, she left, locking the door behind her. The store lay just a quarter mile away on the narrow campground road. For a moment she stood on the porch, eyes darting nervously from side to side. But she was tired of being terrified, and now that they'd lost the weapon, she didn't know how they could kill the creature, anyway. She was in just as much danger trapped inside the cabin as she was on the move out here, surrounded by people.

Screwing up her courage, she stepped off the porch, heading for the store.

Around her she heard the typical sounds of summer in the forest, the chirping and trilling of Douglas squirrels, the *chee-dee-dee* of mountain chickadees, the occasional police whistle–like call of a varied thrush. And always the scent of sun-warmed pine. It was a comforting smell, one that reminded her of endless happy hours spent hiking in the wilderness. She found herself smiling in spite of the dire situation. Sometimes nature reminded her of bigger things than her own problems. It whispered of ancient forests, the advancing and retreating of glaciers, the everyday foraging of birds and squirrels in the underbrush. Here these animals were, carrying on with their lives day after day. They foraged and gathered and stored, slept through winters and explored the springs. Trees weathered countless snowstorms, fierce winds, and mild summers, with the chattering of squirrels in their branches. They did this, year in and year out. The constancy of nature.

It always calmed her mind, the chaos of her problems seeming smaller, the panic subsiding. Time was she had worried about how to hide her gift, about not having any friends, about her parents' aversion to her gift.

Today she worried about her own death. But still, even that seemed smaller, just one organism in the cycle of life, born one day and returning to the earth the next, her body food for coming generations of flowers and worms and trees.

This thought didn't make her sad; it liberated her. The best she could do was make the most of the time she had left, whether that was seventy years or a day. She would live every moment to its fullest, and she would fight until the very end.

Madeline padded along the paved road until she reached the camp store area. A pack of kids rushed by her, screaming and running this way and that, attacking each other with robot action figures. A woman in a St. Louis Cardinals sweatshirt yelled after them, "You all better be back for lunch! I ain't gonna say it twice!" She piled into a monstrous RV and slammed the door.

Ah, camping, thought Madeline, feeling a little better, her spirits brighter than they'd been in days.

She strode up the four wooden steps to the camping store,

only to find the place overflowing with tourists buying suntan lotion, cedar boxes sporting coyotes, and walking sticks decorated with bear bells. It was one of those stores that sold both souvenirs and groceries and was perpetually packed from June through September.

This day was no exception. The line for the register ran the length of the store, and everyone in it looked sweaty and impatient. She did notice one couple, though, happily kissing in the middle of the line, somehow miraculously able to tune out the droning masses, the wheezing of vacationers who've spent their last recreational dollar on postcards and gimmicky T-shirts, the whines and pleas of kids who want just one more gobstobber to stick in their sibling's hair.

A family at the end of the line was buying bear bells for each of its five members. The three kids whined and complained about who got which bell until they got distracted by a bin of rubber spiders and scorpions and began dumping them on each other. She cast an annoyed look at the parents, who were jangling the bells, as if giving them a test run. Many times she'd encountered bell wearers on what she had hoped to be peaceful, rewarding hikes.

The clanging of the bells now rankled her memory.

Jangle jangle jangle up the trail.

Jangle jangle jangle down the trail.

And the real crime of it was that there was no solid evidence bear bells even worked; some specialists believed they were nowhere near as effective as the human voice. As predators, bears exercised a certain degree of curiosity, and sometimes were even attracted by the bells, wanting to know what they were. One Canadian boat captain Madeline had met called bear bells "dinner bells."

She squeezed down the aisle between a cluster of people eying glass tankards with grizzly bears and walked to the refrigerated section. Grabbing a couple of turkey sandwiches and two cans of soda, she steadied her nerves for checkout.

She got in the end of the long line. Shoppers swarmed in every aisle and around every display shelf, pawing ceramic bells that touted Glacier National Park and digging through bins of enough cheap rings to turn every American finger a deep shade of gangrenous green. One portly woman in her fifties, wearing a polyester pantsuit sporting butterflies, couldn't decide between a monkey made entirely of seashells and a Day-Glo orange apron that proclaimed, Kiss the Cook.

Frankly, Madeline didn't see what either trinket had to do with Glacier National Park, but that was her own tastes. In the end, the woman chose both. Madeline pictured the woman's house, shelves bulging with bric-a-brac and kitsch, worm-eaten Indian corn necklaces and fake rubber spears with yellow and green chicken feathers. The woman looked completely stressed about the whole buying endeavor, graying black hair escaping in wisps from her ponytail, her brow furrowed.

But perhaps she enjoyed the purchases when she got home, Madeline thought. She imagined the woman chasing a grandchild around the living room with the rubber spear, the kid screaming with delight.

The line moved forward with the speed of rush hour traffic in San Francisco. She gained one foot. Then two. At the front of the line, a sunburned man in khaki shorts and a too-tight T-shirt was complaining about the price of film. Then his credit card wouldn't work, and the manager had to be called to clear the register and start over. Finally he dug some crumpled bills out of his pocket, but it only made him complain more about the inflated prices.

With him gone, she moved forward another foot, and the new person at the front of the line dithered over whether to get a small sewing kit in a leather pouch or a tiny spoon that read Glacier National Park on its handle. The cashier kept ringing one up, then voiding it out when the customer changed her mind.

The woman dithered for well over three minutes. Madeline stretched, gazing out the door toward escape. It was a good thing the creature didn't burst in right then, ready to do her in. She just might take him up on it.

Finally the lady chose the spoon, and the line crept forward another foot. In five more minutes, her head beginning to pound from all the shouting and shrieking children, she at last reached the register. Fishing out her wallet, she paid for the food and gratefully left the swarming, trinket-shopping masses.

When she got back to the cabin, she tucked the grocery bag under her arm and fished around the loose jeans for her key. Her fingers found the large plastic key chain, and she tugged it out. Inside, she set the food down on the small table, quickly locking the door behind her. Crossing the front room, she stopped at the bedroom door.

Noah still lay there in the same position, only now his eyes were open and staring again at nothing in particular.

"Noah?" she said softly. "I brought you some food."

He didn't stir.

She retrieved the food and brought it into the bedroom. Sitting down on the edge of the bed, she pulled out the sandwiches and unwrapped his. "Noah?"

He continued to stare, eyes red and swollen, mouth set in a thin, gray slash. A rope of clear mucus dangled from one nostril, clinging to the pillow on the other end. Noah was beyond caring. Slowly, his wide, tired eyes closed, and a long exhale escaped his lips.

Still he didn't move. She put a comforting hand on his shoulder. For several minutes she sat there, watching over him, and at last wrapped up the sandwich again and placed it on the bedside table along with a can of soda.

Feeling helpless about Noah, she took her own lunch into the main room and sat down at the small table. She unwrapped her sandwich, the soggy white bread falling to one side as she pulled it free of the cellophane. A pale tomato and wilted lettuce adorned the layers of pressed turkey, but Madeline was so hungry the concoction looked like a rich Thanksgiving feast. She bit into it hungrily, the flabby bread sticking to the roof of her mouth. Prying the bread free with her tongue, she chewed and swallowed, took another bite, and finished the sandwich in minutes.

She popped open the chilled soda and downed a few gulps, wondering what she should do. Noah looked in no way ready to continue his pursuit of Stefan. She herself didn't know what they'd do, even if they did manage to hunt him down. But just sitting there not even knowing what Stefan was up to or what he planned next was maddening and almost more terrifying than knowing what his plans were.

She thought of the images she'd gotten in the cabin when she touched his sheets, Stefan twisting in the blankets, mind obsessing on her like some raving stalker, the need to have her.

She shuddered, thinking of the night before, of him on top of her, looking so much like Noah, but not Noah. How dare he? Moisture fled her mouth as her heart began to pound with fury. *Why? Why?*

"I've traveled for so long. You can see the journey I've had. You could know me. Without me saying a word."

So this creature, however old he was, possibly ancient, had traveled alone . . . like the legendary vampire from folklore, watching everyone grow old and die around him. Or watching everyone die at his hands. No one to know the anguish he'd experienced, the anguish he'd caused. And now he'd been alive for so long that he couldn't even explain it to someone. Too long. Too many lives, too many memories. No one could possibly understand.

Except me, Madeline thought.

She could touch him and see where he'd been, whom he'd loved, if he'd loved, whom he'd killed and hated and wanted to be. Whom he lusted after, the cities he'd prowled, the dark, subterranean worlds he'd infiltrated and conquered. Every time he'd felt a blade or bullet tear into his anguished flesh, each time he'd taken the form of some hapless street musician, or cook, or ranger . . .

She could know all those things without him saying a word. Compliments of her "gift."

Slamming the can down on the table, Madeline stood up, knocking the chair to the floor. Her hands shaking violently, she tried to calm the angry pounding of her heart.

This was *not* what she wanted. This was everything she *didn't* want. She'd come here to get away from her abilities, from people, from the pressure. Instead she'd met a monster, become irretrievably entangled with a centuries-old hunter, and now faced the ultimate choice between living life for herself and risking it to fight an ancient evil.

Three days ago she'd met a monster.

It had stalked her, pulled at her legs in the icy throes of a glacial flash flood, dragged her down. Though she was free of those icy, crushing currents, still the creature threatened to drag her down, down, into the freezing depths where death, or rebirth, awaited.

Worriedly, she stooped over the small table, crumpled up the plastic wrap, and threw it into the beige wastebasket. Drank another slug of soda.

She paced to the bedroom door, then back to the table, the wooden boards groaning in protest beneath her feet. She had to do something. Couldn't just wait there.

Steve, she thought suddenly. *Maybe Steve will have some news.* Ensuring that she had the key by patting the pocket in the jeans, she turned the small lock in the doorknob and shut the door behind herself.

After double-checking that it was locked, she walked off in the direction of Steve's cabin, the same route she'd taken two nights before.

In the daylight, the journey was completely different: brighter, friendlier. Where shadows had clustered beneath the thick trunks of Douglas fir trees, now chickarees thrived, darting quickly from stash to stash, digging up and burying scavenged seeds. Large huckleberry bushes now hid only mountain chickadees and sparrows instead of every imaginable horror her mind could cook up.

Wondering if she'd see the bear again and peering into the tall undergrowth of ripening berries, she almost stepped in a large berry-encrusted pile of grizzly scat. The size of a football, the black mass with red seeds lay right in the middle of the camp road. Its freshness let her know that the same bear likely laid this present the other night when she saw it.

Giving the dark mass a wide berth, she continued along the road, breathing in the fresh scent of pine. Above her the sky shone a brilliant, deep azure, with a few puffy cumulus clouds drifting near the horizon. One was so tall it contained the unrealized potential for a thunderhead. Its upper layers caught the gleaming intensity of the sun, and its billowing ivory masses stood stark against the blue of the sky.

She turned down the little road labeled Park Residences. Ahead she could see Steve's cabin. She looked at her watch: 3:30 p.m. The windows were all shut, a strange thing on a hot day like this one. She didn't see a window air conditioner.

She walked up the narrow dirt path to his doorstep and rapped on the door. An osprey cried out overhead, and she followed the sound to see the brown and white bird sweeping across the sky, probably heading toward the lake to hunt.

Returning her attention to the door, she knocked again. Not a sound came from within. He wasn't home. Turning on the doorstep, she wondered where he might be. Maybe he wasn't on duty today. Maybe he'd gone down to Missoula to visit his sister as he'd intended to do before.

She strolled around the cluster of ranger residences, hoping to run into someone who might know where he was. She didn't feel right about knocking on doors. She wasn't even supposed to be there, since they were private residences. Steve's reaction when she'd first knocked on his door convinced her that annoying people frequently ignored the signs that said Private Residence. It was highly likely Steve didn't know anything more than she did, anyway. Since he wasn't the creature's target and wasn't currently in the way, she guessed he was safe for now. And would stay safer if she just stayed away.

She wondered how long Stefan would take to heal and how soon it would be before it chose another victim, if it hadn't already. She strolled briskly back toward Noah's cabin, her mind racing and anger swelling with each passing moment of uncertainty. Why hadn't it killed her when it had the chance? Had it truly changed its mind, or was this just part of the chase?

She cursed aloud. Inaction wasn't the answer. She had to convince Noah to get up, to find another way to kill the creature.

When she got back to the cabin, she unlocked the door quietly in case Noah was finally asleep. He definitely needed it after his sleepless night, and she wanted him fresh to think of new ways to tackle Stefan.

Quietly she shut the door and crept across the main room to the bedroom doorway. But when she peered inside, surprise hit her. He was gone.

The sandwich and soda sat untouched on the bedside table, where she'd laid it. She searched for a note on the bedside table and bed, then returned to the main room and searched the table and chairs. No note. Nor had there been one on the door.

Maybe he'd only stepped out for a moment. But her gut told her a different story altogether. It coiled and provided images of Noah distraught, maybe even crazy with hopelessness. What would he do in that state of mind? He'd go after the creature in a blind rage. Maybe right now he was lurching up the gravel road in his Jeep, burning to kill Stefan, even if it meant sacrificing his own life in the process.

He'd confront Stefan back at his rented cabin, which is likely where he'd gone to heal. If Noah had gone up there, he wouldn't have left her a note, wouldn't have wanted her to follow. Trouble was, if he did confront Stefan unarmed, he most certainly would end up dead before he succeeded.

Quickly she rushed to the back bedroom window and looked out. His Jeep was gone. She bit her lip.

Damn.

It was suicide.

And maybe suicide was exactly what he wanted.

16

MADELINE jumped in her VW Rabbit and started up the engine. The strong smell of the fire still filled the confines of the cab. Backing quickly out of the pine needle–strewn parking space, she pulled onto the main campground road, heading in the direction of Stefan's cabin.

She didn't get far.

The road was blocked about a thousand yards down the road. A line of traffic formed behind a ranger's truck, the lights of which whirled and flashed, playing over the metal of the cars behind it. She couldn't see why the ranger's car was pulled over, though; the hulking masses of lined-up RVs saw to that. Most were so tall she couldn't even see two cars in front of her.

Madeline tried to see what the holdup was by craning her neck and leaning over into the passenger seat. No luck. She could only see one corner of the ranger's truck. She rolled her window down and instantly heard someone screaming angrily. A few people were out of their cars looking in the direction of the commotion. Some had even pulled out binoculars and stood on the doorsills of their RVs. The holdup showed no sign of clearing up quickly.

Madeline's brow furrowed. She had to get to Stefan's cabin. And this was the only way out.

"Goddammit!" she heard the angry voice scream. It was a man's voice, but so hysterical and raging the guy barely made sense. What could have happened? Had someone tried to feed a bear and met with his just desserts? Was he even now cradling the stump of an arm or a chewed face, cursing at the park service?

The driver of the vehicle in front of her, a heavyset man with an Oregon Ducks sweatshirt on, was deep in conversation with the RV owner in front of him.

She tried to listen in.

"I don't know," Oregon Ducks was saying. "Just went crazy, I think."

She wondered if he was referring to the screaming man or the possible bear who had mauled him for behaving stupidly.

Morbid curiosity tugged at her to go look at the source of the turmoil, but she knew she'd just get in the way. If some guy was injured or "going crazy," the rangers would need space to work.

For three more minutes she sat in her Rabbit, and still the screaming persisted, though now it was completely incomprehensible.

"Why don't they just tranquilize the guy or something?" murmured Oregon Duck to the other RV owner. "We've been here forever." He had walked in front of the other guy's RV, had his binoculars out, and was surveying the scene.

Finally Madeline decided to climb out and see what the fuss was. She shut the door behind her, pocketed her keys, and walked up to Oregon Ducks.

"What's going on?" she asked him.

He answered without removing the binoculars from his eyes. "Some crazy guy is down there screaming at the rangers in the middle of the road. He's poured gas all over himself but doesn't have a lighter. He keeps telling them they've got to set him on fire. Can you believe it? They're trying to talk him down. Jeez! This is just like an episode of *Real Trauma*!" The man's face positively gleamed as he took in the scene, delighting in the stranger's ordeal.

He made her sick.

She had no idea what *Real Trauma* was, but she suspected it was one of those reality shows where they showed people getting eaten by sharks or falling off bridges.

"You don't understand!" she heard the man scream. "If I can't kill him, what fucking use am I?" The suddenly coherent though still maniacal voice was uncannily familiar.

Madeline raced forward, down the line of cars to the front. Oregon Ducks yelled "Hey!" behind her.

When she reached the ranger's truck, she immediately saw the law enforcement ranger Suzanne, who'd helped her the night she arrived desperate and wounded from the backcountry. Steve stood next to her, both talking quietly and serenely, their hands out in supplication. And in front of them stood Noah, doused head to foot in gasoline.

His Jeep was parked off the road with a dripping hose hanging from the gas tank.

"Help is on the way," Steve was saying.

"I don't want fucking help!" Noah yelled. "I want a fucking match and you people to leave me the fuck alone!"

For a moment, though the voice belonged to Noah, Madeline couldn't even believe the figure before the two rangers was actually him. His blond hair lay plastered to his face, eyes red and enraged, fingers tensed into fists at his side, neck muscles and veins bulging. He stood hunched over, glaring at them with an intense hate she'd never seen in someone before, like a force of violent energy striking out in pulsating, visceral waves. If he had a gun right then, she had no doubt he would have shot the rangers. His demeanor made her think of a rabid dog, all sense of peace and logic gone, just a snarling, snapping beast in agony, lashing out at anyone stupid enough to approach it.

"If I can't kill him, what fucking use am I?"

She couldn't imagine the hopelessness Noah must be feeling. He'd followed Stefan for two hundred years, finally had the perfect weapon, the only weapon, to destroy him, and now it was gone.

But this—this was an insane, hateful way to end things.

None of them had seen her yet.

Now she stepped out behind the ranger's truck and approached them. "Noah," she said, when she'd reached Steve's side. "This is crazy. Please don't do this."

He took her in, rage-filled eyes roaming over her. In a rain of spittle he uttered low and threateningly, "You goddamn, lousy sack of worthless shit! I'd still have the knife if it weren't for you! I should kill you before I kill myself, reach in your belly and rip out your intestines, tear your face apart, you foul, useless shit!" He advanced suddenly, and Steve stepped quickly in the way, holding out his hand in protest.

Noah went on. "I'll take you down with me before you have the chance to fuck up someone else's life! You're a goddamned joke!" Stopping in his tracks, he suddenly cocked his head to one side and said in a mocking voice, " 'I'll help you stop him.' " She remembered saying those very words to Noah when she'd returned in the middle of the night after the forest fire ordeal. She'd meant them. Her mouth fell open, his words cutting to the core. He continued to mock her. " 'But ooops! Gosh, did I let the creature get the knife?' " Then he roared in her face, rushing forward and colliding with Steve's outstretched hand. " 'Yes, I fucking did!' " Spittle rained over her face.

The reek of gasoline was unbearable. She staggered backward, her eyes stinging as a huge lump formed in her throat. She hadn't let the creature have the knife.

Suddenly she wondered if he *was* the creature, once again taking on Noah's appearance, saying these terrible things to drive them apart. They'd be less of a threat individually. It made sense.

But one look in his eyes told her that this was the genuine article; his grief-stricken face was the same face that had relayed to her the story of Anna's death. The creature could be convincing, but not this convincing.

He continued to scream at her as Suzanne gently pushed

her back, out of his reach. "I should have fucking left you for dead on the mountain. Or better yet, used you for bait. While he was feasting on your ruined corpse, I could have snuck up behind him and finished him off once and for all."

"Noah!" she cried, wounded and retreating. Her mind spun. The rage in his eyes took on an almost physical manifestation. The veins in his neck bulged, his lips drawn back cruelly from his teeth as he shouted.

He hated her. Truly, utterly *hated* her.

Suzanne took hold of Madeline's face to get her attention. "Honey," she said. "You need to move back. You're making things worse. He's deranged. Just move back."

Once again Madeline thought of a rabid dog. The way the ranger spoke of him, he might as well be.

Steve pushed hard against Noah, trying to restrain him, gas soaking the naturalist's clothes as well. "Help!" Steve said to Suzanne. "I'm not trained for this sort of thing."

The law enforcement ranger moved in. She grasped Noah in a painful-looking hold, with his arm twisted severely behind his back. Noah grimaced and sucked in breath sharply. She pushed him against the car and pulled out her handcuffs. Slapping them on his wrists, she cursed, "Where the hell are the other rangers? We radioed them ten minutes ago!"

As if on cue, sirens blared in the distance then died out just as quickly. Two park service trucks pulled onto the campground road, approaching rapidly.

Noah twisted in Suzanne's grasp, but she held on tightly, one strong hand on his shoulder.

The two rangers driving the trucks leapt out and rushed to her side.

"Took you guys long enough," she said.

They grabbed Noah, one on each side.

"And be careful. He's covered in gasoline."

"He's not the only one," Steve put in.

"So we smell," quipped one of the backup rangers.

Madeline rushed forward to Suzanne's side as the two rangers wrestled Noah into the back of one truck.

"What are they going to do with him?"

She squinted at the truck as it pulled away with Noah inside. Through the window he glared at Madeline with palpable hatred.

"Unfortunately, we can't do much. We're not cops. Unless a serious crime happens, we don't even call in the Feds."

Madeline stood stunned. *A serious crime. What, like murder?* she thought sarcastically. *How about five of them? And that's just so far.*

Suzanne went on. "He didn't hurt anyone, though he seemed pretty ready to do you harm." She paused, scrutinizing Madeline. "Do you know what he was talking about?"

She froze.

"Was it the same thing you say you saw on the mountain?"

Finally she nodded.

The law enforcement ranger looked at her with concern. "Maybe you should talk to a counselor when you get home. Surviving a frightening experience like a flash flood can be traumatic and have deleterious effects."

Madeline opened her mouth to protest and looked over at Steve, who was vigorously shaking his head no behind the ranger's back. "I think several of us are going to need a therapist when this is all over with," she said.

"Can I get a phone number so I'll know where they're taking him?" But even as she said it, the painful lump that swelled in her throat descended heavily to her gut. She was unwelcome. She had made things worse.

With a shudder she recalled the burning look in his eyes. Had she really messed everything up? For once in her life she'd felt a purpose, had begun to make sense of her gift and how she could use it to benefit others. Had she been so caught up in self-righteousness that she got careless and made things worse?

He had been ready to kill her just now. Only Steve and Suzanne had stopped him from trying.

That cut her deeply. Her protector, her knight from the mountain, wanted her dead. Her head began to pound.

Suzanne pressed a small card into her hand. It had the number written on it.

"Thanks," she said shakily and turned away.

"Wait!" Steve called. He caught up to her. She could actually see the shimmer of fumes rising from his clothes. "Are you going to be okay?"

Clutching the card, she looked at him, trying to swallow back the painful lump that had risen once again at his kind words. "I don't know," she said honestly. "But I think I'm going to go home. There's nothing I can do here now."

She started to walk back toward her Rabbit. Steve followed, throwing a cautious glance back at Suzanne. She was climbing into her car, well out of earshot. "But what about the . . . thing?"

She stopped and looked at him, squinting in the bright afternoon sun. "It's still out there," she told him. "And I have no idea what it's planning next. I only know we've lost our only weapon and our best warrior."

She turned then and walked back toward her car. Steve didn't try to follow. When she glanced back, he had turned, walking slowly back to the truck one of the backup rangers had left behind.

She felt bad, just leaving him like this. But if Noah was right about the creature, then unless Steve got in the way again, he was safe from Stefan. She couldn't say the same about herself. But because the creature had had the opportunity to kill her and hadn't, the fear that once consumed her had dulled slightly. *That can make you careless,* she thought.

With RVs and cars pulling around her as the road cleared, she walked slowly back to her car, wondering about Noah and if she'd ever see him again.

And if she did, would he be waiting some night with jagged claws, eager to tear through her flesh as the creature had longed to do—the hero having become the monster?

17

MADELINE opened the car door and climbed in, closing it with a soft click. In front of her most of the RVs and other cars had started their engines and driven off.

Instinctively Madeline locked the door. Home. That's where she would go now.

There was nothing left for her to do here. If the creature came for her now, she may as well be home instead of here. At least there she had friends who could help her.

A couple cars impatiently moved around her, and her attention returned to the present.

Inserting the key into the ignition, she started the car. It roared to life, and she checked the mirror and pulled forward. The car sputtered, jerked, and went dead. She tried to start it again. It tried to turn over but didn't catch. She let it sit for a moment. The reek of gasoline was still strong, and she rolled down the window in an attempt to get some fresh air.

Instead, a fresh wave of gasoline fumes bloomed into the car. Madeline coughed, tried the engine again. For a moment both car and person sputtered simultaneously. She looked down at the gas gauge. Impossibly, it read empty, even though she'd filled it a few days before and had driven it only thirty miles since.

She turned the key off, opened the door, and climbed out, pulling the neck of her shirt up over her nose to filter out some of the overpowering reek. She walked around the edge of her car and saw a large puddle of gasoline pooling beneath it.

Three cars drove by, no one stopping to see if she needed help, just concerned to be on their own hurried way.

Kneeling down, she peered under the car where the gas tank was. The metal fuel line lay broken and twisted, hanging down to the asphalt. The fuel filter was completely missing, and through a gash on the underside of the tank dripped the last remnants of fuel.

Something had utterly demolished her fuel system, and fear seized Madeline like a plunge into an icy-cold lake. Snapping her head up, she gazed frantically in all directions.

Another car drove by, the passenger giving her an unfriendly look that said, "What are you doing parked in the middle of the road?" No offer of help. No "Are you okay?" Just "Get out of my way."

She straightened up, heart threatening to beat right out of her chest. The thing must have done it while she was talking to Noah. It was possible Stefan had damaged her car earlier, but the stink of gasoline surely would have tipped her off when she climbed into her car back at the cabin.

No. This was fresh.

He'd done it while everyone was focused on Noah. Which meant Stefan had healed.

The damn creature had snuck up here while she was only yards away and tore up her precious VW. And with Noah hauled off by the rangers, it was her only means of escape.

Frantically she glanced around, feeling more vulnerable than she ever had before. Until now she'd had Noah, and Noah had the knife. Now she was alone, weaponless, with no idea how she'd get away from the creature if it decided to attack. She couldn't outrun it, couldn't defeat it in a fight. Safety now lay only in movement and escape.

But for several moments she stood rooted to the spot, listening for any sign of the creature lurking nearby.

Several more cars passed. Mountain chickadees fluttered and sang in the trees nearby. *Chee-dee-dee. Chee-dee-dee.* A chickaree warbled and darted quickly up a tree, chirping agitatedly as it went.

Forcing her racing mind to slow, she thought logically. Her car needed to be fixed. She would tow it to the repair garage in nearby West Glacier, just outside the west entrance of the park.

Luckily it was Wednesday. Hopefully someone would be at the garage.

A beat-up old Subaru station wagon approached, slowed, and to her amazement stopped. Two women rode in it, both with shoulder-length blonde dreadlocks, braided hemp necklaces, and worn and faded T-shirts. They looked like sisters, both with similar freckled faces and the same sloping, upturned noses.

"Hey," the passenger said. "You need help?" She was young, somewhere under twenty-five, Madeline guessed.

Madeline nodded quickly, stooping over so she could look at the driver, as well. "Yes. My car sprang a fuel leak. Can you drive me to the garage in West Glacier? The one just up the road?"

"Sure," said the driver. "Hop in!"

"Thank you!" Madeline said gratefully. "Just let me get my car off the road."

"You need help?" asked the passenger.

Madeline looked at the level ground and shook her head. "No, thanks. It'll just take me a sec." She jogged back to the driver door, stooped in, and inserted the key. Then she put the car in neutral, disengaged the emergency brake, and started pushing the car off the road. The Rabbit was light and easy to push on such level terrain, and in less than a minute, it was safely parked in the short grass along the road.

She locked up her car and moved to the back door of the Subaru.

"Oh, shoot! Carly, can you move some of your stuff?" the driver asked hastily.

As Madeline opened the door, a heap of gear spilled out, including a tent, an unrolled sleeping bag, as well as a bunch of bananas, a well-worn boot, and two unwrapped toaster pastries that looked older than the boot.

"Sure thing," Carly said, turning around in the passenger seat and helping Madeline pull in the unruly gear and place it back on the seat.

With a small space cleared, Madeline sat down and closed the door behind her. Her fingers touched the vinyl seat of the car.

The two sisters hiking in the high country, backs laden with heavy packs, stopping at a rock pile to watch for pikas . . .

Carly as a teenager, sitting in the backseat of the Subaru on the way to a piano recital, nervous as never before . . .

The other sister, crying, ankle broken after a fall on a skateboard, Carly driving her to the hospital . . .

Their mother, in mid-lecture, warning them of the dangers of not following a more traditional path, wanting them to be lawyers or bookkeepers . . .

She pushed the myriad images to the back of her mind. The driver took off, and Madeline gave a long, mournful look at her faithful VW. *I'll be back,* she mouthed to it. *Don't worry.*

It was the only time she'd ever had to leave it somewhere like that. In all the time she'd had it, it had never broken down once. Now ragged holes gaped in its underside.

"I'm Meg," said the driver.

"And I'm Carly," added the passenger.

"Madeline," she answered, smiling at them.

Meg sized her up in the rearview mirror. "You been out here for long?"

"Standing on the side of the road or camping in the park?"

She laughed. "Camping."

"Not long. Four days. But it's been one hell of a four days. What about you guys?"

Carly scratched her head, the dreadlocks on that side moving up and down. "We've been out for what, three . . . three and a half years, I think."

Madeline's mouth gaped. "Three and a half years?"

Carly nodded, turning to the side in her seat so she could see Madeline. "Yeah . . . it's been awesome. We just go from job to job, you know? Meg here's a cook, and I mostly do housekeeping—you know, changing sheets and that kind of thing."

Meg nodded. "We just go from park to park, depending on the season, finding odd jobs and room and board."

The idea of such a carefree life appealed immensely to Madeline. She studied the two women with admiration. "That's terrific!"

"Yeah, we sure think so. Mom doesn't so much though."

At the mention of their mother, Meg laughed. "Nope. Definitely not. She wants us to be stockbrokers."

"Or work for a PR firm."

"But not us."

"Nope." Carly pushed a handful of dreadlocks out of her eye and smiled. She was beautiful. A stunning, natural beauty. "We're free spirits."

"You two are sisters, then?" she asked.

"Yup," Meg answered. "You got a sister?"

They were nearing the intense traffic of the trinket store and restaurant area of West Glacier, and they slowed to a crawl behind a line of cars waiting to get gas at the little service station.

"Only child," Madeline answered. But she thought of Ellie and smiled sadly. She was the closest thing to a sister that Madeline could ever want.

She took in the pile of gear in the backseat next to her and in the trunk. "Looks like you two are heading on to new adventures," she remarked.

Carly nodded. "Yep! Meg here scored a job as a cook in a backcountry chalet here in Glacier. I'm going with her to hopefully talk them into hiring me on in housekeeping."

"Sounds like a great life," Madeline said. She thought of

her last few dark days and tried to envision a cheery future for herself full of travel. Failing that, she just tried to envision a future. But she couldn't see past the horror and terror of the last few days, couldn't imagine what lay in store for her in the next few hours, let alone the next few years.

"You okay?" Meg asked, watching her in the rearview mirror.

"Yeah," she lied. "Just really tired."

By now they'd made it to the far end of the gas station's parking lot, moving steadily in the flow of cars. Meg pulled up at the garage. "Front door service," she said, grinning.

"Thank you!" Madeline opened the door, careful to keep more gear from spilling out. "Take care," she said, stooping to look through the window. "And good luck on your adventures!"

"Peace!" Carly said.

"Get some rest," Meg added.

"Will do." Madeline managed a smile, and the women pulled away, leaving her standing in front of the repair garage.

An hour later Madeline sat in an uncomfortable red vinyl seat in the repair garage waiting room, perusing a two-year-old issue of *National Geographic*. They'd towed her car back to the garage, and an elderly mechanic with a shock of white hair had been checking it over for the last ten minutes.

He entered through the employee door of the waiting room and walked up behind the counter, thumbing through pages on an ancient wooden clipboard. "Miss Keye?" he asked, looking questioningly around the waiting room, even though she was the only one there. She put down the magazine and walked to the counter. She fished around in the back pocket of Noah's jeans for her wallet and realized she'd left it back at the cabin in her rush to leave.

"Yes?"

"Well, I've looked over your Rabbit," he said softly. The sympathetic look in his eye did not do much for her confidence. "I'm afraid it's bad. Now, I can weld some of the damage and get new fuel lines and a tank and filter, but the problem is that it's an import, and I don't have many VW parts here. The ones I do have are for the buses. Darn popular with campers, those buses. They got the pop-up top and those sinks and stoves and whatnot. Darn handy. But I don't have any Rabbit parts. I'll order them."

She raised her eyebrows. Somehow she knew ordering them was going to take a long time. She asked the question.

"Two weeks," he said. "Maybe a week and a half. Depends on if they're making another shipment up this way. Otherwise I just get parts every two weeks."

"Darn," she said, using the old man's word of choice. "That long? Are you sure?"

"I'm afraid so." His soft blue eyes gazed on her kindly. "What do you want to do?"

She thought a moment, fingers drumming on the black and greasy Formica counter. What could she do? Towing it even as far as Missoula would cost her a mint. Leaving it here until he could fix it was the best bet. But she couldn't very well stay here, with no friends and no escape car. No. She would leave the Rabbit here, get home somehow, and come back for it. She hated the thought of leaving her beloved car, the sense of familiarity it brought her, but it was the best choice.

"Can I leave it here until you fix it?"

"Sure can," he answered. "Got a lot out back."

She nodded. "Then that's what I'd like to do. I've got to get back home, though. I'll leave you my information so you can contact me when you finish or call me if you have questions."

"Good enough," he said, and produced a tablet from under the counter. In block letters he painstakingly wrote down what was wrong with the Rabbit and then handed the pen over to her to fill in her information, the car's year, make, and model and sign at the X to authorize repairs.

"Thank you," she said.

"It's what I do." He grinned, his blue eyes sparkling beneath the crop of short, white hair. She smiled back and hoped desperately that she was leaving her Rabbit in good hands.

Now she just had to find a way home.

Her first thought was George. No one else would be willing to drive five hours to get her.

Exiting the relative peace of the repair garage waiting room, Madeline entered the chaos of the parking lot beyond. Cars still circled endlessly, waiting to fill up on gas; kids screamed; parents yelled.

Across the street, Madeline spotted two public telephones. At one a gaggle of redheaded children and their parents gathered, each taking turns talking into the mouthpiece. On the other phone talked a lone woman in her mid-forties, with graying hair in a loose ponytail and a point-and-shoot camera in one hand. Her T-shirt advertised, God, Guns and Guts Keep America Free.

Madeline approached the telephones. Reaching in her back pocket, she remembered again that she'd left her wallet at the cabin. Luckily, though, she had her calling card number memorized. And at least leaving her wallet at the cabin was better than if she'd been carrying it during the flash flood. If she hadn't stashed it in her car, her calling card, along with her two credit cards, her driver's license, hell, even her Mothershead Library card, would be somewhere in the river, swept far downstream by now or sunk to voluminous depths along with her expensive, well-loved pack that she'd never see again.

She waited patiently as God, Guns and Guts chatted quietly with someone, and the red-haired family yammered away loudly to the grandmother of the familial clan.

As she stood there, baking in the afternoon sun that beat down between pine needles, she fantasized that someone walking along a beach in the Pacific Ocean would one day stumble across her backpack in a tumble of sun-bleached driftwood. They'd find the name tag on her pack and give her a call. Or maybe the pack would wash up in Hawaii or Japan. Maybe she'd have to go to Oahu to claim it, and would end up scuba diving with dolphins.

After she waited for a few more minutes, God, Guns and Guts hung up. As the woman walked away, she threw Madeline a gruff look over one shoulder. The woman's face was tough, tanned, and leathered, and the eyes spoke of a rough life that hadn't had too many lucky breaks.

Madeline smiled at her, and the woman managed a smile back, then turned away.

She walked to the phone and picked up the handset, getting a wave of psychic white noise as she did so. It hit her powerfully, and she dropped the phone, letting it swing at the end of its cord. Shaking her head lightly, she picked up the handset again, trying to tune the visions out, but the buzzing in her head only allowed itself to be reduced to a low hum instead of disappearing entirely. Normally she'd be able to tune out such a thing. But she was exhausted, and probably a hundred people had used the phone already today, leaving a sea of fresh vibes behind.

She thought about visiting the park in the off-season sometime, but that thought was immediately followed by an image of the Sickle Moon Killer, pursuing her relentlessly through the abandoned campsites and parking lots in front of boarded-up restaurants and gift shops. Vividly she could see his dark, whiskered face, deep grooves carved into his aging face from years of frowning and brooding over the fourteen-year-old who'd put him away. In her mind's eye, with his dark eyes glittering over a crooked nose broken in a prison fight, the Sickle Moon Killer caught up with her, a knife gleaming in one down-swinging hand.

Madeline pushed the image out of her head. The phone uttered its annoyed staggered tone; she'd left it off the hook too long. Holding down the receiver and then lifting it again, she listened for the dial tone and then started pushing numbers.

At the special tone that sounded like a small gong inside the phone, she entered her calling card number.

George answered on the second ring. "Hello?"

"Oh, George. Is it ever good to hear your voice!"

"Madeline? You're back early. I thought you weren't coming back till next week."

"Well, a lot has happened. I feel like I've been away for months."

"What's wrong?" he said immediately, sensing the despair

in her voice. He was a good friend, she thought. She was lucky to have such a good friend in the world.

"A lot's wrong. I can tell you about it in person. But the thing that's the most immediately wrong is that I'm not home; I'm still in Glacier."

"You need me to come get you?" he asked, his tone bright. "'Cause I can."

She sighed. "Yes. Please. I can pay for your gas, if you need—"

"Don't even give it a thought. I'll just grab some snacks for the road and be up there in what . . . four hours?"

"Five from Mothershead." She grimaced.

"Five it is. George to the rescue."

"Thanks so much."

"But what about your car? Where is it?"

"It's here in the park. I'll have to come back and get it in two weeks. But I'll deal with that then. And don't worry," she added after a pause. "I won't ask you to drive me back."

"I would, though, if you needed me to." Then, after a thought, he added, "It's beautiful up there. I wouldn't mind."

She was glad he'd said it. Made her feel less like she was putting him out. She looked around at the swaying pines and the snow-encrusted mountains. "You're absolutely right, George. I almost hate to leave."

"So why are you leaving early?"

"I'll tell you about it on the way home. It's a thrilling tale of adventure." Making light of her situation felt hollow and false, but she didn't want to worry him. When he arrived and saw that she was safe, then she could tell him.

"You sure you're okay, Mad?" He'd taken to calling her Mad now and then, the nickname Ellie had used on occasion. She didn't mind his adoption of the term. It made him feel more like a friend than ever.

"Yeah. And I'll be even better when I see you and we get out of here."

"Then I'd better leave now. Anything you want me to pick up? Potato chips? Pretzels, that kind of thing?"

She smiled. "No, thanks."

"Where exactly are you?"

She thought a second. She still had to go back and get what little she had out of the cabin. "I'll be at Lake McDonald, near Apgar. They'll give you a map when you enter the park. But it's not far from the west entrance. I'll be waiting in front of the camp store there at the lake."

"Okay. Then I'll see you soon. Hang tight."

"Thanks, George."

"No problem."

They hung up, and as she turned away from the phone, she saw that God, Guns, and Guts had returned and was watching her from the shade of a nearby pine. She wasn't smiling, either.

Fear crept silently through Madeline's mind as she watched the woman's gaunt expression, mouth a colorless slit in a drawn face. The woman stepped out from the shadow and moved deliberately toward Madeline, who stood staring.

She hated this. Stefan could be anyone around her. Madeline stepped away from the phone and began moving in another direction, away from the woman. Immediately the gray-haired woman's eyes left her, and the stranger continued to the phone, where she picked up the receiver.

Madeline shook her head and picked up her pace, glancing once more over her shoulder to see the woman begin to dial. She'd only wanted to use the phone again, and Madeline had already ascribed some sinister motive to the woman.

Suddenly Madeline wondered how long she'd be like this, paranoid of strangers, not knowing whom to trust. She wondered if she could recognize Stefan by his eyes. She hadn't right away when he was posing as Noah. But maybe now that she was expecting it, she could.

But she didn't want to be expecting it. She wanted to put this whole thing behind her, not be paranoid about everyone she met.

Madeline looked around at the horde of rushing tourists with dripping ice cream cones and sunburned feet in vinyl flip-flops. Five hours. What could she do for five hours?

Noah was her first thought. She wanted to visit him, talk to him. Had he really meant the terrible things he'd said? What would he think about her returning to Mothershead? It had to be better than being alone in the open like this.

She pushed the thought of Noah out of her head. He'd been crazy back at his Jeep—the chilling way he'd looked at her.

She walked slowly to the edge of the parking lot, crossed the street, and began walking down the main road that led into the park. Soon she came to the bustling Lake McDonald area, where the Apgar Visitor Center, backcountry permit station, and a collection of gift shops clustered. Weaving among the throng of visitors, she finally sat down on a picnic bench under the shade of a hemlock tree. Putting her chin in her hand, she watched the swarm of tourists pour in and out of the camp store and souvenir shops, and knew that this was the ideal place to wait. With this many people around her, she didn't think the creature would even try to attack her. It wouldn't risk the exposure.

Besides, she thought dryly, *it isn't his style. He's far more subtle than that.* It seemed he thrived as much on the subterfuge and chase as he did on his victims' flesh itself.

She resigned herself to a long wait.

To pass the time, she braved the camp store and bought a soda with some cash she found in her pocket. Sipping the cool liquid, she crossed the street and perused the Apgar Visitor Center. After looking at a display showing the topography and relief of the park, she took in a display with a mounted immature bald eagle. She read the plaque. Someone had shot the endangered bird and tried to hide his crime, only to be discovered later and prosecuted.

Feeling sad about the magnificent eagle, she meandered over to the book section. Among the ever-present full-color books filled with gorgeous photographs of wildlife and wildflowers, she spotted a few choice books that probably wouldn't be the greatest thing to read, given her situation: books like *Survival Above the Timberline, The Harrowing Escape: One Climber's Tale of Catastrophe,* and *Into Thin Air.* She read the back of a few of these survival books, and at last, despite herself, settled on *Encounters with the Grizzly,* which featured accounts of people who had been mauled by grizzly bears, and how future attacks might be avoided. She figured it would be cathartic enough to keep her mind off things.

She fished more cash out of her pocket, and after spending only a record ten minutes in line, she returned again to the fresh air, the gravel crunching beneath her feet. Beyond, the lake glistened in the midday sun, waves sparkling. The quiet lapping of the lake at the shore drew her attention, and she walked in that direction.

A photographer stood on the shore, setting up a large-format camera on a tripod, bag upon bag of gadgets strewn at his feet. Sometimes she'd seen camera enthusiasts set up hours before sunset to get that perfect alpenglow shot, when the setting sun bathed the distant peaks in an intense, rosy glow.

An elderly couple walked by her, eating huckleberry ice cream cones, the afternoon heat causing the purple ice cream to drip off their fingers. They laughed, enjoying themselves, and she smiled. She didn't know if she'd make it to be their age, but if she did, she hoped she'd be eating a huckleberry ice cream cone in this gorgeous place.

Tucking her book under her arm, she looked for a comfortable place to sit. She liked reading in unusual places: along whitewater streams, or perched on boulders above the treeline. Later on, when she thought of the particular book she'd read in each spot, she could easily conjure images of how the wildflowers looked that day or how the stream burbled and flowed over moss-laden rocks and driftwood.

She looked at her watch. She'd only killed half an hour in the gift shop.

Scanning around, she saw a sun-bleached log on the shore of the lake with a long, smooth spot, perfect for sitting. Little foot traffic passed by the log, yet it was still close enough to the swarms of tourists that she'd feel safer there. She started off in that direction, squinting in the bright sun.

Eventually she'd have to go back to the cabin to gather her meager possessions: the burned cotton shirt, jeans, and her new toothbrush. But most importantly, she needed her wallet. She dreaded the thought of returning to the cabin, one place the creature knew she might be, but she didn't want to leave her driver's license there for the creature to find. She didn't know if the creature knew where she lived in Mothershead, but just in case it didn't, she didn't want to arm it with any more information than it had. Plus, she realized with an audible gasp, she'd written down her future address with student housing in San Francisco on a slip of paper that was in her wallet. She had to go back and get it before the creature found it.

She wondered if she should go right then and looked toward the path that led to the cabins. No one walked on it. The desolation of that shady trail invited doubts to gnaw at her, and she decided she'd just wait until George got there. It wasn't worth definitely risking her life now to avoid possibly risking it in the future. She'd wait until more people filled the path or until George arrived. Preferably both. To find her future address, the creature would have to go to the cabin, find her wallet, dig through it, and recognize the importance of the slip of paper she'd written her address on. She hadn't marked it "My future address" or anything. It was just a number and a street. She looked with uncertainty at the path again. Still empty. No, she would wait. But she definitely wouldn't leave without it.

And when she went back, she could also grab her pocket knife. Her mom had given it to her when she was five, after the incident with the wildfire. It had bailed her out of several tough situations in her life. Once she'd used it to scare off a creepy guy who had followed her home from the diner in Mothershead, and another time she'd used the little magnifying glass to start a small fire when she was in danger of hypothermia in the backcountry of the Canadian Rockies. Plus she'd used it endless times to make repairs on her backpack during overnight hikes. Though it wasn't very big, it was the one sharp weapon she had, and it made her feel safer. The knife held much sentimental value, and had been with her on every trip. She was superstitious that way.

Stepping off the parking lot onto the pebble-strewn incline that led to the beach, Madeline veered for the log. She sat down on the smooth spot with her back to sun and opened her new book.

Three hours dragged by, with Madeline checking her watch every ten minutes, reading, and staring at tourists. The book was amazing and fascinating, though, filling the three hours with gripping accounts of hikers and hunters mauled by grizzlies, almost all surviving the attacks. In the past, Madeline had always played it smart with grizzlies, making noise while hiking, getting the hell out of an area if she stumbled across the carcass of a game animal, backing slowly away quietly the two times she'd come across a grizzly on the trail. The gigantic omnivores couldn't afford more problems with humans. Montana's population of the bears had greatly dwindled since the arrival of settlers from the East, and she didn't want to be another reason to get one shot.

The book gave her even more respect for the gigantic omnivores and had some very helpful tips to avoid confrontations with grizzlies. But the most interesting part had been the attitude of the victims. They didn't wish harm on their attackers but instead had a sense of awe for nature and for the sheer power of the bears. She found it fascinating.

So fascinating, in fact, that at one point she realized her butt had long since fallen asleep. She shifted on the log, her back muscles groaning in protest. Finally she stood, stretching, and looked out over the lake. The sun was far lower in the west, and the photographer with the large-format camera was busy changing plates.

She looked at her watch. Less than an hour until George got there.

She held the book up, looking at its cover, a close-up of a snarling grizzly's face. She knew then why she'd chosen this particular book. She'd been looking for some insight into the mind of a survivor who had faced a powerful predator and lived. She wanted to know what they'd done to survive and how they'd dealt with the incident after the fact.

But what she'd come away with didn't help. It didn't even

pertain to her situation. These people had faced grizzly bears, powerful creatures indeed, but seldom predaceous, and then only when desperate for a meal or threatened beyond reason. Most of the time when a grizzly attacked, it stopped when the person played dead or was no longer a threat. In only very rare cases had grizzlies eaten people.

A powerful force of nature, a symbol of a healthy ecosystem, the grizzly didn't make it personal when it attacked. It hadn't selected its victim from a series of newspaper articles, or from word of mouth as people chatted with each other about friends with extraordinary abilities. The victim mauled by a grizzly wasn't selected at all but just happened to be the unlucky person who stumbled across a mother grizzly and her cubs or a big male eating a moose carcass.

But the creature she faced was no bear. It was undeniably predaceous and calculating, selecting each victim for the precise purpose of devouring the person's flesh, for acquiring a talent or gift.

It had specifically selected her. And it wouldn't stop when she played dead. It would keep coming, teeth sinking into her, devouring her flesh. And then it would have her "gift." The power that would give the creature staggered her. It would know intimate details about its victims, where they were going, their routines, their deepest fears. It would twist and compromise her ability, finding endless, horrific uses for it; it would contort the "gift" into a thing of evil, extending it to a place of darkness she herself never would have taken it.

She glanced around nervously, scanning the lake's edge, the gift shop and lodge, feeling oddly possessive of her gift. She may not have asked for it, but she sure as hell wasn't going to see it used for evil.

She wondered where the creature was, why it hadn't even made a single appearance since the night before. Here she was, sitting alone, and though she was among a swarm of pulsing, vibrant tourism, she thought at least she'd feel its eyes burning into her back or catch a glimpse of furtive movement in the trees at the lake's edge. But she'd seen nothing in her three hours of reading and watching.

The extent of its injuries had been considerable. It might still be healing, though it had been well enough to rip out the underside of her car. Still, no ordinary weapon had torn the gashes into the creature's flesh, and if Ffyllon's journal had been correct, then those wounds took longer to heal.

She continued to glance around, briefly watching a couple in their fifties holding hands and strolling along the lake's edge.

She looked again at her watch and thought about George. He didn't know what was going on. If she asked him to go to the cabin, she'd be endangering him. She looked at the path to the cabins. Presently, quite a few people strolled on it. If she hurried there now, she'd be in public and could get her wallet and knife.

Tucking the book under her arm, she set off down the path, nodding at families as they walked by, surreptitiously watching them for any suspicious behavior.

Then suddenly she *did* feel someone watching her. Peering around, her eyes fell on a dark figure in the trees behind her, some two hundred feet away, just at the edge of the riverbank. A man, definitely watching her, stood there silently, unmoving. She tried to make out his face, but he was too far away. She looked closer, peering intently. He didn't react at all to her noticing him, and this made her nervous.

Normally when you caught a stranger staring, he looked away.

The cabin area wasn't too much farther. Madeline decided just to continue casually in that direction. She walked down the path, chancing a glance over her shoulder. The figure was closer. Much closer. Only a hundred feet away now, though she hadn't seen him move at all.

She turned around fully now and walked quickly backward, not taking her eyes off him. He vanished behind a cluster of hemlock trees. She continued her backward progress, watching for his reappearance. Branches swayed a mere twenty feet away. When he did reemerge, he was only ten feet away. She took in the familiar features: the long black hair falling in waves about his shoulders, the olive skin, the lithe, muscular body.

Voices startled her, and she backed into someone. "Sorry, darlin'," said a man with a Texas accent. She spun, muttering apologies, and realized she'd stumbled into a group of retired tourists, all of whom wore matching T-shirts that read Sunshine Tours.

They filed past her, and the last tourist, with a kind, wrinkled face, smiled at her. "Young love," she said. "I can remember being distracted myself. And who can blame you? He's a handsome one." She winked and continued on.

Madeline turned, intending to see how close the figure was. Instead, she bumped into someone else. Intense, green eyes stared down into hers. Handsome face with high cheekbones.

The creature.

He wore a dark red shirt and black jeans, and Madeline wondered whom he'd killed for the outfit.

She started to backpedal, her feet moving before she'd even told them where to go. Stefan reached out quickly, gripping her upper arm. "No," he said. "Wait." He held her fast, and she jerked her arm free, wanting to tear away from there. He bore no mark of the fight the night before. At least, none that she could see. The gashes in his chest from the weapon could still be there, beneath the shirt, but his face had completely healed.

Adrenaline flooded into her, making her hands shake, and her breath came up short. If he wanted to tear her to pieces right there, would the presence of other people stop him? She couldn't kill him, but she sure as hell wasn't going to go down without a fight. If he did attack her, she'd fight with everything in her: tear at his throat, his eyes, till nothing but a bloody pulp was left. He would live through it, but it would still hurt like hell.

More voices on the trail caught her attention, but she didn't turn in their direction. A couple in their twenties walked by, arguing about where they would eat that night, the man complaining about being "out in the middle of nowhere." The creature stepped forward, suddenly wrapping his arm around her as they passed. She wanted to cry out to them, ask them to help her, but there was nothing they could do. Except die.

The creature wasn't the least bit interested in them. He didn't even look as they filed by. Instead he studied her face intently, his other hand moving along her jaw. The couple was so caught up in their argument they didn't even acknowledge Madeline or Stefan.

She let the creature pull her head toward his own, and he kissed her temple. She realized he wanted the couple to think they were the same, just two normal people out for a romantic walk in the woods. Not hunter and hunted. Not predator and prey.

She felt his strong hand on the back of her neck, her breath barely coming. This close she could smell him, and the power of that scent crashed into her. Her breathing slowed even more. That powerful, alluring scent washed over her, the same one that had made her so heady the night before, that exotic, sensual smell. She drank it in, leaning closer, her head feeling light, fingertips buzzing and trembling.

The couple continued down the path, and though they were far away now, she didn't move, didn't pull away, but instead stayed close, lips slightly parted, breathing in the scent of him.

He said nothing, moving his fingers through her hair. His other hand curled around her back, and a heavy sensation of anticipation crept into her belly. His lips traced down her face to her neck, teeth lightly grazing her skin there.

Still she didn't move. She didn't want to. He felt so good. Smelled so desirable.

Somewhere in the logical side of her brain, a niggling feeling pestered her to pay attention. But the feeling wasn't strong enough to push through. She couldn't even concentrate on it.

It didn't go away, either, and she thought she remembered something from biology class. Something about chemical attractants.

So attractive.

Pheromones. Yes, that was it. Powerful chemical attractants. Is that what this was?

Her head felt muddled and light, as if she had drunk too much wine. Most of her didn't even care. His lips reached her collarbone, kissing along the sensitive skin there. Her skin broke out in chills.

He eats people, the voice continued. *And now his pheromones are lulling you into complacency so you don't notice when he starts to tear out whole chunks of flesh.*

I'd notice that, she countered the voice, as he began to move his lips upward again, over her jaw, her cheek, the corner of her mouth. His lips brushed her own, and she could feel his skin burning. Then they kissed, a deep, drunken kiss that sang in her mind, her body tingling with pleasure. She'd read it in a ton of hokey books before but had never experienced it till last night, but he tasted sweet, like apricot or honey, a rich, fruity taste that conjured images of a tropical paradise.

His tongue met hers, his legs moving closer until their bodies pressed flush against each other. Madeline didn't even raise her arms. She continued to stand, hands at her sides, as if in shock.

A distant part of her whispered warnings, begged her to pay attention.

But her lips moved, her tongue met his, and she drank him in.

18

THE creature's kisses grew passionate, fiery. Hands on Madeline's arms, he backed her up against the trunk of a tree just off the path, the boughs draping down over them. He moved against her, their bodies pressed tightly together. Her hands reached up, tangling in his long, black hair as their tongues touched. The merest hint of a spark surged through her with every touch, and she closed her eyes against the pleasure.

His hands ran down her sides to her hips, and he grasped her there, pulling her into him, rhythmically pressing against her.

Her hands clasped behind his neck, his dark locks framing their faces as they kissed. His bare skin there was deliciously hot—

A young archaeologist, laboring in the hot sun at the ancient Mesopotamian city of Ur, looking up, startled, then terrified as claws and fangs rend him apart, tongue darting into the spurting throat and red cavities filled with warm, soft organs. Sweet knowledge of ancient times, intoxicating power.

Madeline's eyes snapped open as she jerked her hands

away violently. The very tongue she touched had tasted the flesh of that archaeologist. Stefan's dark eyes watched her curiously.

"I can feel what you see," he breathed, closing his eyes in ecstasy, bringing a hand up to her face. She knocked it away harshly. He remained close, still pressed against her.

She turned her head away, fighting with a fog that surrounded her senses, dulling some sensations and stoking others feverishly. Putting a hand on his chest, she tried to push him away, but he brought his hand up and closed it over hers. The warm olive skin was callused, and he stroked her hand.

The phenomenal scent swept over her, filling her head, singing to her mind and body. She tried to shake it away, but it engulfed her in a voluptuous cloud, like the smell of an incense-laden Buddhist temple. He bent his head closer, breathing her in. His arms wrapped around her back, one hand gripping the tree behind her.

Closing the distance between them, his lips brushed against her cheek, then her lips. His scent effused her very being, and she couldn't concentrate on what she'd just seen, could barely remember it. The exquisite haze drifted around her, luring her until her fingertips ached to touch him, and she trembled with desire.

The red cotton shirt he wore buttoned down the front, and she slid her hand inside, feeling the muscles of his chest move as he held her.

In the vast white expanse of the Arctic, a French-Canadian explorer running desperately across jagged ice, slipping in smooth spots, sharp edges slashing through his boots. Behind him drips of blood trail across the pale surface of the ice. The creature, running close behind, licking blood from the ice, breath frosting in the frigid air, alive with the hunt, excited as it draws to a close. It leaps on the explorer's back, ripping through the fur coat, the shrill cries of agony music to the predator's ears. Biting deeply into hot, steaming flesh, tongue lapping up the coppery blood. Dragging the body off to enjoy, to digest, to ingest knowledge, the explorer's memories of the far corners of the earth.

Madeline shoved the creature away. He lost footing on an exposed root, stumbled, and righted himself a few feet away. Drawing the back of his hand across his mouth, he looked at her with hungry eyes.

"What are you doing to me?" she asked, bringing a hand to her forehead.

Still, the dizzying mist swam around in her head, clouding her judgment. Chemical attractants. That's why she found him so irresistible. He was a killer. A violent predator who devoured his victims. And through her visions, she'd seen him do it, felt him do it.

"You're a murderer," she said, feeling so light-headed she had to grab the tree to stay standing.

"Yes," he said, straightening up. He walked back toward her.

"I've seen your victims." She shook her head lightly, trying to dispel the cloud.

He closed the distance between them. The exquisite scent of him filled her senses again, called out for her to touch him.

"And that's just it," he said softly. "At first I desired your ability. Can you imagine the power? I would know where my victims would be next. Stalking them would be all the easier. I could know what they were thinking, when the best time for attack would be." He brought a hand up, stroked her hair. She pushed him away, but war erupted within her, half of her repulsed and the other inexorably drawn. "But that night on the road, you amazed me. I had no idea how . . . fine-tuned your gift was. You saw things I had done, places I'd been and even I'd forgotten. I could feel you filling me, feel your thoughts, your visions, as forgotten memories ignited inside me. You drew those experiences out of me. The power of your mind was unequaled to anyone I'd tasted before."

He kissed her feverishly, cradling her head in his hands. He tasted so *good*. It couldn't just be chemical attractants, could it? Could they be this powerful? She wanted him. In the core of her being, she wanted him. Her body ached, throbbed at the thought of it.

He pulled away, eyes sinking into hers, peering into her. "I've been alive for a long time, Madeline. Traveling from country to country, century to century. Even I don't remember all the places I've been or the people I've known. I've acquired so many memories that talking with people has grown painful for me. I'm so aware of how much younger they are. They'll never know everything I know, never be on a par with my experiences. They don't have a chance in hell of ever understanding or even knowing me. I'm so old that sometimes I feel insane, filled with the world and its wonders, its terrors and tragedies.

"And I have become one of those terrors, Madeline."

He embraced her. Her face pressed into the warm crook of his neck, his long hair enveloping her. She felt sharp claws sprout, digging into her back. "I never feel more alive," he said, "than when I'm tasting someone, devouring their being. I learn what life meant to them. What scared them, what made them love. Through their flesh I experience their childhood, their first love, marriage, and talents . . . oh, the talents. Those are the best part. Being able to play the violin like a virtuoso, or map any sea route you could want to take, to know the heavens as if you've spent a lifetime studying them as a Mayan astronomer, to understand the secrets of the universe as the Newtons and Einsteins of this world do."

He pulled back, watching her again, his eyes no longer green but deep red and reflective, with no pupils in the scarlet pools. They flashed with an inner luminance and ancient power. "I know darker secrets, too, Madeline. Some secrets I've almost forgotten. And some secrets I'll never forget for what they've done to my body." He lifted his right hand, the fingers grown into sharp, black claws.

With his other hand he continued to hold her, breathing in her scent. "You could know me," he said, eyes flashing again. His right hand became scaled, reptilian, skin there a multitude of greens and grays. Then the olive skin returned, the claws withdrew to long fingers. "I want you to know me."

Intoxicated, she stayed there, next to him, filled with a passion that suffused her being.

But somewhere in the recesses of her mind, the murdered ranger swam into view, bleeding body hanging over the rafters. Noah followed that image. Noble Noah, who had hunted the creature tirelessly. Obsessed Noah. She thought of his sandy blond hair, kind green eyes. Of those last desperate hours before he'd completely lost it. He'd been trying to stop a killer. *Her* killer. What was she doing here then? What was she thinking? "Noah . . ." she whispered, wondering if he'd ever regain himself again, fight and crawl his way back to sanity and once more find purpose.

"Your thoughts are still with him? After all the terrible things he said to you?"

Madeline tried to find words. Couldn't.

He grasped her hand. "You and I are closer than he ever will be to you. He could never understand your depth. He's old, yes, but he's single-minded. He has thought of nothing but revenge for the last two hundred years."

She looked away to where the sun sparkled on the river.

"I can give you so much more. You're already so powerful. I can add to that power."

She looked at him questioningly.

Sensing her unasked question, he said, "I can give you the eternity of youth. The ability to heal. The freedom to change forms in a single moment."

Her eyes narrowed. "I'd never want to be like you."

The corner of his mouth turned up in a smile. "And you never will be like me. We're far too different. And you're too determined to do the 'right' thing. But I can live with that."

For a moment she let him take her down this proposed road that lay in a shadowed future not too far from here. Not only would she be a freak for her visions, but she'd be infinitely more so for her ability to sprout fangs and claws. Sounded like a real promising future. And she'd even have a newfound friend complete with cannibalistic tendencies. *Cannibalistic if he was ever even human, that is,* she thought grimly.

But the ability to change? To be a chameleon? She wondered how powerful the ability was. Would she be able to turn into mist? To fly? Before she'd only thought of the creature's terrifying capability once her gift was his own. Now she pictured herself with those skills. A shape-shifter, a psychic—there would be no end to what she could do. Her life wouldn't be filled with the horrors of crimes or hours spent with the police poring over cold cases, hoping for a lead. And it wouldn't be filled, because it never could be filled. The richness of that life hit her powerfully. She could travel the world over as anyone she wanted to be. She didn't have to be the "Weird Girl." Anonymity, true and abiding, could finally be hers.

"You're intrigued," he said, sounding encouraged, watching her mind churn over the possibilities.

"Offer someone the fountain of youth, and they're bound to be intrigued."

"True, but that's not the part that fascinates you, is it?"

She met his gaze, trying not to let herself fall back into that dizzying place of potent desire. Her lips burned to kiss him, hands ached to roam over his body. But it was just chemicals. She had to resist. She bit the corner of her lip, and he smiled.

"What's wrong?" he asked, stepping closer, tongue lashing out to lick the corner of her mouth.

She was about to say "Don't," about to place a hand on his chest to keep him at bay. But instead her tongue met his, and she kissed him, his irresistible taste flooding into her.

No. She stopped, lowering her head, letting the luxuriant cloud dissipate around her. Pheromones. Nothing more. It wasn't magic. Wasn't love. It wasn't anything more than chemistry, issuing from a killer, no less. A beast with a thousand forms, none of which she could trust. All of which could tear her apart and eat the soft insides.

He took her hands in his and looked at her with desire, his eyes flashing. "I hunger for you," he said. "But not in the way you think. Not like I did up on the mountain, before I . . . experienced you."

Madeline's mind crashed back to that terrifying day, running down the mountain, frozen and soaked with river water, teeth chattering. She thought of the night she spent crammed into the rock crevice. Could this really be the same creature who hunted her that night? That black creature made entirely of shadows, with red saucer eyes that gleamed in the dark? He'd seemed so alien that night, so outside of anything she'd experienced. Yet now she'd felt inside him. She thought of her race to the ranger's station, and of what she found there in the bathroom, slung over the rafters: the creature up there with the corpse, cracking bones between its teeth. What had it gained from eating that person? Intimate knowledge of the backcountry. Especially of that particular area. An efficient predator indeed.

"You're a killer," she repeated.

"Yes."

She thought again of Noah, of how long he had tracked the creature. Of his despair and hopelessness when he'd lost the weapon he'd carried for so many years.

"And your greatest hunter now has no way to kill you."

"I was growing tired of being hunted."

She remembered him saying the same thing the night in the cabin when he'd pretended to be Noah. She'd forgotten that till now, assuming at the time that he'd been her rescuer from the mountain.

"It's hard to sleep," he said, "knowing someone's out there with the ability to kill you, and they're drawing ever nearer, tracking your every move."

She almost laughed at the hypocrisy. "Don't you understand, then, how your victims must feel?"

"Yes, I do. And I think it makes me all that more of an efficient hunter. It lets me know how people are likely to react, lets me remember fear." His hand came up under her chin, lifting her gaze to his own. "But all that commiseration is over now. Noah no longer has the weapon."

"And that means you're unstoppable?" she asked, scrutinizing him.

He didn't answer, just continued to look at her.

"Are you?" she asked again, fear tugging at her. She glanced up and down the path, wondering how she was going to get out of this. No one had come by in awhile.

"Would you take up his sword?" he asked her.

"Will you continue to kill?"

His unspoken answer filled his eyes, red flashes of hunger, the gleam of victims yet to be explored and devoured.

And in her heart burned her own answer: *Yes.* A great floodwater broke within her. Years of reluctance to use her gift washed away before a newfound determination.

He sensed it, and she knew he did. He'd offered her something amazing and terrible, and she stood before him, not only refusing, but fighting him.

He pulled away, dark hair fluttering in the breeze. "You would destroy me when I offer you so much?"

"Would you destroy me if I turned you down?"

He crossed his arms, a puzzled expression on his face. After a long, strained moment of silence, he said, "Well, I can't have you trying to stop me."

Her mouth went dry, feet sinking into the ground, suddenly heavy as boulders. She was stupid. *Stupid. Should have played along.* Maybe it wasn't too late. Maybe if she said the right thing, she could think of an advantage.

"I wouldn't go following you, Stefan. I just want to go home, regain some semblance of the normal life I had before all this."

"And your talent?"

She raised an eyebrow. "What of it?"

"Are you going to waste it?"

She didn't answer, though she knew now she'd use it.

"Because I certainly wouldn't." He uncrossed his arms, slouched forward slightly. "Waste it, that is."

So there it was. If she didn't use her gift, then he'd kill her for it. But she couldn't very well tell him she'd use it for good . . . could she? "I won't waste it. I've seen what I can do with it, what I want to do with it."

He laughed, taking her off guard. It was no laugh of malice, but of genuine amusement. "We could be a pair! Can you imagine? Me taking lives, you saving them. Century after century. The wonders I've seen just since I've known your friend Noah. The waltzes of Strauss. Swing music. Two world wars. Photographs from the Hubble Space Telescope. Think of what lies ahead."

She did think of it. But the road was darker than the one he painted, filled with the wraiths of his future victims. Perhaps he could overlook her saving lives as a whimsical facet of her personality, but she could never overlook his murdering innocent people. *And what of guilty people?* she suddenly thought. *Do they not count? You're not very broken up about the guys who tried to attack you.* But murder in the defense of someone else in no way made up for all, or even a majority, of the creature's kills. She knew that.

"Stefan," she said, watching him closely. "Those men you killed near the cabins. Did you do that so you could be the one to kill me?"

He didn't answer right away, looking up and down the path. The breeze blew his hair across his face, and he moved it aside with his hand. Then he met her gaze, the red flash gone from his eyes as they returned to green. "No."

She waited for him to expand. The burbling song of the river filled the silence between them. "Why did you then?"

He exhaled. "I killed them because they were pathetic swine," he answered, his tone so abrupt it surprised her. He was angry. The muscle in his jaw clenched. "People like that kill and break things because they're stupid, bored, and impotent. They have no concept of the power, the wonder of life. They seek only to take it away because they themselves can't feel it. They seek to destroy people from the inside out but don't even have the consciousness to understand why." He fisted his hand. "I killed them because the world was no more the poorer for it. And those who enliven the world would be freer for it."

She stared, unable to find words. "It's terrible, and maybe I shouldn't say this, but I'm glad you were there that night." She stepped forward and took his hand. His skin was hot under her touch.

"Let me tell you something about death," he said. "Humans have shaped this world to revolve around them. They talk of the tragedy of earthquakes or floods. But natural forces aren't tragedies. What humans forget is that they are just another animal that can drown, or freeze to death, or yes, even be eaten.

"They've hunted all of their natural predators nearly to extinction. They'd like to believe they're invulnerable, on top of the food chain. And what has this mentality done for them? Disease, overpopulation, war. Humans aren't separate from nature; they're a part of it. Everything they do impacts the very natural processes they'd like to ignore.

"Humans are meat for the predator as surely as cows are meat for them. Without natural predators, overpopulation is inevitable. Thousands of years have shown me this. I've seen the world grow from a few pockets of people to cities, to civilizations, to one continuous stream of concrete and roads, towering buildings, and mass destruction wreaked with the push of a button—nature plowed under and destroyed in humanity's wake.

"I am not the monster. My prey is the monster."

She stood silently, his words striking her. He gripped her hand tightly when she tried to back away. The scariest part was that he made sense to her.

He looked down at their hands, then brought hers to his lips. "My name," he said, lips brushing her fingers, "is not Stefan."

She gazed back, puzzled.

"That's just the name Noah knew me by in Vienna."

"What is it then?" she asked, forcing herself to talk, to crawl up out of the tumble of thoughts his words had left her with, struggle to act through the veil of delicious energy between them.

He laughed. "Practically unpronounceable. But it's not Stefan."

She thought again of the sheer sense of ancient she'd felt that night on the road and wondered what the name could be, what culture he was from—if he was ever human, as Noah had speculated, sometime long, long ago.

They stood there together in silence for several minutes, and Madeline's mind raced over everything that had led up to this moment. Her escape into the backcountry from her tiny town of gossip and ostracism. The creature stalking her in the wilderness. Noah begging her to help him. This very moment next to the river. She frowned. Everything hinged on her psychic ability. If she wasn't psychometric, she wouldn't be out here in the first place. The creature wouldn't be stalking her. Noah wouldn't have enlisted her help. The creature wouldn't be trying now to seduce her.

Her whole life she'd been measured by her psychic prowess. Either she was too weird to have friends, or people wanted her close in order to take advantage of her ability. This moment was no different. The creature was no different. And now he was telling her that if she didn't use her ability, he'd alleviate her of it at the expense of her life.

A long-simmering anger that had been building since childhood reached boiling point. Wasn't she worth knowing without her ability? Who would ever bother to find out? She was so much more than psychometric. Her soul itself had been crying out for twenty-one years, and no one had heard it. And now this creature threatened to squelch that soul in order to get at the very thing that had made her life miserable. Her ability. Her "gift." Her soul, personality, vibrancy, and life would fall to the wayside so this shape-shifting thing could get another advantage.

The anger flared into rage, which threatened to overflow. The creature stood before her, still holding on to her hand, clawed fingers laced in her own.

A seething, bubbling primal force of fury welled up within her, and she brought her other hand up, shoving the creature away violently. Quickly she raised her foot high, connecting with his stomach with a sickening *thunk*. She kicked hard, shoving him back, where he stumbled over the exposed root, this time too quickly to right himself. Careening backward, he crashed into a ten-foot granite boulder, head connecting with a sharp corner. He cried out in surprise and pain as it bit into his skull with an audible crack.

She ran forward as his body jelled, and he fell limply to the ground. Grabbing his hand, she pulled him up, adrenaline flooding through her veins, rage straining in her neck. She could feel the muscles standing out there and uttered a low, angry roar as she dragged him to his feet and shoved him back again, where he stumbled onto the path.

Groggy from the blow to his head, he brought his hands up ineffectually, and she knocked them away, landing another solid kick to his gut.

"You can go to hell!" she screamed, spittle raining from her mouth. "I'll kill you!"

The world fell away, narrowing to a tiny beam of focus before her. The creature. The roaring river behind him. There teal waves crashed over huge granite boulders slick with algae. Stefan brought his hands to his head, disoriented, as blood streamed down his forehead, dripping from his hair. She kicked him hard in the head, then shoved his chest with her hands, knocking him back inexorably toward the water.

To her horror, he grabbed onto her arms with the last shove, trying to take her with him. But she brought her hands up lightning fast, connecting with the underside of his chin. His hands came free, releasing her as his head snapped back.

She dropped low, kicking her leg out, and delivered two shattering blows to his knees. He staggered back, stumbled, and fell, arms windmilling in the air, until he hit the water hard.

His body disappeared in the foaming white water. She ran to the edge of the river, eyes searching. She saw him bob up limply a few feet away, swiftly borne on the current, his head connecting sharply with the edge of a slimy rock. Blood frothed in the water, and he cried out in surprise.

She thought of his long fingers pulling her under in the flash flood. He'd been scared then, a creature not at home in the frigid, tumbling water.

She'd just put him back in that unforgiving place, and turning, ran away as his body flopped helplessly downstream.

19

MADELINE looked at her watch. Five p.m. George would be there in just a few minutes. Once the creature crawled out of the river, though she hoped he'd be swept far downstream by then, the cabin was one of the places he knew he could find her.

If she was going to get her wallet and keep the creature from knowing her future address, this was her only chance.

Breaking into a run, Madeline followed the path toward the cabins, the dirt and small pebbles of the path crunching underfoot. As she rounded a turn in the path, ducking under a low bough of hemlock, she passed several startled-looking people who stared at her as she went by. She gave them a curt nod, as if that would convince them she wasn't a mad person fleeing the scene of a crime. She supposed she did make something of a spectacle, tearing down the path at full tilt, not even having the decency to wear jogging clothes and thereby explain her haste.

She continued on, and soon through the white trunks of the aspen, the cabins came into sight. She jogged to hers, reaching into her pocket and producing the key.

Before she inserted it, she glanced over her shoulder at the cabin parking area. No Jeep. Noah hadn't returned yet. She felt torn about seeing him again. She had grown to care for him and longed to see him. But if he truly hated her, honestly wanted her dead, then she hoped she wouldn't run into him again. It hurt her more than she wanted to admit. Her whole life she'd tried to create a tough shell around herself so that if people rejected her—which they usually did, thanks to her lovely gift—it wouldn't hurt so much.

She opened the door slowly, and though she knew the creature couldn't possibly have beaten her there, she quickly scanned the main room and dashed to the small bedroom to check it, too.

It was clear.

She grabbed her wallet off the little table in the main room, and then the toothpaste and toothbrush Noah had bought her, along with the Swiss Army pocket knife. Thankfully she'd had it in her pocket when the flash flood hit. Had it been in her pack, it would be lost in the drink. She slipped the knife and wallet into the roomy back pocket of the jeans.

Not wasting a moment, she crammed the toothpaste and toothbrush into the paper bag she'd brought the sandwiches back with and quickly left the cabin, locking the door behind her.

Once again she scanned the parking area, but Noah's car was nowhere in sight.

She glanced at her watch. George should be here any minute. She just wanted to jump in the car and drive straight to Mothershead. She probably wouldn't be any safer there, but at least there she knew the territory. If the creature still insisted on pursuing her, she'd be ready.

Picking up the pace, Madeline hurried toward the camp store, where George and she had agreed to meet.

When she reached the parking lot in front of the cabins, she saw his familiar light blue Toyota Celica pull up. Behind the wheel, George scanned over the tourists for signs of Madeline. She waved, jogging over to the car.

When he saw her, his face lit up. He stopped the car in the middle of the parking lot, much to the chagrin of the cars waiting behind him, great white sharks ever vigilant in their circling for a parking place. He stepped out of the car. "Madeline!"

"George!" She knew she'd be happy to see him, but to have him there in the actual flesh was more comforting than she'd realized. The sun streamed on his long black hair, making it shine in the bright light.

He opened his arms, and she raced into them, resting her chin on his shoulder. His familiar scent washed over her: the smell of his lime shaving cream and floral shampoo, the hint of Egyptian Musk oil he wore on occasion. "George, it's so good to see you," she breathed. "Let's get out of here."

Impatient drivers behind them started pulling around, squeezing between George's car and the parked cars beside it. Several glared at them poignantly.

"But . . . already? I just got here. It'd be nice to stretch my legs. It's just as beautiful as I'd remembered. Haven't been here for a long time." His gaze wandered out to the breathtaking expanse of Lake McDonald, with the mountains beyond growing golden in the oncoming sunset. "Wow."

"We can come back," she said quickly. "And I can drive if you're too stiff."

He looked back at her, studying her face. "What's wrong?"

She sighed. This wasn't the time to explain everything. "Tell you on the way."

"Is everything okay?"

"It will be if we get out of here now." With each passing moment, she pictured the creature dragging itself out of the river and shaking itself off like a beast upon the riverbank, then coming to find her and finish its job.

"You looked really spooked."

She went around to the passenger door of his car and lifted the handle. "I have good reason. Please, George, just get in and drive me back."

He nodded, gave a last look at the soft ripples of the

darkening lake, and climbed back in his car. Closing the door after himself, he studied her once again. "Straight back to Mothershead?"

She nodded. He threw the car in gear and navigated through the parking lot, the backup of cars behind him restlessly creeping along behind them, tailgating.

George wound around one end of the parking lot and started toward the exit, driving by several trinket shops and the backcountry ranger station. Madeline kept her head low, not wanting Stefan to spot her. Once out of the congested area, George turned onto the road that led toward West Glacier, the small community just outside the park. Madeline lifted her head once the speedometer climbed to twenty-five miles an hour on the main park road.

"Mind telling me what this is all about?" her friend asked, peering at her out of the corner of his eye.

She looked over his car. Three bags of chips lay empty and gutted, crumbly remnants covering the driver's seat and clustering beneath the emergency brake. A half-empty bottle of Pepsi sat in a cup holder near the stick shift.

"I appreciate your coming on such short notice."

He smiled. "No problem."

In the backseat lay several paperback novels, some old CDs, and an umbrella. On the floor behind the driver's seat lay crumpled wet clothes.

A red shirt lay under a pair of sodden black jeans.

"Why are your clothes wet?" she asked, trying to remain calm.

He frowned. "They're not."

She took in his current outfit, a black T-shirt and faded black jeans. "I'm not talking about what you're wearing. I'm talking about these!" She grabbed the wet clothes and brought them forward, slapping them down in George's lap.

He started at her sudden move, then just stared at her.

"Well?"

After a pause he said, "I got caught in a sprinkler system at a truck stop. They were watering this little grassy stretch where people can walk their dogs—"

She wrenched her hand up quickly and grabbed George's hair in her fist. It was completely dry. But that didn't mean the creature couldn't create hair that was dry when he shape-shifted.

"Then how come your hair's not wet?" she said, releasing it.

He looked at her incredulously. "Because it happened a couple of hours ago, on my way up here. I changed my clothes right after it happened. And my hair just air dried."

Madeline squeezed the dripping clothes in her fists. Water streamed from the fabric, and it smelled musty, like river water. "These are not two hours dry."

He turned to face her, momentarily taking his eyes off the road. "Madeline, are you okay? What's wrong?"

It was then she noticed the faint bruise on the underside of his chin, black and blue precisely where she had struck the creature back at the river. The extent of healing matched the timing of the blow.

She reached up, placing her hand on the cool of George's headrest. Nothing but white noise flooded into her, interspersed with a vivid flash of a short, muscular man, a previous owner of the car, stepping out to pump gas, thrilled about landing a new job. She pressed her hand there a moment longer, seeking visions of George. None came. She withdrew her fingers and stared back at him.

Had the creature killed George and replaced him? Or worse, had George ever existed in the first place? She thought of when he'd come into her life. He'd been so accepting. So easy to get along with. None of the problems cropped up that she'd had with other would-be friends. No adjustment period after he learned about her "gift," almost as if he'd already been prepared for it. And she'd met him about seven months ago, and Noah said the creature had been hunting her for months. George never told her in specifics where he'd been prior to that, only of his future plans to attend college in Missoula. In fact, he'd been evasive when she asked about his past. Her racing mind went over the details of the death of Noah's lover, how the creature had insinuated itself into her life. Posed as a suitor in order to get close. Learned who her circle of friends were. Waited for the perfect moment to strike.

George had known about her solo backcountry trek. Worse still, she'd even given him a detailed map of her route. He'd known what trail she'd use on any given day of her trip and even where she'd be along that trail.

Turning in her seat, she cracked him hard in the face with her elbow.

George cried out in surprise and pain. His hand flew up defensively, the car swerving into the oncoming lane. He slammed on the brakes as a Honda Civic honked and swung wide around them. The Celica screeched to a halt, the smell of burning rubber filling the car. Grabbing his head in her hands, Madeline smashed it hard against the glass of the driver's side window. Blood streaked down the window as she let go. She released her seat belt and leaped out of the car, taking off into the trees beyond.

Not daring to look back, she ran, dodging between white aspen trunks that glowed in the slanting light of the setting sun. The ground lost elevation, and she darted down a rise and slipped in a section of mud. Her boots lost all traction, and she came down hard on her back. Quickly flipping over onto her stomach, she peered up to the top of the rise, expecting at any moment to see a sleek, black shadow appear at the top of the hill, eyes red and gleaming, eager for the hunt. She tried to listen over her own labored breathing and the deafening sound of blood pumping through her burning ears.

She was only a quarter mile or so from the town of West Glacier. Getting her bearings, she realized that the car lay between her and the town. She'd either have to make a wide arc around the car or charge back the way she'd come, hoping the creature hadn't had time to recuperate. If she took a wide arc, it could easily recover and then lope after her, quickly covering the ground between them.

She chose to retrace her footsteps.

Rising to her feet, wiping muddy hands on her shirt, she bounded up the rise. Running diagonally so she wouldn't pass directly near the car, she raced toward the road. In a few seconds the black asphalt came into view, along with George's light blue car. She passed quickly over the road, not stopping, but glancing at the car as she did so. He was still in the car, slumped over the wheel, one window dripping red.

She made it over the road and entered the trees on the other side, heading toward the tiny refuge of West Glacier.

20

SOON the trees parted, and another road came into view: the main road that ran through West Glacier. She broke through the treeline and stopped at the side of the asphalt, scanning up and down. Across the street lay the West Glacier Motel, and next to it a line of gift shops and a restaurant. She jogged along the road without crossing, sprinting across the parking lot of a small camera store. Inside, customers browsed over the racks of filters and film.

She passed the store, then ran across the parking lot of a gas station, where patrons stared at her as she darted through the maze of cars.

She forced herself to stop running, to slow to a walk and figure out what to do. Chest heaving, she stopped altogether, bending over to catch her breath. Before her stood the impressive stone building of the Alberta Visitor Center, a tasteful structure of gray stone with large windows. The Canadian flag flapped in the breeze above it.

She wanted to get out of the open. Glancing back at the road and seeing no sign of the Toyota or "George," she walked to the visitor center and opened the tall entrance doors. Inside, a cluster of visitors stood at the information desk while Canadian attendants busied themselves handing out maps and giving directions.

To one side of the desk stood a massive false rock face with a taxidermied mountain goat on top. She ducked down a narrow passageway to her left, winding by displays on logging and early tourism industry in the Canadian Rockies.

Finally she found a quiet little corner by a luge display and sat down next to its red and white sled. What could she do? What were her options? She could rent a car, but she didn't know of any nearby places, and it would take her a while to find them. She'd also have to scare up a ride to the rental location if it was too far away.

She could hitchhike. But at this point, paranoia was tightening its already considerable grip on her perceptions. The creature could be any person who picked her up along the road. Stefan would just have to steal a different car, assume a different form, and nonchalantly pick her up from the side of the road.

She put her head in her hands.

"You okay?" asked a young voice next to her. A little blonde-haired girl stood there, a rubber lizard in one hand.

Madeline smiled. "Yeah. Just got a headache."

"You should take aspirin. My mom gives me this orange-flavored aspirin. It's pretty good."

Madeline guessed at the girl's age. Five. Maybe six. Kate's age. In all the panic of the last few days, she'd nearly forgotten about the little girl she'd pulled from the dam. She hoped Kate was okay.

"Cool lizard," Madeline said, indicating the girl's rubbery companion.

"It's a gecko. His name's Dexter."

"Hiya, Dex," Madeline said.

The girl laughed. A woman walked up behind the child and put her hands on the small shoulders. "Ready to go? We'll go get ice cream."

"Really? I'm ready!"

She turned without a word and grasped her mother's hand. Together they walked away, rounding a corner beyond further displays.

Madeline returned her head to her hands. "What am I going to do?" she whispered.

Outside, the distinct shriek of a train whistle sounded. She lifted her head.

The train. Lots of people would be on it. And the station was just around the corner from the visitor center. The whistle pierced the air again.

She was out of the visitor center in a flash, pushing past a family that was dithering over a map of Banff National Park in the doorway.

Outside, she ran up a small rise and saw the silver of an Amtrak train sitting at the station.

Scanning the road, she saw no sign of George or the car.

She rushed toward the station, hoping the train would stay at the station for a few more minutes.

Madeline ran to the ticket window, trying to catch her breath to talk to the cashier there. An elderly man with a neatly trimmed white mustache, he waited patiently while she gasped and tried to swallow away the dryness in her throat. "Does this train go through Mothershead?" she asked.

The cashier shook his head. "Nope. This is the Empire Builder. It goes west from here but stops along the way in Whitefish, and you can take a bus from there."

"Great," she said between gasps. "Is it leaving soon?"

"At 5:46 p.m." He looked at his watch, a gold-banded thing with a black face. "That's in about twenty minutes."

"Terrific." She pulled her wallet from the roomy back pocket of Noah's jeans. Fishing her credit card out, she passed it across the counter.

He totaled up her ticket and finished the sale, handing her a small folder with her ticket inside. Then he pulled out a piece of paper and wrote something on it. "These are the bus times out of Whitefish," he explained, "and directions to get to the bus station from the train." He slid that paper across the counter, too.

"Thanks," she said, taking the offered paper and envelope.

"You can go ahead and board, if you like. Might be a good idea. You can get a better seat."

She nodded and turned away from the counter. Light from the setting sun streamed into the little train station, and she squinted against the golden brightness.

Outside the train waited, and uniformed Amtrak employees stood by the doors to assist passengers. She left the small station and crossed to the closest attendant, a young woman with cocoa-colored skin and long, braided hair swept up under her hat. "Go up to the second level and sit wherever you like," she told Madeline. "The conductor will come by later and take your ticket once the train's in motion."

"Okay, thanks," Madeline said, smiling at her. She scanned up and down the platform. She was alone except for the train workers.

She stepped up into the train and climbed the small staircase to the first level. Racks of baggage rose on either side of her, suitcases stacked neatly next to army duffels and back-country packs. To her right stood another staircase, this one taller than the first. She climbed its carpeted steps and emerged on the second level in the heart of coach seating.

Most of the seats were empty, and she was glad for it. She'd been hoping to have a couple seats to herself so she could stretch out. She chose a seat on the right side of the train so she could look out that way in the direction of George's car and the park. Only five people occupied the car: a couple near the front sat sound asleep; a woman in her fifties read a Dorothy Gilman novel; a young guy in a cowboy hat sat listening to headphones with his eyes closed; and the last one, a Caucasian dreadlocked guy about her age wearing a batik shirt, sat staring out of the window and looking as if he'd just left the love of his life behind. She could feel sadness wafting off him.

She sat down, bombarded momentarily by the white-noise

Bus Seat Effect, which she tuned out. Leaning forward in the seat, she waited impatiently for the train to depart, watching out of the window with unease.

Madeline started awake with a jerk. She hadn't even realized she'd dozed off. Her exhausted body had made the choice for her.

The train lurched out of the station, and her drowsy head knocked against the seat's headrest. Out of the window, Glacier National Park stretched into the distance. The sun had dipped below the horizon, and shadows filled the forest. They chugged away from the station, slowly passing through the tiny town of West Glacier. She watched the Glacier Highland Resort go by out of the opposite window.

Gradually the train picked up speed as it chugged by the small, scenic towns of Hungry Horse and Columbia Falls on its way to Whitefish. When they'd been under way for ten minutes, Madeline stretched and got out of her seat. Her stomach rumbled, demanding a visit to the café car. She started for the rear of the train, bouncing around the center aisle as the train made its turbulent way down the tracks. On one lurch, she almost ended up in the lap of the woman reading Dorothy Gilman. The older woman smiled up at Madeline from beneath a flowered hat.

Madeline reached the end of the car and pressed the large metal button on the car's door. With a noisy whoosh, it slid open, admitting her to the loud area between her car and the one behind it.

She pressed the square button on the next door, and with a whoosh was admitted to the next car. This one was even emptier, with only two people occupying it. One was a man in his fifties working on a laptop. He looked up as she entered, smiled faintly, and returned to his work.

The other passenger was a haggard, furtive-looking woman who was crocheting what looked like Christmas stockings. She gave Madeline's muddy shirt an unfriendly once-over and returned to her hook and yarn.

Madeline walked to the end of the car, pushed the door button, and entered the confines of the place between the cars. When she pressed on the next button, the noisy door opened to admit her to the next car.

The first thing she saw when the door opened fully was George, standing up in the aisle, facing her, with a wad of paper towels soaking up blood from the nasty gash she'd given him.

He saw her. She backed up, the door sliding closed without her passing through it. He raced forward, pressing the button on the door just as she was pivoting to get back into the previous car. The door opened, painfully slowly, and Madeline was halfway through it when he caught her by the shoulder and pulled her back.

"What the hell is going on?" he demanded, shouting above the din of the train in the confined area. She flung his hand away. "You're my friend, and I'll give you the benefit of the doubt, but I'd sure like to know why you asked me to come all the way up here so you could smash my head open. And I'm still trying to figure out why I was crazy enough to follow you onto this train and abandon my car back in the park. I just saw you duck into the station, and my brain went out of the window. I wanted to help you." He gingerly fingered the bandage on his head. "What was left of my brain, anyway."

She studied him intently, the face she'd come to know as her friend's face, the eyes she'd once trusted.

"I've read Noah's diary," she warned him. Behind her back she reached for the door button.

George lifted his eyebrows. "What?" He threw up his hands in exasperation. "Who's Noah?"

She shook her head. "I know your MO. What you've done here is really clever, and I didn't figure it out until it was almost too late. What did you plan to do? Drive me somewhere desolate where no one would interrupt you while you stole my life?"

George looked thoroughly confused. He put one hand to his temple, the other still holding the wad of red-soaked paper towels. Blood dripped down into his eye. "Okay . . . hold on.

Have you completely lost it? What in the world are you talking about?"

Her searching hand found the door button, and the door slid open. She backed into the car, then turned and ran down the center aisle, the train lurching and throwing her off balance repeatedly as she went.

She glanced over her shoulder. George hadn't followed. She could still see him between the cars, staring at her through the door's window.

She passed through the doors into the next car, wanting to find a conductor or, even better, a large group of people. She thought of the observation lounge, the car on the train comprised almost completely of windows, including the ceiling. Usually they were packed. It would be near the rear of the train, back by the dining and café cars. And George blocked the way.

She'd have to think of some way to get around him or barge by him. She ran through the car and entered her own. Her eyes fell on the stairs leading down to the baggage area, where she had first boarded the train.

Quickly she bounded down them, finding the area much as she'd seen it before. No one was down there, just suitcases and duffel bags. A door lay to her right, and she pushed the button to open it. It didn't budge. Beyond the door window it was completely dark. She guessed the sleeping cars were somewhere on the lower level. Perhaps this was one of them. Or some kind of off-limits train crew room.

She was going to have to get past George. Briefly she entertained the notion of climbing outside the train and up onto the roof, then leaping along from car to car like in so many thrillers she'd seen. At first the thought seemed crazy, but it started to grow on her when she thought of coming face-to-face with the creature again.

Tentatively she went to the door through which she had boarded the train. Feeling like she was shoplifting or hot-wiring a car, she reached out and pushed the door's button. Nothing happened. She tried it again. The door didn't budge.

Part of her was relieved. Taking her chances inside the

train with the creature seemed only slightly riskier than stumbling along the top of the lumbering locomotive. She pictured tunnels with low clearance and tremendously cold, mountain winds that could sweep her off the smooth steel roof.

She turned away from the door and crept to the bottom of the stairs. Staring up the stairwell, she saw no sign of her pursuer, but she knew he was up there somewhere, choosing the best place to ambush her.

If only she could hide somehow. But the hiding places on a train were greatly limited, especially if one didn't have a sleeping car. No matter how easy old movies made it look to completely hide from someone on a train, riding coach on Amtrak was a completely different story. Her options were in plain sight in a large group, locked in a toilet stall in the woman's bathroom, or lying down inside someone's duffel bag after throwing all their stuff out.

None of them seemed too hopeful.

With growing dread, Madeline returned to the stairs and peered upward. She listened for anything unusual above the trains clackity clack on the tracks. She didn't hear anything.

Slowly she climbed the stairs and looked over the car. The same people still sat there. No one new. No one looked alarmed, all just reading or staring out of the window as scenic Montana faded into night.

She crept through her car, then passed into the next. Still, the two passengers sat there, not even looking up this time. Stefan could be one of them. She could file by them, and he could reach out and grab her, sinking teeth into her neck.

She rushed down the corridor and entered the next car, the one where she'd originally seen George. He still stood there, still clutched the paper towels to his head. He saw her enter the car, and she stopped.

"Madeline," he demanded, "what the hell is going on?"

She wanted to know for certain if he was the creature. A desperate part of her wanted her friend George to be real. "What were you doing before you came to Mothershead?"

"I lived somewhere else."

"Yeah, I know that part. But where?"

He wrinkled his brow. "Does it matter?"

"You know damn well that it matters. Answer the question!"

He visibly fumbled for an answer. "I was living in Billings."

"Doing what?"

Again, he hesitated, caught off guard. "I worked as a bookkeeper. For a law firm."

"Why were you so evasive when I asked you about your past before?"

He winced, pressing the paper towels closer to the wound. "I was embarrassed, okay? Bookkeeper. Law firm. Not exactly exciting."

It was a lame excuse, but the creature was obviously not willing to give up his deepest cover with her. "What does exciting matter?" she asked.

He paused. "It's just that . . . when I met you, you were always hiking or rock climbing, all this exciting stuff. I was so boring. I just didn't want you to know how boring."

She shook her head. This was going nowhere. She wanted to see his wound. By now it should be nearly healed. If it was, or if he refused to show it to her, she would know. "Let me see your head."

"What?" he asked exasperated, still covering it with the towels.

"Let me see it!" she yelled, suddenly aware of the other passengers in the car, who stared at her and then looked away quickly when she met their eyes.

George backed up. "I don't think so," he said.

"Why?"

He paused warily. "I don't trust you," he said finally.

She didn't know how she was going to get past him. He completely blocked the aisle.

The other passengers stared. A couple in their thirties entered the car ahead of them.

"George," she suddenly gushed. "Oh gosh, you don't look so good. You look like you're going to pass out!"

He wrinkled his brow in confusion. "No, I'm not. I—"

"Oh, yeah," she went on. "Your pupils are completely dilated. You need immediate medical attention!" She turned to the couple as they approached. "Excuse me," she said. "Can you help me take my friend to the train's clinic? He's really in a bad way."

"Sure," the woman said quickly. Her husband gave her a withering look. "We'd be glad to help."

George shook his head. "Really—I don't need—"

"Nonsense," Madeline said quickly. Then to the couple: "I really appreciate it. He's so stubborn. And I don't think his balance is too great with that bump on his head."

"No problem," the husband grumbled, giving in to his wife's good nature.

Madeline slid her arm around George's waist, and the husband did the same on the other side. They began slowly walking him toward the rear of the train, where the medical attendant's area lay. The wife walked ahead of them. "Are you okay?" she asked George.

He exhaled in exasperation. "This is totally unnecessary!"

"See how stubborn he is?" Madeline said to the wife. Inside, though, she knew it wasn't stubbornness but calculated strategy. If he showed her the wound now, she'd know he was the creature. His refusal convinced her he was in fact her hunter. She had to get away while he was distracted.

The woman rolled her eyes. "Tell me about it. My Reginald is the same way."

When they pressed the door button and entered the space between the cars, Madeline suddenly cried out in alarm, "Oh, no! George, I left your wallet with all our money sitting on the seat! I have to go get it!" She turned to the kind woman. "Will you see that he gets to the clinic?"

The woman nodded. "Of course."

"Thanks!" Madeline let go of George's waist and returned to the previous car. She'd wait there for a few minutes, long enough for the couple to escort him down to the clinic, and then she'd move forward to the observation car.

When she'd waited another five minutes, she passed

between the cars and entered the observation lounge. About ten people sat around in the molded plastic white seats, most staring out at the sunset beyond. A businessman read a newspaper, a teenage boy relaxed with an MP3 player. Two kids about five years old pounded each other with their fists while their dad told them in an annoyed voice to cut it out. No sign of "George." He'd have to play along with the couple till he got rid of them. He wouldn't risk killing them out of annoyance in such a public place.

Madeline slumped down next to an older man in hunting coveralls reading a newspaper in the bright overhead fluorescent lights. She exhaled. Tried to work out some tension in her shoulders with her fingers. She shut her eyes briefly, then opened them, taking in the tremendous black peaks silhouetted against the golden sky.

The older man next to her lowered his newspaper and turned his head to stare at her. Unsettled, she tried to ignore him, but he watched her so pointedly that at last she turned and met his gaze. Terror swept over her. The sad eyes. The kind, fatherly face that had deceived so many. The wicked mouth turned up in a grin, revealing crooked, chipped teeth.

Sam MacCready, the Sickle Moon Killer.

He looked at her with interest, then pivoted to fully face her. "You look surprised," he said, his voice trembling with anger. "You didn't buy that killed-in-a-prison-fight story, did you?"

"How did you . . . ?" she said, her mouth gone dry.

"Find you? With the right . . . persuasion . . . men can give away even their deepest secrets. It cost your dad a lot of skin, but eventually he caved."

Madeline stared. The terror she'd known since losing Ellie gripped her, freezing her to the spot. It was him. The Sickle Moon Killer. Same worry-creased brow, but the hair gray now, the physique muscular from years of prison weightlifting. From his hairy arms to his glowering expression, he was exactly as she'd seen him in nightmares haunting her since that day by the river.

She stood up silently and backed away, her movement in

slow motion as in a dream. But this was no dream. Everything was too harsh. The reek of cigarette smoke, the vibration of the train, the echoing voices of chattering train passengers.

She backed up to the car's door, mind numb. She should stay where she was, she thought. By all these people. He wouldn't try to kill her by all these witnesses. And he was human. She could hurt him. She could kill him, if necessary, to save her own life.

He stood up, walked over to where she stood by the door. She moved off to the side, keeping an escape route open. Several people climbed up the stairs from the small snack bar below, talking animatedly and pointing out the mountains to each other while crunching on nachos. They sat down where she and the Sickle Moon Killer had rested moments before. She didn't take her eyes off MacCready, making note of the other passengers in her peripheral vision. Even still, the flash of the knife darted out so quickly she barely had time to leap away. The blade tore through her sleeve, nicking her.

"What the hell?" cried a familiar voice. George's head appeared in the stairwell from the snack bar, and he bounded up the remaining stairs. She'd almost convinced herself it couldn't really be MacCready but must be the creature. But seeing George—that meant one of them was the creature. Didn't it? She furrowed her brow.

Throwing himself at the Sickle Moon Killer, George knocked the old man sprawling, both of them landing violently amid the seats.

"Someone call train security!" George yelled out.

Madeline gripped her arm where she had been cut. Blood seeped through the material, soaking her hand.

The observation car exploded with activity, people crying out in surprise and yelling for security.

George struggled with MacCready on the seats, restraining the hand with the flaying knife. Madeline darted forward, twisted the hand painfully, and wrenched the knife from the man's grip. His face contorted in fury when he saw her. Old, powerful rage and fear welled up within her, hatred filling her mind. Creature or not, she hated this man for what he had done, for haunting her all these years and killing the only person who had ever really loved her.

Her hand balled into a fist, and before she'd made the conscious decision, she pounded him in the face, his nose exploding with an audible pop. Blood sprayed out, flecking George's face as he struggled to keep the man down.

"I fucking hate you!" she yelled, pounding him again, this time connecting with an eye. Her left hand joined the rain of violence, and she landed blow after furious blow, including one to the throat that left him choking and gagging.

And then uniformed officers grabbed her and pulled her off MacCready. One restrained her while the other pulled George away.

"Are you okay, sir?" the portly, younger officer said to MacCready, obviously seeing him as some sort of elderly, innocent victim of a violent attack.

"He's the killer!" Madeline yelled. She thrashed in the restraining grip of the officer behind her, so angry she just wanted to pound the old man and the cop into oblivion.

By now all the passengers in the observation car and the snack bar below had gathered around the fight. "She's right!" a man said. "The guy had a knife!"

"He cut her!" another added.

"Is this true?" asked the officer who held her, a lean older man with wispy white hair.

"Yes, damn it!"

The cop released her, and she grabbed her arm again, the sleeve completely soaked now in her blood.

"Madeline," George said to her, pushing past the portly train cop to come to her. "Are you all right?"

She saw that his head had been neatly bandaged where she'd injured him.

She backed away, not sure what to make of him. "Stay back," she warned, fists still balled at her sides.

Behind him, the older cop approached, pulled out his handcuffs, and stood the Sickle Moon Killer up on his feet while his hefty partner looked on.

George frowned. "I don't understand. You leave without even saying good-bye. Then you ask me to come up here to get you and practically bash my brains in!"

Madeline stared at the Sickle Moon Killer, feeling half in a nightmare. It didn't mesh in the real world. She looked back at George then, puzzled. "What do you mean, I left without saying good-bye?"

Before he could answer, the Sickle Moon Killer suddenly threw his arms up, throwing off the older train cop before he had a chance to snap cuffs on the powerful hands. "You're dead!" he screamed at Madeline, spittle raining from his mouth.

He kicked the train cop in the gut just as the officer scrambled to get a hold on his prisoner. The flaying knife lay nearby on the floor, and he dived for it. Wiry fingers closed around the handle, and MacCready brought the knife up, connecting with the officer's stomach. A long, red line appeared as blood seeped through the man's torn button-down shirt. He staggered back, clutching his stomach. His young partner rushed to him as he fell, screaming for someone to get a doctor.

The Sickle Moon Killer advanced, eyes crazed and locked on Madeline.

She glanced around for a weapon but saw none, only bolted-down seats and other passengers staring on mutely. Her eyes fell on a hard-sided briefcase, and she picked it up, then hurled it at him. It connected with his shoulder, and he winced with pain.

Then the passengers started to panic. Some ran out of the observation car, piling into the dining car and sliding the door closed behind them. Three passengers came forward, two men and a woman in their forties who seemed to know each other. They moved forward as a single mass, shoulder to shoulder, and leapt as one at MacCready, grabbing his hands.

But the Sickle Moon Killer was amazingly strong, and his armed hand came free, flaying knife striking out at them, aiming for faces and arms and soft middles. One of the men screamed, a gash opening in his chest, and the woman crumpled to the floor when the knife tore open a pulsing artery in her arm. MacCready flung the last man to the side, and he clattered down the narrow stairs to the snack bar below, crying out in surprise and pain.

Now George and Madeline stood in the car with Mac-Cready and the two wounded Good Samaritans, who groaned and lay sprawled on the floor. One train cop was performing EMT duties on his partner, who lay prone, the color washed from his face.

The Sickle Moon Killer advanced on Madeline. She backed up, throwing everything she could find at him. A basket of nachos with dripping cheese. A copy of the *New York Times*, which rattled and fell at his feet. An abandoned backpack with a heavy book inside. The MP3 player. They bounced off him ineffectually.

George moved to the side, keeping out of MacCready's reach, furtive eyes searching for a way to restrain him. Madeline tried to think of the train's layout. The only turf she knew for certain was the cars behind them. She glanced over at the two train cops. The uninjured one leaned over his friend, applying pressure to the slice. Both had guns on their belts.

A *whoosh* admitted a woman in a white coat to the observation lounge. Taking in the situation and wounded people, she rushed first to the fallen cop.

"I got it from here," Madeline heard her say to the younger officer.

At that, the cop leaped to his feet, pivoting angrily.

As the Sickle Moon Killer steadily advanced on Madeline with the flaying knife, the cop unholstered his gun and aimed. A series of deafening shots rang out in the small confines of the car. Madeline clasped her hands to her ears as blood exploded from MacCready's chest in four places, raining over the white plastic seats.

A surprised look spread over his face, and he paused, the knife sliding from his hand. It clattered on the floor, and Madeline stepped forward quickly and kicked it away. MacCready swayed, opening his mouth. Blood spilled out, bubbling on his lips as he tried to suck in a breath. Then he crashed forward to his knees, looked up at her angrily, and crumpled face-first onto the floor. He lay there for several long, agonizing moments, trying to draw in breath, the blood seeping across the floor as it spilled from his mouth and chest. His back spasmed, arcing backward at an awkward angle. Then he went still.

Madeline crept forward. Kicked his arm. No reaction.

The surprised eyes still stared, glistening and wet.

The train's EMT stabilized the cop, then attended to the three Samaritans, the last of whom had just dragged himself up from the snack bar below. The EMT gestured to the wounded officer and the woman with the sliced artery, and said to the young cop, "We're going to have to get these people to a hospital in Whitefish." The officer didn't answer right away. He just stared at the fallen body of MacCready, gun still drawn. Crinkly eyes that looked like he'd known a lot of laughter in his time now looked gaunt and gray. At last he lowered the gun, put it in his holster, and turned back to his partner.

Madeline looked back at MacCready's body. As she watched, the eyes began to film over. He was dead.

George rushed to her side, placing a hand on her shoulder. She couldn't look away from the body. All the years she'd lived in terror, the never-ending flashbacks. She didn't think they'd go away now. She thought they'd get worse. Now the killer truly was free to roam anywhere, no longer confined to a body. His ghost would haunt her forever.

George's fingers squeezed her shoulder.

She jumped and spun around, flinging off his hand.

"It's okay, Mad. It's over."

She looked into his dark brown eyes. "It's far from over," she said. "What did you mean, I didn't say good-bye?"

"You just left. I thought when I didn't show up at the diner you'd at least stop by."

Her brow creased in confusion. "Didn't show up? But you were there. We had a long talk."

George took a step back. "What? No, I wasn't. I got jumped on the way." He pointed to the underside of his chin. "See this bruise? This crazy guy beat me up! Didn't even take anything. Just beat me up for the hell of it."

She stared at him in shock, looking again at the fading bruise under his chin. "You really weren't there?"

She thought of how alluring George had looked that night, when he never had before. How attracted she'd been. She took him in now. It was the same George she'd known for seven months—nothing strangely attractive about him at all now—and it hit her. Pheromones. It was pheromones that night. So Stefan had jumped George and replaced him for one night, in order to learn Madeline's route through the desolate backcountry. But she had to be sure. "If this is true, then why have you always been so evasive about your past? And don't give me that crap about being a bookkeeper."

"What does that have to do with anything?"

"Just answer the damn question," she demanded.

He looked down, ashamed. "I'm afraid you won't feel the same way about me anymore if you know."

"Just tell me."

He exhaled sharply. "I was in prison. Okay? I got involved with these guys who held up a gas station in Billings. But it was a long time ago, and I've really changed my life around now. Going to college. Moving to a new town. Meeting you."

She couldn't believe it. The answer wasn't at all what she'd expected. "Let me see your head."

Dutifully he peeled off one corner of the bandage, and she peered closely. A dark, painful-looking bruise surrounded a tear in the skin. It was a regular, human-looking wound.

She threw her arms around him. "George! You're you! You're human!"

He patted her back, trying to keep her at a distance, still distrustful. "Great news. I'm human. What a relief." Then he pulled back and looked at her in bewilderment.

"I'll explain everything when we get home," she said, glancing around the train car. Behind them, the EMT applied a tourniquet to the woman's arm and helped her and the chest-sliced victim out of the observation car. The last Samaritan remained with the injured cop, holding his hand.

At her feet, the Sickle Moon Killer's blood spread widely, dripping now into the stairwell leading down to the snack bar. An announcer stated that the train would be arriving in Whitefish in fifteen minutes.

A hand closed around her boot.

With a shriek she looked down, trying to jerk her foot away. The Sickle Moon Killer's eyes were no longer filmed over but gleamed red, luminescent disks housing no pupils. MacCready lifted his head, mouth opening to reveal rows of hideously pointed teeth.

She tried to kick the hand away, but it held fast, the other hand reaching up to grab her leg. Pale, white skin gave way to inky black sharkskin, graying brown hair vanished into shadow, and the creature rose to his feet, sliding toward her in the blood.

Releasing his grip on her, he tore away the hunting coveralls, emerging like a hideous black insect climbing from a camouflaged cocoon. A sharp gasp issued from the man sitting with the injured cop. Madeline glanced over there. He sat staring with horror at the creature, the same way she had that first night on the mountain.

"Madeline," George said in alarm.

"George, get the hell out of here."

"What?"

"Just get the hell out! He'll kill you!"

"That's right," said the creature, nodding at George. The coveralls fell in a heap at Stefan's feet, and he kicked them away. He extended his left arm, and the black glowed brightly to become gleaming silver, the hand sharpening into a point, fingers vanishing. The spike. She remembered the devastation on the guys in the campground. Turning, she shoved George away violently. He stumbled over the edge of one bank of chairs and fell on his back.

"Get out!" she screamed at him.

Then turning, she tackled the creature.

21

MADELINE didn't think the creature would risk stabbing her with the spike. Her flesh would bubble and dissolve, be reduced to ashes. Nothing left to eat. Until he tore out her throat or heart, she was safe.

She slammed into him, knocking him off balance. He sprawled on his back in the center aisle, and she landed roughly on top of him, straddling his body. With both hands she grabbed the shimmering spike and aimed it at his stomach. Then with all her weight she jumped up and landed on his upper arm, trying to drive the blade into his own body. But the minute it connected with his abdomen, the spike reduced itself to a hand again, the palm falling flat on the belly.

She grunted in frustration, bringing her fists down hard on his solar plexus. He groaned, deflecting the blows and knocking her to the side.

Behind her, George got to his feet. He rushed forward, grabbing Stefan's legs. She slid to one side and seized his hands. He tried to twist them free, but sheer rage gave her tremendous power, and she held fast.

Kicking his legs out, he tried to throw George off, but her friend wouldn't let go, even when he fell to the floor, banging his knee harshly on one of the seats.

Madeline struggled to get to her feet, constantly thrown off balance by Stefan's thrashing. Finally she managed to stand up and began dragging him toward the nearest door. "Help me carry him!" she yelled to George.

He got to his knees, still gripping the creature's thrashing legs. "I'll try!"

Both of Stefan's hands instantly extended to metal spikes.

Madeline choked up her hold and shifted her position, now gripping him under the arms. She managed to heft him up off the ground. With his spikes now free, Stefan stabbed at George repeatedly, but her friend was too quick, dodging from side to side to evade the blows.

Madeline backed into the door and pushed the button with her back. It slid open, and with a struggle they dragged him into the space between the cars. The noise of the train grew to a loud din as they banged into one wall and then were thrown into the opposite.

The door slid closed behind George. To Madeline's right stood an emergency exit door, a large red button on it. The train went into a turn and she lurched off balance, then regained it as Stefan once more tried to pierce George. Madeline jerked him back, destroying his reach, the spike falling short.

With her hip she hit the red button. The door slid open, and a ringing alarm erupted throughout the train.

"We need to get him closer to the door!" she urged her friend. But in the tiny area, to get Stefan next to the exit would mean they'd have to fold him up, and he'd be in striking range of George. "Drop him!" she yelled over the din of rushing air and *clackity clack* of the train's wheels surging along the tracks.

"Are you crazy?"

"Just do it!"

George dropped the creature's feet. Stefan immediately

planted them and bucked his torso upward. Madeline clung to
his back, kicking one wall with her boot. They pivoted violently, and she lunged toward the open door. "Don't let me fall
out!" she shouted to George.

When Stefan stood on the lip of the exit, she let go, held on
to the walls on both sides, and kicked her feet up, positioning
them firmly in the creature's back. Then she shoved.

He sailed out of the train into the night, landing harshly in
scrub bushes on the side of the tracks, then tumbled out of
sight down a steep embankment.

George rushed forward and grabbed her as she regained
her balance, pulling her back from the door as it closed.

"Damn!" George yelled happily.

Madeline held up a celebratory fist. "Yes!" She turned and
hugged her friend. "We did it!"

"Yeah! We kicked its ass right off the train!" They jumped
up and down in the tiny space, shouting and hooting. Then
George said, "What the hell was that thing?"

The door opposite the observation car opened, and the
young security officer appeared. "Was that you guys who
opened the emergency door?"

They nodded exuberantly.

"Is everything okay?"

"For now," Madeline said.

George looked at her nervously. "For now?"

The cop glanced out of the window. "We're heading into
Whitefish now. Going to unload the people who got injured.
Ambulance will come for the guy I . . . killed." He worked
hard to get out the last word. She got the feeling he'd never
even shot a person before, much less had to kill one.

Madeline glanced back toward the observation car. "Don't
feel too bad about shooting that creep," she said. "You didn't
kill him. He got up. In fact, he just got off the train."

The officer raised his eyebrows. "What do you mean?"

She pushed the button for the door leading to the observation car. It slid open. "See for yourself," she said.

The train cop pushed by them and entered the observation

lounge. He stood there motionless until the door closed again behind him. She heard his muffled "What the hell?" as the door clicked into place.

"Your arm," George said, gesturing at her blood-soaked sleeve.

In the excitement, she'd totally forgotten about it.

"We should get you to the train's EMT. She fixed my head up pretty good."

Madeline smiled, taking in the small bandage. "She sure did." After a pause, she added, "I'm really sorry about that. I think when I explain it all, you might find it in your heart to forgive me."

George shook his head and held up his hands. "If you've been dealing with this kind of crap lately, I can see why you'd totally flip out."

She looked out of the window as the train slowed, heading into Whitefish. Huge log cabin–style resort homes lit by dusk-to-dawn lights streaked by outside the window. "I was going to catch a bus to Mothershead from here. But we should go back and get your car. I'm sorry I ditched you."

"I'd like to get my car, too. I just left it in a gas station parking lot when I saw you get on the train. I hope it hasn't gotten towed. But first I want to know what's going on."

"Well, I hate to tell you this, but that thing we just threw off the train is practically indestructible, and it'll be back. We've just bought a little time, is all." She thought a minute. "Maybe we'd safer getting on the bus. It might be looking for your car."

"It's that smart?"

She laughed sardonically. "It's brilliant." She brought a tired hand to her forehead. "Let me think a minute. It knows where I live, but taking the bus just might buy us enough time to at least get back to Mothershead and get more help. Maybe we can overpower him again somehow. In a more permanent way."

"You keep calling it 'him.' What is it?"

Madeline looked up at George and almost smiled. She had asked Noah the same question that first night on the mountain. Now she was the one in the know, and her poor friend was trying to understand. She put her arms around him. "It's so good to see you," she told him. Then, wondering when exactly the bus left Whitefish, and where she should catch it, she pulled away and reached into the back pocket of Noah's jeans to pull out the slip of paper the train station clerk had given her.

Her fingers closed around a piece of paper, but it wasn't the clerk's note. She fished it out. It was the receipt from the cabin they'd stayed in.

Immediately powerful visions hit her.

Noah, distraught, devising a plan to get Madeline to leave the park by acting crazy to get her out of danger . . .

Noah planning to go to the creature's cabin to lie in wait, believing that if he ingests more blood, he will be able to manifest his own metallic spikes and kill the creature . . .

A gasp escaped her lips. He didn't hate her. It had been an act—all those hateful words he spat at her—just an act to get rid of her, to protect her. Relief flooded over her as the hurt she'd felt so deeply was replaced by hope, and then fear as she thought of the danger he was in. He couldn't face the creature alone and unarmed. Clutching the receipt, she pushed the door button and ran into the observation car. George followed. Dashing between the seats, she grabbed up the camouflage coveralls the creature had been wearing. She let the visions come.

The creature fantasizing about dragging her back to his rented cabin, slowly tearing her apart and eating all the soft parts, splitting open bones to get at the marrow. Later, after digestion, he'd go outside to test out his new psychometric ability . . .

Then . . . revenge. Killing Noah, his annoying hunter of so many years, before moving on to the next victim, reveling in the choices . . .

But first he'd go back to his cabin, get a chance to really recuperate, completely heal the wounds caused by Noah's special knife . . .

She dropped the coveralls. "Oh, no . . ." she breathed,

staring blankly out of the window, not seeing anything but her visions.

"What is it?"

Madeline turned to look at her friend, her eyes wide. "My friend Noah. He's going to get himself killed."

22

As soon as the train screeched to a halt at the Whitefish station, Madeline looked out one of the windows. The police had arrived, and an announcement from the conductor told them that no one was allowed to leave the train until questions had been asked.

Madeline clenched her teeth. "Damn!"

The other passengers who wanted to get off at Whitefish groaned and complained, standing impatiently in the aisles. They obviously hadn't heard yet about the disaster in the observation car.

"C'mon!" She grabbed George's hand, and they darted to the opposite side of the train from the platform. Another set of tracks lay on that side. She pressed the emergency release button on a door on that side. The alarm was still jangling from before, so no new alarm went off to draw attention to them.

"Are you crazy?" George shouted.

"I don't have a choice." She grabbed him harshly around the wrist and dragged him out of the train, bounding over the tracks. Large pools of light illuminated the station on this side, and she quickly ran to the extent of the light and darted into the shadows. Dark shrubbery and trees swallowed them on that side of the station, and they ran on.

She listened carefully for signs of pursuit. She didn't hear any police officers call out or hear anyone crashing through the bushes behind them. They reached a quiet, urban street, all the stores locked up for the night. She released her grip on George, who followed breathlessly, demanding to know where they were going. She shushed him rudely, not stopping to explain until they were several blocks from the station.

She turned down a shadowed, suburban street and stopped, waiting for him to catch up.

"I don't think they followed us. It was pretty chaotic back there."

"Okay," he said panting, trying to catch his breath. "Now you explain?"

She nodded. "Okay. As best I can. And while I'm talking, we have to find a way back to your car."

He brought his hand to his head. "I thought you'd decided on the bus?"

"No. The creature is headed back to his cabin. And my friend Noah is waiting for him there. I have to help him." She gazed up and down the street, trying to spot the way to Highway 2, which led back into the park. "Let's walk while we talk." She picked up the pace to a jog, heading toward a gas station where she could get directions to the highway. "We'll have to hitch," she said.

They reached the gas station, and she went inside the snack store. A burly man sat behind the counter, eating a long piece of round jerky. "Can I help you, miss?" he asked, swallowing.

"Which way to Highway 2?"

He pointed out of the window. "It's about seven blocks that way," he said. "Just go straight. You can't miss it."

"Thanks," she said and quickly left the store, George still following in bewilderment.

She spotted a pay phone and stopped. "I have to make a phone call. Got to know my dad is okay. I'll be right back."

She walked to the phone and dialed his house. Her father answered on the second ring. When she heard his voice she paused, not knowing what to say. They hadn't talked in over a year, she realized. Tempted to hang up, she remained gripping the phone. "Dad?" she said finally.

"Maddy?" he answered. "What's wrong?"

A painful lump in her throat swelled up, and she forced a swallow. For a second she was four years old again, still his little girl. She longed to tell him what had happened, ask for his advice, his help. But instead she remained quiet. She hadn't been his little girl for years now, not since the divorce. "Nothing," she said at last. "Just wanted to see how you were."

"You have one of your visions or something?" The coldness in his voice cut her.

"No, Daddy. Just hadn't talked to you in a long time."

"Yeah," he answered simply, sounding distracted. She heard the TV in the background: football.

"So you're okay?"

"Why wouldn't I be?" He cursed at the home team, then went quiet.

"Well, I'll let you go, then," she said, her heart heavy.

"Okay," he said, and hung up the receiver.

Madeline replaced the handset, and still holding on to it, burst into tears.

"Mad," George said gently, walking over to her. He turned her around to face him, then took her in his arms. "I'm so sorry."

"So am I, George." She desperately missed the family she'd once belonged to. Sitting on the couch watching movies with her mom. Hiking with her dad. She'd become a pariah, even to them. Some nights, sitting alone in her tiny apartment, the grief was palpable. She had never felt so alone in her life than she did then, sitting on her worn couch, with only memories as companions.

She put her head on George's chest, felt his hand stroking her hair. Her dad was fine. And she suspected Steve was okay, as well. "This must be pretty serious for you to call your dad.

That can't have been easy. You want to tell me what all has happened?"

She wiped her eyes on her sleeve and pulled away, embarrassed for breaking down. She started walking briskly in the direction the clerk had indicated, and he followed. "Okay," she said, sniffing and taking several deep breaths. "Here's the deal. That thing on the train? It eats people. And it wants to eat me, to get my psychometric talent. Only I'm not going to let it. And Noah is this guy who's been hunting it for centuries. Only now he's on some suicide mission, and I've got to stop him." She paused for breath. "Make sense?"

George didn't answer. He continued to walk quickly beside her. "Yeah," he said finally. "Given what I've seen today, I'd definitely say yeah."

"This creature can look like anyone," she said further. "I thought you were him."

George touched the bandage on his head. "Oh."

"Sorry about that." Madeline started to jog again, feeling the strain in her exhausted body. But she had to keep going. The cut in her arm had finally stopped bleeding, and her blood-soaked shirt was positively stiff. Luckily, the shirt was dark green, and people wouldn't notice the blood so easily now that it was night. "Let's scare up a ride." She marched toward the highway and the uncertain future that lay before her.

After ten minutes of standing on the side of Highway 2, Madeline and George were picked up by a young man driving a red Ford pickup truck. Squeezing onto the front bench, they drove the twenty-seven miles to West Glacier, she and the driver, Phil, talking animatedly. He was spending his summer helping with his family's ranch. Despite her dire mood, Madeline found Phil quite funny and laughed at more than one of his jokes about his family and long, hot days spent mending fences.

George, on the other hand, remained completely quiet.

"I've never seen people hitch into Glacier without at least a backpack," Phil commented as he dropped them off near George's car.

"Our gear is stashed at our friend's house here," Madeline lied, feeling a little bad about it but knowing she couldn't go into the actual story.

Phil nodded.

"Thanks!" she said, closing the door.

George waved, though he still didn't say anything. Phil drove off, and George walked like a zombie toward his car.

"Are you okay?" she asked him.

He nodded.

She wondered if the insanity of the situation had finally caught up to him. "You don't look okay."

They walked in silence to his car, which was parked in one corner of the gas station's parking lot, the same station that doubled as the repair garage. Her Rabbit stood at the other end of the lot, next to the large bay doors of the garage. She felt sad seeing it sit there forlornly.

When they reached his blue Toyota, he looked up, his eyes haunted. "I'm fine," he said robotically, as if the question had just registered in his brain. He fished out his keys.

She stared at him for several long minutes. He looked out of place there, her friend appearing in the midst of a nightmare. He was part of the world back home, where, as lonely as things were, they still made sense.

"George," she said finally. "I don't want you to come with me."

He furrowed his brow. "What? Are you crazy? You can't go against that thing alone."

She shook her head. "That thing is practically unstoppable. I don't want to be mean here, but it just wouldn't matter if you were with me."

George threw up his hands in exasperation. "It took both of us to throw it off the train!"

"Yeah, but there isn't going to be a train up there. Just miles of desolate backcountry and a remote cabin to get killed in."

"I could help get your friend out of there."

"If he's even still alive when I get there."

"Well, you must believe he is, if you're going to go through with this."

She hoped he was alive, though the creature could still beat her there, loping through the woods on all fours in a direct route while she had to stick to the roads.

She sighed and took a minute to collect her thoughts. George simply couldn't come, as much as she wanted him there for sheer comfort's sake. In reality, she was likely heading up there to her own death. She didn't want him to get killed, too. "George, please listen to me. That thing has killed hundreds of people, maybe more. I don't want you to go."

He crossed his arms defiantly. "I'm not going to let you go alone."

Since the creature had shown up, Madeline had enlisted the help of numerous people. Steve could have been killed. George, too. The ranger in the backcountry station didn't even have a chance to meet her before the creature killed him. Now Noah had gone to face it. She had a stake in this and had to go up there to do something. But she couldn't live with herself if her only friend got killed in the process. This thing wanted her, and she was going to face it alone.

George didn't belong here. He could die here.

Suddenly Madeline knew what she had to do. Lunging forward, she pushed George to the ground. He cried out in surprise, landing on his shoulder. Wrenching the keys from his hand, she fumbled with them quickly, located the car key, and inserted it into the lock.

"What are you doing?" he asked, suddenly come to life. He started to get up. She aimed a well-placed boot at his chest and knocked him back down, robbing him of his breath. Twisting the key in the lock, she unlocked the door and wrested it open.

George coughed, bringing his hands to his chest as she jumped in the driver's seat and slammed the door behind herself. Her hand quickly snapped down the lock, sealing her within.

Staggering, George got to his feet and grabbed at the handle. His fists landed on the glass of the driver's window. "Madeline! Don't do this!"

She started the car up and pulled away slowly, being sure not to run over George or his feet. She gave him a sad look through the window. "I can't be responsible for your death, George," she yelled through the glass.

"And I don't want to read about yours!" he shouted back as she drove away.

She placed her hand flat on the window, silently said goodbye to her friend, and roared out of the parking lot, heading toward the cabin.

Madeline didn't know what she'd find as she closed the final mile to the cabin. Maybe the creature would already be there, gleaming spike driven deeply into Noah's bubbling flesh. Maybe she'd beat the creature there and could talk Noah into leaving with her. Her hands felt slick on the wheel of George's car, and she worried for her friend she'd left in the parking lot.

Ahead, lights came into view.

Madeline slowed the bouncing Toyota on the pitted, dirt road and came to a halt, switching the headlights off.

The lights ahead, perfectly square, gleamed from the cabin only three hundred feet away. She studied the windows for any hint of movement, but it was simply too far away to see.

Not switching the headlights back on, she pulled the car off the road and parked it beneath a large hemlock. She switched the motor off. As quietly as possible, she opened the car door and climbed out. Locking it, she pressed it closed with her hip and pocketed the keys with nervous, trembling hands.

Ahead lay darkened clusters of pine trees and the glowing windows of the cabin beyond. She crept around the car and moved forward, the pine needles muffling her approach.

Two hundred feet.

One hundred feet.

As she drew closer, a large, hulking shape came into view, obstructing the light from one of the windows. Madeline's heart jumped until she realized it was just the bulky, dark dimensions of Noah's Jeep. He had parked right in front.

Bold.

Or stupid.

If Noah was alone in there, he was going about his assassination attempt in a dangerous way, parking his Jeep in full view and turning on all the lights. It wasn't something she thought he'd do. He was either desperate and not thinking clearly, or something had gone wrong.

Ducking down low to stay out of the cabin's light, she crept to the front door. Squatting next to it, she reached one shaking hand up to the handle.

Noah arriving at the cabin, full of despair, sobbing . . .

Leaving the safety of the Jeep, tentatively approaching the front door, determined and full of terror . . .

Reaching in through the broken pane of glass in the door, letting himself in. Planning to lie in wait behind the bedroom door, intentionally leaving his car in plain sight so the creature would know he was there and be braced for a confrontation, perhaps get his heart pumping so that when Noah cut him, the blood would flow that much more freely into Noah's waiting mouth . . .

Noah imagining himself manifesting the gleaming spikes from each arm, impaling the screaming creature against one wall of the cabin, then detaching the spike so the creature could never rise again . . .

Madeline released her grip on the handle and exhaled, clearing her mind. Bracing her back against the cool wood of the cabin's wall, she remained in shadow. She studied the front door of the cabin. She saw the broken pane but didn't know if Noah had entered already, as he'd intended to do in the vision. She would have to touch the inside doorknob to know that.

Silently, heart threatening to beat right out of her chest, mouth gone dry, knees trembling, Madeline approached one of the front windows at an angle. Trying to remain out of sight, she stared in from one far corner, keeping her distance from the pane.

She didn't see anyone, just the empty front room and the kitchen beyond.

She strained her ears.

The wind in the boughs.

A bat emitting a high-pitched squeak as it hunted moths in the tree canopy above.

Crickets singing.

The roar of a distant waterfall.

Stepping forward, she pressed one ear against the wooden wall of the cabin. For several long moments she remained there, straining to hear anything within.

She heard nothing.

Ducking beneath the window, she crept toward the front door again, her feet shuffling in the soft bed of pine needles. She waited a moment, wide eyes searching the darkness around the cabin to be sure she was alone.

Then, standing up slowly, back pressed against the wall, she peered in at an angle through the windows in the front door. She saw tile and a well-worn welcome mat.

Biting her lower lip and holding her breath, she snaked her hand in through the broken pane, fingers groping for the door-knob on the other side. Her hand closed around a cold, metal knob.

Noah unlocking and opening the door. Walking inside.

Exploring the cabin. Finding it empty. Returning to relock the front door and then lie in wait in the bedroom.

An agonized scream rang out, clipped off abruptly by a strangled choke.

Startled, she withdrew her hand, cutting it accidentally on the broken glass.

She recognized the scream, had heard it that first night on the mountain and later at this very cabin. Another long shriek pierced her eardrums, followed by wretched sobbing and pleading before the screams began again.

It was Noah. And this time, she feared, he was not going to live.

Remaining where she stood, she summoned up the dregs of her courage. Then she opened the door.

23

LEAVING the door open, Madeline entered the cabin.

In the bedroom, Noah's anguished screams reached an intolerable pitch. She wondered how anyone could cause such agony in another being, especially how someone could enjoy doing it.

And she had no idea how to go up against someone like that.

She pulled out her pocket knife, which suddenly looked too small. Extending the large blade, she gripped the handle in one hand. Then, eyes darting over an assortment of kitchen objects, she looked for anything else she could use as a weapon. Her eyes fell on the well-worn chairs with the aluminum frames.

Not waiting to lose her nerve, she tiptoed into the kitchen. From here she could see into the bedroom, but the door was mostly closed, and through the crack she only saw part of the rumpled bed.

Fingers closing around the frame of a chair, she lifted it and moved swiftly to the bedroom door as another shriek reverberated in the confines of the cabin. Windows rattled. A spoon on the Formica counter vibrated to a new position.

Madeline readied herself and kicked the bedroom door as hard as she could. It thrust open, slammed against something meaty, then gave way again as the mass fell away to one side. She burst into the room, eyes taking in the situation as her shaking hands gripped the chair and knife with clammy fingers.

Drenched in so much blood that she could barely make out his features, Noah hung from a hook on the opposite wall, white shirt in ribbons around his waist. Madeline blinked. No. Not a shirt. His skin. He had been flayed alive. Visions of the Sickle Moon Killer leapt into her mind—his euphoria in cutting and eating his victims—the scene was intolerably familiar to her.

"Madeline," he breathed, peering at her with eyes delirious from pain.

On the floor lay Stefan, in what Madeline had come to believe was his original form, a muscular, olive-skinned man with shoulder-length black hair. Noah's blood covered his hands, and he gripped the same flaying knife he'd used on the train. She'd knocked him over with the door.

She stepped forward, bringing the chair down as hard as she could on his head. His hand went limp from the shock of the blow, and she kicked the knife out of it. Then she stabbed her pocket knife into his heart. Grasping the handle, he pulled it out, and she brought the chair down again, knocking the pocket knife out of his grasp. It skittered across the floor, landing under the dresser.

His hand lunged out to retrieve the flaying knife at his feet as she brought one leg of the chair down onto his hand. The sharp metal leg drove deeply into his flesh there, and she heard the distinct snapping of bones. Not having time to grab it herself, she kicked the knife across the room.

Stefan rolled over on his back, taking her in.

She brought the chair down hard into his face, one leg entering his eye. He screamed, thrashing, his legs kicking her where she stood. She stumbled, fell to one knee, her weight slamming down onto the chair. For a brief moment Stefan lay nailed to the floor, the leg of the chair embedded deeply in his skull.

Metamorphosing, clawed hands reached up and grabbed the chair leg, gripped it firmly, and wrenched it out. He cast the chair to one side with Madeline still leaning on it, and she rolled harshly to the side, banging her head against one leg of the bed.

In an instant Stefan was on his feet, standing over her. She rolled over, clutching her head and stared up at him in a daze from the blow. He lifted a leg and drove it down on her knee. She heard a sickening pop and excruciating pain flooded through her. She grabbed her ruined knee, struggling to sit up. His clawed hand closed around her neck and forced her to her feet.

Her knee screamed in protest as her weight hit it. Stefan stared at her in fury, one eye destroyed and streaming with blood, the other glowing fiery red and widening into a luminescent disk.

She brought her fists up in a flurry of powerful blows, connecting with his gut, solar plexus, throat, and ruined eye. Then she drove her thumb into the eye socket and, screaming, he released her. Her knee buckled, and she stumbled but regained her balance, staggering back against the metal bed frame. She grabbed the metal eagerly, trying to remain standing.

The chair lay just to her left, and she grabbed it again before Stefan had a chance to recover. Swinging it high in an arc over her head, she leaped forward and struck him once again on the head, then brought it up, uppercutting his chin and then shoved it forward, driving him against the wall. The same sharp leg that had claimed his eye now slid into his abdomen.

He stared at her, disbelieving, from the other side of the chair.

With all her weight, she bore into the chair, driving it deeper inside him.

His eyes narrowed, and a solid, bony spike erupted from

his chest, rib cage deforming and re-forming into a single lethal blade. Reaching up, he grabbed her hands where they
gripped the chair, and he pulled her toward him with tremendous force. The chair legs pierced through him and drove into
the wall beyond, raining bloody plaster over the carpet.

She felt a terrible rip in her being, a searing, hot penetra-
tion that pierced her skin and entered her chest, punching
through ribs and ripping into a lung. The lung collapsed, and
she gasped for air as the blade drove further, breaking ribs in
her back before bursting through on the other side. Her mouth
opened, eyes involuntarily shuttering in the back of her head
as blood bubbled up and dribbled down her chin.

The creature, now just inches away, licked the blood from
her face with a single, long stroke of his tongue.

He pushed her away, and the agony reached an unbearable
level. As the bony spike withdrew from her, so much blood
entered her lungs that she coughed and sputtered, no longer
able to breathe.

When she was at arm's length, he yanked her forward
again, the spike entering her abdomen this time, tearing de-
structively through her organs with unimaginable force, snag-
ging on her diaphragm and jerking the last breath from her
one good lung.

Madeline fought off a wave of unconsciousness, then realized with a panic that it was actually death sneaking up on
her, not blissful unconsciousness at all.

Stefan pulled her nearer, the bony spike piercing her kidneys before it burst through her back once more. Hot liquid
streamed down her back, and the stench of bile and urine
filled her nose. Images of the Sickle Moon Killer devouring
the skin of his victims reeled in her head. What had always
repulsed her could save her now. She could do it herself for an
entirely different reason. But she wasn't going to vomit Stefan's blood and flesh back up like the Killer had done. She
had to devour him. Become one with him.

Then she was back next to Stefan, impaled on the jagged
spear, lips inches from his throat. Those haunting images
would work for her this time. She had done this before, reliv-

ing the Sickle Moon Killer's memories countless times, and
she knew she could do it again. Only this time it would not be
to cause pain but to end it. With her last bit of strength, Madeline strained forward, the spike driving even deeper inside
her, tearing a wider hole in her back. She closed the last inch
separating them and brought her mouth to his throat.

Biting down hard, she shook her head, tearing a gash in
his neck. But she didn't let go, though parts of his skin and
muscle tore off in her mouth. She swallowed them. Sucking
powerfully, she drew his blood into her mouth, taking full,
deep swallows of the hot liquid.

He twisted beneath her, tried to angle his neck away, but
she clung on, taking in gulp after gulp, resisting the urge to
vomit.

He pushed at her, the bony spike withdrawing back into
his body, re-forming into his rib cage. She sank her teeth in
tighter, sucking and consuming as much blood from his veins
as she could physically swallow.

He shoved her away. Her teeth took a large swath of skin
with them as she stumbled backward. Bringing her hand up to
her mouth, she shoved the skin inside and chewed it, forcing
the hot, meaty mass down her throat.

A dizzying warmth spread through her body, a tingling
fire that swept over the pain and drowned it out completely.
Her eyes rolled back in her head, and she collapsed, spilling
onto the floor. The warmth spread, singing to her in a chorus
of sweet voices, extending to every part of her being.

She could no longer see. Her vision made out only a brilliant glow, and she lay in ecstasy as the song filled her body,
entered her bloodstream, her breath, the synapses of her
brain. She closed her eyes.

And visions filled her head.

*Beyond the magnificent gates of the Sumerian city, the
olive-skinned young man standing above the strange, dark
void, seeing the flash of movement, something wet and sinuous, down in the depths. Reaching in to touch it and hit with
a fiery light that knocked him hundreds of feet through the
air . . .*

Awakening, later, no longer human, but a thing that could change shape . . .

Wandering, lost and alone through a desert, starving . . .

Stumbling upon a band of nomads and falling into a feeding frenzy, ripping them apart and devouring the soft insides, drinking their water, stealing their clothes . . .

Later, stunned that the memories and experiences of the nomads were now his own, the knowledge of desert survival and so much more, he becomes addicted, desiring to eat more, vowing to eat more . . .

Learning to control the changes, to heal superficial and grievous wounds alike, to appear as anyone the creature desires, to manifest weapons from his very body . . .

Madeline's eyes snapped open. She rose to her feet.

Power surged through her. With every pulse of her heart, the creature's blood coursed through her veins. And with each heartbeat, her body touched that blood. Her psychometric gift could feel everything about the creature, all of its experiences and memories, all of its abilities. She knew every terrifying and wondrous detail. Knew so much that she didn't know where she ended and the creature began.

Every muscle in her body tightened with that knowledge, her mind focused on the creature across the room. She lowered her head and brought her arms up. Healing surged through her, closing her wounds in a single instant.

Still standing against the wall, the chair embedded deeply in his body, Stefan struggled. He gripped the chair's seat and pushed forcefully, freeing the legs from the wall. He tossed the chair to the side and stepped forward.

Two long, gleaming spikes emerged from his arms, ending in vicious points.

Madeline didn't move. She no longer knew fear, only power and purpose. Focusing the fiery energy singing within her, she lifted her hands higher, breathing out, flesh transforming instantaneously to reflective silver, the metal sweeping down her entire body until she was solely comprised of the deadly alloy.

As the creature swung one speared arm, she ducked to the

side and thrust her hands forward. Each metallic finger detached, hurling into him at high velocity, disappearing deep within his flesh.

He staggered back, one arm spike returning to flesh as his concentration severed.

Fresh metallic fingers surged out, replacing the old. She extended an arm up and summoned a sharp saber, its hilt and her hand joining in a single mass. She lunged forward, driving the sword into his belly. He howled in agony, stumbling backward. Her hand severed from the blade, leaving it embedded inside him.

She summoned a second, matching sword, and as Stefan's body crashed onto the floor, she drove the blade into his chest, crunching through ribs until she struck the wooden floor beneath. Her hand separated from the blade.

Stefan twisted on the ground, screaming. His body passed through torturous changes, forming into victims past, then lumps of bone and sinew, then arms flailing in a bloated mass of bleeding tissue, finally returning to his original form once again. Then he fell still, one tremendous disk eye forming and blinking in shock. It withered and returned to a human eye as he gulped for air. A single tear pooled and spilled down his face. And then he was gone.

The metal in her body receded, revealing flesh once more. She looked down at herself, her body completely healed, untouched. No hole in the chest. No ragged wound in the abdomen. Even her knee was perfect.

She rushed over to Noah, who still hung on the wall. He looked up at her with tearing eyes, intense pain clenching his jaw shut.

Carefully, she cupped her hands under his arms and lifted him up off the hook, amazed at her own strength, but at the same time already knowing she had it. She could feel every ability of the creature just waiting for her to use it.

Gently she laid Noah on the bed. The creature had stripped all the skin off his chest, but Noah's back and face luckily suffered only superficial cuts. Blood seeped into the linens as he lay back on the sheets.

Tenderly she moved each strip of skin back to its original place while Noah cried out and shuddered in agony.

"Just lie there," she told him when she was done, "and you'll heal." She kissed him on the lips. "Just like always."

Before her eyes, the skin began to knit back together over the muscle beneath. She sat down next to him on the bed, holding his hand. In an hour, though the cuts were still deep and evident, the skin had completely reattached itself. In another hour, the cuts were only deep red lines in his skin. Wolves began to sing in the darkened forest beyond.

In the third hour, he reached up and curled his hand behind her head, pulling her down to kiss him.

Noah and Madeline dragged the creature's body out to the middle of a meadow and dug a deep hole, working through the small hours of the night. They dumped him inside it, still full of metallic spears, and threw dirt over him. Then they rolled several large stones on top of the location to mark it in case they ever needed to go back.

But both of them hoped they'd never have to.

Then they climbed into George's car and drove back down to West Glacier, talking excitedly and holding hands the entire way. Noah didn't know what to do with his life now. He was free, and so giddy about it that a few times his bouncing in the passenger seat almost made Madeline drive off the road.

She felt the world differently now; new abilities within her waited to be explored, and she looked back on the experience in the cabin with a mind full of wonder.

At the gas station in West Glacier, they found George sitting miffed on the hood of Madeline's Rabbit.

It was 4 a.m.

"There weren't any vacancies in any hotels around here, you know," he snarled, but only after he hugged her so tightly she thought her ribs would break for the second time that night.

Noah and George shook hands, and she convinced Noah to return to Mothershead with them.

"Why not?" he said, throwing his arms around her and kissing her. "We can do anything we want!"

They climbed back into the Toyota, George driving this time. As she got into the passenger seat, George looked over at her and said, "You seem different."

She smiled. Her eyes flashed red in the dark, and George jerked in alarm. "If you thought I was a freak before," she said, "wait till you see me now." Seeing his surprise, she clasped her friend's shoulder, reassuring him.

Hesitantly, he turned and started up the car. "Now that you've beaten me up twice *and* stolen my car *and* returned with a mystery boyfriend and glowing red eyes, you sure as hell need to give me a better explanation on the way home."

Noah leaned forward and clasped their shoulders from the backseat. "Do you want to hear it from the beginning? 'Cause that might take a while."

"Even longer than you think," she said to him over her shoulder, thinking of the ancient Sumerian city and the black, encompassing void.

George looked at his watch. "We've got five hours," he said, "not including stops for snacks."

"Snacks!" Madeline cried. "Oh, yes. Please. I'm starved for some good, old-fashioned junk food."

"I hope that's the only kind of food you've got an appetite for," Noah said, arching one eyebrow.

She turned to face him. "So far," she said, running her tongue over teeth gone sharp.

Alice Henderson has long been enchanted by Glacier National Park, the setting of *Voracious*. She holds a master's degree in folklore and mythology, and revels in tales of supernatural creatures and mysterious places. She lives in San Francisco, where she is at work on her next novel. Please visit her at www.alicehenderson.com.

Don't miss the page-turning suspense, intriguing characters, and unstoppable action that keep readers coming back for more from these bestselling authors...

Tom Clancy
Robin Cook
Patricia Cornwell
Clive Cussler
Dean Koontz
J.D. Robb
John Sandford

Your favorite thrillers and suspense novels come from Berkley.

penguin.com

M14G0907